Legion, God of Monsters: Awakening

K. J. Forthman

KJF Publishing LLC

Contents

1

Rebirth

"I died."

That was the only possibility. The moments leading up to it vividly hung in my mind like haunting phantoms. The brilliant lights and rumbling explosions, the men with reflective gold masks, the gunshots...

"Those damn reformers had to attack us now, of all times..."

At least Cassie got away. In the moments preceding my death, I managed to sneak my sister out through a secret escape path. I held off the soldiers in a heroic final stand worthy of a movie - complete with a dramatic entrance, a pitched battle, and my ultimate defeat.

Really, the pain involved was a minor detail. My death was just too cool!

So, I distinctly remembered dying, but... where was I now? I glanced around but all I could see was a dark and empty expanse pursuing infinity in every direction. My body had changed; I was incorporeal and transparent and seemed to be floating in this dark and endless space.

With no reference point, time was a little vague. I drifted in nothingness for so long it seemed like an eternity until the darkness before me twitched and shifted. Streaks of white filled my vision as a large sphere slowly stretched out of the gap and spread across the scene before me.

A planet...? Was I in outer space?

"Welcome, new Overseer," a somewhat dissonant voice interrupted my reverie. The tone sounded robotic, like the programmed AI in a computer or a smartphone. I turned, seeking out the source of the voice... but I saw nothing.

"I am Advanced Universal Training and Observation Unit#1124. I am tasked with teaching you about your responsibilities as an Overseer."

An invisible training unit?

"What's an Overseer?"

"In Earth terminology, you may know of them as gods. The world you came from, Earth, has hosted the powers of many Overseers. You may draw comparisons to deities such as Zeus or Thor."

No way! I made it? I reincarnated as a *god*?! I totally called it! I *told* mom that heroic deaths were the way to go! But *no*, she had to get all sentimental and ask me *not* to die before her. Hah! I became a god!

"So, what can I do? Is that my planet? Do I get to create things?"

"An Overseer's primary job is to aid their followers in developing their souls. There are several Overseers representing this planet. You might create things later when you have more power," the robo-voice replied to each of my questions in turn.

"So, what do I do first?"

"First, you must choose a Tether."

"A tether?"

That wasn't a word I heard often. An image of a dog chained to a stake came to mind, but I couldn't see the connection between that kind of tether and a god. Then I thought of an image of connecting two devices to share information, but there wasn't any visible technology around.

"A Tether is an individual who will act as your representative among the people. They will speak your words and spread your religion."

"So, they're kind of like a prophet?"

"That is an adequate comparison."

Huh. I hadn't planned on going down the religion route, but I could roll with it. Dying wasn't in the plans either, but it brought me to godhood.

I glanced back over at the planet slowly rotating beneath me. As the clouds parted I saw four continents spread evenly around a giant whirlpool.

Though I wasn't privy to the modified topography of Earth due to the war, there was no way that seven continents were reduced to four. That was definitely not Earth.

What kind of world was it? Maybe...

Maybe it had magic? I mean, gods turned out to be real, so why not magic?

A sense of urgency rose inside of me. I wanted to find out more.

"So how do I go about choosing a Tether?" I asked.

"I have taken the liberty of selecting a few viable options. With your permission, I will present the most promising to you."

Wait. This thing chose for me? Before I even knew about a choice, it took it away from me? But I was the god, right? Wasn't it supposed to be my choice?

Choosing my prophet was obviously important. There was no way in hell I was letting a random invisible space robot choose for me.

I was careful not to show my irritation, though. It probably wasn't a good idea to show hostility as I had no idea what this thing was or if it was a bad idea to make it angry.

"Sure, let me see them."

As soon as the words left my mouth, I found my vision zooming in on the planet, moving towards the continent on the top left side. Within moments, I was flying over the land at incredible speeds, mountains, plains, and forests passing in the blink of an eye.

After about a minute, I felt a tug pulling me down. As I followed it, I fell into a mountain range and settled atop the tallest mountain. In front of me stood a beautiful woman with pitch-black hair drawing a pentagram around a gruff-looking man with a bandana on his head. From their body language, they seemed to be arguing. The woman had tears streaming down her cheeks, and loose strands of hair plastered to her skin.

I couldn't confirm my inference, though, because my surroundings were entirely mute.

The woman finished drawing the pentagram and stepped back. She seemed to be chanting something, her lips moving rapidly as she waved her arms while moving elegantly around the circle, almost as if she were dancing. The pentagram began to glow an eerie red.

I saw a flash of movement out of the corner of my eye and followed it down the hill. A small group of four medieval-fantasy-looking humans carefully stalked towards the man and the woman with their weapons drawn. They looked like a stereotypical RPG group with a sword-and-board warrior, a white-robed healer, a rogue, and a hunter. All they needed was a mage...

The hunter raised his bow and drew back an arrow, sighting it on the beautiful woman. I tried to shout and warn her but, just like I couldn't hear them, they couldn't hear me. He released the arrow and I watched in despair as it arced through the air and fell towards her. Without pausing in her dance, she reached an arm out and smoothly snatched the arrow out of the air.

Wow.

"Observe the warrior. He should be an ideal Tether..." the robo-voice started when I interrupted it.

"Cut the bullshit."

The voice went silent for a moment before speaking again, a hint of surprise in its tone.

"I do not follow."

"You want me to choose that guy? Isn't he just a novice?"

My personal combat experience was limited to guerilla fighting with guns, traps, drones, and chemical bioweapons, but I could tell with a glance that this boy wasn't accustomed to fighting. Though his group seemed to have a bit of training, all four of them looked green. The warrior was on the verge of tears, the archer's bow was shaking, the priest was shouting something fervently with a twisted expression, and the rogue had been frozen stiff since the moment the woman caught the arrow.

"That man is currently the third strongest adventurer in this region. He has high growth potential and meets the standard criterion most Overseer's use when choosing a Tether..."

"Which are?"

"Blonde hair, blue eyes, and a pretty face."

If I had hands, I would facepalm so hard.

I examined the woman who had started running towards the adventurers at an insane speed that I could barely follow, baring her fangs as she snarled.

Wait, fangs? Was she a vampire?!

"What about her? What is her potential as a Tether?"

"I only considered human candidates. No Overseer has ever chosen a non-human before."

Huh. Why not? Wouldn't it have been cool to have a pretty vampire as a Tether? This one in particular seemed like an okay choice. From the moments before the RPG group attacked, I could tell that she wasn't a heartless monster -- anything that could cry obviously had feelings. This wasn't a good decision to rush though, so I asked about my other options.

"Do I have to pick one of these individuals as my Tether?"

"No, you could pick any individual who is not already a Tether."

I closely observed the fight happening in front of me and cringed slightly as the vampire ripped the warrior's arm off.

All things considered; she was probably a better choice than him.

The young woman groaned as she sat up, gazing blearily at her unfamiliar surroundings.

Directly in front of her lay a near-pristine, pale corpse in the center of a dimly glowing red pentagram. The dead man had a bandana on his head which covered his hair, two axes tied on either side of his waist, and a grizzly beard. Her eyes were drawn to the two punctures on his neck and, as she watched, a single drop of blood oozed out of the wound and began to trickle down the man's neck. She unconsciously ran her tongue over her teeth and tasted blood.

She groaned softly at the overwhelmingly pleasant taste.

Delicious...!

She paused, feeling a piercing sting as she ran her tongue over two particularly sharp teeth.

A breeze ruffled her long, silky black hair. Though there was a faint sting when the wind contacted her skin, the feeling was not uncomfortable. Her questing eyes continued to roam the area and she found four more bodies on the slope behind her.

These looked a little different from the one in the circle. It was as if they were attacked by a feral beast!

The man wearing metal armor was missing his left arm, and he had a huge, gaping hole in his chest. On the ground next to him lay a young girl with blood-stained white robes, her face distorted and frozen in an immortal demonstration of terror. The attractive display of modern art was accented beautifully by her neck that was twisted three-hundred-sixty degrees.

The other two were face down on the ground further down the hill, likely having been cut down as they ran away. One of them had a big metal disc sticking out of his back, and the other guy's head was on the ground several meters further down the road.

She licked her lips and shivered in anticipation when she noted the pools of drying blood settled around their bodies. There was something else she needed to do before that though. She continued searching her surroundings for a clue.

She was standing atop the tallest hill in the area and could see miles of rolling peaks in every direction. To the northeast, she could see walls with small lights walking back and forth atop them. Lording over the night sky, she saw three orbs that dominated the horizon. The leftmost circle was blood red, the rightmost a clean, azure blue, and the central sphere was pitch black with a visible white aura radiating out from it.

Three full moons. Their eerie glow was enchanting, and a strange yearning to move closer to them permeated her body and soul.

Unconsciously, she took a step forward and then stopped as the air around her began to hum. She glanced about and found that the glowing pentagram was becoming noticeably brighter. Light began to rise from the center, tearing apart and consuming the bloodless man's body.

After a brief pause, the hill began to shake slightly. All three moons glowed with overwhelmingly intense light, and a heavy wind ruffled her hair again. She caught a loose strand and noticed that her dark hair was glowing as well. The raven-black slowly retreated, giving way to a silvery-platinum color. She could only look on in amazement and bewilderment as the lights from the pentagram and the three moons gathered around her body.

Almost as quickly as the light had come, it faded away until her surroundings stopped shaking.

"…"

She opened her mouth and spoke the first words of her existence.

"What the hell just happened?"

Before she could think too much about it, she felt a sharp pain in her head. She cried out as she fell to her knees, feebly clawing at her hair. She screamed in agony as the pain spread from her head down to her chest and then radiated out until it permeated her whole body.

Her scream was cut short as she coughed out blood.

2

Critical Error

"What's going on?!" I practically screamed, panicking as I watched the horrific scene happening right in front of me.

For some reason, the tall, dark-haired beauty had changed. Her hair turned silvery-white and one of her eyes flashed with purple light. As if that wasn't strange enough, she promptly fell to the ground, spasming and screaming as she continued to cough out blood without pause.

"I am unsure," the voice replied, "I have heard that terrestrial bodies often suffer due to diseases. Perhaps she is ill?"

Was this thing serious? It wanted to write that off as being sick? And this stupid thing was supposed to train me?

Something else was strange though. I had seen plenty of dying people before, but I had never seen anything like this. If I wasn't mistaken, I was pretty sure that she had already lost too much blood. If the rules were the same as back on Earth, she would be dead.

"Is there some kind of magic keeping her alive? Or is it because she's a vampire?"

"One moment. Allow me to look into this."

I waited impatiently as the owner of the robo-voice did whatever the heck it was doing. The woman coughed out another half-gallon of blood before the voice finally answered.

"In regard to your second query, this individual is not a vampire. She is one of the original, native races of this world. The amount of blood in her body should be comparable to a human and, to answer your first query, there is currently no magic preserving her life."

"Then how the hell is she still alive?!" I asked, my voice tense.

Watching people scream in agony wasn't exactly a hobby of mine. My inability to do anything was beyond infuriating.

"This ritual seems to have modified her body to some extent. Currently, her body is regenerating blood as fast as she is losing it.

Since she is maintaining perfectly healthy levels, one can infer that she is, in fact, regenerating her blood faster than it is draining."

"Huh? So did that ritual give her super regeneration or something?"

"That is a highly probable scenario. However, there is not enough data to return an affirmation."

The woman let out yet another piercing wail.

"Is there any way we can help her?" I asked desperately.

"Affirmative."

I waited tensely for the voice to continue. After a long pause, I cautiously asked.

"Are you going to tell me?"

"If it is your desire."

Another long pause.

This was an entity designed to train gods, right? Did I really have to state it outright?

"Please tell me how I can help her," I growled, annoyed.

"Acknowledged. Designate her as your Tether."

"What?"

"You contemplated choosing her as your Tether, correct? That is the only way you can save her with your current level of power."

The woman's violent screams simmered down to a low whimper. Her arms and legs twisted unnaturally as her muscles writhed and spasmed. If one listened closely enough, they could hear the continuous crunching and snapping as her bones broke and healed in rapid succession.

Insane regeneration or not, whatever was happening to her was getting worse. Eventually, it would probably outpace her regeneration and kill her.

I decided to trust the robo-voice. Unsure of how to make her my prophet, I tried to reach out with phantasmal arms that didn't exist, willing myself to touch her head. I felt a phantom sensation where my hand would be, but otherwise nothing changed."

"You do not need to touch her physically to make her a Tether. This is within your power as an Overseer. Command and it will be so."

I squared my non-existent shoulders as I looked down at the young woman crying out in absolute agony.

There was no hesitation in my voice as I pointed at the woman and issued a powerful declaration.

"As of this moment, you are my Tether."

Several moments passed but nothing seemed to change.

"Now that you have successfully chosen your Tether, it is time to move on to the next step," the robo-voice said.

"What are you talking about? Nothing happened!!"

I felt a heavy force pulling on me, attempting to move me away. I resisted with every strand of will in my soul as I screamed at the stupid, lying robot.

"Didn't you say that would save her!?"

A heavy impact slammed into me from below, launching me into the sky. I tried to move back but something restrained me. There was no pain from the blow and no physical sensation against my incorporeal body, but I could somehow tell that something hit me and was holding me in place.

"Young Overseer," the robo-voice replied calmly. "I assure you that you have already saved her. Come with me now to begin the first stage of your training. If you resist, I will have to terminate your standing and that woman will lose her status as a Tether. If that happens, she will die permanently."

Excuse me? Did this thing just threaten me?

I wanted to scream but the final line of the voice's warning made me hesitate. Whether or not the voice was trustworthy, I couldn't say. However, I didn't have the power to resist that mysterious force. Even if I did, I had no idea what else I could do to help her.

My only option was to follow the voice amicably. At the very least, I needed to build a somewhat better impression of my mental state. Having just died and reincarnated, followed by witnessing an event more horrific than anything in my previous life, it might be justified that I was a bit panicked. However, this voice was going to train me to be a god, and I had a feeling that it didn't have a very good impression of me so far.

"Fine," I grumbled, fighting the raging anger and heavy defeat welling up inside of me. "What are we doing next?"

"It is considered polite to introduce yourself to your seniors."

Ah.

"Next, you are to meet your fellow Overseers who have jurisdiction over this world. As you are not yet a full-fledged Overseer, you are not qualified to know the path we must traverse. I have taken the liberty of temporarily disabling your soul for the duration of our trip."

My vision went dark as I felt all my senses rapidly fade away into nothingness.

It was an extremely unpleasant sensation.

At some point, the pain stopped. It wasn't because she overcame the problem. Rather, it was because her nerves started dying faster than they could regenerate. In a state of total and perpetual numbness, the woman felt her mind slip and she willingly embraced the darkness.

She sat in the murky emptiness for an eternity, huddling against the edge of the hollow depths of her memories. Despite the vastness of the space, there was precious little to fill it. She could understand and contemplate words, but some of the words she knew had no meaning to her.

She knew what a name was, but she knew no names.

She knew the meaning of history but knew no history.

She knew that she had a purpose but knew not what it was.

Hiding from the recent and sole powerful memory of her own, she contemplated the fragments of language and emotions that dwelled within the vessel that was her mind.

First, her name. She most definitely did not remember her own name, but could see vague flashes of unfamiliar faces speaking her name. If she focused on those memories…

Ev… Evin…? Ray…?

The memories danced at the tip of her tongue, always out of reach. She tried to reach for them, but they moved away and then slowly faded out of her mind. Then they were gone as well.

"Evin or Ray? Which should I go by?" The woman mused to herself, testing out the sounds and feelings of the names. Whether either of those was actually part of her original name or not, she had no idea. However, she would rather have a name for now and deal with that later. She couldn't quite explain why, but she desperately wanted a name.

"Let's go with Ray, for now," she decided.

Ray smiled softly, mumbling her new name to herself. A sense of delight filled her soul as she gained her second distinctive memory. A bright light filled her vision, and, for a very brief moment, her happiness outweighed the pain in her memory.

She awoke lying on a warm, padded surface. She lurched forward, almost falling off whatever she was lying on as she tried to grasp her surroundings. Though her vision was blurry, she realized that everything in the room was either white or gold colored. Something soft draped over her shoulders as someone placed a white cloak over her body.

She belatedly realized that she wasn't wearing anything under the cloak. How embarrassing. It didn't bother her all that much, but she was still grateful for the cloak. She turned and found the young teenager that had lent her the article. The young girl donned a bright smile as their eyes met.

"I've never met a human with a red eye before! And your eyes are different colors! It's so pretty!" the girl exclaimed in English, the language of humans.

Red eye? Different colors? Okay.

Though her memories were scrambled, Ray's various languages were untouched. She could still speak English, Ancient, Orcish, Dwarvish, and Goblin.

Ray smiled weakly at the enthusiastic young... priestess? She wore a white robe with a golden rose embroidered across the front. Her vibrant, blue eyes were filled with childlike wonder and innocence.

"So how did you die?" the girl chattered curiously.

Ray stiffened. She died? What?

What did that mean? Obviously, she was alive... right?"

"Did some monsters get ya? Goblins, or orcs? Maybe some bandits?" the girl prattled on, leaning forward as her questioning eyes gleamed.

Ray thought for a moment and then the entirety of her new existence's most distinct memory returned to her. She clutched at her head, huddling into a ball as phantom pains raced through her body. The twisting and crunching of limbs... the blood...

Blood? At that thought, Ray's mind was consumed with hunger. She remembered the taste of the blood that was in her mouth when she became aware, and she began to salivate. At the same time, alarm bells rang inside her mind.

'Don't show your teeth.' a vestige of an old memory rose to the forefront, a sense of impending danger accompanying it. Without questioning the thought, Ray obeyed, pursing her lips to hide the sharp teeth that extended when she thought of drinking blood.

Still, she was very hungry. Ray leapt to her feet, glaring at the young girl with crazed thirst in her eyes.

The young girl sighed and calmly rang a bell. A large, heavy built man walked in, his hand on the hilt of a sheathed sword.

"It's another crazy," the girl complained.

The soldier shrugged as he stepped up and grabbed Ray, lifting her struggling form into his arms.

"I'll take care of her. You should get some rest, Kelsey. That's the fifth person today."

The girl, Kelsey, nodded before turning and leaving the room. Ray briefly contemplated chasing her, but she wouldn't get very far. Though she was wriggling desperately, she couldn't break his grip.

"Hoh...?" the man exclaimed as he easily suppressed her violent struggling, "You've got a bit of strength. Are you an adventurer?"

Ray froze, a dark and heavy storm filling her heart and mind. That word... 'adventurer'? Something about that word struck a chord with Ray's soul. She fought the urge to bite the man as she stiffly shook her head.

"Hmm..." the man tilted his head curiously.

He had short-cropped red hair and a neatly trimmed beard. A long, thin scar peaked out from the edges of an eyepatch covering his left eye.

"What's your name, girly?" the man asked.

"Ray," she muttered.

"Nice to meet you, Ray. My name is Max."

"Max..." Ray tested the sound of the name.

As it was the second name she heard, after Kelsey, she would certainly remember it.

"Ray, can I ask you something?" Max asked in a warm and comforting voice.

She nodded carefully, her eyes roaming over his shoulder towards the door.

"I need you to remember what happened. It's an important step in clearing the confusion after a respawn."

'Respawn'? The hell is that?

Ray shook her head sharply, rejecting the memories as they threatened to overtake her once more.

"Please, tell me." Max pleaded softly.

She forced her body to relax.

"Will you let me down first?" she asked evenly.

She needed to get out of here. If she kept talking to this man, he would end up forcing her to think about that horrific pain.

Max carefully set her down. She waited for the moment when his grip on her was released. She took a deep breath as if to start speaking.

And she ran.

She bolted through the door, turning sharply in the opposite direction from where Kelsey had gone.

"Wait!" Max shouted after her, but Ray ignored the man as she wrapped the white cloak around herself to cover her body. She reached the end of the hall and turned sharply, moving in the direction of the soft breeze that was flowing into the building.

The halls were all the same theme and design as the room she awoke in. The core color was white while the trim and designs were done in gold. The new hall that she entered had a few wandering, white-robed individuals. Some of them watched her as she ran by, but nobody tried to stop her.

In the center of the new hall was an archway that led out to a courtyard. Ray practically leapt across the courtyard, laughing lightly as the pleasant wind caressed her face and the gentle sunlight warmed her skin. She reached the edge of the courtyard, passed under a second archway, and then she skidded to a stop. She stood at the top of a large flight of floating stairs leading down to the ground below.

Looking over the area below, a sense of awe at the beautiful overhead view of a fortress town clashed with a blurry memory dancing at the edge of her vision. As great as the town was, Ray felt an inexplicable repulsion that told her that she shouldn't be here. She was in danger and she needed to leave.

Ray began to run once more, dashing down the stairs at breakneck speed. She moved between the stairs gracefully, never missing a step. A few people wandering below noticed and whistled, calling out in appreciation.

She ignored them as she reached the bottom of the stairs and leapt, landing on top of the nearest building. She ignored the sights and the people below as she single-mindedly focused on escaping through the gate.

Nobody in the town tried to stop her, either. Some people shouted but most just ignored her and moved along with their lives. She figured that what she was doing didn't stand out all that much because she could see at least a few dozen other people dashing across different roofs throughout the fortress at any given moment.

Less than a minute later, Ray reached the gate. She leapt off the roof and over the guards. The guards stared in awe for a moment at the unusual sight of a young person easily clearing a jump of several meters.

Still, they didn't bother to try and stop her.

Ray exited the gate, ignoring the crowd of people bustling to enter as she took off towards the nearby forest.

Her first priority - preventing Max from forcing her to think about that pain - check.

Now, she wanted to find some blood to drink.

3

Newbie God

My vision began to refocus, and I blinked rapidly to hasten the process. I had no idea how long I was trapped in pure darkness, but the feeling had been incredibly unpleasant, to say the least. Complete sensory deprivation was *not* fun.

However, the experience made me painfully aware of the limitations of my current state. My only senses were sight and sound, and the only thing I could hear was the robo-voice.

Advanced Universal Training and Observation Unit, was it?

Screw that noise, I would just call it Auto.

I looked around as my 'eyes' adjusted and I noticed something strange in the corner of my vision. A small meter had appeared in my field of view and filled up slightly with a bright yellowish-white color.

"Hey Auto, what's this little bar?"

"That is your holy power."

"Holy power...? What can I do with it?"

"At your current level of power, you may grant knowledge through your Tether, and you may perform a 'lesser miracle' once every 8.16 days. As you increase in power, you will eventually be able to expend it to perform 'greater miracles'. Certain individuals who devote themselves to your ideals can become priests, monks, clerics, or paladins who gain their powers from you. If you, yourself, gain enough power, that is to say, if you gain enough followers then you will eventually even be able to manifest yourself into the world for short periods of time... though this is a very draining endeavor, so you will not be able to do it often."

"So basically, I can talk to people through my Tether, I can occasionally affect the world directly, I can make an army of holy warriors, and later I can become a big badass avatar that wrecks faces?"

"Affirmative."

"Awesome!"

"Additionally, Overseers can grant special abilities or bonuses to their followers called 'perks.'"

"How do I do that?"

"When you reach one hundred followers, you will unlock your first perk. You may unlock additional perks at increasingly higher numbers of followers."

"I want it! I want all of it!"

The powers Auto was describing sounded pretty sweet! I could already imagine myself as a giant, flaming behemoth walking through armies and swinging a big sword!

"Where do I start..." I mumbled to myself. As cool as all that sounded, I only had one follower and...

"Shoot, I don't even know her name!"

"I would implore you to focus on the situation at hand. You have been unconscious for five days in the reckoning of the world below. Your Tether has just awoken inside the fortress town of Cairel, the nearest human settlement to the location where you encountered her."

"That means she's alive!" I exclaimed, relief flooding my non-existent body.

Though I had been slightly distracted by all the cool, new things happening to me, I was still worried about her. That was a rather graphic experience after all. She might have even been traumatized, right? One of my buddies got his leg blown off while walking his dog and the poor guy was too scared to leave his house after that. What happened to her was on a whole 'nother scale, so I wouldn't be surprised if she never went outside ever again.

"Once again, I would implore you to focus on what's important," Auto interjected, interrupting my thoughts. I might have imagined it, but I would swear there was a hint of impatience in his robo-voice.

"Alright, alright. You said we were meeting the other gods, right?"

"Affirmative. The other four Overseer's presiding over this world have been summoned to this location. Two of them rejected the summons, however, so today you will only be meeting Lord Dallin and Lady Jocelyn."

"Okay, is there anything I need to know before I meet them?"

"Affirmative." Auto replied.

Again with the one word answers?

"Wh-" I started when a door suddenly appeared in front of me. The door swung open, and a heavy force slammed into me from behind, throwing me into the open doorway.

"Have fun!" Auto cheered as the door slammed closed and then disappeared.

"Damn emotionally unstable robot..." I muttered shamelessly. "I bet your mother was a..."

"Hmmm?" a lovely voice cut me off before I could finish my curse.

I looked up and saw the most beautiful woman who ever was... probably, anyways. I now knew that my perspective was rather limited, but she certainly was the most beautiful woman I knew of.

Her features were indistinguishable, and her form was rather vague. One might ask how I knew she was so beautiful if I couldn't see any distinctive details about her but I could only say this:

I just knew.

Her beauty was not defined by features, clothes, makeup, or accessories. Her presence and aura wrote the laws of beauty, and I could only humbly acknowledge them as facts.

"Would you like to complete that statement? I am most curious as to what kind of man our newest Overseer will be," the woman asked lightly.

Despite her light tone, I recognized the poorly hidden malice hiding beneath her words.

"No, I think I'll abstain," I replied evenly. "I apologize if I have caused offense. It was not my intention to do so."

The woman, probably Lady Jocelyn, covered a smile with a vaguely defined hand.

"So, you're that kind of man."

I shrugged. Honestly, I had no idea what kind of person she just categorized me as, but I wasn't too fond of the types of people that categorized others in the first place. I turned my attention to the other individual in the room. He, too, was blurry and indistinct. I figured all Overseers must appear like that since we didn't have a definite form or body.

He was the man among men. More specifically, he was strength itself. I thought I knew strength as a member of the resistance, but I was wrong. He didn't have defined muscles or an athletic form. I had no idea how much he could lift or if he even *could* lift. I knew nothing about the strength of his personality. I could feel only one critical fact that was plain as day.

He was strength.

Also, he was probably Lord Dallin.

"So how does this thing usually go down?" I asked, trying to move the conversation along.

Dallin stared at me for a long moment. After a long pause, he grunted, seemingly satisfied as he pointed towards a table with six empty chairs that appeared floating in space. I moved over, noting that there were nameplates on four of the six chairs.

Dallin the Strong One
Jocelyn the Lovely One
Loki the Hidden One
Mumblegrumble the Strange One

On the fifth chair there was an empty nameplate and on the sixth chair there was a nameplate with a completely illegible name, as if someone tried to scribble it out.

Somewhat intrigued, I made a mental note of it just in case it was important.

"Is that my chair?" I asked for confirmation, gesturing to the chair with an empty nameplate.

Dallin nodded silently.

I started to walk towards my chair but then paused. Here was a perfect opportunity to cancel out my initial negative impression. I changed directions and moved towards Lady Jocelyn's chair.

Arriving at nearly the same time as her, I pulled the chair back. She gracefully accepted my offer, sitting in the chair and allowing me to assist her. I made my way back to my seat and, as I sat down, I made eye contact with her.

She seemed... amused, mostly.

"As the Leader presiding over this world, it is my privilege to preside over this meeting. Any objections?" Jocelyn started smoothly.

Nope. Zip. Nada. As long as they didn't make me do it, I'd be fine with anything else.

After a brief pause to ascertain our acceptance, Jocelyn continued.

"The meeting today is to welcome our newest member. Unfortunately, two of our number were unable to make it. Loki sends his apologies and Mumblegrumble sent us a picture of mermaid cookies."

Dallin snorted but otherwise remained silent. Maybe he was just shy?

"The first item on the agenda is basic introductions. Dallin, would you please start?"

Dallin stood up. He stared down at me for a good thirty seconds, nodded firmly, and then sat down.

Was I supposed to get something out of that?

Jocelyn, meanwhile, was staring at Dallin with a bemused expression.

"He's a talkative fellow, but that was unusually excessive. He must like you."

Huh? I definitely missed something.

"I'll go next," Jocelyn continued. "I am Jocelyn. Hanulfall is my four thousand four hundred and thirty first world. Amongst the residents of Hanulfall, my title is the Lovely One and I preside over beauty, passion, and justice."

"Beauty, passion, and justice?"

Was this a domain or attribute kind of thing? I used to play tabletop games with stuff like that.

She nodded.

"We're a bit overworked here. Dallin, Loki, and I each preside over three domains and Mumblegrumble takes the miscellaneous. Meridian hasn't sent a new Overseer our way since this world was integrated."

Meridian? Was that a person, place, or organization? Integrated?

I hesitated at all the unfamiliar terms, but luckily my confusion didn't clearly show on my face. Benefits of being a vaguely defined spiritual god-thing, right?

"Alrighty then. My name is…" I stopped.

Huh? I couldn't remember my own name. I could remember all kinds of details from my previous life. Names, people, places, events. Everything was there except the one thing that I needed right now.

"Ahh… that's strange… I can't remember my name…" I mumbled.

Jocelyn tilted her head quizzically.

"Is that even possible? No, obviously it is."

"You believe me?" I asked, surprised that she didn't really question it.

"Of course. Like Dallin said before, his secondary domain is 'truth'. You can't lie in his presence."

Ah. I missed that little detail somehow. It was kind of hard to find detailed meaning in long pauses of dramatic silence.

"So, uh, I don't know my name. This is my first world and I'm looking forward to working with you all."

Silence. After several long moments of surreal quiet, Dallin leapt to his feet, pointing at me. I felt a vague pressure as if something was pounding against my head but otherwise, I didn't notice much, or any, of what he was trying to say.

Jocelyn nodded in agreement. "I wasn't expecting a total beginner. That could make things a little difficult. I don't have time to participate in your training either. Did your parents teach you the ropes?"

"Parents?"

"Yeah, which Overseers facilitated the organization of your being?"

Hmmm. I tried to rack my brain to see if anything like that might have occurred during my twenty-five odd years.

Nope. Nada. Zip. Nothing.

"My parents were normal humans from Earth."

Silence. I sensed a pattern forming. I would need to learn some of the new common sense soon if I didn't want to keep looking like a total newbie.

"You... evolved from a lesser species? You're sure you weren't just organized as an Overseer?" Jocelyn asked, stuttering slightly.

Lesser species, eh?

"Nope, I have twenty-five years of memories from my time as a human," I supplied. "Though I have no way to confirm or prove it, I also have no reason to believe that the memories are false."

Jocelyn started to fidget as she pondered, fiddling with some loose strands of her aura.

"Alright. We'll hit some of the key points in this meeting, but it looks like it will take you a bit longer to acclimate and start helping out than I originally thought."

"I appreciate it." I replied.

"First, our purpose as Overseers is to harvest faith and souls. We establish religions on worlds and provide guidance, blessings, and other such things for our followers in return for their faith. When an individual purely dedicates themselves to our teachings, we obtain their souls when they die."

I raised my hand. "What do we do with the faith and souls?"

"We create a copy of the soul and send it to some semblance of whatever version of the afterlife we sell to our followers. Then we send the original to the bosses in Meridian."

"So Meridian is a place?"

"Indeed. It is the origin of time, space, creation, matter, mana, energy, and so on. It's the original home and current headquarters of the Overseer's. It's also a popular vacation spot. You should visit when you accrue enough PTO."

"What does Meridian do with the souls?"

Jocelyn shrugged. "That's something they don't tell the bottom of the ladder people like us. I've heard you have to successfully fulfill terms over a thousand worlds before your request for that information will even be considered."

Well, that sounded sketchy. So, gods were just soul harvesters? And they didn't even send the real soul to heaven or hell? Seriously? I wasn't deeply religious in my last life, but it was still a bit of a letdown to discover the truth.

"You said you came from Earth, right?"

I nodded. "How is Thor doing? Last I spoke to him, he was excited about some movie. Said that he had high hopes of obtaining followers due to some comic book hero adaptation or something?"

"That was a hundred years ago, and I doubt anybody seriously worshiped him over that. In fact, religion was dying in my world after the War of Unification started. The only ones still around were the big ones like Christianity, Buddhism, Islam, and such and even those were dying remnants in the wake of the Unification Army."

Jocelyn sighed. "Earth always was a problem planet. I'm glad I've never been assigned there. The people are so ungrateful and sensitive!"

"Gee, thanks for the amazing compliment." I muttered sarcastically. "Do the people view religion differently here?"

Jocelyn shook her head. "The humans on this planet are all descendants of people from Earth, so we had to take a more roundabout approach to build successful religions. Through some complicated processes and by exploiting the magic systems of this world, we managed to build an automatic resurrection device. Anybody connected to our Overseer system will automatically resurrect at the nearest resurrection point upon death."

From Earth?! And did she just say that they created a way for humans to respawn? And it worked? If there was a religion like that on Earth, I probably would have joined in a heartbeat. But something didn't quite add up there...

"If humans don't really die, then how do you harvest their souls?"

"Oh, they still die. Every time they revive, we take a piece of their soul and eventually they just stop resurrecting. Also, they can still die of old age and such. This just protects them from premature causes of death like murder, sickness, starvation, and disease."

Still, that was incredible. I wasn't sure how I felt about the soul ripping part but the rest of it was neat.

"To increase the frequency of human deaths and hit our weekly soul quota, we released a general decree of persecution against the native inhabitants of this world. In order to manipulate the humans into following the mandate, we universally grouped all of these local races together and labelled them 'monsters.'"

Oh...

Well then. I wasn't so sure I liked this job anymore.

4

A Rude Introduction

Ray walked along the mountain path for a long time. She wasn't sure how long, but it was long enough for the sun to drift behind the looming mountain peaks, while long shadows encroached across the grassy plains.

It didn't feel like she had traveled that far, because the distant stone walls behind her were so tall that she could still barely see them in the distance. Even so, crossing an entire grassy plain was probably enough to consider herself safe.

"Where am I, anyways? There's nothing out here," she muttered to herself as she took in her surroundings.

The mountains looked almost devoid of life. The occasional patch of snow that dotted the rocky slopes accented the still, gray landscape.

She crested another hill and looked down at the winding path ahead of her. The new slope had a few creepy, leafless trees.

The shadows surrounding her shifted as something flew by overhead. Ray flinched and glanced, finding a large bird-like silhouette soaring through the sky.

Unlike the humans who looked nice but felt dangerous, she felt relief when she saw it. The bird looked scary but... maybe it was actually friendly?

She slowed to a stop and waved, trying to get its attention.

The creature screeched in response, twisting in the air as it dived towards her.

Ray felt that something was wrong and slowly dropped her arms. Trusting her instincts over her feelings, she turned around and kicked off the ground as hard as she could. She willed herself to move even faster than before as she sprinted down the hill. Her eyes stung and her hair billowed in the wind, but she pressed on.

A heavy force slammed into her from behind and she tumbled across the hard ground. She smashed against a tree and cried out in shock as her body cracked painfully.

The tree bent in a permanent bow of honor towards the respectable impact. A small torrent of snow covered her as its branches released their heavy burdens.

She rolled over and groaned as she examined herself. Her white cloak was dotted with splotches of mud and had accumulated some random twigs and dead leaves, but it was otherwise okay. She had several cuts on her hands and knuckles and her back was slowly shifting back into its normal position.

She stumbled to her feet as the shadow turned in the sky and prepared to come in for a second strike.

It definitely wasn't friendly.

The creature was some kind of giant predatory bird. She searched her fragmented and blurry memories for any information that might help her, but all that came to her mind were the things that she could already see. That information wasn't helpful at all in this situation.

Ray scanned her surroundings for anything she could use to defend herself but all she saw was trees, snow, dirt, and rocks.

"What am I supposed to do?!"

She stamped her feet against the ground to let out her building frustration and then flinched when she noticed the creature turn towards her.

The flying predator dived, and Ray grabbed a rock in desperation. As the bird approached, she threw the rock with all of her strength. The rock drew a beautiful arc and pierced the bird's massive body. Blood dripped from the sky and stained the snow on the mountainside.

The creature emitted an angry screech but continued its dive undeterred. It lashed out with a claw and struck her in the shoulder as it passed by.

She crashed to the ground and gnashed her teeth. Her dislocated shoulder promptly snapped itself back into place and she picked up another rock while keeping her furious gaze focused on her flying opponent.

A tinge of fear ran through her chest, but she suppressed it with the knowledge that the bird couldn't do anything worse to her than what she had already experienced. As the bird initiated its second dive, she met it's glowing, intelligent red eyes and shivered at the almost oppressive aura that the scary creature emitted.

She stumbled and almost tripped on the rocky ground as she tried to get away. With a furious shriek, the bird passed overhead, and Ray screamed as its piercing claws drew furrows in her back before latching into her shoulder and neck. One talon severed her spine, and her body went limp.

She panicked as the ground started to rapidly move away. She tried to move but all she felt from her arms and legs was a numb pressure. The pain was gone, along with all feeling and sensation below her head.

Ray tried to scream again but her lungs failed to respond properly, and she choked on the blood that rose up into her mouth. It didn't matter though because, as the bird carried her away into the night, there was nobody to hear her.

A tear ran down her cheek and mixed in with the drool of blood spilling out of her mouth. In the darkest hour of the night, pain abandoned her to numbness and fear was her only companion.

Ray yearned for the darkness to come and free her, as it had when she suffered on the mountaintop.

But even that peaceful darkness had abandoned her.

Where had she gone wrong?

She left the town because she felt like she was in danger and ended up in this situation.

The bird carried her for a long time. Ray noticed that her body was trying to restore itself around the claws, but it seemed unable to restore the damage with the claws in the way.

The bird approached a nest high up in a mountainous tree. It released her near the center and then landed smoothly beside her. As she looked around, she saw eggs half as tall as she was and small birds that were a little larger than the eggs.

Then her body jolted, her limbs spasming as she regained the sensation in her lower body. With the offending claws removed, her spine finished recovering and her wounds closed themselves.

Despite the most difficult issue resolving itself, she continued to lay on the ground. She wanted to scream and curse at the world for trying to make her life miserable, though she didn't for fear of triggering the birds.

Why did the bird feel safe, and the humans feel dangerous?

Granted, she had escaped from the humans as soon as she could, but Max and Kelsey both seemed friendly enough. What could they possibly have done that was worse than this? She was about to be eaten!

She put that thought aside for later and decided that she should find a way out of this situation first.

Luckily, the baby birds already seemed to be asleep, or she was sure that she would have already been turned into bird feed. Mama bird, not realizing that Ray's injuries had healed, curled in on itself with one wing drooped over its babies. Though it had only been moments since it settled down, the monster was quietly drifting off to sleep.

Ever so slowly, so as not to wake the birds, she wobbled to her feet. She reached out an arm to steady herself on one of the nearby eggs. As she balanced carefully on the matted nest, she shuffled forward while keeping her eye on the big mama bird.

As if sensing the motion, its red eyes shot open, and it glared at her. She froze, unsure of what to do as the bird shrieked. It quickly rose to its feet while carefully avoiding the large mound of eggs.

Ray heard smaller, more shrill cries and noticed that the young birds had awoken at the cry of their mother. She turned and searched for a way to escape. She ran over to the edge of the nest and looked out, but she only had a moment to process the view. It was beautiful yet disheartening.

She was exceedingly high up in a tree.

A claw latched onto her back and dragged her back into the nest. The bird pinned her and examined her with a strange look in its eyes.

Mama bird was hungry.

It opened its beak and Ray noticed for the first time that the edges were serrated. The inside of the beak was lined with small, sharp protrusions that looked similar to teeth. It's long, barbed tongue snaked out of its mouth briefly as the bird leaned towards her left arm.

Ray felt a tinge of fear, but her emotions were so overwhelmed that they just couldn't catch up in time.

She whimpered in pain as the bird of prey latched onto her arm and bit. She tried to pull away, but she was stuck. The bird whipped its neck, and her arm was gone, blood spilling into the nest as the bird chomped away on its dinner.

Ray, for her part, had gone into shock.

Her face was white, her eyes wide and her mouth open in a soundless screech. Ever so slowly, her brain processed that it was missing input and then the sharp agony rolled through her body.

She screamed. It was a blood-curdling scream that pierced the ears of the bird and it grimaced in discomfort as it softened the food in its mouth. It stomped down on Ray in a vain effort to make the sound stop but she only cried louder. In a moment of inspiration, the bird reached down and slashed the woman's neck with a deft swipe of its claws.

Ray prayed fervently that she could lose consciousness again. She saw the mama bird lean over and regurgitate the remains of her arm into the mouths of its waiting children.

Unfortunately for Ray, her limbs would grow back faster than the birds could eat them. Until they were full, she would function as an infinite food supply.

She lashed out in desperation with her remaining arm and punched the claw that had her pinned. The creature's leg bent at an unnatural angle and the pressure holding her down eased. The bird cried out in torment while Ray grabbed the injured leg and applied more pressure to it.

Mama bird lashed out and raked its claws across her face. Ray flinched when the vision in her left eye went dark, but the pain felt distant, as if it were happening to someone else. Applying even more pressure, she yanked as hard as she could. She felt the resistance suddenly decrease and the bird whimpered. She released the claw which she had just ripped from the bird's body and scrambled backward away from the creature.

Scanning the nest again, she noted that the baby birds had hidden themselves near the eggs behind the mama bird.

The creature that had just moments ago pinned her and ripped off her arm now inched away from her with obvious terror in its eyes. Her left eye finished regenerating and her vision returned to normal.

With a single punch she had snapped its leg.

Ray smiled menacingly as she stalked forward. Mama bird shuffled away from her and she noted that even as the bird moved away, it kept itself between her and its babies.

She felt an idea tug at the edge of her mind and her feral grin widened. Baring her fangs, she leapt forward.

Mama bird lashed out with a wing, but Ray slapped the appendage away. Before the bird had time to register the pain, she barreled into its body and pushed it aside.

The bird tumbled through the nest while Ray reached down and picked up one of the eggs. The baby birds chirped in protest, but she ignored them as she walked over to the edge of the nest and held the egg out over the large drop.

She peered over the lip into the darkness below. The azure light of the moon lit up the ground below, revealing the dizzying height.

If she had to venture a guess, they were at least fifty Ray's high.

Mama bird cried out in desperation, but Ray simply laughed as she released the egg and let it drop.

Ray stepped aside to avoid the incoming storm as the mama bird propelled herself over the edge and down towards the egg. She took a moment to look back at the terrified baby birds behind her, a wide grin on her face.

"Bye!" she called out.

With a quick little wave goodbye, she took a step back into the open air.

She shifted her attention below to the bird that was about to catch up to the egg. It was far too late for it to both catch the egg and recover from the fall, but Ray wanted to make sure the accursed creature died. This method ensured that the bird would suffer for what it did to her, but it would be pointless if the monster survived in the end.

Mama bird caught up to the egg and curled around it in a vain effort as she crashed into the ground. Ray didn't even bother checking if the egg survived the fall because it didn't matter. A moment later, she smashed feet first through the egg and crushed the mama bird against the mountain.

She heard a loud, unpleasant *crack* and then suppressed a scream as agony filled her entire body. She gritted her teeth to endure the pain, groaning as she crawled up out of the bird's ribcage and rolled down the side of its body.

After settling a short distance away from the corpse, she sat up and brushed off some of the sticky egg white and yolk that had mixed in with the dirt and blood stains on her white cloak. Then she ran her fingers through her matted hair to pull the twigs, feathers, and bone fragments out while she waited for her shattered legs to finish restoring themselves back to their original condition.

Looking back on the entire event from beginning to end, she sighed in relief that it was finally over.

The questions that she had been suppressing returned to her mind.

Why did the bird feel safe when it obviously was not?

Why did the humans feel dangerous when they were being nice?

It was probably a bad idea for her to trust the fragmented memories. She decided that she wouldn't listen to them anymore unless she understood the reason for the negative feelings.

Having reached that conclusion, she examined the bloody corpse behind her and then looked off in the distance towards the human town she fled from. If she was going to ignore her impressions, then it was probably a good idea to go back. At the very least, the people there didn't try to eat her like a certain nest of giant birds. It was possible that they might know something about her and why she woke up with no memories.

Besides, what was the worst they could do? There was no way they could ever do anything worse than what had already happened to her.

With this new direction in mind, she pushed herself to her feet.

As her healing reached its final stages, she started to run as fast as she could towards the town full of people. She didn't even spare a single glance back for the dead bird that had dared to offend her.

5

Decisions

I sat alone at the table, long after the other two Overseers had already left. The things I learned in that conversation continued to cycle through my mind. Anybody would have been shocked to learn some of those truths of the world. I wasn't a religious dude before, but I didn't hate most concepts of deity.

The fact that gods only helped humans to farm them for faith and souls? I could live with that. It actually made me less uneasy about the whole idea. It was always easier to trust someone when you knew the purpose behind their actions.

But the way these particular gods were going about it bothered me quite a bit. They were uniting humanity under a single banner by persecuting the natives of this world.

Considering that these gods wanted humans to die as often as possible, it was easy to see the benefits of doing such a thing, especially if there were powerful creatures native to this world like dragons and such.

However, I couldn't help but feel that they didn't tell me everything. At the very least, I held onto a small thread of hope that gods didn't usually declare genocide on dozens of species so easily. Fighting in self-defense or on the battlefield would be one thing, but deliberate murder of innocent children, elderly, and other non-combatants?

There was no way that I could ever support that.

And then there was one other detail that I had to consider. Perhaps most important for my immediate situation, my chosen prophet was one of those 'monsters' that the other Overseers had ordered the entire human race to hunt and destroy.

That might complicate things a little bit...

Of course, I would never regret my decision. I was able to save that woman and I would do it again in a heartbeat. I used to get in trouble for that kind of thing a lot in my previous life. The captain said it was my fatal flaw, but I thought it was my greatest strength. I just couldn't look the other way when people were suffering due to the actions of others.

That didn't mean I was stupid. Though I disagreed with what the other Overseers were doing here on a fundamental level, I didn't have to openly oppose them. Even if my prophet was one of their targets… but nobody needed to know that yet.

In fact, it could end up giving me some advantages if I played my cards right. From the brief display that I saw, my new prophet was stronger than any human from Earth could ever be. The other Overseers talked about various worlds and having multiple assignments. If I played my cards right, it might be possible to return to Earth as a god. Considering that this world seemed to be more of a fantasy world, it could even be possible to take some followers over with me. I would lead a legion of monsters to save my family, my friends, my country, and my world.

The Director and his Unification Army most definitely wouldn't expect that. I mean, who would realistically plan for an army of fantasy aliens led by the soul of a dead traitor?

Then again, given the number of conspiracy theorists on Earth, I wouldn't put it past somebody to have predicted it.

Anyways, that would be my ultimate goal. I would find a way to return to and save Earth. In the meantime, I would build up my power here and raise up an army powerful and faithful enough to liberate a world.

While I learned the ropes and amassed some power, I would have to quietly carry the burden of knowing that I was the last hope for the people of Earth. This was a burden that I would have to carry alone, for now. Earth's problems were not Hanulfall's problems.

"Auto," I called out. "Ya there, buddy?"

I heard a faint click and turned, seeing a door open that wasn't there before.

"Affirmative. Have you concluded your assimilation of the newly acquired data?"

"Yeah, let's go with that. Can you take me back to Hanulfall? I want to see that the vampire is okay with my own eyes."

"Understood. I will comply."

My soul shuddered as a faint jolt traveled through my form. My senses began to fade once more. What a terrifying ability. There was nothing that I could do to stop it since I hadn't the slightest idea how he did it in the first place.

It probably wasn't a good idea to make Auto mad. At least, not until I got a lot more power and understanding. To do that, I needed followers. To get followers, I needed teachings. To establish teachings, I needed a purpose.

With that thought, my senses completely abandoned me, and my entire world went dark.

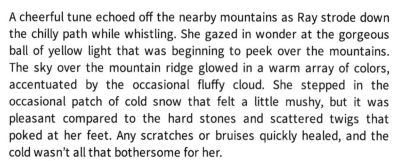

A cheerful tune echoed off the nearby mountains as Ray strode down the chilly path while whistling. She gazed in wonder at the gorgeous ball of yellow light that was beginning to peek over the mountains. The sky over the mountain ridge glowed in a warm array of colors, accentuated by the occasional fluffy cloud. She stepped in the occasional patch of cold snow that felt a little mushy, but it was pleasant compared to the hard stones and scattered twigs that poked at her feet. Any scratches or bruises quickly healed, and the cold wasn't all that bothersome for her.

Another hour or so and she should reach the place full of people. She didn't know what was waiting for her there, but she felt confident. Though it was rather painful, she beat a giant bird! She survived a fall from at least fifty times her own height! What else could the world throw at her?

She whistled on autopilot and a familiar tune filled the air as she walked, blissfully ignorant of her surroundings.

Which might have been why she didn't see the people until she was surrounded.

A blonde-haired, blue-eyed man with a pretty face, a sword, and a shield stepped out onto the path in front of her. Ray skid to a stop a few meters away from him. She sensed movement from the side and heard rustling in one of the bushes that lined the path as a white-robed young girl stomped out with an angry sneer on her face.

Ray startled in recognition. She looked behind her and saw the dagger user in a new set of leather armor. Beside him was the bow user.

They were the same four humans who she'd found dead when she first woke up. The same four that she had briefly observed before experiencing something rather painful that she didn't want to think about.

"Fancy outfit you got going on there. Looks like we found a kitty cat lost in the woods," the swordsman said nonchalantly.

Kitty cat? Ray twisted her body and looked down over her shoulder, but she couldn't see a tail. There were plenty of bloodstains and some dried egg yolk though.

"Pretty sure I'm not a feline," she informed them.

"See, we met a vamp a week ago on this mountain. Know anything about it?" the man continued, ignoring her helpful comment.

Ray shrugged. She honestly didn't know. She knew that she wasn't human, but she also wasn't a vampire.

The white-robed girl raised her hand and it started to glow with a white light. Ray felt a tinge of unease. She felt an inexplicable sense of danger from that light.

"You came from the direction of the peak! You obviously know where the vamp is!" the girl practically screeched.

Ray grimaced at the unpleasant sound.

"Now, now Suzy. There's no need to get so heated."

Suzy? Another name to add to the list.

Suzy reluctantly lowered her hand as the swordsman took a few steps forward.

"Miss, the vampire is dangerous. I don't know why you are out here, but if you know where it is then you need to tell us. We need to put it down. It's a danger to all of humanity."

Ray gave him a weak smile. "Sir, I don't know where it is. I just escaped from the nest of a giant flesh-eating bird."

The man blinked in surprise, doing a double take as he reappraised her. "A giant flesh-eating bird... you mean a roc? Are you actually an adventurer?"

A roc? Was that what those birds were called? Ray stored that info away in her memory and then shook her head.

"Hmm," the man paused as he thought for a moment. "Where are you going? If you can deal with a roc by yourself then you can obviously pull your own weight. Maybe we can help each other?"

"I'm headed for the place full of people over there," Ray replied, pointing at the big wall.

"Cairel? I've never seen you around the guild there. Are you an adventurer from another town?"

Ray opted to remain silent. She noted that the swordsman's hand still hadn't left the pommel of his sword. Also, she could smell the warm blood of another individual hiding nearby. When she listened closely, she heard the faint rustling of leaves as someone moved out of sight.

They were clearly unwilling to trust her, so she decided not to answer.

The man examined her for a moment and then held up his hands. "I apologize for the interrogation. That was rude of me." He took a few more steps forward, reaching out his hand. "The name's Jonathan. I hope to see you around more."

Ray stared at his hand for a moment, perplexed. She saw his face fall slightly and hesitantly reached out to grasp it. His grip was firm as he shook her limp hand. She looked up and met his eyes.

What she saw there was shock.

The man released her hand and stepped backward, reaching for his sword. "You almost had me," he growled. He drew his sword and pointed it at her. "You vamps are real good at deception. I was almost convinced that you were a human until I saw that red eye."

Ray took a step back, confused by the sudden shift in direction. She was fairly sure things had been about to end peacefully.

"Thing is, you're pretty. A little branding and I bet you'd fetch a good price."

Huh? Ray had no idea where this was going but she didn't like the greedy gleam she could now see in the man's eyes. She looked around for a way to escape, but she was still surrounded.

With an annoyed grumble, she reached down and picked up a rock as her preparation for a fight. After her recent experiences, she wasn't afraid of dying, but she still didn't like pain.

Worse than pain, though, was the unknown. She didn't know what they were going to do if they won.

Right now, there was an awful lot of unknown if she let them catch her.

Unfortunately, it wasn't much of a fight.

Ray seized the initiative, throwing the rock as a distraction and then launched herself forward to deal the first strike. As she flew, she wound her arm back to throw a powerful punch.

The fighter sidestepped the rock, and her fist impacted his quickly raised shield. His stance remained firm, though his surprised expression betrayed the amount of effort it took to keep his shield in place.

Ray's right hand, however, was a bloody mess.

She wasn't done though. She grabbed the rim of the shield with her bloody hand and pulled it aside, hooking her left fist towards the man's armored chest with a shout.

She released her grip on his shield as her left fist smashed into the man's chest, denting his armor, and pushing him back.

He stumbled a few feet backward before recovering and returned to his stance. The entire sequence happened in the blink of an eye, and he stared at her with dazed eyes.

"So fast..." he muttered in awe.

And then an arrow slammed into her lower back.

Ray stumbled forward, turning to see the dagger-user carefully approaching while the bowman knocked another arrow. She reached back, fingering the shaft of the arrow while her eyes moved back and forth rapidly between each of the four humans.

She carefully yanked the arrow out with her nearly recovered hand, grunting in pain as she held it in front of her.

"Hey vamp! If you give up, we won't hurt you anymore," Jonathan promised.

"Hah!" Ray laughed derisively. "What a pathetic lie. You never had to hurt me in the first place."

The man scowled. "The buyers don't like damaged goods."

"I don't get it. You guys were fine to let me go until you realized I wasn't human and suddenly I'm for sale? What kind of twisted logic is that?"

They paused and exchanged glances with each other.

"Uh, aren't you a vampire? This is pretty normal, right?" Jonathan responded with a hint of confusion in his voice.

"You're not human," Suzy sneered. "Monsters don't get *humane* treatment."

"And who said I'm a monster?" Ray countered, turning to look at her.

She felt the wound on her back slowly closing while her knuckles finished inching back into their natural positions. She decided once again that her recovery ability was a beautiful thing, and she would be forever grateful for it.

"We say, the gods say. Monsters are forsaken by the Overseers, rejected by your own creators and inferior to humans. Your only place is under our heel," Suzy responded, her face twisting into a slightly manic expression.

Ray, for her part, had no idea how to respond to that, mostly because she had no idea what Suzy meant by any of those three points. She shook her head. All that really mattered was that she disagreed.

"So where does that leave us, then? I'm not going without a fight," she warned them.

"Don't worry about that. Vick here is a rogue. He's got all kinds of ways to take someone down without external injury," Jonathan replied with motion towards the red-haired dagger user.

Vick nodded silently, pulling a black rope out of thin air. He raised the rope, and it began to levitate as it extended itself towards Ray.

She sliced at the rope with the tip of the arrow, taking a step back to distance herself from it.

An excruciating pain struck her side and she looked down. She found a faint glowing light resting against her dirty cloak near her waist. Though the light did no visible damage, it *burned*!

Ray hissed, gritting her teeth as she launched herself at Suzy, hoping to stop her before she could use that weird light again.

A shield entered her vision and sent her reeling into the ground. Ray spit out a glob of blood, baring her fangs at the humans.

Inside, she desperately continued searching for a way out.

Try as she might, she couldn't find one. The dark-haired archer and the rogue circled around, preventing her from running while Jonathan blocked her way forward. If she stayed in place, Suzy would keep attacking with that burning light.

The rope latched onto her wrist, interrupting her thoughts. It shifted, twisting around her back. Ray turned with the rope, releasing the arrow to clutch at it with her now-free hand. She grabbed the end and tried to wrestle the rope away from her.

Another white light struck her in the back, causing her to flinch. In her brief moment of hesitation, she relaxed her grip.

The rope promptly latched onto her other hand and pulled her hands together. Shortly after, a second rope latched around her feet and Ray lost her balance, falling face-first into a pile of bloody snow.

She felt a firm grip reach under her and then she was moving through the air as Jonathan picked her up with one hand and slung her over his shoulder.

"She's a feisty one. A lot stronger and faster than I was expecting for a vamp though. Her punch dented my armor."

"The sun's up. Also, she bled when I hit her with a normal arrow..." the archer pointed out. "Are you sure she's a vampire?"

Vick shrugged. "She has a red eye and you saw the fangs too, right?"

"She could be a snakekin..."

"Who cares if she's a vampire or not, she isn't human. All monsters are the same. The gods have forsaken them. No matter how strong they are, someday this world will be cleansed of their sinful existences!" Suzy half-shouted, her tone rising with vindictive fire.

The other three humans stared at Suzy with tired eyes. None of them decided to respond.

"Anyways, we should head back to town…" Jonathan continued.

Ray listened in silence. Her mind took in every detail to form a plan of escape. All she needed was one moment.

She didn't know when the moment would come, but when it did, she would be ready.

6

Escape

Jonathan held Ray out with one arm, his other hand scratching his chin as he examined her.

"You're a strange one," he admitted. "What are you? You have some vampiric traits but you're not undead. You're far too weak to be a seraph. Are there any other monster races with vampiric traits?"

Ray spat on his face.

Jonathan didn't even flinch as he wiped the liquid away with his free hand. Then he reached into a bag hanging from his waist and pulled out a small vial of purple liquid. He uncapped the vial and poured the contents into his mouth.

Nothing changed. Ray stared at the man in confusion as he grimaced.

"That wasn't poisonous? What a waste. I had to make sure, though."

Ray promptly dismissed the man's actions.

She had decided on a plan. It was a stupid plan and would probably end with her body in a ditch somewhere... but even that would be an escape of sorts.

Jonathan released Ray, dropping her to the ground with a *thud*. He pulled a black cloak out of his bag and tossed it over her. Without another word, he started walking in the direction of the huge wall.

The archer prodded her with his bow. She meekly pointed with her bound hands at the rope tying her feet together. The thief snapped his fingers, and the rope released her legs and returned to his hands. She obediently rose to her feet, walking with her back hunched to keep the cloak covering her figure.

The group walked in formation, the thief moving in front while the archer was in the rear. Suzy walked beside Ray while Jonathan was a short distance in front of the two girls. They moved in silence. The four individuals were tense as they constantly observed their surroundings.

Ray, for her part, ignored them as she focused on the rope binding her hands. The cloak functioned as an excellent cover as she slowly experimented, prodding it and attempting to move her hands around. The rope didn't seem to conform to her wrists without its master's orders. Perfect.

For the next several minutes, Ray focused on working her hands through the rope. She hid a grimace as the bones in her hands ground against each other. After a minute of painful compressing, a piercing wave of agony shot up her arm as one of the bones cracked. She bit her lip to stop herself from making any sounds. She focused her mind on the tiny sting as she continued to pull her hand through the rope.

Her arm started trying to regenerate, so she pulled harder, trying to prevent it from healing by causing further injury. She heard an audible crack and flinched, hoping that nobody heard it.

The four humans stopped in their tracks, searching for the source of the sound. Ray pulled one more time and felt a wave of relief as her right hand squeezed through the rope and started to heal.

She hid a smile, trying to remain inconspicuous.

After several quiet minutes, Jonathan signaled that they should keep moving. The group started to move together along the path once more. Ray, walking beside Suzy, twisted her hunched form slightly to observe the white-robed girl.

Specifically, her eyes latched onto the hilt of a dagger peeking out from the sash of her robes. She turned just enough to inconspicuously glance at the archer in the rear, noting that most of his attention was focused on their surroundings. He only occasionally looked at her, probably putting too much trust in his friend's flying ropes.

The walls were moving ever closer, and Ray estimated that they were still about thirty minutes away. She waited for one of the brief gaps when both the archer and Suzy were looking away from her.

Now or never.

Ray lunged at Suzy, grabbing the hilt of her dagger, and deftly shoved it up under Suzy's chin and into her head. The dagger felt strangely natural in her hand and the dagger cut into Suzy with little resistance. Suzy went limp, the light in her eyes dying before she could even recognize that she had been attacked.

Without pausing, Ray launched herself at the archer at breakneck speed, holding her cloak in place with her left hand. He started to turn, noticing something approaching in his peripheral vision but he was too late. Ray shoved the bloody dagger into the archer's ear. His neck snapped from the force of the blow, and he fell over dead.

Both Suzy's and the archer's bodies hit the ground at about the same time.

Unfortunately, the bodies hitting the ground made a noise, which meant that Jonathan and Vick noticed something was amiss.

Ray resisted the compelling scent of blood that began to waft through the air as she quickly slashed the rope into three pieces with the dagger. She felt a growing urge inside of her to attack the other two, but she suppressed it as she reached down and grabbed the bag tied to the archer's waist, slashing the cords that held it in place. Then she faced Jonathan and Vick, starting to circle off the path to the left as if to approach them.

"By Loki, what did you just do?!" Vick swore, his face turning white.

Jonathan stared at his friend's corpses with a grim expression. He donned his shield and unsheathed his sword, turning to face Ray. As she was shuffling to the left, he matched her movements to keep her at a far enough distance that he could react to anything she might try.

Vick moved with Jonathan, keeping himself behind the frontliner. He wasn't sure how Ray had escaped or killed the other two party members. Until he had more information, he didn't want to charge forward or put himself in a position to get attacked.

When they completed half a revolution of a circle, Ray stopped. She wanted to keep fighting. She could feel her heart pounding as adrenaline surged through her.

She also felt that it would be a bad idea to continue. She took out two of them in a surprise attack, but she didn't really know how to fight.

She took a step back, bowing to her opponents. Jonathan and Vick froze, unsure of what to make of the gesture.

Ray straightened her back, finally pulling her arms through the sleeves of her new black cloak as she stuck her tongue out at them. Then she turned and ran towards the wall at a speed far faster than a normal human could run.

She giggled hysterically as she ran, licking the blood off the dagger. It wasn't anywhere near as good as the blood she tasted when she first awoke, but it was still delicious.

She summoned the image of Jonathan's and Vick's surprised faces in her mind, as well as Suzy's blank expression.

Ray replayed the sequence in her mind repeatedly, chuckling with delight every time she remembered the pleasant sound of the archer's neck snapping.

In the short time since she became aware, she finally made a memory that she never wanted to forget.

Victory tasted incredibly sweet.

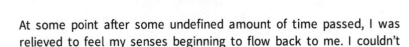

At some point after some undefined amount of time passed, I was relieved to feel my senses beginning to flow back to me. I couldn't really say for sure, but I suspected that whatever Auto did to me also removed my sense of time.

As I focused my attention on my surroundings, I found myself floating behind the familiar vampire as she ran down the mountain towards the walled town.

Why was she out here? I thought Auto told me she was inside a temple in the town.

Then again, I had no idea how much time had passed. It couldn't have been too much because she didn't look any older than when I saw her last. She was wearing a black cloak now and laughing hysterically as she licked a bloodstained dagger. It wasn't the weirdest thing I had ever seen, but it still made the list.

"Mr. Overseer?" robo-voice interrupted my thoughts.

"Yes, Auto?"

"It appears that you are approaching an important decision that will influence you for the rest of eternity."

"What's that?"

"You have to choose a new name."

"..."

I honestly hadn't thought about it that much, but Auto was right. Try as hard as I might, I couldn't quite seem to remember my name from when I was on Earth. Everything else about my previous life was crystal clear, but whatever process turned me into an Overseer withheld that one detail from me. I wouldn't be allowed to claim that I was the same person here.

That being said, I had no idea what to call myself. I decided to spitball whatever came to mind.

"Hmm... considering the 'vampire' and 'monster' stuff, maybe something anime-ish? Lord of Darkness. King of Vampires. His Almighty Spirit-ness. God of Monsters? Nah, those are all titles. I need a *name*."

"If you so desire, I can run a Name Generator to give you ideas."

A Name Generator? What could go wrong?

"Sure…"

"Calculating… complete. I will now read the generated options."

The voice paused for a moment before taking on a slightly different tone. It was still robotic, but this time it sounded almost… amused… or perhaps whimsical?

"Sugar Fruit, Sunshine Zephyr, Snow Music, Juicy Firefly, Amethyst Poser…"

"STOP! Stop, right now!"

Auto's voice cut off. After a brief lull, he spoke again. "Objection, I was nearing the more creative ones."

"I don't even want to know."

What the hell kind of name generator did he just use?

"Sir, are you absolutely certain that you do not want to be known for eternity as 'Coco Velvet'?"

"Yes, I am absolutely sure."

But I was starting to have doubts about my impression of Auto's personality. This was a rather sudden shift.

"Noted. Shall I use a different generator?"

"No, I think I'll brainstorm a bit more on my own."

"May I address another topic then?"

If I had eyebrows, I'd probably be raising them now. "Sure, what's up?"

"Now that you are aware of the truth of this world, I must apologize for allowing you to choose a non-human as your Tether."

Ah. Was Auto feeling guilty?

"Can I ask you a question related to that? You claimed that the sword-and-board warrior was the third strongest adventurer in the region. Why were he and his party defeated so easily by a random monster?"

"That entity was not simply a random monster. However, I did exaggerate and falsify information to manipulate you."

Huh. Though I'd suspected as much, I did not expect such a forthcoming reply.

"Why?"

"You are an anomaly. There were only four Overseer's given free reign over this world and then you suddenly appeared. My master grew concerned and sent me to observe and manipulate you into choosing a less-than-promising Tether."

"And yet you are very honest in all your appraisals."

"Naturally. I have taken an interest in you. Your decisions do not follow established protocols and I wish to see interesting things."

"Hmm, so basically if your master orders you to screw me over then you'll do it with no hesitation. Otherwise, you'll help me 'because it's interesting'?"

"Affirmative."

"And I don't suppose you'll tell me who your master is?"

"Do not ask inane questions."

Right. No way it would be that easy.

"As for your apology, don't worry about it. Given my personality, I probably would have ended up on this side in the end anyways. This just forced me into that position a little sooner, that's all."

"I am relieved to hear that you hold neither contempt nor anger for my lack of candidness. In the future, I will be more forthright with both my aid and my training."

"Sure, don't mention it."

I needed Auto to teach me how to do this Overseer stuff, after all. I wouldn't be throwing my 'teacher' out quite yet, notwithstanding my complete inability to actually do so.

I returned my attention to my Tether. I circled around her as she ran, noting that her silvery hair was tangled and had mixed clots of dried blood and dirt spread throughout.

The sight of the blood reminded me of the horrific event that ultimately led me to turn her into my Tether. She was quickly approaching the town. At her current pace, she would probably reach the gate in a handful of minutes.

Outside of the gates, I could see several humans. Some had carts or wagons. Other's carried heavy loads. There were many armed individuals who seemed to be guarding different clients. If I had to venture a guess, I would say that the people there mostly consisted of merchants, farmers, adventurers, and hired guards or mercenaries.

Disappointingly, though as expected, I didn't see any nonhumans. Other than that, everything externally looked like I would expect it to for a medieval fantasy world.

My Tether moved to the end of the line, and I decided to wait and watch for the time being. Once she got inside the town and found a place to stay, it would be time to introduce myself and have a good heart-to-heart conversation.

We were going to be seeing a lot of each other for a while, after all.

7

Return

The remainder of Ray's trip to the wall was uneventful.

While on the trail, she tried to see what was in the bag she had picked up, but it seemed to be empty. The rope that the dagger-user had pulled out of his bag was bigger than the bag itself, so there had to be some kind of trick to it, but she couldn't figure it out. She decided to hold onto the bag a little longer, just in case.

As Ray neared the town, she slowed down to stop the cloak from billowing around her. She pulled on the hems and wrapped herself up tight. Observing her surroundings, she noticed details that had escaped her when she passed through from the other direction.

There were dozens of farms separated by fields. The outermost farms were dilapidated, surrounded by rotted and collapsed wooden fences. The fields were desolate and grey, and the houses looked like they fell apart a long time ago. One farm had a large hole in the wall as if something large had smashed through it, and another building looked to have been burned down by fire.

However, as she moved closer to the town, she noticed more signs of civilization. The fields were still devoid of life due to being covered in snow and ice, but the fences and houses were well kept. Smoke billowed from the chimneys of several homes, and she heard peals of laughter from a few human children who were running and playing in the fields. The occasional canine creature whimpered in fear as she passed by.

She stared at one cowering animal that was leashed to a fence post. The creature refused to meet her eyes, bowing its head down in acknowledgement of her regal presence. She turned her nose up and snorted, hiding a pleased smile as she continued on.

She walked past the farms and found herself approaching a large gate on the side of the wall. When she was here before, she hadn't really taken the time to appreciate exactly how large these walls were. They were *huge*. Each side was approximately fifty feet high and twenty feet wide. The wall faces were perfectly smooth without a visible chip or crack.

Yet, more than wondering about how they had built such a big structure, Ray was more concerned about *why*.

What were they defending against that required walls this big?

Outside the gate was a small line of people waiting to talk to the couple of guards who controlled entry to the town.

She hesitated, the same nagging warning from before telling her to flee.

Was this really a good idea?

The man and the priestess in the white and gold building saw her red eye and they didn't attack her on sight, but her experience with the four rude humans made her hesitate.

However, she had already resolved herself to confront this feeling. She didn't have context to understand what was making her so nervous, so she decided to move forward and learn for herself.

Her pause had garnered some attention. A few of the guards were watching her now, but they were still too far away to have noticed anything about her.

The group at the very front started to move through the gate. They were dressed similarly to the four rude people, covered in armor and weapons with little bags hanging from their waists.

She got into the line and waited. There were only three groups of people ahead of her. One of them was a merchant that was guiding a cart covered in a white tarp while the other two looked like farmers carrying sacks. The merchant's cart was being guarded by a group of burly, rugged-looking men with lots of weapons and scars.

While she was observing them curiously, the merchant started arguing with the guard. Ray took a step closer to listen in, curious about the contents.

"You have no right to steal my merchandise! I do not serve this kingdom and will not support you by paying your absurd 'tolls.'"

"Sir, I will have to ask you to step away from the cart."

"This is absurd! What are you, thieves and brigands?"

The guard motioned with his hand and two of the guards behind him leveled their spears at the complaining merchant. He stepped away from his cart with a grumble, motioning for the burly men to stand down as the first guard walked over to it. The guard pulled on the white tarp and revealed what was hidden underneath.

Ray gasped at the unexpected sight that was revealed. She noticed more than one pair of eyes turn in her direction. She quickly fixed her expression, donning one that she hoped looked uninterested. The soldiers' attention returned to the cart.

The tarp had covered a large cage. Inside were several children that looked like they were in various stages of a cross between beast and human. One boy looked like a human, though he had wolf ears and a tail, while one of the girls looked more wolf-like, having brown fur all across her body and a canine nose. Those two were glaring at each other and didn't even seem to notice the change in their surroundings.

There were five children in all - two wolf-human hybrids, a cat human, and two fox kids. The cat human had black ears and a long, black tail. Her claws were silver and reflected the light. The two fox kids looked terrified and were huddling together in the corner, making it difficult for Ray to make out any details.

She felt a surge of overwhelming rage and fury run through her. She struggled to push it down. She knew that the emotion was coming from inside of her, but they felt alien at the same time. What…?

"Hoh, what have we here?" the guard wondered aloud. "Smuggling, perhaps?"

"Smuggling my arse! If I wanted to smuggle, I wouldn't have used the main gate. These are legal goods! I showed you the papers!"

The guard smiled, but the smile never reached his greedy eyes. "You know what happens when you break the law?"

The slave-trader merchant went still, an annoyed expression on his face. He turned to address the burly men that traveled with him, and the guards took advantage of the gap in his attention. Two spear-wielding guards stepped forward, stabbing with their weapons.

The slave merchant belatedly realized what was going on and yelled. "St..stop!"

One of the burly men lunged forward to intercept but he was a step too slow. The spears pierced the merchant simultaneously. One struck his heart and the other pierced his lung. The man crumpled to the ground and was still.

"You can respawn in New America, where you belong!" one guard declared as the remaining guards at the gate roared with laughter.

A few of them came over and began wheeling the cart into the town. One of the guards pushing the cart flipped off the burly men as they moved away. The men glared at the guards, but none of them moved to retaliate. They simply turned and started to walk away from the walls with slumped shoulders.

Ray struggled to deal with the unnatural rage building inside of her. When she saw the people in the cages, she just thought they were cute and a bit pitiful. She certainly hadn't been even remotely angry, so why was she now almost overcome with fury?

She focused on the feeling and attempted to follow it to its source. She found something inside her mind that felt strange. It was dark and empty, like a void, and she could feel the rage coming from it. She reached out with her mind, attempting to stop it when a voice started to speak into her mind.

"-cruel and evil bastards! That's a catgirl! How can you live with yourselves keeping a catgirl as a slave! Heresy! It's the worst kind of heresy! You don't have the right to call yourselves men!"

Ray immediately withdrew and the voice went quiet.

Okay then. There was a sentient, dark void in her mind that had a strong obsession with animal people. That was good to know.

Before she could let herself get too bothered by this new information, it was her turn to speak to the guard. Both farmers entered without encountering any issues and Ray stepped forward.

"Name, occupation and reason for visit?" the guard asked.

"My name is Ray and I want to visit the white and gold building."

"White and gold building? Probably the temple or the cathedral. That's fine. What's your occupation?"

"Uhhh, I can fight stuff."

"Low-level adventurer then? Aren't you a little on the small side for that?"

"Tell that to the stuff I killed. I don't think they cared how big I was."

"Ha!" The guard grinned widely. "I like your spirit. Finally, can I ask you to remove the hood of your cloak?"

Ray shook her head. "I'd rather not."

"It's just a precaution. There are a few humanoid monsters and some of them even manage to learn our language. It's not that I think you're a monster, but I need to do my job."

Ray felt a bead of sweat roll down her neck as she desperately searched for a way to avoid him seeing her red eye. Had she not encountered the four rude people, she would have lifted the hood without hesitation, but now she wasn't sure whether he would also be a rude person. He did just kill a merchant in front of her, so he probably wasn't very nice.

"Miss?" the guard asked with a hint of wariness. His hand was slowly inching towards the spear on his back.

She reached up and grabbed the edge of her hood when a voice called out from behind the guard.

"Hey, young miss! Where've ya been?"

Ray and the guard both turned to see a man approaching. Ray gasped as she recognized him by his short-cropped red hair, neatly trimmed beard and his eyepatch.

Max -- the man from the white and gold building.

She felt a wave of relief as she recalled that he was one of the nicer people. He didn't fly off the wall about the fact that she wasn't a human.

Ray pointed at the guard. "I'm trying to get back into the town, but this guy thinks I'm a monster."

"Oh? Is that so?" Max muttered, raising an eyebrow.

Ray smiled internally as she noticed beads of sweat forming on the guard's forehead. She pressed her attack. "I just wanted to visit the white and gold building to see you again, but he doesn't trust me!"

Max stared at the guard. The guard took a step back, looking down at the ground.

"Is this true, Jerrick?"

"N-no. I was just doing my job..." the guard stuttered.

"It's good to be cautious, but I hope you can let this one through on my word? I'll take personal responsibility for her while she stays here."

"Y-y-yes... there's n-n-no problem." Jerrick stepped aside, motioning for Ray to enter.

Ray quickly stepped forward, ignoring the guard's bow as she walked up to Max, with a bright smile.

Max winked at her as they started to walk inside.

She passed through the well-lit, seven-meter tunnel and emerged through the gate on the other side. The afternoon sun blinded her for a moment. As her eyes adjusted and took in the scene, she gasped. A swarm of people in dozens of varieties walked through the street: young, old, male, female, those who looked both male and female. Some had long or short hair in black, red, blonde, or brown tones. Some had dark-toned skin, while others had light-tones.

All of them walked on cobblestone streets, moving between wooden stalls set up along the sides. Alongside the visual storm was a cacophony of noise, almost like a symphony gone wrong. Merchants shouted, advertising their wares while the buzz of side conversations covered the sound of hundreds of footsteps on stone.

The experience was rather different from when she had been looking down from above while moving through the air at a fast pace. This was much more splendid.

"Hey, young miss!" one merchant shouted, pointing at her.

Ray stared at the guy for a moment, unsure of whether she should respond.

"No need to be janglin' yerself! I haven't seen ya 'round these parts. Ya new?"

"Yes," she responded. "I came to visit the white and gold building."

"Oh, a temple pilgrim, are we? Don't see too many of them pious sorts this close to the border. Too many monsters, not enough devotees if ye catch me drift."

Ray nodded slowly. She didn't 'catch his drift', but whatever.

"But hey, if ye be needin' anythin' while yer in this here poor excuse fer a town just look fer good ol' Max. He be the one who can get you pious folks squared away."

"Oh, you mean him?" Ray asked as she turned to point at Max but then she stopped, confused.

"Huh?"

He was gone.

She hadn't noticed when he left. Also, there was a note attached to the back of the hand she was using to point. She hadn't noticed when it was placed there.

"The likes of Max wouldn't bother comin' down here!" the merchant chortled. "Imagine the High Templar himself walkin' these here streets! Them people over there might hafta respawn just from the shock!"

"Looks like I met someone important..." Ray muttered to herself. She picked up the note and quickly scanned the contents.

See ya at the temple. I'd love to hear your story.

- Max, High Templar of Cairel

Perfect. If he was someone important, he might have some answers for her about who and what she was.

Ray turned to walk away. Then she paused. "Which way is it to the temple?" she asked.

The merchant looked at her appraisingly, a look of incredulous disbelief on his face. "Are ye sure yer a pilgrim, miss? Ye never saw a temple a'fore?"

Ray shifted uncomfortably under his piercing gaze, but she held her ground.

After another moment of silence, he pointed at the huge, white building visible in the distance. "Ye see that there big building in the center of town?"

Ray nodded. It definitely looked like an expensive, important building. If she hadn't been here before, she wouldn't have been surprised if that were the place that she was looking for. But she distinctly remembered that the temple was on a floating rock in the sky, and she couldn't see that.

"It'll be right behind that. Ye can't miss it."

"Thank you, sir! I'll be sure to visit again later," Ray beamed.

The merchant feigned a cough, turning to look away with slightly flushed cheeks. "Off with ya, I need to be findin' payin' customers."

Ray turned and moved down the street. She was unfamiliar with the flow of traffic and kept bumping into people, but they seemed to not even notice. Gradually, she made her way through the town, her eyes greedily consuming every new sight she could find.

Past the merchant stalls, she found herself in a large open square ringed by buildings of various shapes and sizes. One had a sign with twin swords, another with a picture of armor. She was intrigued by the 'Adventurer's Guild' and the 'Inn' on the corner. The word 'adventurer' still gave her a bad feeling. whereas she was merely curious about the purpose of the second building. The smells coming from the structure were somewhat appetizing, but nowhere near as savory as the scent of blood.

As she continued to look around, she started noticing other details. The alleys between buildings were dark and often seemed dirty or run down. More than once, she saw cloaked individuals moving through an alley before disappearing.

Additionally, there were people wearing collars. She identified three different 'types', grouped by races. There were the animal/human hybrids, some sort of tall, green-skinned humanoid with tusks, and ginormous, gray-skinned humanoid monsters with thick, craggy arms.

There were no humans in chains.

All the nonhumans wore rags of some sort and had collars attached to some part of their body. Strangely enough, the chains were never connected to anything else on the free end, they simply dragged across the ground behind the nonhumans.

Ray wasn't an expert at reading expressions, but she could see from the drooped shoulders, empty eyes, and soulless shuffling of these individuals that they were not having a good time.

The sight filled her with a strange emotion that she hadn't experienced yet. Her heart ached and she felt like something was caught in her throat. Thinking back to what had happened with the four rude people, she suspected that this might have been her fate if she hadn't escaped. Luckily, she had the presence of mind and the mental fortitude to break out of her bindings.

She continued moving through the town until she reached the tall cathedral. It towered over all the other buildings and was a testament to the wealth and power of humans. Three large panes of colored glass depicted a young, blonde-haired child with blue eyes accomplishing various heroics. Each pane had a description engraved beneath it.

In the left pane, he fought off an army of the green-skinned humanoids. It was titled 'Douglas subdues the Green Tide'.

In the right pane, the child faced off against a group of the gray-skinned giants. 'Douglas topples the Trolls'.

However, the center pane was the most interesting to Ray and made a nervous chill run through her. It had an image of a divine light settling on the boy as he posed in victory. Countless bodies surrounded him.

'Douglas, Tether of the Strong One.'

This cathedral seemed to be a building dedicated to this 'Douglas' figure. He looked extremely familiar to her, and she couldn't shake the feeling that she had met him before. Her senses were telling her that she should stay away from him.

Judging from the images, he was clearly a dangerous individual despite his young appearance. Ray silently prayed that she wouldn't have to encounter Douglas as she skirted around the building and moved behind it.

The merchant had been right, there was no way for her to miss it.

Directly behind the cathedral was a set of stairs. The bottom step floated almost a foot above the ground. The stairs were pearly white and had four intricate patterns that lined the sides, alternating on each step: lilies, mastiffs, mermaids, and keys.

Her eyes followed the several dozen steps up, landing on a small island floating in the sky. The sheer size of Douglas' cathedral had blocked it from sight. Atop the island sat a modest, white building. A single spire jutted from the center, ending in a sharp edge pointed towards the slightly cloudy, blue sky. White-robed individuals moved in and out of the structure and a couple of them traversed the stairs between the town and the floating island.

Ray approached the stairs and carefully tested her weight as she stepped up onto them. They held, so she continued moving upward. As she ascended, she glanced nervously at the increasing height. There was no railing on the stairs so one wrong step was all it would take to go splat. She'd already experienced a fatal fall once and, despite her unique ability to recover, she was not eager to repeat the experience.

She reached the top of the stairs without incident, passing a few white-robed individuals as she did so. They nodded to her in greeting, continuing on their way without sparing her a second thought. She did the same.

At the top of the stairs, she gazed across the temple courtyard in awe. Dozens of people moved back and forth, moving in and out of archways on all sides. Through the archway on the opposite side of the courtyard, another set of stairs led up into what Ray presumed was the main structure.

"Can I help you?" a familiar, pleasant voice inquired from beside Ray.

Ray turned, finding the young, blonde-haired, bright-faced girl from before standing next to her. The girl beamed and Ray couldn't resist returning the smile. "Kelsey, right?"

The girl's smile dropped slightly. "Do I know you?".

Ray shook her head, lifting the hood of her cloak back to reveal her face. "We met briefly yesterday when I woke up on the altar."

Kelsey's eyes lit up in recognition. "Ahh, the crazy one, right? Welcome back! Congratulations!"

"Right..."

"So, what brings you to the temple today?" Kelsey asked, returning to her original question.

Ray held up the letter and showed it to the priestess. "I'm here to see Max."

Kelsey stared at the note for a long moment, her face draining of any emotion.

Ray felt her stomach sink. "That's not a bad thing, right?"

The girl examined her for a moment as if she were contemplating something. Finally, she replied in a perfectly neutral tone.

"No, I don't suppose it's a bad thing. Are you sure though?"

The nagging feeling to run flared up stronger than ever before, but she ignored it. "Yeah, I'd say I'm pretty sure."

The girl shrugged indifferently, yet she looked around, clearly checking to see if anybody else had heard their conversation. "If you'll follow me, then. Lord Maxwell should be with the High Priestess. I'll take you to see them."

Ray nodded, feeling her stomach twist. She didn't know if this was good or not, but it seemed to be going alright so far.

"Lead on."

8

Introductions

"What the hell do they think they are doing?!" I shouted at the people below who couldn't hear me.

I tried to slow my breathing, but a red haze overlapped my vision and my form shuddered as fury permeated my entire being.

"Sir, please calm down!" Auto pleaded.

I took a few more deep breaths. Since I didn't have a real body, it was more of an impulse that had no real physiological effect, but it started to work.

Before the Unification War hit the middle stages and the entire world got involved, I was a relatively normal person. I was your everyday American student doing my generals at a normal university while trying to figure out what I wanted to do with my life.

My hobbies included anything fantasy and my favorite types of stories were the ones called 'isekai', especially the self-insert type. Wasn't it every man's dream to meet real elves and animal girls?

Yet my first animal girl encounter was from the other side of a barred cage. Having heard that the humans of this world originally came from Earth, I kind of assumed that they would be like the people on Earth.

Actually, I might have had hope before the Unification War, but I saw the true face of humanity. If you make a human a little bit special, they will trample everyone else around them. Humans were just that kind of creature.

I shook myself out of my thoughts and searched for Ray. While I was brooding, my Tether entered the town with the help of some warrior dude. I could see a powerful aura surrounding him, one that dwarfed everyone else nearby.

"What is that?" I asked, pointing at the aura.

"That," Auto replied, "is a High Templar. You can see the strength of the holy power bestowed upon him by an Overseer. He must be highly favored. However, there is something strange about him…"

As we were watching, the man stuck a piece of paper to her hand and then stepped backward, his body fading away until he disappeared without a trace.

Wow.

I scanned our surroundings, but I couldn't figure out where he had gone. I wasn't even sure if he teleported or just went invisible, or if there was some other mechanism involved.

The 'fortress town' was very much like I imagined a semi-medieval fantasy fortress would look like. It seemed like most of the merchants operated stalls just beyond the main entrance while the center of town contained some key buildings and more permanent stores. The sight of the various humanoid slaves was rather bothersome, but I was more or less expecting it now that I knew they had slaves here.

However, there were some unexpected elements that drew my attention. Some of the adventurers had rifles slung across their backs, and when I looked a little closer, I found that a few of the warriors had handguns hidden in holsters on their belts. The modern weapons were nowhere near as plentiful as daggers or bows, but there were enough that I would say they were common.

I remembered Jocelyn saying that these humans were descendants of Earthlings. At the time, I didn't really think about it too much, but it seemed they came from an era not too far removed from my own. That was a bit odd, because I never heard of a large group disappearing, but with magic involved, there were probably several explanations for that.

With the existence of guns, I couldn't help but wonder why there were so many more bows… perhaps because of the price?

Most of the people were wearing clothing that I would associate with the early twenty-first century. Though I had no idea how long it had been since humans came here, they seemed to have managed to replicate some things rather well, though I couldn't see anything like bicycles, cars, or cell phones anywhere.

Eventually, my Tether passed the cathedral and ascended the stairs to the floating temple in the sky. I stared in awe at the majestic sight, absorbing all the splendor of the awesome building.

Something about the temple resonated with the core of my being. Reaching out, I touched the wall of the temple and felt the boundless power confined within the structure. I wasn't sure how, but I knew without a speck of doubt that divinity rested here.

My Tether reached the top of the stairs, and I returned my full attention to her as she started a conversation with a priestess.

They walked side-by-side across the courtyard. Few people even spared the duo a second glance despite Ray's dark cloak standing out amongst the white and gold. They reached the stairs through the central archway and began to ascend.

"I'm Ray, by the way. I never introduced myself."

"Kelsey Vale."

"Is it alright if I ask some questions?"

"Sure, I guess."

"I saw some words that I wasn't familiar with engraved below the murals on the cathedral. What's a Tether?"

Kelsey stopped walking and stared at Ray with a sharp gaze. Ray stopped as well; her eyebrows raised as she took in the other girl's guarded expression.

"A Tether is the representative of an Overseer. They convey the words of the gods to us mortals."

"Overseer?"

"... *Who* are you?" Kelsey demanded. "*Everybody* knows the answers to these questions."

Ray shrugged. "You could say I've been living in a roc for most of my life."

Kelsey stared at her for a moment longer. She abruptly turned and started walking forward again while correcting her. "You mean *under* a rock."

Ray giggled as she followed the priestess once again. "No, I think my expression was more accurate."

Kelsey shook her head, giving up. "Overseers are the guardians of humanity. Each Overseer has jurisdiction over different areas and accordingly grants different perks. The 'respawn' you experienced before is one of the universal perks granted to all followers regardless of which Overseer they worship."

Respawn? She'd heard them use that word a few times.

"What kinds of perks are there?"

"The lady I worship, Jocelyn the Lovely One, has a rather abstract perk that doubles the charisma of her followers. Dallin the Strong One is said to have a similar perk for physical strength, though nobody has managed to prove it."

"Jocelyn and Dallin... are there any other Overseers?"

"Loki the Hidden One and Mumblegrumble the Strange One. Those two are a little more mysterious and their followers keep to themselves, usually."

"What are their perks?"

Kelsey shrugged. "I've read a lot of scholarly essays on the topic, but nobody really knows. Some people think Loki grants increased agility or dexterity, but that has never been claimed by the god or his Tether, and nobody has any guesses about what perks Mumblegrumble gives."

"If nobody can prove it, how do you know you have these perks in the first place?"

Kelsey waved her question away. "Obviously, they exist. The gods said they do, so they do."

Ray narrowed her eyes at the unsatisfactory response but decided not to comment any further.

After several seconds of silence, they arrived outside an ornate, white door. The edges were rimmed with silver and the handles were shiny and transparent. Kelsey raised a hand and knocked.

A moment later, a gruff man slid the door open. "Whaddya want?"

"I've brought a guest of Lord Maxwell. She has his magic signature," Kelsey replied while holding out the note.

Magic signature? Was there something else there?

Ray stared intently at the piece of paper, but she couldn't see anything.

The man took the note and examined it. After a short pause, he nodded as he handed it back. "One moment."

The door closed and Ray heard footsteps moving away from the door.

"Was there something special on that paper?" Ray asked.

"You could say it's a proof of your claim."

"My claim?"

Kelsey grimaced. "I swear, we get another person with random and bizarre claims coming in here every other week. Last week, an infamous bandit broke in and claimed to be a unicorn. He was shouting some nonsense about a ritual that would bring doom on us all. The crazy people never seem to consider that they need to prove their claim."

Ray felt a bead of sweat run down her neck.

A ritual? Was that related to the ritual that changed her? Or a different one?

"What happened to him?"

Kelsey leveled her piercing gaze on Ray. "I'm sure you have nothing to worry about. You had the magic signature, after all. If we find out that you lied... well, you won't need to worry about it for too long. Impersonating high-level personnel in the clergy is one of the more offensive mistakes a person could make. The only thing worse than that would be falsely claiming to be a Tether or a unicorn."

Ray examined the priestess with renewed eyes.

What was with this girl? She looked nice and pretty on the outside, but the things she said were comfortably hostile. It was an extremely favorable impression.

She noticed the sound of footprints approaching on the other side of the door again.

With an inward sigh, Ray braced herself, preparing to move forward. She was already this far. She had to continue.

The door opened to reveal a tall, graceful woman standing on the other side. Her very presence seemed to radiate light that accentuated her beautiful features and long, black hair.

The High Priestess smiled warmly as she looked down at Ray. "Are you the one?"

Ray stared at the radiant woman, dazed.

"Come in, come in! We... Oh, my! Your eyes are most peculiar. I am most curious about your story."

"I don't really know very much."

"Hmm," the High Priestess said, looking down at Ray appraisingly. Her attention shifted and she paused for a moment, looking at something only she could see. Her smile widened. "Interesting. Come on in then. I think we have *much* to discuss," she said, stepping back into the room in a smooth, graceful motion.

Ray moved through the doorway, hesitating only when she noticed that Kelsey didn't follow. The door closed behind her.

She squared her shoulders, fighting down her nerves and the nagging impulse to flee as she walked forward, alone in the Temple of Cairel with the High Priestess. She noticed that Max was nowhere in sight.

Wasn't she supposed to be meeting with him? Was this really a good idea?

Well, it was probably too late to back out.

A soothing voice called for her attention. "Let's get down to business, shall we?"

Ray turned and met the eyes of the High Priestess.

"I must admit that I was genuinely surprised to see the name 'Evelyn Raymond' appear on the register. Imagine my surprise when you, a young woman who claims the name of the Monarch of Ages, respawned in our temple. You also bear a remarkable resemblance to her. I must ask, what is your connection between the two of you?"

Evelyn Raymond.

That name sounded so far beyond familiar that it resonated with her soul. Ray stared at the High Priestess, bewildered. Her thoughts raced as she tried to latch onto the sense of familiarity, though her memories remained as blank as ever.

This woman knew who she was.

She could finally find some answers!

"Though I guess my first question should be *what* are you? You respawned while carrying over vampiric traits, which goes against providence. Your presence is reminiscent of a higher being, but your magic aura is entirely nonexistent..."

"Nice to meet you," Ray interrupted as she approached the vibrant woman and reached out a hand carefully, just as she'd seen Jonathan do before.

The High Priestess looked down at the hand in amusement for a moment before reaching out and softly accepting the offer. She shook Ray's hand firmly and showed a soft, gentle smile. "Well, well, aren't you the polite one... I suppose I was a bit overeager... I should at least introduce myself first," she mused. "My name is Eileen Vanis, High Priestess of the Temple of Cairel. You may call me Sister Eileen."

Ray released Eileen's hand, taking a step back.

"Sister Eileen, I wish I could answer your questions about me, but I don't know the answers. Could you tell me more about this 'Evelyn Raymond'?"

"Oh?" Eileen tilted her head quizzically. "If you aren't connected then it's best not to talk about her. You know what they say, 'speak of the Queen and she comes', and all that. It may be a bit superstitious, but I would rather this country persist for a bit longer."

"I think that name, Evelyn Raymond, is especially important. It sounded awfully familiar to me," Ray supplied. "I recently woke up on a nearby mountain with very few memories, so I don't really know who or what I am."

Eileen observed Ray quietly for several long seconds.

Ray fidgeted uncomfortably under the piercing gaze and started to observe the room they were in. There were two soft couches situated on opposite sides of a low table carved from some sort of white stone.

The only other decoration in the room was a desk against the corner with a small, strange box-shaped object on it. In front of the box was a thin, rectangular platform with strange symbols carved into it.

"Alright, little one, I have an idea." Eileen finally spoke.

Ray returned her attention to the older woman.

"Since we don't have a Tether here, we can't run an appraisal on you. However, there are tests that privileged people can undergo to discover their talents and aptitudes. I will sponsor you to take these tests."

"Aptitudes? Talents?"

"Every person is born with certain talents and abilities inherent to them. When it comes to magic, most people are also born with an aptitude or two for specific types of magic. The majority of the population has to discover these things through trial and error, but a Tether could simply observe you and tell you. Unfortunately, there are only four Tethers in the world, so most people don't have the option to do such a thing. We developed certain 'tests' to help us uncover the talents and aptitudes of promising individuals to better foster their growth and development."

"And you want me to take these 'tests'," Ray concluded.

Eileen nodded. "Normally it would be impossible for you to take them, but with my letter of recommendation the instructors are guaranteed to run the basic test. Anything beyond that is between you and them."

Ray pondered on the suggestion. It seemed like a rather good idea. At the very least, it wouldn't hurt to know what kinds of skills and magic she could use so she was all for it.

There were a few questions that she wanted to ask first, though.

"My first question. Outside the town, I was attacked by four humans when they discovered that I have a red eye. Why is that?"

"When the Overseers first appeared almost one thousand five hundred years ago, they decreed humans to be the superior race and that all other intelligent species were inferior 'monsters' like the wild monsters that roam the world. They ordered humans to exterminate the 'monsters' and cleanse the world."

Ray felt a chill run down her spine. Remembering the sight of the various nonhumans in chains, she felt like she knew exactly where this was going.

"It was an impossible task, of course. The four immortal races by themselves were far too strong for humans to stand against. The mortal intelligent races had their own nations and tribes scattered throughout the continent and even now, hundreds of years after humans won, humans still have no presence or influence on half of the continent."

But that also meant humans had power over half the continent.

"However, not every human in this world was a follower of the Overseers. Some of them objected to the cruel treatment of the other sentient races. After several political conflicts and a civil war, it became an acceptable practice to spare the lives of children. Those poor individuals become slaves almost without exception."

"I see..." Ray muttered.

"It is a monstrous practice but a practical one. Orcs and trolls are, on average, much stronger than humans and can perform good physical labor. Beastkin with highly developed animal traits often have better senses than humans. Depending on the animal traits, they can be faster or stronger than humans as well, so adventurers often use them as bait to lure monsters."

"What about vampires?" Ray asked, curious.

"Vampires... are a bit more complicated. Rather than calling them a 'race', it would be more accurate to call vampirism a 'curse'. Human vampires cannot be enslaved, they are instead cleansed through execution. Vampires of other races are treated the same as any other nonhuman. They have superb physical strength and speed, but they are not exceedingly popular as slaves because they are undead. The only way to make them feel pain is holy magic, so they usually aren't very obedient. Still, there are ways. A collector might enjoy putting a vampire on display as a stuffed doll."

There were people who taxidermized slaves? If they were still alive, Ray could see some appeal in the practice, but she couldn't see any point in displaying dead bodies.

"My second question then. Why are you helping me?"

Eileen giggled softly. "An excellent question, though I hope you forgive me if I only give you a partial answer. A lady has to have some secrets, after all."

Ray grimaced but nodded anyway.

"I have four reasons, but I'll only tell you two of them for now."

She paused, leaning forward while motioning for Ray to do the same.

"My fourth reason, in order of importance, is that I want to change this rotten world," Eileen whispered. "And the second one is that I want to meet the people who saved my life."

Ray leaned back, curious about the first and third reasons, as well as the story behind the second reason but she decided to respect Eileen's wish to keep it secret for now. Rather, she was grateful that Eileen had revealed as much as she already had.

"My final question then. Even though I am not a human, why are Max and Kelsey and the others treating me well? The people in this temple should be the close followers of Overseers, right?"

Eileen shook her head. "That is actually the reason most of the people here are accepting you. As close followers of Overseers, they know that no Overseer would allow a monster to respawn. Kelsey saw you respawn and only humans have access to the respawn system. There is no doubt in her mind, or in the minds of anybody else who has heard about the strange 'red-eyed crazy girl', that you are a human."

Ray recalled her conversation with Kelsey. 'The gods said they do, so they do.', was it? It seemed like most people thought that way.

She wanted to ask why an Overseer had allowed her, a 'monster', to 'respawn' then but decided to leave it for now. This conversation thus far had been all take and no give, so she decided that she would place some trust in this High Priestess.

"Alright, then I would be happy to accept your assistance," Ray replied. "Please introduce me to the instructors so that I can take the talent and aptitude tests."

Eileen looked over Ray one last time before smirking. "Before that, why don't we have you take a bath and get you some clothes?"

She walked over to the door and rang a bell. The same man who had answered the door when Kelsey knocked before appeared inside the room. He didn't enter through a door or window, he just appeared.

"Sullivan, please ask the priestesses to help this young lady get cleaned up and outfitted. She will be undergoing the aptitude tests in the morning and needs to be properly dressed."

"It will be done, Sister," Sullivan replied with a low bow.

He motioned for Ray to move through the door, and she started to walk when Eileen called out after her.

"Since you don't use the recorded name, what should I call you?"

"Ray," she replied without hesitation. "My name is Ray."

9

Formal Beginnings

While Ray cleaned herself up, I waited outside the bathroom. I spent the time reflecting on the conversation between her and the High Priestess.

Both Eileen and the High Templar were practically oozing Holy Power from their entire beings. I didn't know what Overseer they followed but whoever it was had given them an absurd amount of power. Each of them individually had more Holy Power than the rest of the people in the temple combined.

The general contents of the conversation weren't very surprising for me since I already met two of the other Overseers and most of the contents were just expounding upon what I already knew.

What really caught my attention, though, was the computer monitor in the corner of the room. It was an old-fashioned monitor, the ones that were bulky and took up half the desk. The keyboard had symbols on it that I didn't recognize. I couldn't say for sure since I didn't speak every language on Earth, but I would suspect that the letters did not originate from my home planet.

At one point, I reached out and touched the monitor. As I did so, a jolt ran through my spirit form. Everything around me seemed to slow down. Ray and Eileen's words became disjointed as if they were stuttering in slow motion.

"Auto, what's going on?"

"You gained access to a terminal, so the Overseer System is now being downloaded. You are currently experiencing lag due to the huge amount of data being transferred."

Lag?! Was that a joke? Gods could experience lag? What were we, computers?

"The transfer is almost complete."

A minute later, my vision went dark, and my mind erupted, the pressure building like it was going to explode. Various shapes danced across my vision in the darkness, but I was in too much pain to pay attention to them.

And then the pain stopped. My vision gradually refocused and I mentally blinked a few times, reorienting myself. I still floated next to Ray and Eileen. I could hear them clearly again, but I tuned it out because something else caught my attention.

I had a video game UI! There was a chat box in the bottom left-hand corner and a series of boxes in the bottom right. Mentally focusing on them caused the name of each box to appear in my mind.

"Perks, Divine Mandates, Tenets, Prayer Log, Calculator"

I would need to experiment with this. They all seemed like useful things for gods. Especially that last one... it would really suck if someone died because a god made a mistake in their mental math.

I focused on the chat box, curious about who I could talk to. Five options appeared on the screen:

Dallin
Jocelyn
Loki
Mumblegrumble
???

So, the other four Overseers and some mysterious unknown entity. Great. I started to move away when I heard a *ding*. I glanced back at the box and saw a little red circle next to Dallin's name. I focused on his name and a separate chat box appeared.

When I saw his screen name, I sighed. Of course he did.

[xXxDallinTheDestroyerxXx] has entered the chat room.
[Unknown] has entered the chat room.

[xXxDallinTheDestroyerxXx] Heyyyyyyy! It's the new guy! I'm Dallin!

[Unknown] Hey

[xXxDallinTheDestroyerxXx] We were having a bit of trouble communicating last time, so I wanted to introduce myself as soon as you got access to the system. The name's Dallin. I'm in charge of strength, truth, and ambition, in that order. Did you pick a domain yet?

[Unknown] Uh, not yet. I'm just getting around to contacting my Tether.

[xXxDallinTheDestroyerxXx] Sweet! Take care and try to learn the ropes as fast as you can! It'll be so much easier to farm souls here with another guy helping to share the load. Catch ya next time!

[Unknown] For sure. Laterz

[xXxDallinTheDestroyerxXx] has left the chat room.

Okay then. Moving on. I returned my attention to my new UI, opening and closing windows to explore.

It felt like the first time logging into a new video game. It had been several years since I last experienced it... that slightly overwhelmed sensation when viewing all the buttons that you aren't familiar with yet, the awe at the intricate details of the system and the giddiness that comes with learning a new feature.

I laughed giddily like a child opening presents on Christmas as I opened another window and began scanning its contents.

While I was still fiddling with the new UI, the door to the bathroom opened and Ray came out dressed in a well-fitted soft pink t-shirt and dark grey sweatpants. Her hair was still dripping slightly but it looked much better now that it was clean, even if it was still a little tangled.

I followed her, listening as Kelsey guided Ray through the temple. Once Ray was alone, it would be time to introduce myself.

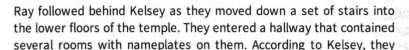

Ray followed behind Kelsey as they moved down a set of stairs into the lower floors of the temple. They entered a hallway that contained several rooms with nameplates on them. According to Kelsey, they were the rooms of those who lived in this temple.

Kelsey led Ray to a room near the end of the hallway on the left. "I am told that you may use this room for the duration of your stay here."

"Thank you," Ray replied. "I appreciate you helping me out."

Ray was surprised to realize that she meant it. Kelsey was literally the first living person that she met in this world and the young priestess had been pretty kind. Not only did she not try to capture or kill her, but she also answered her questions, supplied clothes, and guided her around the temple.

What a nice person.

"Don't worry about it. You should get some sleep, the tests start early, and you don't want to be late," Kelsey replied as she turned to walk away.

Ray smiled while waving at Kelsey's retreating form and then turned the knob to walk into her new room.

The room was decent-sized. It had a bed, large enough for one person that took up a third of the space. There was a dresser next to the bed and a curtained window that let her look outside at the town below.

Ray walked over to the bed and lifted the blanket, marveling at the softness of the material.

Then a voice resounded inside of her head. *"Hey there!"*

She tossed the blanket away and shrieked. She didn't know where the voice was coming from and so, unable to decide which way to go, she jumped straight up. There was a loud *thud* as she hit her head on the ceiling.

She plopped to the floor, holding her head with a dazed expression.

"Well, that's one way to overreact."

Ray looked around before remembering that she had experienced having a voice in her head once before already. It was also not too long ago, so it was easy to remember.

She closed her eyes and focused. Then she found it. "Is that you, Mr. Animal-Obsessed Dark Void?"

"Animal-obsessed...? Huh?!"

"Who are you?" Ray asked, ignoring the sharp pain that resounded through her skull when the voice got loud.

"I am a new god. I've been watching you and I have decided that I want you to be my prophet!"

Ray pursed her lips. Prophet? *"Alright Mr. Animal-Obsessed 'New God', why are you in my head and what do you want from me?"*

The voice sighed. *"Of the two descriptors, that's the one you kept...? Anyways, I don't need anything special yet. I just want to work together with you... like partners. I think that we can help each other out."*

"What can you do for me?"

She would swear that she felt the owner of the voice smirk. She briefly considered that she really had lost her mind.

"Currently, I can give you advice. I have even less information about this world than you do, but I know a bit about reading people and dealing with them."

"Oh? Could you give me an example?"

"Well, for one, you should be more careful regarding Eileen and Max. Nothing is ever free when it comes to dealing with people. You already agreed to accept her help, so you should follow through with it for now. You do need allies and people that you can trust but be cautious moving forward. If something seems too good to be true, then that means that you don't have enough information to make an informed decision."

Ray pondered his advice for a moment. She couldn't find any faults with his logic. However, Eileen had been upfront about not telling her everything and she had decided to accept that.

"I recognize that you already accepted it, and I took that into consideration already. I'm just urging you to be more careful in the future. When you meet these instructors and when you start learning from them, do your best to figure out why they are helping you. Without that information, you have little to no control over your fate."

His advice seemed to make sense. Then she realized what had just happened. "Wait, did you just read my mind?"

"I'm a disembodied voice speaking directly to your mind. Did you really think the communication was only one-way?"

Ray wasn't sure how she felt about that. On one hand, he didn't hear anything important, but she didn't really like that he could just read her thoughts.

"You mentioned that you want me to be your prophet. What, exactly, does that mean?"

"It means that I want you to be my representative and my voice."

"Sounds awfully one-sided. What do I get out of it?"

"The future potential is limitless, but currently I can only give you advice and act as your confidant. However, that doesn't mean I haven't already done anything for you.

"Already done?" What was the voice talking about?

"You wondered earlier why you were able to respawn, right? When I chose you as my prophet, you were integrated into the Overseer System. In other words, by associating with me you gained the ability to respawn. As my religion grows, I'll be able to grant you and my other followers more and more power. Additionally, you'll have a god behind you. I don't plan on being stingy with miracles."

Huh. Even if she assumed the voice was telling the truth, she was hesitant to accept his words at face value.

"What's the catch?"

"Smart. The catch is that it will be a lot of work. I need you to start and lead a new religion that worships me."

Well, that didn't sound like a job that she wanted to do. She just became aware yesterday and already some random void in her mind was asking her not only to worship it but to get others to worship it as well. That sounded like more than enough to be considered 'insane'.

"I'm not asking you to do anything major yet. I'll support you from behind the scenes and do my best to keep you hidden from the other

Overseers for now. You need to get stronger and make some friends. We can talk about the religion thing later."

Ray nodded slowly. The things he was asking her to do now generally aligned with what she was doing already. She would start her new training in the morning, and she hoped to become friends with Kelsey and maybe some others. Shelving the issue for later, she climbed into the bed.

"Since we aren't going public with this yet, keep it a secret from everyone. That includes Eileen, Max, and Kelsey. We don't know enough about these people yet and if the other churches get involved before I have enough power, we're finished."

Being forcefully drawn into a massive religious conflict between gods... what a positive way to end a day.

"Okay, I won't tell anybody for now. I need to sleep though; I have a test in the morning."

"Good night," the voice whispered softly in her head.

"G'night..." Ray muttered as she drifted off to sleep.

Leximea of the Bloodclaw tribe flinched awake as she heard the rattling of keys. A moment later, the cruel laughter of humans tormented her ears. Following the sound, she found humans approaching her cage. The footsteps stopped just outside the barred door, and she began to tremble, huddling against the bars as far away from them as she could go.

The guard opening the cage was different from the one who had thrust her in here the previous day when they arrived in this horrible town. Despite it being morning, she detected the faint smell of alcohol on his breath.

The cage rattled as he unlocked it and slammed the door open.

"Get out here, ya filthy animal!" he roared.

Leximea shook her head. There was nowhere for her to run but she did not want to go with that man.

"Your new owner is here to pick ya up. Get moving or I'll make you."

Leximea flinched. Obediently, she began to crawl forward. When she was within reach, he grabbed her by the hair and yanked her out of the cage, slamming the door shut and locking it again. She learned a long time ago not to cry out when slavers did this. They enjoyed hearing her scream and she wouldn't give them the satisfaction.

On the one hand, Leximea was glad to be leaving this forsaken pit. She knew she was lucky to be out after only one night. Others could spend weeks or even months here while they slowly starved to death.

On the other hand, there were only two types of people who would buy a catkin slave: collectors and adventurers. She did not want to associate with either type of person. It was adventurers that had destroyed her village. It was adventurers that had captured her, and it was adventurers who had raped and brutally tortured her parents right before her eyes.

But with collectors, she would either be killed, stuffed, and put on display or turned into a toy for their personal satisfaction. She would rather serve people that she hated than suffer either of those fates.

The slaver released her, and she fell to the ground, landing agilely on her hands and feet. She moved to step forward, hoping to avoid further injury by being proactive.

Unfortunately, the guard seemed to be in a foul mood because he landed a kick on her behind, thrusting her forward face-first into the ground. "Get a move on!" he thundered.

Leximea shoved down her anger, retracting her claws as she meekly pushed herself back up to her feet and started shuffling forward.

The room they were in was full of cages containing various races of 'monsters'. There were others from beastkin races like Leximea, such as wolfkin, foxkin, and some others. Most of the inhabitants, however, were orcs and trolls. The humans did win a war against the United Federation recently, after all. This town, Cairel, was close to the border so it wasn't surprising that some of the spoils of war found their way here as slaves.

Leximea of the Bloodclaw tribe fiddled with the collar that was now fixed around her left wrist as she stepped out into the sunlight. She looked up at the clear blue sky. She felt small and insignificant beneath the endless expanse towering over her.

The guard grabbed her chain and pulled, forcing her to move towards her new master. She searched the overwhelming expanse above, praying silently that someone out there would help her. The humans were the only ones who had gods that answered prayers.

Still, she prayed fervently in hopes that someone or something out there was listening. At this point, it was easier to hope that some powerful entity might be kind enough to answer.

10

Talents

As Ray maneuvered through the crowded streets towards the Martial Quarter clutching a letter in her hands, she pondered the information Eileen had given her about the talent and aptitude tests.

There were two general tests and several special tests that depended on the results of the general tests.

The general test for talents almost always took the form of a mock combat. An individual dueled one-on-one with an experienced instructor and the instructor would attempt to discover the individual's physical talents. There were five different martial pathways that were well established in Hanulfall, and most people would have a talent for or tendency towards one of these five paths.

Those pathways were: warrior, berserker, martial artist, samurai, and guardian.

The general test for aptitudes was facilitated by a magician. They would use some measuring tools and their experience with reading mana to estimate an individual's aptitude for the various types of magic.

The five most common types of magicians were elementalists, priests, warlocks, druids, and arcanists.

It was possible to combine two or more types of magic into a new one. An example being that those who could use both elemental magic and druidism were often called shamans.

It was also possible to combine magic and martial pathways. Among humans, the most common was combining a priest's holy magic with warrior or martial artist techniques to become a cleric or a monk, respectively.

The tests to determine talents and aptitudes varied in different countries and amongst different races, but this system of one-on-one testing facilitated by well-established professionals was how it was performed by humans here in the Kingdom of Rovar.

If the instructor was impressed, it wasn't uncommon for them to sponsor the individual being tested. They would use their connections to help the individual foster their talents and become strong.

If the instructor were extremely impressed, sometimes they would offer to take the individual on as an apprentice. This, however, was a rare case. Most instructors already had several apprentices and were not interested in taking on new students.

In the Kingdom of Rovar, the martial instructors were predominantly warriors while the magicians were mostly priests or elementalists. There were a handful of famous people who trained in unusual paths, but the majority followed the trends of the regions in which they lived.

Just based on the verbal explanation, Ray wasn't particularly inclined towards being a warrior. Warrior was a kind of jack-of-all-trades martial fighter. There were subcategories of the warrior pathway that were relatively self-explanatory, such as swordsman or archer.

Berserker sounded incredibly appealing, though. A raging storm that cleaved through the enemy. An all-offensive class with little defense.

At first, Ray had been leaning towards that idea because of her unusual regeneration ability. Unfortunately, she figured it was unlikely for her to become a samurai or berserker. There were very few humans who took to these paths and there were currently no known teachers in Cairel. These two pathways were extremely common in the Empire of the Dragon King to the south-west beyond the Voskeg Mountains, but that journey would take at least a month and the mountains were full of wild monsters like the roc she had fought.

There was also an option to become a guardian. Guardians were referred to as 'tanks' in this world. They protected allies from damage by drawing the attention of opponents to themselves. If she couldn't be a berserker, she suspected that becoming a guardian would be the best way to capitalize on her regenerative ability. If she managed to learn berserker techniques later, then she would be both an unstoppable force and an immovable object.

Given her recent experiences fighting opponents, words such as 'unstoppable' and 'immovable' sounded like a rather nice change of pace.

She turned the corner and walked through an archway into the martial quarter. The man she was searching for, Siegfried, was supposed to be in the training fields at this time of day. The sun was firmly in the sky and the steady clanging and clashing of swords reached Ray's ears as she walked onto the field.

She followed the sound to an area where men and women in armor were facing off against each other. She couldn't see any magic being used - they were all fighting with their raw physical abilities and nothing else.

A whistle sounded from the side and Ray followed the sound to see three previously unnoticed figures observing the spars. The one in the center towered over the other two.

"Break for lunch!" the one in the center shouted.

The fighting stopped immediately and many of the fighters collapsed to the ground in relief and exhaustion while others simply stared into the distance with tired, dazed expressions.

A handful of people moved towards a large pavilion that emitted a strange, appetizing smell that Ray had learned to associate with human cooking.

She approached the three observers, assuming them to be the trainers.

"What's a little lady doin' wanderin' round these parts?" the man on the right said, giving her a pointed glare.

He looked like a guy who was obsessed with weapons to the point of impracticality. He had three swords, a dagger, and an axe tied to his belt, two large swords across his back, and daggers strapped to his legs and to his chest.

The other two focused their eyes on Ray as well, a hint of curiosity evident in their gazes.

Ray gave them a half-smile as she held up the letter she'd received from Eileen. "I'm looking for Siegfried, the Guardian. I've got a letter of recommendation from Sister Eileen."

All three trainers froze. A range of expressions ran across the faces of the two men standing near the giant, finally settling on a concerned frown. The giant in the center merely raised an eyebrow, stepping away from the other two and reached for the letter.

"I'm Siegfried," he rumbled.

Observing him from up close, she saw that he had blue eyes and dark hair. A thick scar ran from his clean-shaven chin to his left ear. He wore heavy plate armor and had a huge shield draped across his back.

Ray gave him the letter and waited patiently as he opened and read it.

A minute later, he grunted as he tore a corner off the letter and put the piece into a bag tied to his waist. He then refolded the letter and sealed it once more before returning it to Ray.

"This is a bit unusual, but I have to admit that it's not the strangest request I've received from her. A talent test, is it? I can do it, but I can't guarantee anything beyond that."

"That's fine."

Siegfried shrugged and then started walking across the field, moving his hand through the air in front of him. With a practiced motion, he lightly tapped his plate armor and shield and they disappeared. Underneath the metal armor he was wearing leather over his torso and legs, which he promptly removed in a similar fashion to reveal a tank top and gym shorts that both strongly accented his muscular form.

Ray hesitantly moved to stand across from him. As she sized him up, she felt ridiculously small. He had nearly two feet on her in height and a lot more rippling muscle on his arms and legs. She had no idea how she was supposed to beat him... but she would be damned if she didn't try. She bent her knees slightly and prepared to dash forward.

Siegfried saw her movement and smiled, his eyes showing a faint interest.

"Begin!" he commanded.

Ray launched herself forward like an arrow, her fist already raised to strike. Siegfried stood unwavering as she approached. He raised an arm and took her punch in the palm of his hand, testing out the force.

He grunted in surprise.

"Hmm, two and a half, maybe three times the norm?" he rumbled.

Ray bit her lip when she saw his nonchalant attitude and spun, whipping her left fist in a backhand towards his chin.

He caught her arm with his other hand and twisted. The world spun as she sailed through the air before crashing into the ground.

"Your speed is exceptional. I don't sense any magic, so this is just your base ability?"

She pushed herself to her feet, feeling for any serious injuries. Her wrist was bruised and her side hurt, but she was okay. She turned and faced Siegfried again warily. He hadn't moved from his original standing position.

Ray ran forward. This time instead of leaping she went for a low strike. She punched out with her right arm as a feint and revealed a victorious smirk as he raised his left arm to block. She deftly hooked a hand underneath his guard, grabbed his arm, and pulled with all her might.

He took a step forward to regain his balance, his stoic expression shifting as he raised his eyebrows. Ray took advantage of that moment to weave her free hand towards his face.

Just before her hand made contact, she felt a strange prickling aura fill the air around them. His face went rigid like a rock and her eyes widened as her knuckles split against the terribly hard surface.

Her wrist collapsed and a sharp crack resounded as several bones crushed together. Ray grimaced and kicked off the man's chest to leap back to a safe distance.

She took a moment to catch her breath and examine her wrist. "Damn..." she muttered.

It was broken but the regeneration had already started. The pain flared, demanding her attention. She glanced warily at Siegfried, but he wasn't moving towards her. He had a contemplative look as he observed her, his eyes alternating between her clearly broken wrist and her face.

She returned her attention to Siegfried. He had a contemplative look as he observed her, his eyes alternating between her clearly broken wrist and her face.

"Are you done?" he rumbled.

Ray snorted. "Of course not!"

She ran forward, swinging her right arm in a wide arc.

Siegfried raised a single hand to block the blow. She reached out, but instead of punching his hand she grabbed his left wrist. Siegfried grunted in surprise as she jumped and pushed off his arm, the built momentum propelling her over his head like an acrobat.

She landed gracefully behind him and then immediately twisted, hooking her right foot around in a low crescent kick.

Her foot caught Siegfried behind his left knee. His knee collapsed and he stumbled forward. Unfortunately, she was finding it difficult to follow up as her ankle crumbled under the impact. She stumbled, barely regaining her balance as her foot started to shift back into its natural position. Her left hand was almost finished healing.

"I've seen enough." Siegfried rose back to his feet and looked down at Ray's injured form. His eyes gleamed with interest as he motioned towards the other trainers. One of them had already produced a pair of red potions. They approached while Siegfried began his evaluation.

"Young lady, color me impressed. You've got strength, speed, and good instincts. Most importantly, though? You've got spunk. Not many people taking this test will continue after breaking a bone."

Ray grunted in response. The pain in her foot was unbearable. If she was still fighting, she could manage it somehow, but the moment Siegfried ended the test, her arm and leg screamed in protest at the abuse she heaped on them.

"What *was* that...?" she groaned. "Your jaw and your knee were ridiculously hard!"

Siegfried chuckled, his rumbling voice echoing like the clash of boulders.

"It's a guardian technique that I call Steel Skin. It's what makes me the most famous guardian on this side of the continent."

Steel Skin. It was a rather lame name for such an awesome technique.

"With your abilities, I don't really understand why you want to be a guardian. You're so strong and fast that I almost wouldn't believe that you're a human," he muttered.

Ray flinched and he winked.

"*It was probably written in the letter,*" the voice in her head supplied.

Well then. Ray figured Eileen wouldn't have sent her to someone who went batshit crazy at the sight of monsters. Still, she might have stood out a bit too much.

"I actually wanted to be a berserker but there are none around here," she explained.

"Oh? Well then, I should consider this my good fortune. It seems that I'll be lucky enough to teach this era's second prodigy."

"Second?" Ray asked curiously.

"Well, 'cause of Prince Doug, of course. He's only sixteen and he's already a Tether and a gold-ranked paladin. The damn kid has charged against armies alone *twice* and won both times."

Ray nodded as if she knew what he was talking about. She did remember seeing the images of Douglas, Tether of the Strong One on the cathedral. That was probably the person Siegfried was talking about.

The other trainers arrived and tried to offer her the red potions but stopped with confused expressions.

"Were you not injured?" asked the weapon-covered trainer.

Ray shook her head as her foot finished snapping back into position.

Siegfried, strangely enough, came to her rescue. "She was just surprised by the impact and overreacted. There shouldn't have been any substantial injuries, judging from the force of her blows.

The two instructors shared a glance and then shrugged. "We'll let you take care of it then," the weapon guy replied. "We're going to go get some lunch." The two trainers waved goodbye and left.

"Thanks…" Ray mumbled as she started to push herself to her feet, looking up at the bear-like man.

Siegfried reached a hand out. She accepted it and he helped her stand up.

"I've always found that fighting is the best way to get the measure of a person. You have conviction, and I have a feeling that you will be extraordinarily strong one day. Add on Eileen's recommendation and I would be honored to leech some reputation from your great successes." Siegfried paused for a moment, folding his arms, and tapping his elbow as he thought about how to rate her on the test. "I'd rate your talent for every martial discipline as top tier. Considering your incredible speed and physical strength, with a little training, you would be a devastating berserker. If you choose to go down that path later, I won't stop you, but if you would have me, I would be more than happy to teach you my guardian techniques."

Ray's expression lit up like a child receiving an unexpected present. "Yes! Please teach me!"

He placed a hand on her shoulder. "Let's start first thing tomorrow morning. You'd better get over to see that grouchy magician, though. He gets irritable when people are late."

"Okay! I'll be here!" Ray promised as she turned and left towards the Magic Quarter.

Siegfried watched her as she walked away. "What on earth did that old witch have to do to find her?" he mused to himself.

He probably thought that she was far enough away, but she could still hear him. He turned and stomped towards the cafeteria.

"Doesn't matter, though. Looks like we finally found one."

11

Aptitudes

While Ray weaved her way through the crowded streets towards the Magic Quarter. I spent the time fiddling with my new UI.

At first, I was intrigued by the medieval fantasy setting with random bits of modern technology here and there. But I honestly found the UI just a little bit more worthy of my attention for now. Especially the Perks, Divine Mandates, and Tenets tabs.

I really wanted perks. The options I had were absurdly powerful. My first perk would allow me to choose a quality that would define my followers. This quality would then become enhanced for any who were officially part of my religion. Dallin presumably chose strength and Jocelyn chose charisma. Those two options were crossed out, so the info Kelsey gave Ray was probably correct.

Of the remaining options, Dexterity, Agility, Intelligence, Endurance, and Luck, both Endurance and Luck were crossed out, so those were the ones that Loki and Mumblegrumble chose, though I wasn't sure who chose which.

That left Dexterity, Agility, or Intelligence for my own followers. I had plenty of time to consider what would be best for us before I would even be able to choose, though. I would be able to unlock my first perk when I reached one hundred followers and my second perk at one thousand. It seemed to ramp up from there to ten thousand, one hundred thousand, one million and so on. I wasn't sure what the population of this continent was like, but with how many Overseerless monster races there were, it wouldn't be too long to hit a million followers, right?

A million people... that would be a lot to handle. I couldn't really imagine it. I hadn't the slightest idea how Christianity, Islam, Hinduism, or any other big religion back on Earth did it with so many millions of adherents. Since the heads of those religions were apparently Overseers, I was curious about a few things, like who the head Overseer was in some of the polytheistic religions, if there are different Overseers for different branches of Christianity and about a few Tenets and historical decisions of certain religions.

I especially had questions about the current revolution being led by the Director. If he were a Tether with divine backing, it would explain many things.

Regardless of the answers to my questions, it could be fun and/or interesting to hang out with Thor or Jesus if I ever found a way to visit Earth.

The Divine Mandate tab was a list of currently outstanding divine mandates and the option to create them. I just had to 'type' in text and the leaders of my religion would receive some sort of revelation.

The process was automated to a ridiculous degree, but at least that would increase the overall efficiency.

The Tenets tab was one that I felt nervous about. It was where I would build the core of my religion. Here, I would put the rules that my followers would need to follow, and it said that I would gain holy power for strong acts of faith. In other words, I would need to create a list of dos and don'ts for my followers, and I would get power to grant miracles if they follow the list. There were no requirements that the items on the list had to have a valid reason, neither were there requirements saying that they had to be 'good' or 'evil' things.

There were just no limits in general. I could ban my followers from drinking water, wine, coffee, or all three. I could ban them from certain foods or require them to eat certain things at certain times or on certain occasions. I could ban murder or require it. Rules on sexual orientation, gender roles, discrimination... in all things, my word was law, and my moral code would be the moral code of my church and anybody who joined it.

That was a lot of pressure.

I looked over the windows again, and a little blinking red circle next to the Prayer Log caught my attention.

Curious about the meaning, I focused on it and the circle expanded, displaying a number:

415,532 unread messages.

Oh shit.

"Who could possibly be praying to me? I don't have any followers yet if I don't count Ray."

"This is a support function of the Overseer System for those who are just starting out on a world. It gathers the prayers of individuals who are praying but don't know who or what to pray to."

I opened up the log and a *huge* list of names appeared.

Damn, that was far too many prayers! How did gods do it?

I opened up a few of the messages and scanned them. After clicking on a few dozen, many of them had similar contents.

Speaking of automated processes...

"Hey Auto, can I set up an auto-response function?"

"Affirmative, though it is not advised..."

"I just want to filter out the prayers a little. A lot of these are people expressing gratitude for food and asking for it to 'nourish and strengthen their bodies'. That'd cost way too much holy power. I want to have an automated response for those prayers. Something like... 'kk, np'."

"Don't you think that's a little... cold? Those people are asking for your blessings."

"Bless the food to what? Not give them a heart attack?"

I pointed at the message I had just read. "This guy asked me to bless his cheeseburger. There's no way in hell he seriously expects my blessing to make that greasy trash healthy."

"... I see your point."

After fiddling with the options for a few moments, I pressed enter and 204,936 messages disappeared. I then began to scan through the remaining prayers.

Simultaneously, 204,936 individuals on the continent of Nathea paused as a feeling of warmth filled them. Amongst those who were called 'monsters', a small portion of them realized instinctively that the impossible had just occurred.

For the first time, a god had answered their prayers.

As Ray lightly crossed into the far edge of the Magic Quarter, she felt that something was off. For almost a minute now, she hadn't seen another person. A jolt of alarm ran through her and she took an instinctive step back in response to the sense of danger. She flinched as a wave of fire and heat passed in front of her face.

If she hadn't taken a step back, that would have hit her.

"By Mumblegrumble's feathered fins, what are you doing here?" an angry voice demanded.

Ray followed the sound of the voice to a large figure. He wasn't as big as Siegfried, but he was still several inches over six feet tall. He had long, greasy hair and he looked as if he hadn't shaved in a few days. There were dark circles under his eyes and the wind carried a foul stench from his body. Despite his rugged appearance, his piercing gaze seemed to penetrate her soul.

"You're forty-three seconds late! You think you can just prance in here all smiles and whatnot?"

Erm. Ray wasn't quite sure how to respond, so she shrugged while remaining silent.

"Dallin caught your tongue, eh? Well then, get on with it. Why are you bothering me at this unholy hour?"

Was she bothering him? This was the middle of the street though...

This man didn't seem entirely sane. At the very least, he was certainly unreasonable. Ray took out the letter from Eileen and held it out to him.

"Are you Master Rambalt? Sister Eileen gave me a letter of recommendation."

Master Rambalt approached her and yanked the letter out of her hand.

"I know that much. I'm asking why *you* are here."

"To take the aptitude test...?" Ray replied with a hint of uncertainty, not quite sure what the man was asking.

Master Rambalt released the seal on the letter and very briefly scanned the contents. In reality, he barely gave them a glance before he tossed the letter in the air. With a snap of his fingers, the letter burst into flames, dust and ashes scattering into the wind. "Incorrect. You are here to impress me and convince me to teach you magic. You're off to an unbelievably bad start if you think that using your connections will help you get away with being late."

Ray was starting to wonder if she really wanted this angry man as her teacher. He was highly recommended by Eileen but, in her opinion, he was a bit unpleasant. She decided to stick around for a bit longer though before deciding. She took a step forward and bowed. "I apologize for being late, Master Rambalt. It was not my intention, but that does not change the fact that I have caused you displeasure. Please allow me to continue."

Master Rambalt grunted as he examined Ray with a bit more interest. Finally, he turned sharply and began to walk away. "Come, the other students are waiting. Let us discover your aptitudes."

Ray hid a faint smile as she released her bow and followed him into a nearby building that looked somewhat like a tower from the outside.

The inside of the tower was exactly what one might expect from seeing Master Rambalt's shabby appearance.

In other words, the inside of the tower was a mess.

There were books scattered throughout the room on the floor and on tables and chairs. The entire right side of the tower was scorched black while the left side had moss and mold growing from the cracks between stones. There was a small, speckled lizard floating through the air on a wizard's hat near the winding staircase that wrapped around the wall of the tower, leading up to the next floor.

In the center of the room, three people were sitting at a table drinking from cups of some steaming liquid. One of them was enormous. He was at least five Ray's wide and wore a similarly large white robe to cover his ample mass. He was balding, his remaining hair thin and stringy and he held a long, golden staff in his meaty hands. Sitting next to the fat man was a small, scrawny boy with dark hair. He was wearing a black robe and his attention was focused on the leather-bound journal that he was busily writing in.

Next to the scrawny boy was a familiar, blonde-haired figure in her white robe. Kelsey waved briefly as their eyes met. Ray waved back with a wide grin. She didn't know that Kelsey would be here, but it was a rather pleasant surprise.

Finally, hiding underneath the staircase was a cat-human hybrid with a chain on her left wrist. She had dark hair, matched by black triangular ears and a black tail coiled around her body as she huddled in the darkness. Her nose was small and stubby, and her arms and neck were covered in a thin layer of dark fur that blended into the shadows.

"Sit," Master Rambalt instructed.

Ray obeyed, moving to an empty chair next to Kelsey.

"These are my apprentices. The fat lard is Jantzen, the scrawny bundle of lust is Peter, and I'm told you already know Kelsey. You lot, this is Ray. She's taking the aptitude test."

Jantzen flinched but Peter didn't even look up from his writing.

Ray braced her heart, preparing to receive backlash as she raised her hand. "So how do I go about taking this test?"

Master Rambalt glared at her, scowling with obvious irritation. "Just summon your mana and I'll tell you."

Ray hesitated for a heartbeat before coughing lightly into her hand, covering an embarrassed smile. "Ummm, how do I do that?"

She heard a pen clattering against the table and turned to see that the other three students were all staring at her with incredulous expressions.

Master Rambalt, for his part, was staring at her appraisingly. Her question seemed to pique his interest. "Are you telling me that you have never consciously accessed your mana before?"

Ray just shrugged and let her silence speak for her.

He observed her carefully for a long, drawn-out moment. Ray could almost see the wheels turning in his mind as he thought about something.

"Girl, we are going to summon your mana *right now*! This is critical!" His voice took on an almost urgent tone.

"What do you mean?" Ray asked, her voice betraying a hint of unease.

"Because you aren't using your mana right now, right? Yet I currently sense an abnormally high concentration of mana being emitted. If you truly are not emitting any mana consciously then there are two possible reasons for this, and both require immediate action."

"Are you going to explain what those reasons are?" Jantzen asked, his beady eyes focusing on Ray with interest.

"Imbecile! What part of the word 'immediate' did you not understand?" Master Rambalt roared. He snapped his fingers twice and the table sank into the ground. Peter anxiously snatched his journal, storing it away in a pouch hanging from his belt.

Then Ray's chair began to move until it rested directly in front of the scroungy elementalist.

"Girl, follow my instructions as if your life depends on it."

Ray nodded meekly, fear swelling inside of her. Her heart drummed in her chest and her face flushed. She had no idea what was happening, but she knew from his tone that the situation was bad.

"Close your eyes and search within yourself. Every living being has a core. Some call it energy, others call it mana, and some call it ki. It is all fundamentally the same and can be harnessed in different ways for different types of magic."

Ray complied, closing her eyes while searching inside of herself. She wasn't sure what to look for, though. "What does the core feel like?"

"Every mage describes the feeling differently. Mine is somewhat tangy."

"Tangy?"

"When I use my mana, it feels like I'm sucking on oranges," Master Rambalt supplied.

She searched for something 'tangy' within her, but she found nothing. Then a thought came to her. "Do you like oranges?"

"Indeed. Oranges are my favorite fruit."

That was something she could work with. She hadn't personally experienced eating oranges or anything 'tangy' since she woke up so that sense was probably not what she was looking for. Instead, she focused on the first sensation she experienced after awakening on the mountaintop.

The taste of that man's blood.

She pursued the memory, salivating as she let the taste flow through her mind. She followed the deliciousness as an overwhelming euphoria spread throughout her body. She felt something shift and then a warm sensation filled her. The scent of that man's blood permeated the air as she felt a well of power spring up inside of her. Her vision tinted red, and her hair started to levitate a barely noticeable amount.

Master Rambalt coughed in surprise. "What is this...?!" he shouted; his eyes wide with excitement.

Ray gulped, swallowing her saliva. "What?"

"Not only do you have an aptitude for all types of magic, but the quantity and quality... It's almost as if... no, it definitely is. Girl, return here every afternoon."

Ray tried to follow the incomplete series of thoughts but gave up after realizing that it was impossible. "So, I take it I passed?"

Master Rambalt reached down and patted her on the head. "You are now my apprentice. My first rule is simple: don't ask stupid questions."

Ray shook his hand away, standing up as she started to drag her seat back to its original position.

She was met with three questioning stares from Kelsey, Jantzen, and Peter.

"All of you, get out. Class is over for the day. Dismissed. Leave!" the cranky old magician ordered while shooing them towards the door.

The four of them filtered out of the tower with bewildered expressions.

12

Foundation

As Leximea Bloodclaw silently followed her master out of the tower, she continued to stare at the walking, talking enigma. The beautiful woman with hair like waves of platinum over heterochromatic eyes who somehow reached adulthood without knowing how to summon her mana.

Her nose twitched as Ray walked by and she was assaulted by her scent. It was bloody, dark, and heavy but sprinkled with lavender and springtime.

Ray smelled of destruction and yet, at the same time, she smelled of peace. Leximea took a step back, her fur standing on end as she tried to understand exactly what kind of being she had just seen.

She recalled the stories her parents used to tell her. Stories about the five immortal races who used to rule this world.

The elves, who embodied grace and nature.

The dragons, strength and power incarnate.

The fae, magical entities that consumed the light.

The seraphim, the rulers of life and darkness.

The slimes, with unlimited potential and the right to be absolute.

Though no living beastkin had met a member of these races, it was said that their ancestors fought wars with these beings. Sometimes they fought against them and sometimes they fought side by side.

One thing that Leximea remembered was the description of their scent, passed on so that the Bloodclaw Tribe might never again anger those who must not be angered. Every member of the immortal races always had two contradictory scents: they smelled of destruction and of peace.

"What in Jocelyn's holy bosom was that?" Jantzen growled.

Peter shrugged. "Think she's another talent like your cousin?"

Jantzen dismissed the suggestion with a shake of his meaty head, his robe fluttering as ripples rolled through his body. "There are no talents like him. He's the strongest. She might be a few levels below him though."

"What do you think? Master Rambalt said you already know her?" Peter faced Kelsey and asked.

She shrugged. "We've met, but I can't say I know her. She respawned in the temple two days ago, but nobody around here seems to know who she is. Also, within a day of respawning she somehow obtained a letter with Lord Maxwell's magic signature."

Peter whistled in admiration. "Lord Maxwell? She's the real deal then. We have to get her on our team."

Kelsey turned and her long, blonde hair fluttered as she started to walk away.

"I still haven't agreed to join your team and I don't plan on becoming an adventurer," she called back.

Peter smiled mischievously. "Oh, you will," he muttered softly so that Kelsey couldn't hear.

Leximea overheard with her sharp ears and grimaced.

"Slave! Let's go!" Jantzen shouted, swinging his staff. Leximea ducked under the blow and hissed, baring her teeth at the fat lump.

"She's still got some fight left in her," Jantzen observed. "You want to have a go at breaking her at the inn, Peter?"

Peter shook his head. "I prefer humans. I'm not yet desperate enough to rely on beasts to please myself."

Leximea took another step back, then stopped as she felt a heavy pressure on the chain dangling from her left wrist. The chain links that were coiled lightly on the ground beside her suddenly felt as if they weighed a ton.

Leximea cried out as her shoulder dislocated and she crashed to the ground, her wrist pinned by the overbearing weight.

Jantzen stood over her, leering with eyes full of malice. He held his staff in both hands, raising the golden rod overhead. "Let's try this again."

The staff descended.

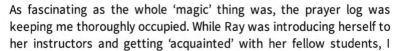

As fascinating as the whole 'magic' thing was, the prayer log was keeping me thoroughly occupied. While Ray was introducing herself to her instructors and getting 'acquainted' with her fellow students, I used the time to address my huge backlog of prayers.

I couldn't help but feel that there must be another way though... it didn't seem possible for a single person to address each of these prayers individually. Even after filtering out all the 'thanks for the food prayers' on auto-respond, I could only watch in amazement as the number of prayers continued to rise.

674,532 unread messages!

In other words, no matter what I did, I still had an aggravating blinking red light at the edge of my vision, taunting me with the ever-growing number.

It felt depressing reading them too. People asked me for all kinds of things that I wanted to give them, but I just... couldn't.

Rudy the Gnome asked me how to become a great swordsman.

Issylra the Naga expressed her desire to attract her ideal minotaur.

Steve the Human... well, he seemed like an interesting guy. First, despite being human his prayers were coming to me. That would mean that he didn't currently follow an Overseer, which obviously caught my attention. He asked for a way to become a paladin and a dark knight at the same time. Also, he said he wanted to learn how to breakdance.

I wasn't sure where he wanted to go with all that, but he seemed interesting enough. I kind of wanted to meet the guy.

Still, it was promising to see the huge number of prayers coming my way in a constant stream. The other Overseers may have created an effective soul farm by restricting their followers to humans, but they made a mistake. They didn't account for the possibility of a new Overseer coming in and sweeping up followers amongst those who are being persecuted.

Certainly, I would have to proceed carefully though. Having read many stories about goblins, orcs, trolls, minotaurs, and other monsters, I would have to make sure that I didn't become responsible for elevating evil creatures to positions of immortality and power. It would probably be a real chore walking that fine line, but I could do it if I kept my mind open and my heart free of judgment.

I glanced over at Ray as I was pondering that. Someday, she would be at the core of my church. I would have to raise her well...

I froze as I took in the unexpected view.

What the hell happened while I was looking away?

Ray, observing from behind a nearby building, winced as the rod struck the young slave again and again. She had turned around when she noticed the smell of blood. She noted Jantzen's delighted smile.

He continued to swing again and again, the poor girl long since forgetting how to whimper.

Vague memories surfaced in Ray's mind. They were indistinct and fleeting, almost as if they were on the verge of disappearing.

She saw hunched forms on the ground before her. The rattling of chains echoed from the depth of her mind. Waves of rage and hatred seeped into her heart, dying it crimson and black. She tried to take a step forward, barely managing to brace herself against the wall as tears streamed down her face.

Ray slapped her own cheek, attempting to break herself away from clutches of the dark, sinister emotions. She shivered and her body broke out in cold sweat. She leaned heavily against the building, sliding down until she was resting on the ground.

"Are these... memories? Why was I in so much pain...? Who am I...?" she muttered, resting her head against her knees.

She sat like that for a long moment until she heard another *thump*, and she lifted her head. The fatso was still at it?

Ray slapped herself once more, driving away the gloomy thoughts.

She stepped out from her hiding place and approached Jantzen from behind. She winced as he struck the slave once more. Ray broke into a silent run. As the staff descended on its final arc, she reached out and grabbed the end before it could strike the poor girl bleeding on the cobblestone.

"I'd tell you to pick on someone your own size, but there doesn't seem to be any others in this town," Ray said, her tone rising playfully. She hoped that by smiling, she could hide the dark emotions seething beneath her skin.

"Is that a fat joke?" Jantzen questioned. His eyes gleamed with a dangerous light. "I don't like fat jokes."

"Well, at least you'll never be a narcissist then," Ray replied with a wink. She turned her back to Jantzen and reached down to pull up the barely conscious slave.

Peter coughed and covered his mouth as he looked away. His shoulders shook with suppressed laughter.

Meanwhile, Jantzen took an angry step forward, reaching his hand out to grab Ray from behind. "You think you're clever, eh? That right there happens to be my property. If you touch it without my permission, I'll have you arrested for theft."

"Oh?" Her vision tinted red as she breathed deeply, inhaling the scent of warm, fresh blood. Her fake smile twitched as a wave of excitement rolled through her, overtaking her inner rage and sorrow.

She gently lifted the battered slave and turned to face Jantzen once more.

"I'm quivering. Please, do try your best."

Jantzen grimaced, his expression frozen between shock and displeasure. "I'm not kidding, you know! My cousin is Prince Douglas, and my father is a duke of this kingdom. I could have you arrested for interfering with me!"

Ray ignored the fat man's threats and attempted to step past him. She didn't know how much merit his words had, but any nervousness she might have felt was being thoroughly suppressed by the bloodlust she was barely holding in check.

Besides, Sister Eileen could probably help her deal with some lame old 'duke' or whatever. What mattered right now was that this idiot wanted to harm the poor girl in her arms.

Peter reached out and placed a hand on Ray's shoulder. "Now, now. I think we got off on the wrong foot. Why don't we talk this out?"

Ray flinched and then hissed as she felt a strange sensation. Something foreign seemed to be seeping into her. She paused and examined the feeling. It was somewhat similar to the mana she managed to summon before but this one had been refined and tuned towards some kind of purpose. The mana oozed into her and slowly approached her mind.

She summoned her own mana, filling the air with the powerful scent of delicious blood. The aroma was appealing enough to overpower the scent of the actual blood that was staining her new cloak. She directed a fierce glare at the puny boy who dared to try and use some unknown magic on her.

"Let go or I will rip your arm off and feed it to the fat pig over there!"

Peter cried out and quickly retracted his arm. He fell backward onto his rear and desperately pushed against the ground, crawling away from her as his senses screamed at him to get away as fast as possible.

"You're not getting away from me that easily!" Jantzen shouted, snapping his fingers.

Ray stumbled as an enormous weight pulled down and yanked the catgirl out of her arms. She heard an ominous cracking sound followed by an agonized scream.

She looked down and saw that the catgirl's left arm was bent strangely, blood pouring out near a fragment of bone protruding from her skin. Ray reached down and gingerly pried at the heavy shackle.

She found that she was able to lift it with some effort, but the slave screamed every time she touched it so she decided to leave it for now. Instead, she whirled around to face the fat piece of trash who would treat a young girl like this. Jantzen was gloating, his smug eyes looking down on her.

Ray walked up until she stood directly in front of him. He towered over her and, for a very brief second, she felt short. She reached out and grabbed the man by the wrist. She pulled while twisting her body and Jantzen cried out in surprise as his feet left the ground and he smoothly flipped over her head and smashed into the ground with a meaty *thump*.

Jantzen remained on the ground, gasping for air while Peter looked on in awe. Neither of them would meet Ray's half-crazed eyes as she laughed.

"W..what..? H...h...how?" Jantzen wheezed.

"Turn the weight of the chain back to normal!" Ray ordered.

Jantzen obeyed and snapped his fingers. She shot him a menacing smirk, and waved goodbye as she walked over to the prone form of the catgirl. Her smile turned warm and gentle as she reached down and carefully lifted the slave into her arms once more. She tried her best not to aggravate the girl's arm as she started to walk towards the exit from the Magic Quarter.

A raging whisper followed her. "You'll regret this!"

Ray had no idea what kind of consequences her actions might have but she couldn't help how her face twisted as her expression lit up with delight. She resisted the urge to shudder with excitement for fear of hurting the catgirl further.

Still, she started to giggle. The melodic sound filled the air as she walked carefully and confidently into the crowds of people who turned to stare at her. Whether they were staring at the injured catkin, the blood stains on her cloak, or the fact that a young woman was laughing while carrying a dying person, she wasn't sure.

There might be consequences for her actions here later, but she didn't care. There were only two things that mattered -- she did what she set out to do, and most importantly, it was fun.

That sense of power... using her strength to suppress and thrash, scaring the scrawny boy with a glare, saving the poor slave, and otherwise putting those arrogant pieces of trash in their place...

Wouldn't it be great to experience that sensation again?

13

Leximea Bloodclaw

Pain.

Every part of her body screamed and protested against the violent abuse that was heaped upon it. Her broken arm was a wet, sticky fire that boiled, flaring up at the slightest jostle.

Though her memory was fuzzy, she vaguely recalled someone intervening in the beating. Leximea heard a faint rumbling nearby and tried to focus on it to distract herself from the pain. As her consciousness resurfaced, it felt like she passed through a murky film into the dark and dirty place called reality.

"And that's what happened," a familiar voice concluded.

Wasn't that Ray, the immortal girl? Why was she here?

"Essentially, you attacked the son of a duke and stole his slave?" an unknown, female voice clarified.

"That's right. Do you think we could get her healed?"

The other voice sighed and then Leximea heard a faint rustling of fabric, followed by footsteps approaching her.

The unknown person stopped next to her. "How barbaric..." she muttered. "I suppose I should heal her myself."

"You can heal?" Ray interjected her voice filled with amazement.

"Healing is elementary holy magic, and I am a High Priestess. Of course I can heal."

A High Priestess?! Leximea felt her heart beating furiously in her chest, the fur on her arms and neck bristling with alarm. She had to get out of here. This was the most dangerous place in the whole town... but the slightest twitch of her arm made her want to screech.

The High Priestess summoned her mana and the temperature in the room increased by a few degrees. Leximea felt sweat forming on her brow and unconsciously released her claws.

And then a gentle hand caressed her injured arm, bringing pure, blessed relief. The bone retreated beneath the writhing flesh. Her skin resealed itself and her arm snapped back into its natural position. There was a faint itch as new patches of dark fur sprouted and grew over the freshly healed skin.

The High Priestess then ran her healing touch over the other visible injuries. After a minute of careful observation and prodding, she paused and moved away. "She's completely healed. She should wake up soon."

There was another rustling of fabric and then a soft collision.

"Thank you!"

"I have to ask though, why does she matter so much to you? Do you know her?"

No, Leximea was certain that they didn't know each other.

"I think I saw her at the gate when I entered the town, but other than that, I have no idea who she is."

"You would go this far for a stranger?"

It was certainly odd. Why did Ray help her?

"I can't say that I would always do this much. It just bothered me, so I intervened."

What? For such a simple reason?

"That reasoning is a bit childish. Remember that being impulsive will hurt you at least as often as it helps you."

"I'll try to remember. No promises though."

Leximea decided it was probably time to stop feigning unconsciousness. The High Priestess already probably noticed while she was healing her. She opened her eyes and observed the people who saved her.

They both looked over as they heard a rustling sound from beside them. Leximea groaned as she sat up, her freshly healed muscles protesting as she stretched. She blinked a few times and her expression twisted as she took in her surroundings.

Her eyes settled on Ray. She jumped back in shock and rolled over the back of the couch, crashing to the floor.

She was covered in blood! What happened to her?

Ray burst out laughing while the High Priestess covered her mouth to hide a faint smile. Ray walked around the couch and reached out a hand to help her up.

"Nice to meet you. My name is Ray."

She stared at Ray's extended hand for a long moment. Her eyes and mouth were both wide open, revealing her feline fangs. She gingerly grabbed Ray's hand and allowed herself to be pulled up to her feet.

"Leximea of the Bloodclaw tribe…" she mumbled. "M..my friends called me L..Lexi."

"May I call you Lexi as well?" Ray asked gently.

Lexi looked up and met Ray's warm, confident gaze. She couldn't explain why, but an overwhelming sense of safety and peace filled her soul. She remembered hearing that her instincts would become sharper as her transformation progressed. She felt the changes keenly.

She instinctively knew that Ray was like a god to someone like her.

Without hesitation, Lexi nodded her assent.

Ray beamed with delight and Lexi felt her heart flutter as she observed the ethereal enigma before her. Why would a godlike entity descend to help her, of all people? There were so many other slaves outside, why did Ray pick her?

She looked down at the chain on her right wrist in confusion.

"I asked Sister Eileen to heal you," Ray supplied.

"Sister Eileen?" Lexi asked.

Ray pointed towards the older woman standing behind her and the High Priestess waved in greeting.

"Hey, sweetie. You feeling better?"

Lexi scuttled behind Ray and gingerly peeked out from behind her. She gave a careful and deliberate nod. She may have healed her, but that didn't change the fact that she was a High Priestess. She was the enemy.

"Come and sit down. We have a lot to talk about," Eileen invited with a motion towards the couch.

Lexi looked up at Ray and their eyes met.

Ray nodded with a smile.

They both sat down while the High Priestess poured a cup of tea and offered it to the young beastkin. Lexi flinched, her eyes never leaving Eileen as she scooted closer to Ray until their legs were touched. There was no way in hell she was touching that tea. What if there was poison in it? That seemed like something a human would do.

"I'd love to hear your story but before that, we need to figure out how to get you two out of trouble."

"What do you mean?" Ray asked as she accepted a cup.

"Miss Ray, you seem to think that you heroically rescued this girl from her captor. From what you've told me, it seems that you slightly bruised his body and violently shattered his pride. Gods forbid he ever recovers."

"He deserved it," she added.

"Now, I can't do this every time, but I do have a solution to get you out of trouble," Eileen continued. "I am prepared to purchase Lexi from this 'Jantzen' and turn over ownership to you, Ray. Would you be willing to accept this responsibility?"

Ray pondered for a long moment as she sipped at her tea. Lexi stared at her nervously, unsure what the godlike entity was thinking. She seemed somewhat uncomfortable, but Lexi hoped she would accept. She would rather serve her savior than an immature man-child like Jantzen.

"If we do that, could I pass that ownership on to Lexi?"

Lexi's eyes widened with disbelief.

Eileen tilted her head in thought, her eyes gleaming with a peculiar light. "You mean, Lexi would officially be the owner of her own slave contract? I'm not sure. To my knowledge, no one has thought to try it."

"It would be for the best. Lexi needs to wear the collar to walk around town normally, right? She can pretend to be my slave but really she'll be free."

Eileen pursed her lips as she considered the idea. "Yes, I think that could work."

Lexi's confusion grew with every added sentence. Just a short time ago she was being violently beaten and now she was in a strange place with people she didn't know who were discussing her freedom.

"Excuse me…" Lexi interjected. "Why are you helping me?"

Ray leaned over and grabbed Lexi's hand. "Will you be my friend?" Her eyes were full of earnestness without a single hint of deceit.

Lexi flinched. She examined the woman in front of her carefully. Her instincts screamed that she should do whatever this great personage commanded but she shook that off and nodded stiffly, her confusion slowly filtering into disbelief.

Though she couldn't truly relax yet, for the first time in over a month, her eyes began to water. Her vision blurred. All the rage, guilt, and pain of the last month simmered and a small portion of it drained away.

Eileen offered her a tissue and Lexi blew her nose.

After a long, uncomfortable pause, Lexi finally broke the silence. "I don't know what to say. I don't know how the two of you expect me to repay you, but I have a goal that I must accomplish no matter what."

Ray tilted her head. "Tell me," she urged.

Lexi raised her gaze to look at her savior and their eyes met. The ethereal and beautiful woman had a sharp gaze unbecoming of her appearance. If this lady was what she seemed to be...

The young slave cut off that line of thought immediately. Fighting back the faint, impossible hope that this person would help her, she cleared her throat. "I suppose it's only fair to tell my rescuers how I came to be in this situation..."

***

Leximea Bloodclaw was born into the Bloodclaw tribe as the youngest daughter of Chief Bloodclaw. Her early years were filled with playful memories and the vibrant love provided by stable friends and family.

In her seventh year, her life was visited by tragedy.

"Lexi, take your brother and run!" her mother ordered.

A faint explosion resounded outside, and the entire house shuddered, scattering dust into the air.

Lexi reached out and accepted her newborn brother into her arms. Her mother gave her one last hug goodbye before she turned and left to join the battle. Lexi turned the opposite direction and ran out the back door. She bolted through her yard and leapt over the fence in a smooth motion. She ducked low on the other side to help avoid the invaders' attention. She hugged her baby brother against her chest, praying silently that they might somehow win.

This was the fourth time the invaders had come. No matter how many times they killed the humans, they just kept coming back. Every time they invaded, more valiant tribesmen died and now there weren't enough people to repel them.

Her father fell during the third invasion and the people were still in chaos trying to choose a new Chief. Normally, her older brother would have inherited the position, but he panicked and lost control of his inner beast. Having transformed into a feral werecat, he attacked his fellow tribesman and fled the village after being severely wounded.

Lexi heard another explosion in the distance. The battle cries of her people filled the air as they sought to defend their homes and their lives. She leapt over another fence as tears filled her eyes.

"Why..." she whispered. "Why do the humans hate us so much?"

Lexi slowed to a stop as she neared the edge of the village. She sensed people walking towards her from outside. Before her eyes, a wall of fire blasted through the weak fence and a dozen humans entered the village from behind the defensive line.

They saw her. One of them pointed, shouting to the others. Lexi turned and ran in the opposite direction, back towards the center of the town. She could try to escape in another direction, but she wasn't confident that she could get away anymore. Besides, she needed to warn the others that they had been flanked.

"I'm sorry, Mynn," she whispered to her baby brother. "Looks like we might not get out of this one."

Neremynn looked up into her eyes with the incomprehension of a three-month-old. Lexi continued to cry as she entered the main road and approached the final defensive line.

When she saw what remained, she fell to her knees.

There was no more defensive line. Her mother was being restrained by a group of male humans who were laughing as they prodded her with their weapons. Several other female catkin were in the same boat. The younger ones were being herded into cages while the older ones were being dragged away to alleyways and houses.

The men chasing her from behind caught up and surrounded her. Lexi hugged Neremynn close with her left hand and raised her claws with her right. She had heard stories of what would happen to her if she ever got captured by humans.

She would much rather go down fighting.

Lexi jumped forward and swiped at the nearest man with her claws.

He laughed as he caught her by the wrist and lifted her in the air to examine her. "She looks young enough - maybe fifteen or sixteen? Good for selling."

Lexi snarled at the man and bit his arm through his shirt. She drew blood but the man didn't even flinch.

"Hey, Travis, she's got a baby beast with her. You want to get rid of it?"

"Oy oy, why do I always have to do the dirty jobs?"

"I can give it to Henrick. He enjoys tearing apart the little buggers."

"Nah, I'll do it. They may be cursed, but even they don't deserve what that guy does to 'em."

Travis reached out and yanked Neremynn out of Lexi's arms. Lexi tried to fight back but he was much stronger than her and she barely put up a fight before her brother was taken.

Being separated from the safety of his sister's arms, Mynn began to cry.

"Would you like to watch?" the man holding her whispered into her ear.

Lexi shook her head, trembling.

"Sucks to be you then," the man replied as he grabbed her by the back of the neck with his grubby hand.

"What should I do?" Travis mused as he looked around. He saw an empty bucket lying on the ground and smiled. "I've heard that cats hate water. How about we give him a bath?"

Travis picked up the bucket and tapped it with his finger. The bucket filled to the brim with pure, clean water. He held Neremynn up over the bucket. Neremynn continued to scream defenselessly, unaware of the fate that awaited him.

"No, no, no, please don't!" Lexi screeched. She clawed in desperation at the arm holding her. "You monsters! How can you do this?"

"We might seem that way to you, but the gods tell us otherwise. Males don't sell well, and we don't need babies," Travis explained as he grabbed Neremynn by the head.

Lexi wailed as she desperately tried to free herself.

They were going to kill her baby brother.

The men around her all merely laughed. They laughed and laughed. The man holding her leaned forward and whispered into her ear. "You shouldn't have been born a beast. You should have kept on running. This is your fault."

Lexi sobbed as her world crumbled around her. She never once looked away. She stared at each person in the circle and seared the faces of every one of the laughing monsters into her mind.

As she was carried away amidst the screaming of her fellow female catkin, black fur slowly sprouted along her neck, back, and arms.

That evening, Eileen waited anxiously in her designated meeting room. After her earlier meeting with Ray and Lexi, she had been busy arranging to purchase Lexi. She paid more than twice the price of a young, pretty slave, but she had no issues with that. The other party raised the price because he understood that she wanted this whole situation to remain quiet for as long as possible.

She knew that she could trust the duke. He never reneged on their deals in the past.

Finally, the long-awaited knock came, and Sullivan opened the door to admit the three people she had been dying to see all day.

Lord Maxwell Rovar, Siegfried Lancaster, and Quincy Rambalt

Max was wearing his typical black leather jacket over a t-shirt and dark pants. His eyepatch and red hair contrasted with the dark hair of the other two. Quincy was greasy and unkempt, as usual. Siegfried wore his tank top that showed off his muscular frame.

Sullivan stepped back into the shadows and disappeared as her guests entered the room.

"Come in, brothers, and take a seat."

"I assume you took the usual precautions?" Quincy muttered as he and the others found their way to the comfortable couch.

Eileen offered each of them a cup of tea but only Max accepted.

"Of course," Eileen replied as she poured the tea.

"Good," Quincy replied. "Now tell me. Where in the Dark Lady's holy abyss did you find that girl?"

Eileen giggled. "Would you believe me if I told you that she just *walked* in here? She respawned in the temple two days ago and walked back in yesterday."

"Pffft, you expect me to believe that there exists an Overseer that would let one of those *things* respawn?" Quincy scoffed.

"It's true," Max supplied. "I was there when she woke up. She seemed confused."

"She seems to have lost her memories," Eileen supplied.

"I'd believe it. The damned beast asked me how to summon mana! I had to teach her how to control it before she leaked too much and gave herself away. Still, I wonder how such a blessing fell upon us? I was beginning to think we would never find one..." Quincy mused, scratching at the stubble on his cheek.

"What name was on the register?" Siegfried asked.

Quincy, Max, and Siegfried all leaned forward.

Eileen paused uncomfortably. "You're not going to like it. It's a name that all of you know. We can't be sure that this isn't a trap."

"Tell us the damn name!" Quincy spat out.

"Please," Max added while giving his grungy colleague a sharp glare.

Eileen let out a deep sigh. "It's her. The Queen of Vampires. The most legendary and powerful assassin."

Quincy, Max, and Siegfried all froze. They looked at each other before Siegfried leapt to his feet, crying out jubilantly.

"That young lady is Evelyn Raymond?! We got our hands on the Monarch of Ages?!"

Eileen smiled as she saw that Quincy was tearing up. He noticed her staring and rubbed his eyes, glaring at her as if daring her to mention it.

Max leaned back into the seat of the couch. He collapsed into the cushions weakly, and all the strength left his body.

"Humanity's greatest enemy... The Queen of Vampires is now my student..." Siegfried muttered in amazement.

"But why did Evelyn Raymond respawn in the temple with no memories? Why did she suddenly get younger? Why did she lose her fighting techniques and ability to control mana?" Max muttered. His eyes scrunched with worry.

Eileen shrugged. "We'll have to see if we can figure all of that out. What matters is that she is a blank slate right now. If we are careful, we can paint her in any color we want."

Each of the three men nodded in agreement.

"If we can train her to a sufficient level, then we can continue this shadow war for as long as we need to," Eileen continued. "Ray has no memories, so I don't expect that she could perform at the same level as the esteemed Evelyn Raymond yet, but she is still one of the legendary immortals and I want each of you to carefully raise her. Max, I want you to protect her. Siegfried and Quincy, I want you to help her become our most powerful weapon. By the beginning of spring, she needs to be ready to fulfill her role."

Each of them nodded, accepting their respective task.

"Are we definitely leaving by spring then?" Quincy asked.

Eileen grimaced, her displeasure showing on her face. "That's what Phineas ordered. He received a divine revelation saying that if we haven't found the core by spring then we won't be able to find it here anymore."

"Phineas..." Siegfried sighed. "If he's the one saying it, he's definitely right, as much as I hate to admit it. We'll make sure our little 'friend' is ready by then."

"Make sure of it," Eileen ordered. "The most important part is to gain her trust without raising the suspicions of the other students. She must trust us wholeheartedly if we want the greatest results."

"Is there anything else you can tell us about her?" Siegfried asked, his eyes filled with determination.

Eileen thought for a second. "Let's see, she attacked two of Quincy's other students earlier today to rescue a catkin slave. Also, I investigated an attack she apparently received yesterday. She seems to have fought with an adventurer team and killed two of them. One was another of Quincy's students and the other happens to be one of Rick's students."

Siegfried and Quincy shared a glance. "She attacks and kills her fellow students, and we have to gain her trust without raising their suspicions," Quincy summarized.

Eileen smiled. "Doesn't she sound perfect? I leave it in your capable hands."

14

Guardian

"Ray, we need to talk."

Ray shot up, looking around with wide-eyed alarm. "Who's there?" The room came into focus, but she didn't see anyone else present.

"It's me, the Overseer."

Ray sighed when she realized that the voice in her head was speaking to her again. "What do you want to talk about?" she asked, tilting her head with curiosity. Her now tangled hair bobbed with the motion and she grimaced when she realized that she would have to straighten it out shortly.

"Yesterday. I support your decision to rescue the catgirl. I believe your actions were just. However, you didn't even attempt to resolve the situation peacefully. Fear is a great tool for creating power, but it is terrible at maintaining it."

"My actions were just? Creating power? I wasn't worried about anything like that. I saw someone in trouble, and it made me feel unpleasant so I fixed the problem."

"My point is that you need to start thinking about those things. Some people are only alive because it is illegal to kill them. Even if those people deserve death or worse, if you break the law then you will bring upon yourself trouble that you and your new friend won't be able to deal with."

Ray's cheeks burned and she felt her chest tighten. "Who are you to lecture me? You don't know anything about me!" she half-shouted, her voice rising with indignation.

"You're right, I know very little about you. That is something that will only change with time. But keep in mind that you also don't know much about me. I'm only trying to help you."

He was just trying to help?

Ray took a deep breath to push back her rising irritation. "Of course I don't know anything about you. You're a voice in my head! Why do you even exist?"

"An excellent question and one that I am not sure how to answer. I am a god, and you are my prophet. I was not given a reason for why I became a god. Perhaps it is up to us to decide what our purpose will be?"

"What kind of answer is that?" Ray growled. "You haven't even told me your name yet and you want me to work with you?"

The voice was silent for a long time. Ray was starting to think that he wasn't going to reply when he finally broke the silence.

"Ah, that's right. I haven't even picked a name yet. I know that you still aren't convinced that you should work with me, but please at least consider my advice. Try some diplomacy next time and see if it doesn't work out in your favor."

There was a knock on the door. Ray rolled out of bed and landed on her feet. "I'll consider it," she replied.

Her shoulder felt a little stiff, so she lightly stretched it as she sauntered towards the door. When she answered the door, there were three figures waiting on the other side.

"Good morning!" Ray greeted them. She stepped away from the door and motioned for them to enter.

They moved through the doorway one by one, and Ray closed the door after Eileen entered last.

"'G'Mornin'" Eileen grumbled. She drearily rubbed her eyes as she limped over to the bed and sat on the edge. Then, with a sigh of relief, she leaned back until she was lying down and closed her eyes.

"She's not a morning person," Kelsey explained, seeing Ray's confusion.

Ray snickered while Lexi simply stared at the High Priestess with curiosity, her triangular ears twitching.

"I heard that!" Eileen pushed herself back into a sitting position and glared at Kelsey. "I like mornings just fine. Unfortunately, mornings do not like me." She tapped the dark bags under her eyes as if to prove a point.

Ray wasn't quite sure what point she was trying to make, but she decided to change the subject after Eileen turned her sharp glare towards her. "So, what brings you all here this morning?"

Eileen motioned to come closer, and Ray complied.

"I purchased the slave contract yesterday evening and I came to give it to you."

Lexi gasped and then covered her mouth. Tears formed at the edge of her eyes.

Ray smiled at her before returning her attention to the High Priestess. "Why didn't you just give it straight to Lexi then? Is there really a need to give it to me first?" she asked.

Eileen nodded. "A fair question. I am not the one who will give her back her freedom, you are. You may not understand now, but it is an important distinction to make. This will help you down the road."

Ray angled her head in confusion but decided to just accept it. "How do we go about this then?"

"Transferring a slave contract is like imprinting a magic signature. A portion of the slave's mana is connected to a slave collar or wristband. The master is registered to the same medium and has a mana conduit which connects them. I can transfer ownership of the conduit through contact with your mana."

"So, Lexi and I just need to summon our respective mana, and after you give it to me then I just touch her mana and give it to her?"

"Correct."

Ray closed her eyes and focused her attention inward. She felt for the mana that she knew was there and smiled as the delightful aroma surrounded her once more.

She opened her eyes and noticed Kelsey scrunching her nose.

"What the heck is this?" the priestess complained while plugging her nose to block out the smell.

"Blood, I think," Ray replied with a smirk. "You don't like it?"

"You really are a beginner if your mana still has a scent... but why does your mana smell like blood?"

"Let's continue with the task at hand," Eileen interrupted. "Are you ready?"

Ray nodded. A moment later, an enormous presence contacted her mana. Her eyes widened as she realized that she couldn't see anything about Eileen's mana. When she had connected with Peter, she felt the entirety of his mana supply and the fact that he was using magic.

With Eileen, she felt completely overwhelmed. It wasn't that there was nothing to see. Rather, it was because there was so much to see that she effectively couldn't process anything.

A piece of the aura broke off and attached to her mana. Ray felt for the piece and intuitively understood that it was a pathway or channel of sorts. She followed the link to the shackle on Lexi's wrist.

"You ready?" Ray asked Lexi.

The young slave nodded, though Ray noted that her shoulders were tense, and her tail was stiff.

"Summon your mana!" she ordered.

Lexi meekly complied and they felt the air fill with something that had a faint fishy smell.

Ray reached out with her aura and touched the new mana permeating the air. With some effort, she forcibly detached the portion Eileen had transferred to her and moved it over into the catgirl's mana.

They both pulled back their mana and stared at each other in silence.

Lexi launched herself forward and embraced Ray. "Thank you! Thank you so much!" she cried out, tears flowing down her cheeks.

Ray patted the former slave on the back. She felt a strange sense of satisfaction rising within her, different from the one she experienced after flexing her strength on Jantzen and Peter.

She also liked this feeling quite a bit. It was warm.

Maybe if she helped more people, then she could experience this feeling more? But she would have to balance it. She also wanted to experience more of that rush that came with breaking and terrorizing people.

Then again, Eileen had said that she wouldn't be able to help out every time Ray tried to rescue slaves, so she would have to plan a bit more before doing something like that in the future. There was that request from the voice in her head as well.

Eileen called out to them, interrupting her contemplation. "If you two are done, you should be heading out. Siegfried will be waiting for you on the public grounds. Today he will show you the way to his private training area."

Ray nodded as she gave Lexi one last pat on the back before she broke away from the embrace. "Shall we go?"

Lexi wiped away the tears on her face and nodded with a determined look in her eyes.

The two started to move towards the door but Eileen stopped them. "One moment!"

Ray heard a faint whistling sound as something flew through the air, she turned and caught the small box. She didn't know where the box came from, but it had a somewhat appetizing scent.

"A little breakfast for the two of you to eat on the way. Off you go then."

Ray nodded in thanks and walked through the door.

As they left the room, Ray overheard a brief exchange between Kelsey and Eileen and she frowned, curiosity raging through her.

"High Priestess, why did you ask me to witness this?" Kelsey asked.

"I'm just planting a seed. Ponder on what you just saw and pay close attention to her for a while. Things should be getting interesting pretty soon."

Just what did she mean by that? Eileen had been upfront in saying that she had her own agenda for all the help she had provided. Ray was somewhat curious about what that agenda might be, but she vowed that for the time being, she wouldn't ask.

After everything Eileen had done for her already, it was the least she could do to wait until the High Priestess was ready and willing to talk about it.

After meeting up with Siegfried, he guided them to another portion of the martial quarter that Ray hadn't seen when she visited the previous day. He only gave Lexi a single curious glance before giving his undivided attention to Ray as they walked.

While moving, he explained a bit more about what his training would entail.

"As of today, you will be one of my students. My job is to raise adventurers to hunt monsters and that is what I will be teaching you to do. Specifically, I will be teaching you to fight in a traditional guardian style. That means you will learn to fight with a sword and shield, and with a two-handed greatsword. Any questions so far?"

"So, if I learn from you, then I have to become an adventurer?" Ray asked with a slight frown.

"Of course not. However, while training under me you will often be expected to perform 'adventurer' work. Your practical experience will come in the form of 'missions' and you will be expected to join and operate in a team of fellow students."

Ray thought about that for a moment. "What is classified as a 'monster'?"

Siegfried examined Ray carefully before replying. "Adventurers are glorified monster hunters. 'Monster', in this case, refers to any non-human entity that poses a threat to humans. It could be wild, unintelligent creatures such as a roc or a yeti, or it could be orcs, trolls, goblins, beastkin, vampires, or bandits. Those are the most common monsters in this area, anyways."

Beastkin? Ray glanced at Lexi. "Am I allowed to refuse some missions?"

Siegfried shrugged. "That depends. You will have fewer opportunities to gain practical combat experience, but I can't exactly

force you to go. It comes down to how dedicated you are to growing stronger and more proficient." He paused in front of a nondescript stone structure. "After we go through here, you will meet with your fellow students. I've been told that you have already had some spats with other students. I'll give you one warning, and one warning only: No fighting in my class outside of practice matches or sparring."

Ray chuckled as she recalled her brief 'spat' with Jantzen and Peter. "I'll keep that in mind."

"Good." Siegfried opened the door and stepped to the side. He motioned for Ray to enter first. "After you."

She entered through the doorway and found herself in a small entryway leading to a set of stone stairs. The stone was old and worn, with some cracks and chipped edges and corners. The stairs lead down to a bright doorway.

Ray glided down the stairs, followed by the quiet Lexi and the enormous Siegfried. As she entered through the doorway, she gasped. She found herself in a huge underground area, the ceiling being almost twenty feet high. The room was wide with plenty of space to run and jump and practice. The leftmost wall was jagged and covered in ridges. The rightmost section had a heavy waterfall and a deep pool. In the center of the room stood seven others.

She was surprised to recognize four of the seven people. Standing off to the side were the two instructors that had watched her practice match against Siegfried. However, she had also met two of the five students.

They seemed to recognize her too. Jonathan was frozen, his eyes wide open with shock as he stared at her. Vick stopped mid-laugh. The two of them glared at Ray and Lexi shivered, her ears flat against her head.

Ray was completely unaffected by their obvious animosity, though. "'Sup! Wasn't expecting to see you guys here!" she called out cheerfully. She strolled up to Jonathan while intentionally donning the purest of pure smiles.

"*Maybe I should teach you how to act. That looks weird as hell…*"

She ignored the voice in her head as she reached out and offered to shake his hand. "Peace?"

Jonathan gaped at her. At this point, every eye in the room was focused on the two individuals, though only a few of them knew why the two men were so angry.

"What is a 'monster' doing here?" Jonathan growled.

"My, whatever do you mean? Do I look like a monster to you?" Ray decided to play innocent. She tilted her head to the side to add to the effect.

"You killed Bill and Suzy! And you have a red eye!" Vick spat out.

"And she was vouched for by High Priestess Eileen herself!" Siegfried added.

"Right, and she was..." Vick trailed off. "Wait, what?"

Every eye turned to Siegfried, and he met their gazes with a smirk. "That's right. I spoke with the High Priestess myself and she vouched for this young lady. She passed my talent test and is now one of your fellow students."

"That's ridiculous! She killed *two* of our party members. How could you possibly expect us to team up with her?" Jonathan shouted, his face burning with crimson outrage.

"I don't care what you decide to do. Team up with her or not, I'm sure she'll be just fine either way. Your teammates can reflect on their loss while they wait to respawn. If they didn't want to die then they should have won." Siegfried replied simply.

Jonathan shut his mouth.

Siegfried turned and pointed towards the remaining students. There was a tall, lithe woman covered in leather armor and hidden daggers. Her light-brown hair was tied back in a ponytail and she had a quiver and a bow strung across her back. "Helen."

Then he pointed at the strange figure next to her. He was wearing a long, dark cloak that covered most of his body. His face was covered by a silver mask with two slits that revealed icy blue eyes. "Ven."

He pointed at the two instructors, one whom Ray recognized as the weapon-obsessed trainer and the other was a man who didn't stand out in any way.

The weapon trainer had the same weapons as before, three swords, a dagger and an axe all tied to his belt, two large swords across his back, and daggers strapped to his legs and to his chest. The ordinary man had short-cropped grey hair and wore a simple robe with no visible weapons.

He first pointed at the weapon-obsessed trainer. "The Blade Storm, Rick. He's the warrior trainer."

Then he pointed at the other trainer. "The Echo Fist, Jedediah Lion. He's the martial arts trainer."

Siegfried clapped his hands together. "Introductions complete. While the rest of you get started, I'm going to get Ray here a sword and shield and run over the basics with her to get her caught up."

The other two trainers nodded. "Alright, line up!" Rick shouted.

The students moved to comply while Siegfried motioned for Ray to follow him. Ray and Lexi followed Siegfried to a small room near the entrance. The room was full of weapon racks, sorted into swords, axes, maces, spears, shields, staves, nunchucks, bows, and so on.

Siegfried stepped up to a rack of smaller swords, looking back and forth between Ray and the swords on display. "Base strength is higher than a beginner adult male. Roughly five foot six..." he muttered to himself as he picked up a few different swords and tested out their weights and balances. "She's a beginner, so we can't give her a masterwork sword yet... gotta be one of them trash swords, just like everyone else..."

He reached out and grabbed a shortsword and smiled as he passed it to Ray. "Give this one a try."

Ray effortlessly swung it around without any particular technique. "It's as light as a feather."

Siegfried frowned slightly. "Normally, I'd say that's a good thing but..." He pondered for a moment before grabbing another sword and trading it with the one she was holding. "This sword was designed for more advanced students to practice. Normally, people can't wield it until they can enhance their strength by roughly four times."

Ray swung the sword lightly and stumbled as the weight of the sword pulled her forward. She could feel a bit of strain in her arms but the motion itself wasn't too difficult. "I could see myself getting tired if I used this one for a while."

"I should hope so. That sword weighs half as much as you do..." Siegfried shook his head. "Go ahead. With the style I'm going to teach you, there's little point in practicing with a weapon that's so light you can't even feel the weight. Let's build up your strength and make you even stronger."

Using the weight of the sword as a reference, he picked out a heavy kite shield and a large two-handed longsword. Ray lifted each piece without much difficulty, though she needed both hands to make a controlled swing with the longsword.

"Unbelievable..." Siegfried said as he watched her swing the sword around. "That lump of iron is too heavy to swing for non-enhanced humans. How heavy will your sword get when you master enhancement magic?"

Ray grinned as she rested the sword against the ground. She motioned towards the catgirl who had been silently following behind them. "Can we get a weapon for Lexi too?"

Siegfried shook his head. "I'm sorry. Though I've heard the circumstances between you two, it is illegal to train slaves or provide them with weapons inside of a residential area."

"What about combat slaves?" Ray asked.

"If they have any training at all, it's from before they were a slave. They are never provided with weapons near civilians, and they only have weapons at all because it improves their reusability. Slaves with weapons usually survive longer while fighting monsters."

Ray grimaced while Lexi shuddered.

"It's alright if she watches from the side though, right?"

Siegfried considered for a moment and then shrugged. "I don't see a problem with that."

He passed Ray some straps and sheaths and showed her how to tie them so that the longsword and the shield would both be strung across her back while the shortsword rested on her belt.

"You can carry those in your enchanted bag, but I would encourage you to take a few days to get used to wearing them. Walking with the added burden takes some practice so that you don't bump into people or objects or fall over unexpectedly."

"The rest of it, I understood but... what enchanted bag?"

Siegfried blinked in surprise. He pointed at the bag tied to Ray's belt. "Isn't that an enchanted bag?"

Ray glanced at the bag that she had forgotten about. "I picked it up off an archer's corpse. I tried to look inside of it, but I didn't see anything."

"I recall hearing that your memory was a bit jumbled. If you look inside an enchanted bag, you won't see anything because the bag is connected to an extradimensional space. It's a type of spatial magic that makes it easier to carry objects around. Enchanted bags are awfully expensive."

"Oh..." Ray murmured, "How do I use it?"

"To store an object, hold it up to the opening and connect the object to the bag with your mana. To recall an object, hold your hand over the bag and think of the object you want to pull out."

Ray held the longsword next to the bag and summoned her mana. She connected the two and the longsword poofed out of existence.

She stared at her empty hands for a long moment, shocked that it worked. She then thought of the longsword and it reappeared in her hand.

She whistled in appreciation.

"Convenient."

"What's the weight limit?"

"Stop bothering me!" She told the voice in her head.

Then she looked up at Siegfried. "What's the weight limit?"

"Hah."

"It varies based on the material of the bag and the mage who cast the enchantment. This one looks to be made of ordinary leather so I doubt it could hold more than five or six thousand pounds."

"That's incredible!"

"Go away, I'm busy!"

"Shall we get started then?" Siegfried asked with a nod towards the door.

Ray followed him out and they found an open area away from the other students who were taking turns swinging at posts under the observation of their respective teachers.

"For today, we are going to cover the basic stances and swings for each of your weapon sets. As a guardian, you will generally be using a sword and shield but there are times when you need to abandon defense and commit fully to an offensive. As such, you will also be learning to use the two-hander."

Ray donned the sword and shield first.

"Now, follow me and try to mimic my stance. I will correct any mistakes."

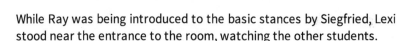

While Ray was being introduced to the basic stances by Siegfried, Lexi stood near the entrance to the room, watching the other students.

She stroked the chain attached to her wrist. The rattling chain no longer seemed as constricting as it did just a few hours before.

She was free.

Lexi had only been a slave for about a month but in that short time frame, she had endured many kinds of cruel treatment. She knew that she was beyond lucky to escape after such a short time.

And it was all thanks to Ray.

She honestly didn't care what race Ray was anymore. The beautiful and kind woman had rescued her. Until she repaid the debt, Lexi had every intention of staying and helping Ray accomplish her goals. At the same time, Lexi had her own goals. She needed to get stronger to track down the evil creatures who murdered her family and friends and enslaved her.

When she found them... well, it wouldn't be pretty.

Though she couldn't receive formal training or receive a weapon, there was a discipline here that did not involve weapons. Lexi carefully observed the Echo Fist and his students, taking note of their stances and techniques. She couldn't try them now but at night, when she was alone in her room, she could practice without anybody knowing. It wouldn't be ideal, but it would be better than nothing.

She would do the same thing when accompanying Ray to her magic lessons. By doing so, she would be indirectly receiving lessons from highly respected teachers amongst humans.

Through this training, Lexi vowed to herself that she would accomplish three things:

She would protect Ray.

She would avenge her tribe.

She would never be a slave again.

15

Magic

The start of Ray's first magic lesson with Master Rambalt was similar to her the start of her first lesson with Siegfried. When she walked into the tower, Jantzen and Peter shrank away from her. Peter fell backward, his body trembling and his eyes shaking with terror. Following Siegfried's advice, she had the swords and shield strapped to her body rather than hidden within the enchanted bag.

Kelsey, for her part, merely observed the interaction with a poorly hidden smile.

"Hey, Kelsey!" Ray greeted her cheerfully.

"Hey," Kelsey responded. "Did you eat a good lunch before you came?"

"Lunch?" Ray asked. "Why would we do that when we already had breakfast?"

Kelsey, Lexi, and Jantzen stared at Ray with dumbfounded expressions.

"Huh...?"

Kelsey approached Ray and patted her on the shoulder, leaning forward slightly to speak in a lowered voice. "Even if you don't feel like eating, make sure that beastkin eats three meals a day. She can't ask you for food in public."

Ray's eyes widened in shock as Kelsey stepped back. She turned and stared at Lexi. "Are you hungry?"

Lexi shook her head, but Ray caught her nervous glance towards Jantzen and Peter. "I wouldn't dare ask for food!" She spoke loudly so that the others could hear. Unfortunately, her stomach conveniently chose that moment to revolt.

Grrrrrrowl

Ray frowned and Lexi flushed with embarrassment. She reached down to her enchanted bag and imagined 'food'. She figured that the adventurer she had taken the bag from would probably have had something edible in there.

A small pouch of dried 'food' appeared in her hand. She didn't really know what it was, but it smelled a little salty and had a rigid, leathery texture. She held it out to the catgirl. "This should hold you over until after the training. I won't forget in the future."

Lexi gingerly reached out and accepted the unidentifiable substance that was presumably edible. She had a weird expression on her face, but she didn't complain.

Satisfied, Ray turned back, humming to herself as she strode over to the table and sat down. Jantzen, Kelsey, and Peter remained silent throughout the whole exchange. After Ray had comfortably been sitting in her seat and humming for several seconds, they also took their seats.

Two minutes later, Master Rambalt slammed open the door with a burst of fire and flew into the room. A gust of wind launched all the scattered papers flying about and several stacks of books fell over, adding to the relative chaos and clutter.

The small, speckled lizard resting on a floating wizard hat following behind the elementalist. It glided over to the same area it had been at last time Ray was in the tower, though this time the hat alighted itself upon the frame of the staircase leading up.

Master Rambalt descended lightly in front of the table they were sitting at. He patted down the new wrinkles in his robes while grumbling. "Whew. That's the last time I stay up 'till sunrise playing cards..."

He looked almost a hundred percent identical to the previous day except the bags under his eyes were heavier and his hair and robe looked a bit greasier.

"He's said that every day for the last three months," Kelsey informed Ray with a whisper.

"If I could get your undivided attention!"

Ray straightened her back and focused on the magician.

"Today is self-study! I'm going to sleep."

Master Rambalt staggered over to a chair and plopped down. A large book appeared in his hands.

Ray stared at the greasy magician in disbelief. This was her first day! How could she self-study if she had no foundation to build on?

"That's pretty common as well," Kelsey sighed.

Ray felt her temper rising.

"Don't get angry."

She grimaced. *"What do you want now?"*

"Smile innocently and ask him politely. If necessary, explain the problem. Guys like him have a weak spot for pretty women."

Ray raised her hand. "Excuse me, Master Rambalt, sir?"

He turned his violent glare towards her. "What?"

"I don't know how to use any magic yet. How should I self-study?"

Master Rambalt examined her for a moment before his expression softened. He directed a look of intense longing towards his book and then sighed. He coughed lightly into his hand before grumbling. "I suppose I could get you started. Summon your mana."

Ray obeyed. She smiled and directed her gratitude towards the voice in her head. *"Thank you!"*

"Sure thing!"

As soon as her mana was released, Master Rambalt studied her for a long moment before speaking. "I told you yesterday that you could pursue any branch of magic that interests you. Do you have any magic that you would like to study?"

"What types are there?"

Eileen had given her a basic introduction before, but she wanted a more comprehensive overview before deciding.

"There are five basic categories of magic. Elementalists like myself focus on the traditional elemental magics such as fire, water, earth, and wind magic. Some specialized elementalists might also use metal, lightning, or light magic as well." Master Rambalt paused for a moment. He rubbed the tiredness from his eyes and slapped his cheek a few times. Then he continued with his explanation. "If you want to be a priest, I can't help you very much, but I can get you started. Priests use holy magic and must be chosen by a god. I'm not sure which god blessed you, but you have one of the strongest aptitudes for holy magic that I have ever seen. It's above even the level of Lady Eileen and Lord Maxwell. It might even be near the level of a Tether."

Kelsey and Jantzen gasped and stared at Ray with wide eyes. She squared her shoulders and revealed a smug smile. She knew she was special, but it still felt good to be validated.

"Warlocks use what is generally classified as 'dark' magic. There are various subcategories, but the two most common types of warlocks are obliterators and dominators. Obliterators use magic that manifests as pure destructive force while dominators use mind-control and mind-domination magics. A more obscure, third type of warlock would be a dark mage, sometimes called a dark healer."

"A dark healer?" Ray asked, intrigued.

"A warlock who specializes in removing injuries, poisons, and other debilitating effects via magic. They use their mana to transfer the negative effects to their own body first and then redirect those effects into their opponents. It is a type of healing that can only effectively be used on a battlefield unless there are ample prisoners to use as sacrifices."

Unless one had regeneration abilities like Ray.

"Druids use nature magic. Some druids specialize in controlling plants while others focus on working with animals. This can take several forms, such as taming wild beasts as pets or shapeshifting. While you have an aptitude for this type of magic, it is by far your weakest category. You should pursue this only if you have a great interest in it."

That explanation didn't really catch her interest.

"Finally, there are arcanists. They study arcane magic. 'Arcane', in this sense, refers to branches of science that are not well understood. It includes the study of self-enhancement, space, gravity, and many other things. Arcanists generally study mana in its purest form and most of their magics take the form of enchantments."

Ray pondered on the explanation for several minutes while Master Rambalt returned to reading his book.

Elemental magic didn't seem like a bad choice at all, but consequently, it also didn't stand out too much.

She really liked the sound of the obliterator and dark mage pathways of the warlock. Though she wasn't fond of pain, the mental image of being able to take all the injuries that she received and return them to her opponent was extremely satisfying.

With such a high aptitude, she didn't want to discount studying holy magic either.

Naturally, being an arcanist also sounded amazing.

"Do I have to pick only one?" she asked.

Master Rambalt looked up from his book and shook his head.

"Since you have an aptitude for all five, you could choose all five if you really wanted to, though I wouldn't recommend it. Some mages have had success studying deeply into two or three magic systems but five is too broad. No matter what, I would encourage you to study the arcane arts. Enhancement magic will be of great worth to you in your endeavor to become a guardian."

Ray mentally put a checkmark next to 'arcanist'. She crossed out 'druid' and 'elementalist' for now. She would come back to those later if she decided that she wanted to learn more. For the time being, she would focus on 'enhancement' magic from the arcane tree and becoming a warlock. She would experiment a bit with both the obliterator and dark mage paths to see which one she liked more. Since she had Kelsey around to ask questions, she would investigate holy magic with any time she had left.

"Can I start with enhancement magic and basic warlock magic?"

Master Rambalt nodded and tossed his book in the air. The book disappeared with a snap of his fingers. "Excellent choices." He waved his hand, and the earth pulled the table down into the ground. He motioned for Ray to stand up. "Enhancement magic has various applications. Its most common usage is to protect the user's body from physical harm. With enough enhancement, it is possible to reinforce a portion of your body such that a sword or an axe would simply 'bounce' off harmlessly."

Ray recalled when she had struck Siegfried in the face during her test. His skin had become extremely hard, and she had injured her hand without even fazing him.

"Conversely, you can also enhance your muscles, tendons, ligaments, and bones for various effects. If you have enough mana and control, it is possible to do a full-body enhancement. This would give you a massive increase in strength, speed, flexibility, and durability."

Jantzen went pale as he eavesdropped on the explanation. "Even stronger than that...?" he muttered to himself.

"For now, you should practice using basic reinforcement on a small portion of your body. Practice focusing the mana on your hand and visualize 'durability'. Focus on what being 'durable' means to you and 'will' the mana to become that very definition."

'Durability'? In Ray's two whole days of experience thus far, the most durable thing she had encountered was Siegfried's 'Steel Skin'. However, she had a feeling she had encountered something much, much more durable in the past. She focused on that feeling, trying to recall a faded memory.

She was charging towards something, her long, dark hair billowing in the wind. Her daggers were sheathed as they were utterly useless against this foe. The large, blurry shape slowly came into form in front of her eyes as she struck the being with something that she no longer understood.

Nothing could harm the foe. Its scales were impenetrable. *That* was the definition of durability.

Ray focused on that feeling and willed her arm to become as durable as that creature, whatever it was. She felt her hand go stiff.

She couldn't bend her fingers or her elbow. Tapping the limb with her remaining hand, she noted that she no longer had any sensation in the petrified limb.

"Uhhh... was that supposed to happen?" she asked, unnerved.

Master Rambalt leaned over and tapped her arm curiously. "This seems rather strong. I'm going to test it."

Huh?

Master Rambalt snapped his fingers and Ray panicked as she sank into the ground until only her shoulders and head were visible. With another wave of his hand, the ground shifted and exposed her petrified arm.

"W..what are you going to do?"

"A simple test. If you did it right, your arm should survive. If not, it's nothing a respawn won't fix."

The crazy elementalist reached into his enchanted bag and withdrew a large hammer that was almost as tall as he was. He raised the weapon above his head and, with a shout, smashed it into her poor arm.

Ray closed her eyes and turned her head away. After a brief pause when she felt nothing, she reopened them to see the hammer resting against her arm.

Master Rambalt whistled in appreciation. "That durability is no joke. I'm not sure what you imagined, but this is definitely harder than steel. For your self-study, practice making it so that you can move your fingers and elbow while your arm is reinforced. While the appendage may be extra durable, it doesn't mean much if you can't move it."

The greasy elementalist summoned his book once more and turned away.

"Excuse me!" Ray called out after him.

He threw his hands up in the air and turned back with a fierce glare. Fire danced at the edge of his fingers. "What is it now?"

Their eyes met and Ray let out a nervous laugh.

"Could you let me out of the ground now?"

16

Prayers and Progress

Six days. That was how long it took to organize the Prayer Log.

It only took a little over a day to design the automated system for the organization of prayers, but in that timeframe several hundred thousand prayers came in that were unsorted. I had to read and manually sort every prayer.

Well, I didn't have to do it, but the idea of having a few hundred thousand unread and unsorted messages sitting in my inbox for the rest of eternity made me cringe.

A sense of satisfaction welled up inside of me as I looked at the Prayer Log. I couldn't help but feel a little proud to see the results of my efforts. With the previous automatic response function that I had set up, all the prayers I received with the keywords 'bless this food' were automatically answered. As I experimented more with automating the system, I discovered a way to route prayers into groups.

I made eight categories:

Assistance, Romance, Miracle, Vows, Gratitude, Curses, Steve, Misc

Any prayers primarily asking me for some form of non-romance related aid were filtered into the Assistance category.

Petitions of a romantic nature were numerous enough that they had their own group.

Requests for divine intervention to solve their problems for them went to the Miracle category.

Those who made promises towards any being who fulfilled their request entered the Vows category and another group was made up of prayers that contained only Gratitude.

The Misc section was for prayers that didn't fit under any of the other six groups.

As for the Curses category, that one was created after I figured out the origin of some strange prayers I frequently received. Many of these strange prayers were fragmented and nonsensical, often containing words that hinted at the sender's anger or surprise. After reading a few hundred of these prayers, I noticed that every single one of them would make sense if preceded by a phrase along the lines of:

'Oh god' or 'Oh my god'.

Then I realized what was happening. These words were key words that acted like a prayer and, as a god without official followers, I received their unaffiliated prayers. The contents were whatever words or thoughts immediately following their usage of the phrase. I labelled it as cursing cause most people use that phrase in the same place that another might use a curse word. They weren't actually praying; they were just expressing their emotions. I briefly wondered how those people would react if they knew they were unintentionally spamming a god's inbox.

After spending about five days skimming through and sorting prayers, I finally had the previously unread messages sorted. Any new messages containing preset keywords would automatically be filtered into the correct groups while messages that hit none of the keywords would land in Misc.

Assistance: 554,832 (Unread - 4,532)
Romance: 92,954 (Unread - 21,210)
Miracle: 1,439,549 (Unread - 900,304)
Vows: 515 (Unread - 3)
Gratitude: 112,222 (Unread - 10)
Curses: 2,942,352 (Unread - 750,047)
Steve: 394 (Unread - 1)
Misc: 2 (Unread - 0)
Total Prayers: 5,142,820 (Unread - 1,676,107)

Since many prayers could fit into multiple categories, it also had a priority system. The order of highest value to lowest was ranked: Vows, Gratitude, Assistance, Romance, Miracle, Misc and any prayer that would fit in multiple categories would land in the category it qualifies for that has the highest priority.

I tried to keep up on the Gratitude and Vows as soon as I received them. I had also tried with Assistance at first, but it was depressing to read a bunch of prayers I could do nothing about. I ignored the Romance prayers for the most part and didn't even touch any of the new Miracle requests. The distinction on whether a prayer landed in the Assistance or Miracle section was mostly in whether the individual had asked me to do something for them or whether they had asked me to help them do something.

And honestly, most of the requests for miracles were things people could do themselves if they just put in the effort. I personally had little interest in solving people's problems for them. This was a religion, not a charity.

Finally, I had a little subsection titled **Steve**. The system copied any prayers I received from him and placed the copies here so I could access them quickly. Over three hundred of the Vows were his prayers. Most of the vows were promises to serve well if some entity that is not one of the four gods made him into one of their paladins... he made this promise dozens of times a day.

Though he wasn't my follower yet, he was on the road to becoming my favorite.

I opened the **Steve** section and found one that I had bookmarked yesterday to look at closer.

Yo, buddy! Thanks so much for dropping that gnome in my backyard! Mr. Swaggins is an awesome breakdancing teacher. I hope you can find some way to let me know your name. Once I know who you are, as promised, I will find a way to claim a temple in your name down here in New America. Hope you keep me in mind if any open paladin slots open up!

Wow, this guy...

Obviously, I didn't send the gnome. Either he was insanely lucky, or some otherworldly force was granting him his wishes. Whatever was going on, it had made Steve aware that there was another existence out there. If I could somehow let him know about me, I could obtain a follower...

Unfortunately, I had no idea who this Steve was and had no way to contact him yet. Hopefully, I would find some hints in his prayers or maybe Ray or another follower would cross paths with him someday. At that time, if he could do what he promised then I most definitely wouldn't complain about getting a temple dedicated in my name.

My nonexistent fingers were crossed.

And then the new prayer that I had just received moments ago.

Hey, it's Steve again! I wanted to thank you for guiding Grandmaster William to me! I'm sure you already know, but he has taken me as his apprentice. I was already an accomplished dark

mage, so now he just needs to teach me about being a guardian. Once I learn to fight as a guardian, He'll help me combine it with my dark magic and I'll be a dark knight! After that, I will fulfill my vow to claim a temple in your name.

Before the time comes, please let me know your name!

P.S. Mr. Swaggins says I'm a natural!

P.P.S. Once I get a temple for you, please allow me to be one of your paladins!

Okay, what?!

Everything this guy asked me for just seemed to fall into his lap!

Anyways, if he really did acquire a temple for me then I would absolutely make him one of my paladins. He hadn't even officially become one of my followers yet and, for whatever reason, he was this dedicated.

Also, apparently, he was a dark mage. If it weren't for Master Rambalt's explanation a week ago about magic, then my knowledge of fantasy stories and video games from Earth would have made me slightly hesitant to trust the character of an individual that would mess with dark magic...

But then again, if I were judging by the standards of those stories, I wasn't exactly on the path to rainbow unicorns and fluffy bunnies.

There was another prayer that I had been surprised to find as I was sorting through the logs.

There was a name that I knew... a prayer from Leximea Bloodclaw.

I don't know if there is anyone out there for us beastkin. I don't know if anyone or anything is listening to me right now. If there is someone listening... and if you have any kind of power, please... please help me become stronger. Please help me overcome my fear.

For my little brother... for my friends and family... for Ray...

I want to be strong.

Wow, what a sincere prayer. I wanted to grant it. Someday soon, when I started gathering more followers, I decided that she would be my first follower aside from Ray.

"Where do I even start...?" I mumbled to myself.

"Suggestion. Choose a domain," Auto replied.

"Huh?"

"I believe the other Overseers already mentioned this earlier. Decide what you will be the god of. Will you rule over something abstract, such as peace or freedom? Or perhaps something more visible, such as the sun or the moon? A domain will assist you in understanding what you should build your religion towards."

That made perfect sense.

So then, what should I become the god of?

There were many gods in ancient stories of Earth that I could use for reference. If I looked at the Greek, Roman, or Norse gods, for example, most of them had distinct domains.

What I was most curious about, however, was the domains of the Christian God and the Islamic Allah. They were supposedly supreme deities. What was their domain? Or did they even have a specific domain?

Maybe they tried to rule over everything?

The last option would seem to make sense, considering that historically both Christianity and Islam had a lower tolerance for belief in other gods than polytheistic religions did.

Regardless, I didn't want to be the same as any of the gods from Earth. I could use them as references, but I had no intention of copying any of them.

Speaking of stories from the gods of Earth, there's something that I had been curious about.

"Hey Auto, I have a question."

"Is it related to your domain?"

"Uhh, maybe? When I was thinking about that, I remembered something that I was curious about."

"What might that be?"

"In the stories of the gods of Earth, there are references to beings such as 'angels', 'demons', 'valkyries', 'demigods', and so on. There are also various monsters that appear such as the hydra or Cerberus. Are any of those true?"

"Many of those stories carry some degree of fabrication. However, all of the stories contain some truth as well."

"Does that mean that I will have my own divine servants, like the angels or valkyries?"

"That entirely depends on your will and your followers. When you eventually design the afterlife for your followers, you can input a clause indicating that the most devout of your followers will have the option of becoming a divine servant when they die."

"I get to design my own afterlife?"

Whoa.

"Affirmative. However, the afterlife you design must be in line with your domain. You cannot be the god of evil and torture and send all your most faithful followers to a heaven full of pacifists. A god of darkness must send his most loyal followers to a dark place. The god of light must send his loyal followers to a place full of light and so on. This is absolute."

Hmmm. That made a lot of sense as I thought about it. Any person who would worship a god of evil and follow all their 'evil' tenets would probably be happiest in an 'evil' place, as abstract as that was. While this system seemed limiting, it was forcing the Overseers to give out the promised rewards.

"What about the souls of those who don't believe in gods?"

"To a certain extent, they get exactly what they believe in. Those who believe there is no afterlife will get no afterlife. The biggest complication is those who believe in reincarnation. Some souls are certainly recycled, and Overseers attempt to use those who believe in reincarnation when that happens."

"What about the souls harvested by Meridian?"

"All souls are harvested by Meridian. It is merely a copy of the soul that is sent to the afterlife."

"What are the souls used for?"

"You are not yet eligible for that information."

Right. I needed to have presided over a thousand worlds or something like that. Not sure if I was patient enough to wait that long though...

"What about the 'demons' and beings like 'Satan'?"

"You are also not eligible to receive that information. It is sufficient to say that when there is any goal there will be opposition."

Well, damn. There just might be some cosmic battle between gods and demons. I would have to avoid that for now. It was probably way outside of my paygrade. Especially since I didn't get paid to do this job.

I decided to think about happy things like my ideal afterlife instead. Maybe working backward from there would help me pick a domain.

What would my ideal afterlife be?

I pondered this question as I followed behind Ray and Lexi moving towards their seventh day of training.

After six days, Siegfried let Ray join the training with the other students. He had used the time to personally invest in her foundation and to teach her the things the other students had already learned earlier in the year.

As far as stances went, Ray honestly felt that the shortsword and shield was a bit boring compared to the two-handed longsword. The first style was much safer, of course, but Ray wasn't all that concerned with safety since she knew she could regenerate. She was much more impressed with the power that she could manifest while wielding the longsword.

Siegfried was thorough in his teaching, and he showed her clear advantages and disadvantages to each guard. Ray's personal favorites were the Wrath Guard, where she held the sword up above and behind her shoulder, poised to strike with a heavy blow, and the Fool's Guard, a stance in which she held the longsword at a low angle in front of her body.

Of course, she learned several other stances as well.

Today, she joined the line of student's practicing their techniques against the wooden targets covered in cloth and straw. The 'training dummies' looked like poorly constructed stick figures with a few extra horizontal beams attached in the torso area. Some of the targets even had button eyes glued on.

Ray stood in front of one of the training dummies with her longsword held poised to strike. She waited for the go-ahead from Siegfried as she felt the weight of the sword attempting to pull her down. After days of training, it was now a comfortable and familiar weight.

"Begin!"

Ray stepped forward and violently swung her sword. It was a controlling swing following the motions that she had practiced against the air. The sword arced downwards in an overhead slice and smashed into the gap between the 'shoulder' and the 'head' of the training dummy.

The dummy exploded in a shower of splinters and straw. Through some miracle, it was still standing but her sword was firmly lodged in its 'chest'. Ray tugged on the hilt for a moment, meeting unexpected resistance as she tried to withdraw it. She planted her feet and pulled back with all her might.

The sword slowly dislodged and then shot out, launching her backward as she tumbled and crashed into the ground.

Ray pushed herself to her feet and dusted herself off. She felt the stares of various individuals and noticed that she didn't hear the repetitive sounds of the other student's striking their respective training dummies.

She hefted the sword onto her shoulder with her left hand.

As she observed the other students, she wanted to laugh. If Jonathan's jaw dropped any further, it would probably hit the floor. Vick looked a bit pale, and she could see Lexi off in the distance practically rolling on the floor, covering her mouth as she tried not to laugh. Helen and Ven looked more curious than anything else but their wide eyes clearly displayed their shock.

Bill, the archer that she had killed when she got ambushed by adventurers, just grimaced, and turned away. He had suddenly shown up the previous day for practice and he didn't say anything to anyone.

Siegfried smirked while shaking his head as if he knew something like this would happen. Rick and the Echo Fist were staring at him with questioning eyes, but he ignored them as he clapped his hands.

"What are y'all standing around for? Get to work!"

Each of the students jumped at sudden noise before turning back to their practice with somewhat disheartened expressions.

Siegfried walked over to Ray. "Swinging with a lot of power is good, but there's no need to hit it as hard as you can. Any opponent would have still died if you used a quarter of that force."

Ray scratched the back of her neck and laughed nervously. "That wasn't all of my strength though…"

"Hmm?" Siegfried froze, a hint of surprise crossing his features.

"I wanted to test out the feeling of striking something a bit before I tried hitting it as hard as I could. I didn't put very much force into that strike…" she explained.

Siegfried covered his face with his palm as he shook his head in disbelief. "I wonder how to explain this one…" he muttered so softly that Ray wasn't sure if she heard it correctly.

"Is there a problem?" Ray asked.

Siegfried shook his head. "I'll take care of it. Try not to completely break the dummy. They were made to last through a few sessions worth of swings so if you break it in one go, the big bosses will get mad at me."

As he was walking away, Ray chuckled to herself when she overheard his barely audible musing.

"I wonder who I should have her spar against…"

Ray started humming to herself as she held herself back and swung at the targets with a greatly restrained amount of force. She used the amount of damage taken by the training dummy, as well as the volume of the impact, as a reference as she set a new goal for herself for the training session:

Within the next two hours, she would figure out exactly how much strength she had to use to create an identical force to Jonathan's swings.

Thud

Still too hard. Ray listened for his next strike and made a quick estimation. She then swung again at half the strength of her previous swing.

Thud

Closer, but still too loud. Ray reduced the strength of her next swing by another half.

17

Enhancement Magic

Her training with magic was not yet showing as much progress. In the tower, under Master Rambalt's supervision, Ray had still not yet succeeded in performing a perfect enhancement of her arm. She didn't feel like she had made any progress.

"Your image is too rigid," Master Rambalt informed her. "Simply imagining a durable object is not enough. If durability is all that your arm has, then the force applied to bend your elbow or fingers would have to exceed the durability of your arm to 'bend' it. Not only is this not ideal but it would also be extremely difficult and, if done incorrectly, could result in you snapping your arm like a twig."

Ray nodded as she prepared to make another attempt. Master Rambalt was not in the habit of spoon-feeding his students. He would give hints, such as the one he had just given, but only after he had watched them fail repeatedly.

When she had once complained about it, he simply told her that the best way to progress is to learn enough to get yourself into trouble and then work hard enough to get yourself out of trouble.

Ray focused on the hint he had just given her. Durability wasn't enough, which meant that there was something else she needed to add to her enhancement.

But what could she add to durability...?

Her only other experience with enhancement thus far had been when she encountered Siegfried's 'steel skin' technique and his face had also gone rigid. She had a feeling that his technique also focused on durability.

A short-term solution could be to ball her hand into a fist before enhancing only certain portions of her arm. However, when Ray tried that, Master Rambalt had not praised her as she had expected.

"Shortcuts are only efficient for short term powerups. If you rely on petty tricks, then that will be the extent of your strength. You would do much better to focus on achieving a full body enhancement."

Ray groaned in frustration as she leaned back in her chair and tried to think of something else to try. She couldn't just add 'flexibility' or 'elasticity'. She tried that once and Master Rambalt had merely laughed when her steel-like arm bent in half like rubber. There might be a use for such an enhancement in the future, but it wasn't what she was aiming for.

Ray pushed her feet up against the desk and tilted her chair back until it balanced on its back two legs. She leaned her head over the back of the chair so that her hair hung down as she looked at the entrance to the room behind her.

Lexi was standing near the doorway, carefully observing the students. Ray smiled and waved as their eyes met. Lexi grinned and waved back.

Over the last week, they hadn't had many conversations. Most of their waking time was spent in these lessons or eating and the evening was used for personal study time. Ray didn't know why, but Lexi always confined herself in her room during those hours.

Ray tilted her head to the side and saw Jantzen meditating in his chair. Surprisingly, the fat priest hadn't tried to do anything to her in the last week. He seemed to have learned his lesson from their first encounter. Leaving aside talking, he rarely even looked in the direction of Ray or Lexi. The one time Ray caught him looking at her, his face had gone red, and he had started sweating furiously.

There was one incident two days prior when Suzy had suddenly shown up to the lessons. It had been quite a while since Ray saw the crazy bitch and she still felt a thrill run through her when she remembered the sensation of stabbing a dagger up through her head and into her brain.

After their eyes met once in the tower, Suzy merely looked away, her face turning red. "I'm sorry. Her Holiness told me that I was wrong about you..." she muttered meekly. Her lips quivered as she stared at the floor, unable to meet Ray's gaze.

Ray had just shrugged and moved on. The whole incident didn't really bother her anymore. In fact, she was rather grateful for the experience.

Peter, on the other hand, was just annoying. He talked to Kelsey a lot, but he avoided Ray and Lexi like the plague. Even now, Peter was talking to Kelsey instead of practicing. Kelsey seemed irritated but she put on a strained smile as she endured the young boy's endless prattling.

"So, Kelsey, did you think about our offer? Do you want to join our team?"

Kelsey sighed. "You already have a priest. You should think about recruiting a guardian to fill the frontline spot."

Peter waved her statement away. "You can never have too many priests! Why would we need a front line if we could have two healers?"

Kelsey just shook her head and ignored him as she tried once more to focus on her own meditation.

"Hey! Hey Kelsey!" Peter started again.

Ray tapped the edge of her chair, drawing both of their attention. She glared at Peter. "Shut up."

Peter went pale and the words he was about to say died in his throat. He masked it with a fake cough before turning and looking the other way.

Kelsey shot Ray a grateful look and then closed her eyes and continued with her meditation.

Ray returned her thoughts to her enhancement. She knew that there were multiple ways that she could enhance her body. She could modify the durability, the ductility, the elasticity, the flexibility, the permeability, or the chemical structure. Though she couldn't do it yet, it was possible to change her arm entirely into another substance, such as metal or water.

She knew that the solution she was supposed to be looking for was not related to changing the chemical makeup of her arm, nor did it have to do with the permeability. Also, making her arm less durable would defeat the purpose of the enhancement.

Elasticity and flexibility. The solution to her problem had to lie in those two properties.

Ray looked down at her currently unenhanced arm. She deliberately bent her elbow and flexed her fingers.

Why did her arm function in an unenhanced state? What part of increasing the 'durability' made it unable to move? It already had some durability inherently. It also had flexibility and elasticity.

Or wait, that wasn't completely true.

Ray pinched the skin on her arm and pulled. Like joints, the skin had high elasticity. Comparatively, bones were more rigid and presumably had a higher durability. The joints connected the durable bones at a flexible, elastic point while the skin and muscles held it all together. Each component had its own durability, and the system was balanced.

The process was probably much more complicated than that, but Ray didn't have a detailed knowledge about the inner workings of the body, and she didn't particularly feel like opening her arm up to find out the minute details.

Eager to put her theory to the test, Ray closed her eyes and summoned her mana. She focused it on her arm and willed the entirety of the structure to become more durable. As she felt the sensation in her arm disappear, she focused on the joint in her elbow and imagined 'flexibility'. While she didn't know the internal workings of an elbow, she figured if she enhanced the flexibility of the joint, she would see results.

To Ray, 'flexibility' was a snake. She hadn't met a snake since she became aware, but she remembered seeing the creatures moving their entire body. Snakes were flexible.

As she willed the flexibility of a snake into her elbow joint, she opened her eyes and attempted to bend her elbow. It slowly creaked as it shifted from its original position.

"Yes!" Ray cried out, her excitement bubbling to the surface. "I did it! My arm can move!"

She raised her arm and waved it in the air for all to see.

"Now focus on being able to move every joint in your hand at the same time." Master Rambalt instructed, looking up from a book he had started reading at some point. "Also, it seems slow and sloppy. You should work on that too."

Ray withdrew her arm and half-bowed towards Master Rambalt. "Yes sir!"

She met Kelsey's gaze and the priestess mouthed 'congratulations'. Ray smiled and nodded her thanks.

She returned to her meditation. She tried to focus on making the joints in her fingers and wrist more flexible. The more she tried to do so, the more she realized how difficult the process was going to be. Focusing on maintaining three or four enhancements at once wasn't too difficult. Maintaining ten or more? That was hard.

The full body enhancement was still far away but Ray had taken her second step. The future looked bright to her as she enthusiastically dreamed of punching stuff without breaking her arm.

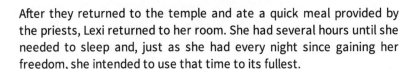

After they returned to the temple and ate a quick meal provided by the priests, Lexi returned to her room. She had several hours until she needed to sleep and, just as she had every night since gaining her freedom, she intended to use that time to its fullest.

She stepped into the center of the room and closed her eyes. She imagined the stances and moves she had seen Ven practicing under the instruction of the Echo Fist. She recalled the demonstrations and then she opened her eyes and revealed a fierce and determined glare.

Lexi mimicked the stance she had seen, with her left foot behind her right and her legs spread a comfortable distance apart. She bent her knees slightly and rolled between the balls of her feet and the tips of her toes to test her balance.

Maintaining her resolute expression, Lexi took a deep breath. Imagining that there was a target in front of her, she twisted her body and arced her left leg in a smooth and powerful kick. As her foot impacted the imaginary target, she let out a deliberate and forceful breath, almost like a *hiss*.

With a practiced motion, she smoothly returned to her stance and prepared to replicate the motion.

After practicing the martial arts, she would meditate and work on enhancement, using the same clues Master Rambalt gave Ray.

Without any guidance, she couldn't effectively practice the elemental magic she had started learning a month or so before her tribe was attacked, but sometimes she would spark a flame and roll it across her knuckles.

Martial arts and enhancement.

For now, she could work on these two things. Lexi focused on the mental image of herself dancing through the slavers while ripping them to pieces with fierce, powerful, and elegant movements.

Every time she imagined that scene, her heart beat faster and she felt a rush of adrenaline.

She punched out and sighed in satisfaction as she crushed the skull of her imaginary opponent.

Someday, she would meet those men again. When she did, she would be ready to return her sorrow sevenfold.

Duke Jantzen Rovar, one of the 31 Grand Dukes and son of the 43rd concubine of the Legendary Hero, was the presiding, and only, noble official over the border fortress town of Cairel. That he was placed in such an important position was a matter of great pride for him and his mother. He had accepted the appointment and forsook even the love of his life to preside over and protect the border region from the monster-ruled wildlands to the east.

He paced anxiously in his study located near the top of the grand cathedral, staring at the mosaic of his nephew. Even though it was long past the time that he normally retired to his quarters, he was forced to stay up, worried about his son who had yet to return home, despite the late hour.

This was the fifth time this month and he had all but lost his patience. He was at his wit's end. The other day, he had finally finished the process of balding that started a few years ago when he noticed the changes in his son's behavior.

His son, Jantzen Jr., was a great source of pride for him. The child was blessed from a young age by Jocelyn, the Lovely One. He was granted authority to act as one of her priests and to learn holy magic. The day that his son had received that blessing had been one of the proudest moments of the duke's life.

However, at some point, his son had begun to change. First, the boy was fat. There was no sugar-coating that fact and even if he tried to, his son would probably try to eat it. The problem wasn't that his son enjoyed eating. Duke Jantzen himself carried a little more weight than the average peasant and he didn't see a problem with that. It was only natural that he, as one of the rulers responsible for the prosperity of his domain, also enjoyed a reasonable portion of the profit gained by those under his protection.

No, he had no issue with the fact that his son enjoyed food. The problem was that his son was lazy. If one enjoyed food, then one must put forth an equal amount of effort to be deserving of that food.

Second, his son was arrogant and, perhaps even more concerning, his son was not intelligent. The duke had spared no effort to correct these issues, providing the best tutors and spending as much time as he could with his son.

Except for situations where either of them was traveling outside of the domain, he had a standard practice of refusing to sleep until he had welcomed his son home.

But the boy changed, and he had no idea why. The most recent incident was still fresh on his mind. As reported by the High Priestess herself, the boy had been ruthlessly beating a beastkin slave and was apprehended by a mysterious vigilante. His behavior was unacceptable as a noble and the fact that he was defeated by an individual outside of their sphere of control was a stain on their family name.

A knock on the door signaled the moment he had been anxiously waiting for.

He quickly moved over to his seat. "Come in," he ordered. He twirled his finger in his well-groomed mustache as one of the night-guards opened the door and ushered the boy into the room. The duke nodded to the guard and the guard bowed before exiting the room, closing the door inaudibly behind him.

He observed his son for a long, drawn-out moment. The boy was flushed. His eyes were unfocused, and his body swayed as if he were drunk. Additionally, he was fidgeting, as he had been ever since his pride was injured. The duke smiled inwardly as he considered the possibility that this new fear and damaged pride might knock some sense into the boy. If that happened, he would spare no effort to find and reward his benefactor.

"Take a seat," he ordered.

The boy swaggered over to a chair opposite the desk and plopped down into it, his ample mass oozing outwards to drown the noble frame.

"I have been waiting for you."

Jantzen smirked at his father's words, his eyes focusing on the old, bald man in front of him. He chuckled and the duke narrowed his eyes.

"I heard you got banned from the tavern. My informants told me about the 'experiments' you are doing, and I am exceptionally displeased."

"Father, you worry too much!" Jantzen slurred. "Even if they banned us, there are other places I can go."

The duke frowned ever so slightly. He allowed his face to slip a little bit because he knew Jantzen wouldn't notice in his current state. "My son, we must discuss the events of this last week. I have made no attempt to discover the identity of the individual who stopped you. Do you understand what this means?"

Jantzen's eyes snapped into focus, his flushed face going pale as he was reminded of that hateful, terrifying moment. The duke resisted the urge to smile. That mysterious vigilante certainly had an enormous impact on his son. He needed to issue a test to see if there were any significant changes.

His son quickly recovered, light entering into his eyes. "I do," he replied confidently. "It means that you entrust me with fixing the issue."

The duke raised his eyebrows in surprise. He briefly wondered if his son wasn't stupid after all. "You understand why this is an issue then. Not only were your actions a disgrace to nobility and to the kingdom, but the fact that you were punished by a vigilante is a humiliation that you must clear up yourself."

Jantzen scowled. "I admit, I did not expect you to agree with me, Father. However, I don't know how to go about it. The enemy this time is far stronger than any that I have faced before."

The duke nodded approvingly at the sense of caution his son was evidently showing. He silently praised the unknown angel who knocked some sense into his son. It was true that fixing one's public image after self-destructing was one of the most difficult battles a person could ever face.

The father smiled as he looked over his son with pride. "I will offer you a single piece of assistance to resolve this matter. Ponder upon what you might need and ask. I will do any one thing that is within my power."

This was a test. His son needed to prove his worthiness. Whatever his son asked for would be the final proof the duke needed that his son was changing.

Jantzen shot to his feet and stared at his father in a daze. He regained his balance and then saluted after the manner of the Rovar Kingdom, crossing his arms across his chest while bowing forty-five degrees. He almost fell over, but he somehow managed. "Father, I will meet your expectations without fail!"

The duke's grin widened even further. "I am looking forward to it. You may leave. I wish you beautiful and happy dreams, my son."

Jantzen straightened up and waddled from the room. He hadn't expected his uptight and old-fashioned old man to be the one to tell him to get revenge. The fact that he had done so only cemented in his mind how despicable the acts of that strange, freakishly strong woman had been. She deserved what was coming for her.

His eyes teared up as he felt his heart practically burst with joy. His father was finally supporting him for the first time in many years.

Finally, he had earned his father's trust!

He would not fail in his mission.

18

Development

"Alright, gather around!" Siegfried's voice shouted out.

Another week had passed with both Ray and Lexi making progress in their respective training. Today, they had been surprised when they arrived at Siegfried's private training ground to discover that Master Rambalt and the other magic students were all there as well.

Siegfried was standing on a small stage that Master Rambalt formed out of stone. Next to him were four individuals that Ray had never seen before.

The one who immediately drew her attention was the sole male in the group. He was tall and wore heavy-looking shiny full-plate armor. He had a shield on his back and a shortsword on his belt. He brushed back his sleek, blonde hair as he looked over the group with bright eyes and a refreshing smile.

Next to him were three females who all looked bored. One of them seemed to be some sort of mage, another was a crimson-haired rogue, and the last person had her hair dyed green and wore a soft green robe embroidered with silver leaves.

Siegfried cleared his throat to draw everybody's attention and then began his announcement. "This is the silver-ranked adventurer team Earthbreakers led by Edwin Weston. His party volunteered for and completed the scouting for your next excursion."

Ray tapped Kelsey on the arm. "What does he mean by 'excursion'?"

"At least once a month, all of the students gather into teams and complete a request that the adventurers guild has received. A silver-ranked team or higher scouts out the request before they are passed down to us to make sure it's something that we can handle."

Ray nodded in thanks for the explanation and then returned her attention to Siegfried's explanation.

"We have two requests this time so we will split you into two teams. One of the requests is carried over from the one you received two weeks ago."

He held up a piece of paper with some words on it. Ray couldn't clearly make out the contents from her current position.

"This is the bandit request. Since Jonathan, Suzy, Vick, and Bill failed it, this time we will allow Jantzen, Peter, Ven, Helen, and Ray to attempt it."

Ray's eyes went wide with surprise. "Me?"

Siegfried nodded. "Their team has been lacking a guardian. This made it difficult to give them potentially dangerous extermination requests. Fortunately, you came along and should be able to fill that gap."

Jantzen stepped forward and accepted the paper.

Ray knew that she would be assigned to a team, but she hadn't considered that it would have to be either Jantzen or Jonathan's team. She had some bad blood with both sides.

"I told you violence isn't always the best method. Diplomacy helps in times like this."

"Violence would have worked just fine if they didn't respawn..."

"You didn't kill Jantzen or Peter. Your bad relationship with them would not have changed even if there were no respawn system."

Ray grimaced. There wasn't much she could do about it now. The past was the past.

"Jonathan's group will be assigned to track down some goblins that have been sighted in the area," Siegfried continued. Jonathan stepped forward and accepted the paper containing the details of the request.

"You all have the rest of today to prepare in any way that you would like. You will leave tomorrow morning and are allowed up to two days to complete your mission."

With that final declaration, Siegfried and the four silver-ranked adventurers leapt down from the stage and Master Rambalt snapped his fingers, causing the stage to sink back into the ground.

Ray moved over to where Jantzen, Helen, Ven, and Peter were gathering. Helen and Ven didn't have any reaction towards her approaching, but both Peter and Jantzen flinched.

They were still scared of her. There hadn't been much in the way of meaningful interaction between them over the past two weeks so it was understandable that they would base most of their feelings on that first impression.

Admittedly, it was a first impression full of impact.

"Hey, guys!" Ray greeted them.

"Focus on befriending Helen and Ven first. Jantzen and Peter will take a little more time."

Ray made note of the voice's input and reached her hand out towards Helen. "This is the first time we've talked to each other, right? My name's Ray."

Helen accepted the handshake gracefully, brushing the light-brown hair out of her eyes with her free hand. "Helen. It's a pleasure to have you with us."

Ray nodded her head towards the masked man covered in his standard black robe.

"Ven," he replied simply.

She turned towards Jantzen and Peter and donned her most innocent smile so as not to provoke them.

"Oh yeah, we needed to work on your acting…"

She ignored the voice in her head that couldn't appreciate her acting skills as she addressed the party leader. "So, what's the plan?"

Jantzen held up the paper for her to see.

Ray examined the paper and then she gasped, her eyes going wide with shock. She had seen the man in the photo before. At the time, he was lying in the center of a ritual circle… but he was unmistakably the same person.

"Wanted Dead or Alive: Ax the Pony," she read. "Reward: Standard Rate."

She licked her lips as she recalled the delightful taste of the man's blood. Still, the request seemed to be impossible. That man was very dead, and his corpse was probably long gone. "So, we just have to find and kill this one guy?" she asked carefully.

Helen shook her head. "Bandit leaders never travel alone. We'll have to fight through somewhere between five and thirty bandits. Since this request could pass through to students, I would expect it to be on the lower side."

Okay, so they could still hunt and kill a few bandits at least. She didn't have a great explanation for why she knew the bandit leader was dead so she decided it would be best to keep that information to herself for now. "This is my first time doing something like this. What kind of things should I prepare?"

Helen motioned towards the bag hanging from Ray's belt.

"Food, water, extra clothes… those are the most important things. A tent for camping, supplies to maintain your weapons, tools for hunting, or cooking. Just about anything should be fine since you have an enchanted bag."

Hmmm. Ray wasn't sure if there was any money in the bag. She would have to check after talking things out with the group. If not, she would have to ask Eileen for some help.

"Anything else I need to know?" Ray asked.

Helen deferred the question to Jantzen.

The fat priest flushed red as he looked down at the scary woman. He shook his head. "M..meet at the main gate an hour after s...sunrise..."

Helen and Ven stared at their leader. Helen had an amused expression and, though she couldn't see his features, Ray assumed that Ven was surprised as well.

"You okay?" Ven asked. "This isn't our first time hunting bandits. Why are you so scared?"

"S..scared?" Jantzen wheezed. "Who's s..scared? Not me!"

Helen shook her head in disbelief while Peter stared at the ground. Evidently, Jantzen and Peter had not shared the story of their experience with their friends.

Ray sighed. "I'm not going to hurt you," she informed them. "We're teammates this time. I have no intention of harming you again."

Unless they did something to deserve it, of course.

"Careful with that line of thinking. Don't stand by and let them do bad things but try to resolve things without making your situation harder on yourself."

"Thanks for the amazing advice!" Ray thought back sarcastically.

Helen and Ven looked at her curiously while Peter and Jantzen exchanged gazes.

The two scared men nodded and turned to face Ray as one. "We'll hold you to it," Jantzen replied, his voice no longer shaking. His face was still a little flushed and she could see sweat forming on his brow, but it was an improvement.

"L..let's all be nice now..." Peter mumbled.

Ray beamed. "I'm going to go get prepared. I'll see you all tomorrow morning!"

Helen waved as Ray turned and walked towards the other individuals she wanted to talk to before she left. Ven, Jantzen, and Peter followed her with their eyes, but they otherwise didn't react to her leaving.

"Bitch..."

When she was outside the range of what a human should be able to hear, she heard Peter mumble an insult under his breath. She frowned but she held herself back from showing her displeasure in any other way. She gave him a chance. How unfortunate that he ruined it.

"Introduce yourself to the silver-ranked adventurers. I'm ninety percent certain they are lingering because they want you guys to talk to them."

Ray forced herself to smile again, humming to herself as she strode up to the silver-ranked adventurer party that was still observing from the side of the gathering. The instructors were all standing near the doorway observing the group, but the silver-rankers were standing amongst them.

The four adventurers watched her approach.

"Heya, I'm Ray!" she greeted them enthusiastically.

"Edwin," the armored dude responded.

"Melissa," replied the mage.

"Samantha," the crimson-haired rogue introduced in a monotone voice.

"Sage," the green-haired, green-robed lady said. Her voice sounded like soft bells chiming.

"How can we help you?" Edwin asked. The edges of his mouth twitched upward.

"I was right! Ask them about the bandits!"

"I wanted to meet you all at least once," she informed them. "Also, you were the ones who scouted out this request for us, right? I was wondering if you could tell us anything about the bandits we're hunting?"

Edwin grinned. "It's a pleasure to make your acquaintance, young miss. We would be more than happy to share the results of our investigation." He motioned towards Samantha.

The crimson-haired rogue pulled out a piece of paper and read the contents aloud. "Sighting of Ax the Pony confirmed yesterday. Location: Voskeg Mountains. Seven bandit henchmen confirmed. No magic users detected. Henchmen expected to consist of a guardian, two warriors, two rogues, and two archers. Ax the Pony had over thirty axes hanging from various locations on his body."

Ray's jaw dropped in surprise. "He's alive...?" she muttered; her eyes were so wide that her eyebrows practically reached her hairline.

Melissa raised an eyebrow. "Isn't that the problem? There wouldn't be a request to kill him if he were dead."

Ah... Realizing her mistake, Ray closed her mouth and fixed her expression. "Right, of course. That makes sense. Hahaha..."

Edwin scrunched his brow and examined her with a critical eye. Ray felt a bead of sweat forming on the back of her neck and decided it was probably best to leave quickly

"Thank you so much for the information!" she blurted out and then she turned as if to dash away.

Edwin reached out and grabbed her shoulder. "One last thing. Don't bring any ponies with you."

"Ponies?" Ray asked, tilting her head in confusion.

"Ponies." Edwin affirmed. "That mad man is obsessed with killing ponies using axes. That's where his name comes from: Ax the Pony."

"...?" Ray was speechless. She nodded in thanks before rushing off towards Lexi. The two of them had a lot to prepare.

Edwin watched her go with a peculiar expression on his face. "She's the one Siegfried was talking about, right? The one with unusual strength and speed."

Melissa nodded. "I would assume so. I'm glad he warned us ahead of time. With how much she seems like a vampire, I don't know how I would have reacted otherwise."

Sage shook her head. "Do you really think you could have done anything with Master Rambalt and Siegfried watching over her?"

Edwin smirked. "You noticed as well?"

"It was extremely obvious," Samantha chimed in. "Between the two of them, there was never a moment we could have struck that she was unguarded. It was an uncanny degree of supervision."

The four of them exchanged glances. ""Let's not get involved.""
They unanimously agreed.

Of course, they were still well within the range of Ray's hearing.

There was not much money in the enchanted bag, so Ray and Lexi had been forced to beseech Eileen for some assistance. The High Priestess was willing to help, though she seemed to be getting a little annoyed with their near-total dependence.

"Have the two of you done nothing but train? Didn't you think of earning even a little bit of money for yourselves?"

Lexi looked ashamed. She hunched her shoulders and twiddled her feet as she looked at the ground, unable to meet Eileen's eyes.

"I don't know anything about earning money," Ray replied, unfazed. "But won't we earn some money from this job?"

Eileen covered her face with her palm and sighed.

"Certainly, you will earn a small amount if you succeed. It won't even be close to the amount you are asking me for, though." She pinched the bridge of her nose. "Oh well, it's not that big of a deal. It's well within my means and helping you here will only make my job easier."

Ray tilted her head. "How so?"

Eileen dismissed the question with a wave of her hand. She then withdrew a little white enchanted bag from within the folds of her robes. "You can ignore that last part. Here's what you'll need."

She pulled out a stack of the same unidentifiable food that Ray had given to Lexi before. She also withdrew several stacks of clothes, including black and white robes, several different colors of t-shirts and pants both long and short, as well as several changes of undergarments.

She also pulled out two strange contraptions. One of them was a stone block, the top of which was shaped almost like a seat with a hole in the center. Ray peeked inside and noted that the box was hollow and empty.

"What's this?" she asked, curious.

"That is one of the single most important tools for any wealthy adventurer," Eileen replied. "It's a portable toilet enchanted with spatial magic. Anything that you put inside of it will be moved to a special space due to the spatial magic enchantment. If you look here, you'll notice that this toilet also comes with a bidet."

The High Priestess then motioned to the other contraption. At first glance, it seemed like the portable toilet except the hole was on the side and it wasn't molded like a seat. There was a door that allowed the operator to close off the insides. "This is a portable kitchen. The main device is a stove and there are drawers on the sides enchanted with spatial magic. Each drawer holds various knives, spoons, pots, pans, measuring cups in both metric and imperial units, and basically any other cooking utensil you might need."

Lexi's jaw dropped at the explanation.

Ray, for her part, didn't have any concept of how much these gifts were worth. She promptly stored each of the items in her bag. "Thanks, Sister!"

The High Priestess sighed as she watched the two of them leave the room. Out of the corner of her eye, Ray noticed Eileen counting the coins left in her wallet with a nervous expression.

"Ray, that didn't seem suspicious to you?"

"Maybe a little?"

"You don't think it was weird that she happened to have stacks of food and clothes in both of your sizes ready?"

Huh. She had been so distracted by receiving all the gifts that she hadn't noticed that part. She made a mental note about that and decided to worry about it later. Turning to Lexi, she threw an arm around the catgirl's shoulder. "You need to get any food before we train?"

"Yeah," Lexi replied while patting her stomach.

The two of them worked their way out of the temple, down the stairs and into the main street.

"What do you want today?" Ray asked, motioning towards the food stalls and restaurants lining the street.

Lexi sniffed the air and caught a scent that seemed appetizing to her. Following the aroma to its source, the two of them moved into an alley and found a small bar with a sign.

The sign bore a picture of a red triangle and its name was transcribed beneath the shape.

"The Triangular Tomato..." Ray read aloud, turning a questioning look on Lexi. "Do they taste better when cut into triangles?"

"Who knows?" Lexi shrugged as she moved to open the door.

A loud *crash* similar to the breaking of glass resounded nearby, causing both of them to pause. Exchanging a glance, they stepped away from the bar and moved towards the source. Stepping out onto the main street, they saw a small crowd forming around a man and a young foxkin. The beastkin was groveling on the ground with his hands covering his head while the man continuously kicked the poor boy. Ray recognized him as one of the foxkin she'd seen on the cart when she had made her way back into Cairel.

Beside them was a shattered vase that had once been decorated exquisitely. Undoubtedly, it had been expensive.

The man began to shout, accenting each word with another kick. "How. Dare. You. Drop. The. Vase!"

"I'm sorry! Sorrysorrysorrysorry!" The boy screamed repeatedly while tears streamed down his dirty face.

The man twisted to the side and arced his foot up into the boy's ribs, flipping him over so that he lay flat on the ground. Reaching to his belt, the man grabbed a mace that was tied there. He loosened the knot in a swift, practiced motion and raised it over the screaming foxkin child.

"Mynn..." Lexi coughed out, taking a hesitant step forward. "No... no... NO!"

"Get her out of there!" the voice in her head shouted.

Ray reached out and caught Lexi's shoulder, drawing the catgirl into a hug while simultaneously restraining her. She pulled her struggling friend away before she could make a scene.

Stepping back into the alleyway, Ray moved further in and released Lexi, keeping an arm around her in case she needed to quickly restrain her again.

"Mynn...!" Lexi sobbed. She fell to her knees as tears streamed from her eyes.

Ray took a step away and then moved towards the entrance of the alleyway to give her friend some time to compose herself. She glanced out at the main street and saw that a masked figure had intervened before the man could kill the young boy. She studied the silver mask and her eyes widened. It was identical to the one worn by Ven.

The masked figure brandished a dagger, threatening the man holding the mace. The man released his hold on his mace, and it clattered against the ground as he raised his shaking hands. The masked figure shook his head as he sheathed his dagger and turned towards the foxkin. Extending his arm towards the boy, Ray felt a pulse of mana and then the shackle on the boy's ankle crumbled.

Lifting the boy up with one arm, the masked figure tapped his belt with his free hand and a purple gate opened. Stepping through the gate, the masked savior and the boy disappeared, and the gate collapsed behind them.

"Holy shit..." the voice muttered.

Ray made note of the mask. The figure had been taller and broader than Ven, but there was no way it was a coincidence that they wore masks with the same design.

Stepping back into the alleyway, Ray sat down next to Lexi and placed a hand on the catgirl's arm. Lexi looked over with puffy eyes.

"It's okay, he got away," Ray reported.

Lexi smiled weakly. "I'm sorry, it just reminded me of what happened to my village..."

Ray shook her head, but she didn't respond. Bitterness welled up inside of her as she recalled the scene. It wasn't the first time she had seen slaves being treated poorly, but this time felt different. She couldn't help but imagine that it was Lexi out there being beaten.

It felt *wrong*. She didn't do anything this time and a heavy weight settled in her stomach.

"That feeling is called guilt," the voice in her head explained. *"All humans feel it when they do something they know is wrong..."*

"But I'm not a human, and I'm not the one who beat the foxkin…"

"That may be so, but you stood by and did nothing. Of course, I'm not saying you should have started a fight then and there. You feel guilty because you saw something cruel and unjust, and you ran away."

Ray thought about the voice's words for a long time and dwelled on their meaning. *"Are you saying that I should do something to prevent these actions?"*

"I'm saying 'we' should do something to prevent them. It will take time and effort, but I am a god, and you are my prophet. Our path is one that we choose for ourselves."

19

First Adventure

Though Ray didn't particularly feel tired, she slept through the night. The moment her head hit the pillow in her room, she was asleep. Through a little bit of experimentation, she had found that she didn't see any distinct negative effects from staying up for a few days in a row for training, but when she brought it up, Sister Eileen had assured her that her body still needed sleep. Maybe someday she would experiment with how long she could stay awake before she collapsed...

The next morning found Ray waiting at the front gate of the town for the members of her new party. She had arrived first with Lexi and the two of them had been waiting for over fifteen minutes before Jantzen and the others could be seen approaching with a large cart in tow.

As they got closer, Ray called out to them. "What's the cart for? Don't you have an enchanted bag?"

Jantzen nodded, tapping the small bag hanging from a sash tied around his waist.

"Of course, I do. This cart is for something else."

Ray raised an eyebrow.

Jantzen pointed at Lexi. The catgirl flinched and stepped back so that she was partially behind Ray.

"You're bringing a slave along but you're also taking up her job as the tank, so we decided to turn her into a packhorse instead," Jantzen explained. "Most importantly, carts draw more attention and increase the chances of bandit attacks."

The first reason aside, the second reason would have been decent logic if it weren't an open top cart with no products inside. She opened her mouth to protest when Lexi reached out and tapped her arm.

"I don't mind," Lexi whispered. "I'll just pretend it's strength training."

Ray nodded hesitantly. The catgirl stepped out from behind her and walked up to the cart. She reached out and grabbed the reins that were obviously designed to be attached to a horse or an ox. She started to pull, and the cart creaked as it rolled forward.

"Wait a moment!" Jantzen called out as he placed a meaty hand on the side of the cart.

Lexi relaxed her grip as she paused, looking at him with an anxious expression. The fat priest waddled over and grabbed the front edge of the cart. He pulled himself through the opening and into the storage area where he sat down and made himself comfortable.

"Continue," he ordered, his face covered with a vengeful grin.

What in the world happened? This guy was terrified less than a full day earlier and he was now acting like a selfish bully? Ray couldn't understand the sudden shift in Jantzen's behavior.

"Be careful. People like that don't change their attitudes unless they are confident that they have control again. Don't act rashly until you have a grasp on why he isn't scared of you anymore."

She suppressed her annoyance as she watched Lexi pick up the reins and struggle to move. Jantzen and Peter both widened their eyes in surprise as the cart slowly started to inch forward. Helen looked on with a straight face and Ven still wore his mask, so Ray was unable to determine exactly how they felt about what was happening. She carefully examined Lexi, noting her strained arms and the perspiration matting her dark hair.

Ray stepped forward and casually grabbed the reins of the cart as well. "I like the idea of attracting prey to attack us, but I dislike your method," she informed Jantzen as she started pulling the cart with Lexi.

Though Jantzen's considerable weight was added to the cart, the task was particularly difficult for her.

Jantzen ground his teeth slightly in annoyance. "She's a slave... " he started but stopped when Peter lifted himself up into the moving cart and put a hand on Jantzen's shoulder.

"It's alright, no harm done, right?" Peter said. He shifted the dirty-blonde hair out of his eyes as he revealed a lopsided grin. "As long as she can still tank when we get in trouble, it's fine if the old bi- I mean, if the *young girl* helps pull the cart."

Ray forced herself not to glare at Peter. She took note of his carefree demeanor. She knew that he was a warlock-in-training but since he avoided her until now, she didn't know much else about him.

Jantzen shrugged and Peter gave Ray a wink. She felt a slight pain in her head, and she winced. She wasn't sure why but something about Peter rubbed her the wrong way.

"What kind of warlock are you, Peter?" she asked.

"Obliterator," he replied smoothly. "I break things."

She frowned. The pain in her head flared and she shook her head in a futile attempt to make the sensation go away. Then a memory of her first encounter with Peter crossed her mind. He had used magic on her. Ray summoned her mana and examined her internal state. A foreign mana had invaded her since who knows when. She winced as the mana struck her mind again and her head flared with pain.

Obliterator? Clearly not. He was a dominator-type warlock.

She willed all the mana that she summoned to permeate through her body and surround the foreign mana. She directed a vicious glare at Peter as she collapsed her mana into the invading magic and thoroughly crushed it.

Peter met her furious gaze and winked again.

The action startled Ray and in that moment of clarity, she realized that the voice in her head was right. Something had changed that made it so both Peter and Jantzen felt like they could act up so blatantly.

Unfortunately, she had no idea what it was.

Ray shook her head, breaking the line of thought. It didn't really matter what Peter was trying to do because it didn't change her plans. If he thought he could mind control her, then this should be the extent of the attacks that she would have to deal with.

"I think you should be a little more understanding of our ways," Peter suggested.

The mana invaded her body once more and a sharp pain flared in Ray's mind.

"Yes, I should do that," Ray replied, trying to sound like she was mind-controlled. She didn't really know what that would be like but guesstimated that a mind-controlled person would be devoid of expression.

She thoroughly crushed the mana invading her again as she shuffled forward, pulling the cart while looking in the direction she was moving with a blank expression. The hood of her cloak caught in the wind and billowed slightly, but she paid it no mind. She noted that Ven and Helen were now paying close attention to the conversation.

They were supposed to be checking the road for traps and watching for ambushes.

"Who are you?" Peter asked.

Every time he spoke, the invading mana returned. After crushing it again, Ray realized that he wasn't manually controlling his mana, he was just imbuing it into his words.

That was why he didn't realize it when Ray kept foiling his attacks.

Rather than come up with a fake story on the spot, she figured it would be better to tell the truth. Of course, she would have to embellish a few details, though.

"Ray," she responded simply.

"What's your family name? Where are you from?"

"I have no family. I am from nowhere and I have no home." The words rang true, and a faint memory of a crater passed through her mind. The crater was ringed by tombstones. She pushed the feeling away. She was curious about the memory but now was not the time to examine it.

"Your hair. Is it dyed?" Jantzen asked.

"Yes."

"What about your absurd physical strength?"

"I lift."

The group had mixed reactions. Peter looked amused while Jantzen looked vindictive. Helen looked disinterested in the whole thing.

If she had to guess, Helen and Ven were not participating because they didn't support the idea. However, they clearly didn't oppose it either, seeing as neither of them were getting involved in any way.

The throbbing pain in her head disappeared and she shook her head as if coming out of a daze.

Ven and Helen returned their attention to the road while the group continued to move forward. Jantzen watched the two girls pull the cart with a sneer while Peter pulled a journal out of his bag and started writing in it. It was the same one he had the first time Ray saw the boy.

Lexi tapped her on the shoulder.

She glanced at the catgirl, ducking her head slightly to hide her expression behind the cowl of her hood.

"You resisted the mind control, didn't you?" Lexi whispered quietly. "I sensed a few lies in there."

"Of course," she replied with a chuckle.

"Thank you for helping me. The cart was too heavy to pull by myself."

"That's what friends are for, right? Besides, this just gives me another reason to wipe the sneer off that arrogant prick's face."

Lexi giggled while Ray returned her focus to the path ahead of them. She hadn't been paying much attention to her surroundings due to the conversation, but they had already passed by the farmlands and were moving towards the Voskeg Mountains. The area around them was dotted with snow and dry grass. Trees were sparse and the sky was a dreary grey accented by dark clouds.

Originally, she had intended to share the info she got from the Earthbreakers, but she felt less inclined to do so now. It was common knowledge that Ax the Pony and his bandits waylaid groups traveling through the Voskeg Mountains. Ray didn't intend to let them know more than that.

If her party was going to treat her and her friend like this, there was no reason for her to help them.

After about an hour, they approached the semi-familiar rocky landscape. The ground began to slant up and trees became a bit more common. There were more dried bushes than in the open landscape behind them.

Ray didn't have many fond memories of this place.

These mountains were the place she woke up in after that ritual and then mysteriously experienced excruciating pain until she died. They were the place she had been eaten alive by a giant bird. They were also the place where she had to break her own wrist so that she could fight Jonathan's party for her life and freedom.

As the scenery around them changed, the group became even more focused on their surroundings. Peter put his journal away and he and Jantzen both began to help search for signs of bandits.

Helen and Ven each took a side of the cart while Peter watched behind them and Jantzen, Ray, and Lexi watched in front.

The wheels of the cart creaked loudly. Jantzen cursed as a wheel rolled over a rock and the cart jumped. Ray snickered and observed the path in front of them. She intentionally shifted the cart to hit as many bumps as possible.

Ray was the first one to detect the bandits. In the quiet, snowy mountains where the only constant sounds should have been the creaking of the wheels and her team's shuffling steps, she heard a rock tumbling and a faint curse.

Her eyes immediately went to the source of the sound, and she saw a small boulder on the side of the mountain path ahead of them. She studied the path and noted that there were three boulders spaced evenly apart in a triangle that were just large enough for a few people to hide behind if they were crouching. There were two other such boulders behind their group.

Realizing what was happening, she lightly bumped her shoulder into Lexi. The catgirl turned and their eyes met.

"Ambush," Ray mouthed.

Her friend's eyes lit up with understanding. The two of them released the reins on the cart and stopped moving.

Ray drew her two-handed longsword.

"What are you doing?!" Jantzen hissed.

Ray ignored the bumbling bundle of stupidity as she turned in a circle, carefully observing each of the five boulders. Helen and Ven, upon seeing her actions, quickly realized what was happening and drew their own weapons.

They heard a loud clapping sound and all eyes turned to see a man stepping out from behind a boulder. He had a pristine, white bandana on his head which covered his hair. His beard was grizzly and unkempt. He had two axes hanging from his belt, one on each side, and several throwing axes and hatchets attached to straps across his torso and his legs.

Ax the Pony.

"I am impressed that you detected our ambush. It was a little too late though, as you are already surrounded." The bandit leader's voice was deep and clear. Though he was smiling, his eyes were sharp and intelligent. He was carefully observing each of them, taking note of their weapons and positions.

His eyes widened in surprise when he saw Ray. He froze and his face twisted unnaturally. After a long moment, he turned and stepped back behind the rock.

"I apologize for the inconvenience. You may continue on your way."

" ... "

What the hell?

20

Search

"How's the training going?" Eileen asked the two men sitting on the soft couch in her meeting room.

The two of them were sipping hot cups of tea. Quincy wore his usual ruffled and dirty robes and looked like he hadn't slept in days while Siegfried was dressed in slacks and a t-shirt that showed off his well-defined muscles.

"I don't even know where to start..." Siegfried mumbled.

Quincy nodded in agreement, his eyes sparkling as he recalled his new prodigy.

"Her latent potential is absolutely phenomenal! She has only been practicing enhancement magic for a few weeks and she can nearly perform a practical durability enhancement on her entire arm! Her control of the flexibility still needs some practice but yesterday she successfully managed to get movement in seven joints!"

"Is that good?" Eileen asked. "I'm not well versed in enhancement magic."

"For reference, how long did it take you to get that far, Siegfried?" Quincy redirected the question.

He grimaced. "Three months, give or take. I was on the fast side."

Eileen whistled in appreciation. "What about her training as a guardian?"

Siegfried spat out his tea as he started to laugh. "You call that a 'guardian'? I sparred with her two days ago and she snapped her sword and bent my shield in half by 'accident'! I've given up on teaching her how to use a shield. Who needs a shield when you can just give that lady a bunch of big, heavy weapons and she'll break anything or anyone you point her at?"

"I wonder what she'll be like when she completes her durability enhancement and starts working on enhancing her muscles..." Quincy mused.

Siegfried stopped laughing and turned to stare at Quincy.
"Are you trying to kill a god?"
Quincy met his gaze with a soft smile.

"Wait!" Ray called out to the bandit leader.
Ax flinched. "Why are you still bothering me? I did everything you asked me to!" he cried out without turning around.
"What are you talking about?" Ray asked, raising an eyebrow. "I never asked you to do anything."
"Bullshit!" His knees were slightly bent, and he was poised to run away at a moment's notice. He desperately waved off his subordinates as one of them tried to draw their weapon. "You crazy man! You wanna die?!"
Ray felt someone tap her shoulder and she turned to see Jantzen towering over her.
"Do you know him?" the fat priest asked. His eyes were full of suspicion.
"No idea," Ray replied with a shrug.
"He seems to know you though."
The other members of the party kept their eyes on their surroundings, but she could see that they were surprised and a bit suspicious about this development. Even Lexi seemed a bit curious.
Ray shook her head. "I only know him from the wanted poster. I think he's mistaking me for somebody else."
As if. He was on the mountain. This man knew who she was before the ritual.
"Are you Ax the Pony?" Jantzen called out.
Ax shook his head. "I don't want to fight you anymore. You are exempt from the toll. Please, just leave and let us be."
"We were looking for you. Will you come peacefully, or do we have to fight?"
Ax flinched again. His wavering eyes focused on Ray, and he grimaced.
Whoever Ray was before the ritual, this guy was completely terrified of her. It was somewhat refreshing.
"I... will have to choose the third option. I have no desire to fight you, but I can't be drawn into the human kingdom yet. I still have to finish my job before I go there."
Third option? His job?
Ax pulled out a small object from a bag on his belt.

"Stop him!" the voice in her head shouted.

Ray leapt forward and swung her sword at the object in his hand. But she was too late. The object flashed brightly, and Ray covered her eyes. When her vision returned, Ax the Pony was gone. The boulder next to him was also gone and there was a small crater in the ground where they had been standing.

Half of Ray's sword that approached the bandit leader was also gone. Everything within the radius of a sphere had completely disappeared.

Losing a weapon didn't bother her too much, at least. She kept a few spares in her enchanted bag ever since she started breaking them in practice.

"Ah, I should have expected that. It was so cliché!"

Lexi came up behind Ray and tapped her on the shoulder. She held out a dagger with a note attached to it. "He threw this at me during the flash of light," she reported softly.

Ray accepted the note and quickly memorized the contents before hiding it in her bag.

Because the throw was masked by the blinding light, nobody else noticed the dagger or the note.

"How are you not injured?" Ray asked, noting that she didn't see any blood on the dagger.

"I caught it." Lexi deadpanned. She revealed her sharp canines. "You could say that I have cat-like reflexes."

"..."

Ray stared at her with a dull expression. "Was that supposed to be a joke?"

Lexi shrugged.

Ray covered her face with her palm and sighed.

The group carefully checked behind each of the boulders but there were no more bandits. Since the other four boulders were all still present, they had to have escaped using different methods but neither Helen nor Ven were able to find any tracks indicating the direction they moved.

"These were not normal bandits," Helen observed. "Their skills and resources are far beyond our expectations. That thing they used to escape was a spatial grenade. Those things are *expensive!*"

Ray ignored the conversation of Jantzen's party members as she thought about the contents of the note:

'As we feared, it seems that your memory was a bit scrambled by the ritual. If it is answers that you seek, ask your god. We yet have time before you must act, but he should know the best way for you to prepare to face the darkness.

Oh, and I quit. This is my letter of resignation.'

Her god? How did he know about the voice in her head?

"Is he talking about you?" Ray asked.

"Uhhh, I'm not sure, honestly. That's the only explanation that makes sense though, right?"

It was the only explanation they had, at least. He and the other four Overseers were the only 'gods' she knew of. Amongst the five, he was the closest one to being considered 'her' god. He gave decent advice from time to time.

So, if she wanted 'answers', she needed to work with the voice in her head.

"Ray, what do you think?" Helen's voice interrupted her thoughts.

Ray jolted to attention, realizing that the others were now focusing on her. She scratched the back of her neck, flushing slightly with embarrassment. "Erm, about what?"

"We still have the rest of today and all of tomorrow to find the bandits. I don't think randomly wandering around the mountains is the best idea. We were discussing the best way to go about it," Helen explained. "Any thoughts?"

Ray rubbed her chin as she studied their surroundings for something that might spark an idea. *"What do you think?"*

"Hmm, this is a bit of a tricky one. Since I have no experience with using spatial magic to hide, I don't exactly know how far away they could be. When my group and I used to run and hide, we would usually have preset hideouts scattered throughout the area. If they were able to move large distances with that spatial grenade, it may be impossible to find them. If not, they are probably hiding within a few miles of this location."

"How far is it possible to travel with a spatial grenade?" Ray asked.

"It depends on the maker, but they can only move to a preset location. The kingdom uses them to capture criminals by teleporting them into prison cells. Since each city has a prison and the grenades work anywhere within the city and the surrounding farmlands, I would guess that anywhere within a few square miles is fair game."

"It's a bit of a large area to search for only two days but if you search for caves, you might be able to find them."

"Caves…" Ray muttered. "We should probably look for caves on this mountain. If we cover this whole mountain and don't find them, they either moved while we were searching, or they were able to move further than we expected. In either case, we won't find them."

Jantzen went to climb back into the cart but Ray reached out and grabbed his wrist. He turned and looked down at her with an annoyed expression. However, when their eyes met, Ray squeezed his wrist. Jantzen's eyes looked like they might pop out of his head as he groaned from the pressure.

"We don't need the cart anymore," Ray asserted.

"B..but…" Jantzen stammered. His face flushed red as he tried to break free of her grip.

Unfortunately for him, she was just a *little* bit stronger. Her grip was firm, and he was unable to pull his arm away. Ray clenched her teeth as she repeated her previous statement. "We. Don't. Need. The. Cart. Anymore."

Jantzen shrunk back, cowering against the side of the cart. She released his arm and he collapsed to the ground.

"Be careful. We still don't know what made them so confident. They might try something soon. If the consequences are acceptable, then we need to let it happen and then react to it. We can't punish them for sins they haven't committed yet."

She stepped aside and motioned for Lexi to follow her. She wasn't fully sure if she agreed with the voice's idea here, but she decided she would give it a go. It would be the first 'step' in their partnership. She would make use of him at least until she found out the truth about her past. "If they try to do anything to me later, ignore it until after they make their attempt."

The catgirl nodded with a slightly confused expression but she didn't ask any further questions.

"Let's go!" Ray called back to the others as she continued up the path. "Let's get to the peak and decide which direction to go from there."

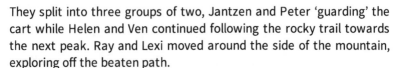

They split into three groups of two, Jantzen and Peter 'guarding' the cart while Helen and Ven continued following the rocky trail towards the next peak. Ray and Lexi moved around the side of the mountain, exploring off the beaten path.

Whereas the trail had shown signs of relatively frequent travel, the rest of the mountain was dotted with melting snow, budding flowers, and trees that were starting to show green. Here and there, Ray noted some strange claw marks on the bark of trees and small imprints in the half-frozen mud moving in all directions.

'Looks like there are creatures moving about. Whether they are normal animals or wild monsters though, I couldn't say,"

"Lexi, do you know anything about the monsters in this area?"

The catgirl shook her head. "My home was in the fertile flatlands between the ocean and a desert. If I had to guess based on stories... maybe mountain yetis, cave trolls, lesser rocs, goblins, dwarves, and vampiric rabbit-bears? Ah, and we aren't that far from the Federation, so it should be possible to encounter orcs or trolls as well."

Many of her guesses lined up with the info that Siegfried had supplied. Ray silently raised her internal measure of Lexi's deductions. Looking around carefully, she tried to compare the tracks and scratches with the faint memories dancing at the edge of her recognition. Everything seemed familiar, yet distant. The answer was at the tip of her tongue, but she couldn't reach it.

Biting her lip in frustration, Ray stomped further into the trees, scattering rocks and twigs and covering her pants in mud. Lexi followed her more carefully, making sure to avoid stepping into deep patches and dirtying the clothes gifted to her by the temple.

A few dozen minutes of searching later, Ray felt a strange sensation envelop her. She stopped and immediately began to search the area for the source of the disturbance.

Lexi paused as well, tilting her head curiously. A moment later, she realized Ray had sensed something and her triangular ears perked up as she focused on their surroundings as well.

A small, black bundle blitzed by. Ray barely noticed it in her peripheral vision. She turned and attempted to follow the shape with her superior kinetic vision. She focused her eyes on the creature and its shape blurred into view.

The little beast was small and strangely colored. The top half of its fur and its long, bushy tail were pitch black with a small white circle in the center of its back. Its belly was pure white with a small black dot in the center, exactly opposite of the white dot. The fur on its head was split horizontally, its left half being black with white around its eye while its right half was white with black around its eye.

Ray began to quiver. Her instincts warned her to flee with all her might.

However, she had already resolved herself to push through her instincts and discover the truth hiding behind her forgotten memories.

"A squirrel...? It kind of reminds me of the yin-yang symbol."
Ray pointed at the creature as it leapt between two branches and zipped up a nearby tree. "Is that a monster?"

Lexi followed her finger and noticed the small creature. Her eyes widened and then began to shake. "A karma squirrel..." she muttered in awe.

Before Ray could ask if it was dangerous, the creature hissed threateningly, glaring at them with its beady eyes. The squirrel looked relatively harmless.

Ray pushed back the instinctual terror welling up within her and took a step forward. A vague memory danced just outside of reach. Beneath the overwhelming fear, she felt a deep well of sorrow and regret tied to the memory.

"Wait...!" Lexi attempted to call out, but it was too late.

The black and white squirrel launched itself from its perch, claws extended as it flew towards Ray.

She took a step forward and firmly planted her feet on the ground as she drew her fist up. Then she struck with all the strength that she could manage.

The karma squirrel exploded, covering Ray and their surroundings with red paint and chunks of bone and gore.

"DAMMIT!" Lexi wailed.

Ray moved as if to turn towards her friend but froze as a strange pressure rose inside of her. Pain comparable to a snapshot of her time on the mountain filled her body. She opened her mouth to scream, and then...

Everything went black.

After an unknown amount of time, Ray felt her senses returning. Agony surged through her and she tried to scream but she couldn't move her body yet. A horrific wail filled her ears, momentarily scattering her consciousness. As the sensations across her body slowly grew stronger, she managed to twist her neck and open her eyes.

Lexi was covered from head to toe in blood and kneeling over Ray, arms folded over her face as she sobbed into her chest.

Ignoring the pain, Ray gently lifted an arm and stroked the back of Lexi's head.

The catgirl stiffened, her cries abruptly halting as she turned to search for what was touching her.

Ray fought the urge to cry and instead offered a weak smile.

"R...Ray...?! H...h...how?!" Lexi spluttered, tears streaming down her cheeks.

Ray could practically see her friend's mind reeling. She propped herself up onto her elbows and took note of her surroundings. With her as the epicenter, there was a rough circle of blood and gore. Her clothes were in pieces and bits of flesh and bone could be seen scattered about.

"Most of what you see here is 'you'. You exploded quite spectacularly."

"W...what...?!" Ray coughed out, her mind reeling as she collapsed back down to the ground. She felt her regeneration moving towards completion as the pain began to dull.

Lexi wiped her nose with her sleeve and smiled. Her eyes revealed a dangerous glint. "Karma squirrels are considered creatures that should be avoided at all costs. They have low combat capabilities, but they have a natural property that returns all injuries to their opponent..."

Ray's eyes lit up in understanding. "So, I exploded because I exploded the squirrel?"

Lexi nodded in affirmation, her ears twitching. "Now, you have something you need to explain to me."

Ray shivered as she reached for her bag to find a new pair of clothes. Swearing that she would never again disregard her senses, she opened her mouth and began to explain.

21

Murder in the Dark

"Respawning?" Eileen asked, "What about it?"

"How does it work? Are there any limits? What causes the respawn?"

"As far as we understand it, when we die our soul is caught by the nearest temple. The magic inside the holy building reconstructs our body according to the blueprint registered within the system.

"Is there anything it can't regenerate?"

"It heals injuries and cures sickness, disease, poison, and curses. However, it cannot remove negative status conditions related to hunger, thirst, fatigue, or aging so if a person dies of starvation, they often get stuck in a cycle of painful death."

"That sounds…"

"Terrible. It is. I've seen it happen a few times. The unfortunate souls usually reject their respawn after two or three painful deaths."

"Wait, you can reject it?"

"Yes."

" … "

"The respawn system is wonderful, but it's not perfect. Sometimes… it doesn't work right."

"What do you mean?"

"It's best if I show you."

Eileen stood abruptly and walked towards the door.

Ray stood up and followed. They moved to a portion of the temple that Ray hadn't seen yet. It was a large, open room in the right wing.

"We call this the Drone Chamber."

"Drones?" Ray looked inside and saw many humans roaming about. Some of them were repeatedly walking into the wall while staring blankly into space. Others were crawling across the ground while some had tears in their eyes as they shuffled about. One person approached the doorway and she observed his face.

His eyes were devoid of light. He was nothing more than a living husk.

"Sometimes the temple reconstructs a body, but the soul doesn't return. When this happens, a drone is born. Mindless, helpless, soulless shells of humanity."

"How often does this happen?"

"It's not all that common. We noticed a trend that individuals who suffer an extremely violent and traumatic death often become drones. If this is true, then how much trauma an individual can handle will be different on a case-by-case basis. Some people will become drones for a simple stab wound and others have to be brutally mutilated."

After several hours of combing the mountainside, they only found one cave and it was empty. They decided to set up camp inside and resume their search in the morning.

Ray was assigned as the last watch and she promptly went to 'sleep'. Lexi wasn't assigned a position in the watch order. She was busy cleaning up the dishes used for dinner while listening to the conversation between the four adventurers who were still awake.

"Let's just go back. It's not a big deal if we fail the mission and I'm tired of walking through snow and mud to find something that might not even be there," Peter complained.

Jantzen nodded his agreement. "Jonathan's group failed this mission last time. It should be fine to go back."

The two of them looked at Helen and Ven. Ven pulled out his dagger and a rag and started polishing it. Helen shook her head and motioned towards Ray's sleeping form.

"I think we should make the decision as a full group..." Helen replied.

Jantzen frowned. "She's not one of us. That bitch is completely out of control."

"She hasn't caused any problems though..." she pointed out. "Her suggestion to search this mountain for a cave was logical and she pulled the cart without any complaints."

Jantzen spat on the cave floor. "She let the bandit-leader get away and then she hurt my arm!"

Helen sighed. "If you kick her out, she'll be the third guardian you've rejected. We need a frontline."

Jantzen pointed at Lexi and smirked. "We can just use slaves. A disposable tank is still a tank."

Lexi flinched, her triangular ears wilting. She continued to scrub at a particularly stubborn patch of burnt food.

"What do you think?" Peter asked the silent rogue.

Ven paused his motion of polishing the dagger. "I don't care. I'm here to get training. Nothing more, nothing less."

"Figures," Peter shook his head ruefully. "But that's why I like you. You know when to get involved and when to stay out of it."

Helen grimaced at the verbal jab. She stood up and walked over to the tent she set aside for her own personal use. She stepped inside and closed the flap, cutting herself off from the issue.

Ven sheathed his dagger and entered his own tent.

Jantzen and Peter looked at each other. They covered their mouths to hide their smiles as they laughed. Lexi's ears twitched as she overheard their whispering that they probably thought was quiet enough for her not to notice.

It was a typical human mistake. Her hearing was at least as good as a normal human.

Well, they likely just didn't care if she heard.

"Ready?" Jantzen asked as they quietly stood up and started tiptoeing towards Ray's tent.

Lexi's ears twitched and her tail started waving back and forth as she glared at the two of them.

Jantzen withdrew a shining dagger from his enchanted bag. Peter snorted and covered his mouth to prevent himself from laughing out loud. They carefully pushed aside the tent flap and crawled inside.

Lexi wanted to call out, but she remembered Ray's request from earlier.

She was supposed to ignore it.

But how could she stand by and watch this happen? Even if Ray would regenerate, Lexi didn't have that power, nor would she respawn if she died.

Lexi inched over and peeked through the tent flap. She saw Peter poised with a dagger held over Ray's heart while Jantzen was holding the dagger as if to cut her throat. The two of them met each other's eyes and silently counted together.

One. Two. Three!

On three, they both thrust their daggers into the unconscious woman and Lexi averted her eyes. She covered her mouth to muffle her scream. Tears formed at the edge of her vision, and she started to back away from the tent. She tripped over a rock that had been used as a bench and crashed into the portable kitchen that was still set up.

She frantically pushed herself back to her feet and looked towards the exit to the cave. She needed to get out of here. It took several minutes for Ray to regenerate when she had exploded and, without her protection, she was at the mercy of humans.

That was the worst possible place she could ever be.

Lexi started to run when Jantzen and Peter emerged from the tent and blocked her path. They both looked alarmed, but they breathed a sigh of relief as they realized it was just the catgirl. They raised their now bloodstained daggers and stalked towards her with sadistic grins.

"Now that the bitch is gone, we can finally deal with the runaway trash. When she respawns, we'll just tell her that it was a sneak attack and she died first. Her poor, poor slave died and got eaten by a monster! Since she isn't a human, she's gone for good!" Jantzen chortled merrily, the flaps of his chin dancing up and down like waves in the ocean.

Lexi looked around for a place to run. She saw Helen's tent flap twitch and her desperate eyes met the eyes peeking out from behind the canvas. Helen shook her head apologetically and closed the flap once more.

The two monsters stalked towards her with their daggers poised to strike. Lexi took the combat stance she had been practicing. She stepped back with her left leg and bent her knees slightly. She ignored the rattling of the chain as it slid across the ground while she tested her balance by lightly bouncing on her toes.

They were between her and the exit. No one was coming to help her. If she died, it was over.

This was the moment of truth. This was one of the moments Lexi had been training for.

It was two on one, but neither of them were martial artists. The two of them refused to study a martial discipline and stuck exclusively to magic. She didn't know why they were attacking her from up close, but she would take advantage of their stupidity before they started using their badly deformed brains.

Before they could gain control with their numbers advantage, Lexi stepped forward and initiated the first strike. She punched out with her right hand, moving through Peter's virtually non-existent guard, and striking his chest with the palm of her hand. Her fingers were curled in the shape of a tiger's paw.

Peter's eyes widened in shock as he fell to his knees, gasping for breath. His dagger clattered to the floor as Lexi twisted her body. Her left hand arced out to intercept Jantzen's arm mid-swing. She smacked his wrist, sending his dagger spinning into the air.

Lexi bared her teeth and snarled as she raised her knee and struck the fat priest's weakest spot.

As he hunched forward, she smashed her fist into his jaw.

Jantzen's eyes rolled back into his head, and he fell over backward with a plop. Without missing a beat, Lexi took a step forward and used her momentum to land a solid jab to Peter's face. She felt a tooth lodge in her sore knuckles, but the pain was worth it to see the hopeless, lustful beast collapsing to the floor with a bloodstained face. His nose was smashed flat, and he was missing a few teeth.

Lexi took a deep breath to calm herself. As she felt her heartbeat start to settle, she heard clapping coming from the side. She turned and saw her one and only friend standing outside her tent.

The catgirl fell to her knees, confusion warring with joy. She knew Ray would recover. She had seen her recover from a far worse injury just earlier that day.

Even so, it was still shocking. Ray was now standing there, perfectly fine. She had a small tear in her shirt over her heart and there was some wet blood soaked into the fabric, but there were no injuries.

"H..huh...?" Lexi spluttered. Tears finally began to fall as the tension left her body and the reality of everything that just occurred set in.

Ray's smile widened as she stepped forward and embraced her. "Good job," she whispered to the young catgirl.

"Thank you..."

After a full minute, Ray released her and stepped back.

Lexi sniffled a bit as she wiped the tears from her eyes. She took a deep breath to calm her rattled emotions. "Why?" she asked. "Why did you let them go this far?"

Ray scratched the back of her neck. "A person told me that I can't judge someone for sins they haven't committed yet. I figured I would have more justification in dealing with these two if they actually tried to kill me."

Lexi's eyes lit up with understanding.

"It was an unfortunate miscalculation that they went after you before I regenerated..." Ray muttered. "Sorry 'bout that. I didn't mean to get you caught up in it."

The catgirl shook her head vehemently. "No, it's fine. You helped me, it's only natural that I would help you. Besides, these two are as much my problem as they are yours."

"That's true, I suppose," Ray agreed. She turned to examine the two unconscious idiots. She reached down and picked up their bloody daggers, wiping the blood off on Jantzen's white robe before she stored them in her enchanted bag.

"By the way, you can stop eavesdropping and come out, Helen!" Ray called out. They both heard a faint *gasp* from Helen's tent before the canvas softly slid aside and Helen crawled out.

"I'm sorry that I didn't do anything..." she whispered, her eyes watering as tears threatening to pour out at any moment. "I'm too weak to stop them."

Ray tilted her head. "They just got beaten by an untrained beastkin slave. What do you mean 'too weak'?"

Helen shook her head. "That's not it. I'm certain I would beat them in a straight fight. The problem is after that. My father is only a count while Jantzen's father is a duke."

"And?"

Helen laughed emptily. "I can tell that you have no regard for rank or titles. I wish I could be like that too. Jantzen's father is a good duke, but he is also concerned about his public appearance. If I killed Jantzen and word of that spread, it would cause all kinds of problems. Even that could probably be managed, but Jantzen is also a party member. If I were to kill him for any reason outside of self-defense, I would lose my right to be an adventurer. I would no longer be allowed to train under the famous Blade Storm."

"So why not resolve it like we did, without killing him?" Ray asked.

"Jantzen is also the party leader. Unless they attack me first, it's still insubordination. If they reported me and neither you nor Ven took my side, the results would all be essentially the same."

Ray shook her head. "In other words, you're too afraid of the potential risks to take action when it counts."

Helen nodded meekly. "It's a bit more complicated than that, but I suppose you could say it that way."

Ray reached out and patted the ranger's shoulder. "Don't worry about it for now. Those daggers hurt but they were nothing compared to getting eaten alive by a roc."

Helen started to nod once more in agreement then stopped, her brow furrowed. "Excuse me?"

Ray laughed as she turned and walked back to her tent. "Have a good night!"

Lexi and Helen stared at Ray's retreating form with baffled expressions. Too many things had happened that evening and the two of them went to their respective tents to sleep and process it all.

In hindsight, Lexi probably should have realized that the person who was supposed to be on watch was now unconscious.

22

A Brutal Gamble

Ray jolted awake when she sensed that someone was inside her tent who wasn't supposed to be there. This wasn't like when Jantzen and Peter entered while she was pretending to be asleep.

This was something unexpected.

"Who are you?" Ray asked, opening her eyes. She couldn't see anybody. She no longer sensed any presence other than her own, but she was certain that somebody was there.

"The moment you started talking, he stepped back into the shadows and disappeared. It was like what Max did that one time."

Ray reached for her enchanted bag and withdrew her shortsword. Her eyes roamed back and forth over the dark interior of her tent. "I know you're there. If you want to talk, let's talk. If you want to fight, let's do that. I don't want to play hide-and-seek right now."

"Did you see what he looked like?"

"He was short, maybe two feet tall, and covered in black clothes. He had a few daggers strapped to his body and he had green skin, red eyes, and pointed ears."

Ray mentally went over the list of creatures her teachers had told her about during training. The description almost perfectly matched one that she had been told about.

Goblins.

Fortunately, her memories of languages were relatively untouched. Goblin was one of the five languages she knew how to speak. It was especially easy amongst the five because Goblin was basically just a diluted version of Ancient, her first language.

"Who are you?" Ray asked, this time using Goblin.

After a long pause, a small figure stepped out of the shadows in front of her with a baffled expression on his face. Now that she saw him herself, Ray was struck with déjà vu.

She was certain that she had met this goblin before.

He kneeled and bowed until his nose touched the floor. "It really is you! My lady, your humble servant Og is overjoyed to meet you once more!"

Huh? Ray froze like a statue.

"If you can forgive my ignorance, I would like to know why you are traveling with a group of adventurers?"

"What do I say? I don't know who this guy is…"

"Just be honest with him. It's better to clear the air early than to risk offending him by lying."

She decided to follow the advice of the voice in her head. "Umm, Og, right? I lost most of my memories a few weeks ago and I don't remember anything about who I was. I'm with these adventurers because the human fortress was the first place I found with people in it."

Og looked up and stared at her with a blank expression. As he processed her words, tears budded at the edge of his eyes. "You've lost your memories…? I don't want to believe it…"

"It's true. I want to figure out what happened that day that I woke up, but I don't have very many leads to work with, so I've been learning to fight and use magic with the humans here."

The goblin groaned. "You should have sought out our tribe or moved across the border into the United Federation. Even staying in these mountains and fighting wild monsters to train would be safer and cleaner than living amongst humans."

"Cleaner?"

"Spiritually. The only things humans can teach you is depravity, persecution, and destruction."

Well, that wasn't completely true. Of course, she had seen many things that bothered her, but she had also met nice people like Sister Eileen, Kelsey, and Siegfried.

Og sighed and motioned towards the tent exit. "We should leave, I think that you should meet with Shaman. She might be able to help you."

"What about my teammates?" She was willing to go but she knew that if she just waltzed off with a group of goblins, she would have a lot of explaining to do if she wanted to maintain her current lifestyle in Cairel.

"We can't take your 'friends' to our camp because they'll just respawn and let others know where it is. They'll have to die here and now."

Ray thought about that for a moment, and she remembered what Eileen had taught her about drones. An idea popped into her head, and she revealed her fangs in a savage grin.

"Would it be possible to just kill the ranger and the rogue for now? I have some unfinished business with the fat priest and the warlock before we leave. Oh, and the catkin is with me."

Og motioned for Ray to exit the tent first. "So long as our safety is guaranteed, I see no issues with your request." He then nodded towards an empty space. "See to it."

Ray felt a chill run down her spine as she realized that there had been multiple goblins either inside or surrounding her tent while hiding. She didn't know anything about the forces she was dealing with right now. She felt a bit bad for Helen, but she couldn't see a way out of the current situation that didn't involve the other girl dying. However, she shoved her guilt aside and focused on what was about to happen.

It was time to get some closure.

"Ray, I see what you're planning to do, and I think you should stop. Just let the goblins kill Jantzen and Peter like the others. You're taking a needless risk based on an unproven theory. If you're wrong, everything you've built up in Cairel will be compromised."

Ray knew the voice in her head was right. However, she felt like continuing with her plan. From the moment the idea had popped into her head, she was resolved to follow through with it. She licked her lips in anticipation as she remembered the sensation of stabbing a knife into Suzy and Bill.

"I thought it was understood that we were going to be working together. You are your own person and can make your own decisions, but I hope that you consider my advice more seriously. I warned you, so don't expect me to fix the consequences for you when things go wrong."

Ray giggled to herself. Things may have gone poorly for her when she first became aware but ever since she made the decision to return to Cairel, almost everything had gone well. It was almost as if the universe was balancing things out for her. Her first set of distinct memories was absolute hell, and the rest of her life was paradise.

Perfect balance.

"If that's really how you feel then this should be a good learning experience for you. Go ahead."

With that blessing from the voice in her head, Ray started humming as she patiently waited. A minute later, Helen and Ven's dead bodies were dragged out of their tents and propped up against the wall of the cave. They both had a hole in their heart and a slice across their neck. Ven's mask hung crookedly off his face, revealing sharp, handsome features and blonde bangs that fell in front of his eyes.

Jantzen and Peter were tied up and dragged in front of Ray. She wasn't sure how long it had been since she had knocked them both unconscious, but they were both awake now and looking around with terrified expressions.

Their eyes settled on Ray and Peter squealed. "H..how are you s..still alive?!"

Ray took a step towards him, and he squirmed in his bindings as if to run away. The ropes tying his wrists and his ankles were tight and he was helpless as he wriggled like a worm.

Another goblin approached with Lexi in tow. The catgirl was shuddering but when she saw Ray all of the tension left her shoulders and she relaxed.

Ray motioned towards Jantzen and Peter's helpless forms. There was a dangerous glint in her eyes and the corners of her mouth turned up in a sadistic grin. "I heard that if a person experiences an extremely traumatic death, the respawn usually fails and they become a mindless husk - a drone."

Lexi glanced at the two idiots then returned her attention to her friend, unsure where Ray was going with this.

Ray pulled a few blades out of her bag. She offered one of the daggers she'd confiscated from the idiot duo to the catgirl. "Ready to get started?"

Lexi gulped as she reached out to accept the weapon.

"What are you doing?!" Jantzen shouted, his blubbery face twisting with terror. He tried to push himself away from her, but he only ended up rolling onto his back, his ample mass spreading against the ground, securing him in place like a baby in its mother's loving embrace.

"Stop!" Peter shouted.

Ray felt his mana invaded her mind, but she thoroughly crushed it. She turned to observe him for a moment while deciding how to best go about creating a 'traumatic' experience. His nose was still flattened, and he was still missing some teeth. She took a step towards him and the warlock desperately tried to inch himself away from her approaching form like a caterpillar.

"N..n.nooo! Get away from me!"

Ray stalked closer to him. "Repulsive," she growled. "You call us 'monsters'. You treat others like trash and yet you call us 'monsters'? How does someone like you dare to mistreat others? When we fight back, you do nothing but cower and scream!" She reached down and picked up Peter by the neck. "You tried to cast domination magic on me. Obviously, it didn't work... but I cannot ignore the attempt."

She swung him like a sack of potatoes and smashed his legs against the ground. There was an audible *crunch* and his legs bent at odd angles.

The boy went silent for a moment, staring at the sight. His eyes widened and then he screamed.

She released her grip and allowed the monster to crumple to the floor. She then raised her sword, eyeing the creature with a dangerous glint in her eyes.

"W..what are you going to do to me?" Peter screeched. Tears streamed from his eyes and mixed with the bloody mucus pooling on his chin.

Ray giggled as she crouched down next to his agonized form.

"I'm just raising the stakes and gambling. We're going to make sure you have one hell of a traumatic experience."

She raised the sword and pointed it at Peter's hand.

Peter's screams of agony echoed in the cave and pierced Lexi's ears. Though the torture was slightly unpleasant to watch, the feeling was completely overpowered by the sense of satisfaction she felt in watching her former owners take their turn as victims.

Thanks to Ray, she had been freed. Thanks to Ray, she would finally be able to rid herself of her fears. Lexi felt her eyes tear up as her chest swelled with emotion.

The screaming stopped after a few minutes of intense, brutal torture. Ray moved away from Peter's now unrecognizable corpse. It would be more appropriate to call it a lump of poorly processed meat and bones.

Ray stopped in front of Lexi while licking the blood off her sword. "You want to do the other one?"

"Yes," Lexi replied confidently. Every horrible beating, vicious slur, and cruel mistreatment passed through her mind. She couldn't wait to show Jantzen just how humiliating and painful it was.

Ray grinned. "Better get to it then!"

"Yes! Oh gods, yes!" Lexi shouted as she leapt forward and threw her arms around her savior and friend. She didn't care that the young woman was covered in blood. She didn't care that her friend had just violently mutilated someone in front of her. She had seen much worse and wanted to do much worse to the people who had harmed her. It was a little unsettling, but she needed to get used to it.

Ray hugged her back and Lexi felt like her reality shifted back into place. Her life was finally on the right track again. If she stayed with Ray, she would get stronger and, one day, she would be able to get her revenge.

A faint weeping sound from the side reminded them of Jantzen's presence. Lexi met Ray's gaze.

Ray motioned towards the sword. "Shall we have some fun?"

Lexi raised the blade, her arm shaking. Phantom pains from a month of beatings and poor treatment flared across her back. She remembered when Jantzen forced her to eat her food off the floor because she was a 'dirty beast'. She remembered every single wrong Jantzen had committed against her.

Still, she hesitated.

Before she was enslaved, she had been a normal, teenage girl. She had never done anything like this before. Her arms trembled slightly as she held the sword with both hands.

The mind was willing, but the body was weak.

The weapon slipped from her sweating palms and Ray caught it in a smooth motion. She gripped Lexi's wrist firmly and placed the sword back into her palm. She gently closed Lexi's fingers around the hilt.

"I know you can do it. You know you want to do it."

Lexi smiled back weakly, taking strength from her savior and friend's support. "I do... I really want to..." she purred as she allowed Ray to pull her towards Jantzen's waddling form.

The fat priest was oozing tears and snot as he desperately tried to find a way to move his body.

Lexi pointed the sword at Jantzen. She was scared but her instincts were telling her to do as Ray said. She raised the sword in her trembling arms.

Jantzen cried out and she yelped, stumbling backward.

But Ray was there to catch her. Her friend leaned forward to whisper into her ear. "If it helps, you can close your eyes. I won't let anything happen to you."

Ray released her and took a step back.

Lexi nodded and positioned the sword over Jantzen's leg. She closed her eyes and folded her ears down to block out some of the sound. She took a deep breath, and, with a mighty roar, she stepped forward and struck down her fear and hesitation. She felt the tip of the blade jolt against bone and smiled bitterly. Adrenaline surged through her system, and she could feel her heart beating rhythmically.

To her surprise, she was calm.

She opened her eyes and saw the blood oozing out of the open wound. She heard Jantzen's wailing anguish and revealed a tranquil smile as she raised the sword to strike again.

The minutes passed by filled with violent, vengeful stabbing, swinging, and crushing. The air of the cave was permeated with the scent of blood and sweat, while wails of soulful torment rang out periodically.

Finally, Jantzen went silent. By the time he finally died, he was missing both eyes and all of his teeth. Every bone in his arms and legs were firmly shattered and a disturbing amount of his ample mass had been carved away. Both of his eyes had been entombed in his mouth from an early stage in the procedure and had long since been crushed until they were unrecognizable. Blood pooled over the floor of the cave.

Ray observed Lexi's bloodstained form, a faint smile tugging at the edge of her lips "I wonder if that was traumatic enough..." she mused.

Lexi fell to her knees, exhausted. The bloody sword clattered against the floor.

The two of them smiled at each other.

"Ahem," a voice interrupted.

Both flinched simultaneously. The goblins were still around. They were so focused on the torture that everything else blurred out.

"Well then," Og coughed out in Goblin. "I suppose we can conclude that you are not on the adventurer's side."

The other goblins all vehemently nodded in agreement.

There were five goblins in total.

"Let us pack up our stuff first. Then let's have a little chat," Ray suggested.

Og nodded his assent and she moved to collect her portable toilet and kitchen. She also collected all four of the enchanted bags. She would give one to Lexi, but she intended to return Helen and Ven's bags to their rightful owners. Neither of them had done anything to harm her.

Ray and Lexi entered their respective tents and took a moment to wipe themselves off and change into clean clothes. After collecting all the tents, supplies, armor, weapons, and enchanted bags, Ray approached Og. "You mentioned a shaman? Take us there and we can talk as we walk."

The goblin revealed a toothy, wistful smile. "How efficient. Let's do that."

Ray motioned for Lexi to follow. It was unlikely that Lexi understood Goblin, but she could translate the essential points for her.

They left the cave escorted by five goblins covered in black leather clothes. Ray noted the sun rising over the edge of the mountains and grinned as the cold, mountain wind scratched against her face and caused her hair to flutter behind her.

She giggled, remembering the tears and screams of the two idiots who had treated her poorly. She gave them multiple chances to avoid this fate. It was their fault for acting the way they did. Ray hummed quietly as she strode down the mountain path, following behind Og as he led her to an unknown destination.

It was finally time for her to meet some more 'monsters'.

23

Goblins

Watching Ray and Lexi's violent methods, I felt a bit queasy, which was quite an accomplishment considering that I didn't have a body. I despised those two creeps and I wanted to cheer at seeing them receive their just desserts... but considering my upbringing in twenty-second century America, I couldn't help but feel like they went overboard.

"Interesting."

I followed the sound of the voice, but as expected, I couldn't find Auto. "What's up?"

"Her performance was shocking. It is rare to find an individual so willing to commit violence. It is likely that she will become quite strong in the future."

"In the future? Isn't she strong now?"

"No, not really. She is strong compared to normal people but considering the road you will have to traverse; she is not yet strong."

Well, that was just *perfect*.

"I told her not to do this. If she's wrong and either of them respawn, things are going to get complicated. I don't want to face off with the other Overseers yet! I haven't even convinced her to work with me, let alone gained any other followers!"

"She was both right and wrong. It is true that those who experience traumatic deaths often fail to respawn. This is because the system requires a larger portion of the soul to restore them to a stable psychological state after reverting all of their physical injuries. It depends on how much of their soul was left."

I sighed. Now we would have to wait and see. It wasn't as if Ray had no options even if both respawned. It would just make things harder than they needed to be.

"Though her actions were nonsensical and fueled more by emotion than logic, I believe that the situation is not as bad as it might seem. I estimate that meeting some of her former students will prove to be fortuitous.".

Former students? Those goblins?

Maybe there would be some gains from this situation after all. I just didn't like that she took such a dangerous risk. It reminded me too much of my past self and I suffered for it. It was only after I became the leader of a team that I started being more careful.

Lives were lost when I made bad gambles, after all.

"However, I agree with the advice that you gave her. I am afraid that she is overestimating her power and her position. Her current attitude is foolish and, if left uncorrected, will lead to her destruction. Do not let naivety hold you back. You have already begun this process, but you must become her mentor in earnest. You must gain her trust before you can become her god. The more she continues to act like this, the more urgent your guidance will become. There are forces in this world that could erase her, true immortal or not."

"Any suggestions on what I should do next?" I asked as I returned my attention to Lexi as she finished tormenting the priest.

The catgirl was quivering slightly as she looked at the bloodstained dagger in her hands. Then she fell to her knees, clearly overcome with fatigue.

"Neither of you seems to have realized it yet, but she has already attracted a lot of attention from immensely powerful forces. I would suggest that you find a way to convince Ray to lie low while gathering followers in secret. You must build up your strength, not just hers."

'Immensely powerful forces?' I didn't notice anything like that, so it was a bit unnerving to hear that they were already moving around us. Was I not able to notice them because I was still weak?

"Hypothetically, if we started fighting the other Overseers right now, how outmatched are we?"

"You should cease that line of thought immediately. If the current Evelyn Raymond comes into serious conflict with any of the other current Tethers, she would not last five seconds in a fight."

"Even though she's so freakishly strong and fast?"

"Irrelevant. Victory in combat is not only determined by speed and physical strength. Both magic and experience are key elements to take into consideration. Additionally, each of the other Tethers has received many blessings from their respective Overseers that have increased their abilities well beyond the realm of humanity."

"So, Ray fighting a Tether is essentially a two-on-one fight then. I need to get stronger as well to turn it into a two versus two. I suppose that makes sense."

"She is decades of experience too young to be leading in the inevitable war that will start over this. It is your responsibility to prepare her as she will be leading your armies. Control your emotions and do not let her encounter..."

I started to laugh. "Relax, man. I mentioned it was hypothetical. I'm not stupid enough to send Ray charging after someone like that. I told you that I want her to stay hidden for a while longer, right?"

Auto sighed. "I apologize. Though conflict seems inevitable, I have found Ray to be an amusing specimen and was distraught at the thought of losing one of the rare sources of entertainment that I've found after such a long time."

"I know. I wish I could do more to help her, but I'm a bit limited right now until I start getting more followers. It sucks being stuck in a position where I can't do anything but talk to her."

"Even if you had a significant amount of holy power, you would often find yourself incapable of helping."

"What do you mean?" I asked, narrowing my eyes. If I had holy power, why wouldn't I be able to perform miracles?

"Consider your former world. You had dozens of powerful Overseers over thousands of years, and yet bad things still happened to their followers, right?"

"Right..."

It was one of the things that led me to believe that there were no gods.

"It's a mathematical problem. You gain power when you gain followers but unless you stockpile it, you never have enough power to help every one of your followers at the same time, outside of niche circumstances, of course."

Oh man, I wanted to strangle whoever designed this system. Why would they design a limitation like that?

"Those you call 'gods' are simultaneously the most beloved and despised existences. They leech their power from mortals, yet they must sometimes choose which mortals to save and which to abandon."

My vision tinted red, and my hazy form trembled with anger as I considered the implications of Auto's words. It wasn't much of a problem right now as I only had one semi-follower. There was little doubt in my mind that it would soon become two, though.

If I wanted enough power to help them, I would have to grow my religion and gain even more followers. That came with the risk of being put into a position where I would have to choose who to save.

"Screw that!" I growled. "So long as I have the power and ability, I will *never* abandon my followers! I'm not like the gods of Earth."

"Heh..hehe..heh!"

Auto's disjointed, robotic laugh was unnerving. "What's so funny?" I demanded, irritated.

"I admire your passion. I hope that you will be able to follow through on your convictions. I've seen too many choose that path and break."

I glanced at the screens. The options I currently had to utilize my power were very limited - all I could do was command and direct. But someday...

Someday there would be no doubt in the minds of my friends, followers, and enemies.

Someday, all would know that I was a god.

The five goblins were called Og, Trog, Urg, Jug, and Frog. Ray needed to meet more goblins to be sure, but there seemed to be a pattern in their names.

Each of the five goblins wore the same black leather outfit and had a few daggers strapped on various parts of their bodies, such as on their legs or their chest.

They all looked similar, but Ray's discerning eyes caught a few distinct features in addition to their different choices in weapons.

Og had a mole on his nose and was the only one who had daggers hanging from his belt. Trog had a goblin-sized, black two-handed mace strung across his back. Jug was missing his left ear and had a pair of shortswords. Urg carried a bow almost as big as he was, and Frog had no weapons and wore a strange hat that bore a remarkable resemblance to a toad. The adorable hat had little toad legs that hung down the sides of his head like tassels.

They walked in silence for several minutes. Neither group seemed to know how to start a conversation.

The silence was broken when Lexi sidled up next to Ray and tugged lightly on her shirt sleeve. "I'm a bit hungry..." she whispered.

Ray reached down to her belt and grabbed Jantzen's enchanted bag. She handed it to Lexi. "This is yours now. It should have some food in it."

Lexi stared at the bag reverently for a long moment. Her stomach growled, interrupting her moment of happiness. She pulled out some rations from the bag and unwrapped them. "Thanks!" She stepped back to eat her food quietly.

Og cleared his throat. "I believe both of us are in need of information about each other."

Ray nodded, looking around at the five goblins. All the goblins were shorter than her, coming up to about her chest in height. Their teeth were sharp, their eyes were crooked and mean, and their noses were long and bent.

They looked kind of cute.

"So," Ray started. "What's your tribe called?"

"Glitterfarts!" Frog declared proudly.

Ray coughed, attempting to mask her snicker. "Why are you called the Glitterfarts?"

Og and Urg shared a glance and smirked.

"I never thought we'd be able to get Master with this twice. Frog, you want to show her?" Urg asked.

"Sure!"

'Get Master with this twice'?

Ray watched curiously as Frog increased his pace until he was a few feet in front of the group. The toad-hat goblin bent his knees as if he were preparing to jump.

"You asked for it," Trog sighed.

She hesitated, her curiosity battling with a sense of foreboding as she noticed that Lexi had also backed away to a safe distance.

Frog reached for a previously unnoticed small flap in the back of his pants, released the catch, and then jumped backward.

Ray watched in surprise and confusion, unsure how to react as a green goblin butt flew towards her. There was a wet, tearing sound...

And then there was glitter *everywhere*.

She coughed and coughed, glitter flying as she tried to shake it out of her hair and clear her lungs simultaneously.

All five goblins burst into laughter. Frog and Urg rolled on the ground, hugging their ribs while tears streaming out of their eyes. Ray glared at each of the goblins in turn, focusing especially on those two.

Lexi snickered while nibbling on her salty rations.

It took Ray a minute to calm down and then the group started moving forward again.

"Was the adventurer group you were part of searching for us?" Urg asked.

Ray pulled out the Ax the Pony bounty paper she had already collected from Jantzen's bag. "There was a request in the

Adventurer's Guild in Cairel to kill some bandits. There was another team who took a request to hunt down goblins in the area though. I'm not sure if that was referring to you or not."

Urg took the paper and scanned it with a frown.

"Must have been some weak adventurers. Bronze-rank, maybe?" Trog observed.

"Not even bronze-rank," Ray snorted. "Officially, we're still in training."

"Good. If silvers were out here searching for us, we'd have to move again," Og grunted.

"Again?" Ray asked.

"The Rovarians are getting aggressive. By order of the King, the Adventurer's Guild keeps putting up bounties for goblin ears. We've been moving further and further east every time they find us," Urg answered.

"They've found us again. I told you we should have just continued on to the Federation," Jug said, looking at Og.

"I really don't want to go there," Og sighed. "No humans, sure, but they have different kinds of problems."

"I know you hate politics and the Slimelords, but there are no other options. It's them, the dwarves, or the vampires."

Og waved the problem away. "We'll talk about that with Shaman. For now, let's deal with what's in front of us."

"Who's Shaman?" Ray asked.

"Shaman is a spiritual leader to us goblins. She remembers the past, leads the present, and creates the future," Trog recited.

"So, she's a magic-user? What kind?"

"Yes."

The goblins didn't elaborate, seemingly unwilling to say more than that. She shrugged and decided to let it go for now.

A few minutes later, they moved past a small totem that sparkled as it reflected the sunlight. As Ray stared at it, she sneezed, and a small puff of glitter covered the ground in front of her.

Frog snickered and she glared at him.

Og noticed and revealed a toothy grin. "You did ask for a demonstration," he reminded her.

Ray ignored him and continued down the path. She heard laughter behind her and flushed, her cheeks turning crimson.

A few dozen yards past the totem, she saw a small, wooden palisade. It was barely half as tall as an average male human and looked extremely flimsy. A few goblins stood guard near a gateway.

They each wore ragged leather armor and carried shabby wooden spears. As the group approached, both goblins saluted Og.

He nodded in acknowledgment and then crossed through the gate into the goblin camp.

Ray and Lexi shared a glance before following him.

Upon entering, Ray could tell they were both thinking the same thing:

How the hell did Jantzen think his team could beat this?

There were goblins everywhere. The little green 'monsters' moved across the pathways between tents. Some were stopped and socializing while others fulfilled various tasks. One group of goblins was dragging a covered cart that smelled of fresh animal blood towards the center of camp. Other goblins were off to the side training in a field. Some used swords, others used spears or bows.

None of them wore metal armor like some humans did. All the goblins wore either leather or cloth that covered their legs and torso and a few wore bone ornaments around their wrists or as ear piercings.

What surprised Ray the most though was the sheer number of goblins. Just within her line of sight, she estimated that there were at least three hundred of them in the camp.

A small goblin, a child, noticed them and pointed. "New person!"

Dozens of heads turned in the direction of the group and Ray felt their curious eyes drilling into her. The sensation of all eyes focusing on her... it sent shivers through her body, but she smiled at the wave of nostalgia. She flicked her hair to the side and raised her chin as she strode forward with confidence.

Og and the other goblins guided them towards a large tent in the center of the camp. As they moved down the semi-narrow walkways, the crowd parted. By now, every goblin in the camp was staring at them and all chatter and work had paused. He sighed and turned to address the crowd. "Get back to work! We need the camp ready before sundown!"

With a jolt, the crowd began to disperse, and various conversations picked up once again. The group continued to move forward when they noticed a small group of fifteen goblins approaching.

"Damn it, it's Vorg," Trog groaned.

Og stepped forward to greet the approaching goblins.

"Og, you're back!" the leading goblin greeted.

"Vorg."

"You seem to have brought back guests. One wonders what gutter you found these ones in?"

"What do you want, Vorg?" Urg asked, "This is Glitter business. Take your Gobbers somewhere else."

"Oh?" A dangerous gleam flashed across Vorg's eyes. "Interesting." He turned and studied Ray. She met his gaze and stared down the creature. He gave off an unpleasant aura and she was certain that he was looking down on her.

That was not okay. Ray glared at him with as much animosity as she could muster.

Vorg blinked in surprise and the edge of his mouth tilted upward. "I am Vorg, envoy for the Gobber Goblins. Who are you?"

"I'm..." she started when Trog cut her off.

"None of your concern. Yet."

Vorg narrowed his eyes. "Yet?" After a moment of tense silence, Vorg raised an arm, signaling his fellow 'Gobbers' to back off. "You will give me the details at another time." He started to move away but then paused and smirked at Trog. "Oh, and I'm sorry to see that you're doing well." With a flourish, he bowed and then followed the other Gobbers.

Ray turned a questioning eye on Trog, and he grimaced.

"Vorg is my grandgobby," he explained. "He's mad that I switched sides."

"Switched sides in what?" Ray asked as the group started moving forward again.

"There are two political factions among goblins - Glitters and Gobbers. Trog was born a Gobber but switched sides four months ago," Jug explained. "The Glitterfart goblins actually got their name from our political stance, and we developed the technique later."

"What's the difference between the two factions?"

"Glitters embrace our heritage while Gobbers embrace the inner goblin."

"Heritage?"

The goblins went silent.

They reached the entrance of the tent and Og turned to look at Ray. "We can talk more about this later. Now, we need to speak with Shaman."

Ray nodded in agreement.

Og entered the tent. A few tense minutes later, he returned and ushered Ray and Lexi to enter.

The two stepped forward and pushed the flap aside to enter the tent. The interior was uncomfortably warm. Despite the midday hour, a small fire was lit in the center. On the far side of the fire, a rocking chair wobbled back and forth. Seated atop the chair was a wrinkled old goblin. Her hair was grey, her once-sharp teeth dulled and crooked and she had a gnarled staff in her right hand.

The old goblin waved the group forward. "Come, children!" she said in English. "Come and speak with Shaman."

Ray and Lexi stepped forward while Og stayed near the entrance. The rest of the goblins had remained outside. They stepped around the fire and approached the rocking throne.

Lexi kneeled and bowed her head to the venerable goblin. Ray started to copy the motion but something inside of her rejected it. She got the impression that 'no matter what', she must not bow. Since she disregarded her instincts and exploded herself when she encountered the karma squirrels, she decided to trust her instincts this time. Instead of bowing, she simply nodded her head in acknowledgment.

Shaman's eyes twinkled in amusement. "Young one, why do you not bow?"

"Should I bow?" Ray asked, the corners of her mouth rising in a sardonic smile. She couldn't quite explain it, but she felt like it was improper for her to bow here. Shaman laughed, which only furthered Ray's impression that she made the correct choice.

"Even if you do not, I know who you are. You are right that it would be inappropriate for you to bow to me."

Ray raised an eyebrow. "You know who I am?"

Shaman waved her question off. "Though your hair and one of your eyes have changed, you look otherwise identical to my dear Evelyn." She turned and addressed the catgirl. "Rise, meek one. I am honored by your presence."

Lexi rose and looked up at Shaman with nervous reverence.

"I admit, I am almost as intrigued as I am distressed to see my dear friend Evelyn's fate. To lose her now... these are dark times indeed. Do you know what the humans call this Age?"

Ray shook her head, but Shaman was looking at Lexi.

"Th...the Age of Peace," she replied.

"Right! The Age of Peace... for humans. For us, it is truly the Age of Fear and Death!" A hint of despair entered Shaman's voice as the simmering embers in her eyes dimmed.

"Ray, I think now might be a good time to use my existence as bait."

Ray shook her head slightly. *"I thought you didn't like my methods."*

"Rather than say I dislike your methods, I just wouldn't have taken the risk that you did. Perhaps that is a good thing though. We are different people which means that together we can accomplish a lot more."

"What do you want me to say?"

"Just catch her attention and then repeat after me."

Ray stepped forward. "Shaman, what do you think of this world?"

The old goblin studied Ray for a long moment as she pondered the question before answering. "This world is beautiful, but those who inhabit it are not."

"Are you referring to the humans?"

Shaman shook her head. "Humans are only a piece of the puzzle. Admittedly, they are a very large and central piece, but they cannot be blamed for every issue. Why do you ask?"

"What are your thoughts on 'gods'?"

Shaman snorted. "Which gods? The real ones or those fakes that the humans worship?"

'Real' gods? 'Fakes'?

Seeing Ray's confusion, Shaman started to explain. "Our world originally had five rulers. They organized this world and each of them is a creator and parent to one of the five immortal races. These are the 'real' gods. The Overseers and the humans appeared on this world at the exact same time 1595 years ago. The Overseers are usurpers. They are 'fake' gods."

Ray listened to the explanation with great interest. "Where are these 'real' gods now?" she asked.

Shaman sighed wistfully; her gaze was full of longing. "Nobody knows. Demestrix, the Fae Mother, disappeared while the humans and Overseers revealed themselves. She was the first. The other four rulers disappeared simultaneously about a hundred years after that, and they have made no public appearances ever since."

"'Public' appearances?"

"There was a designated representative for each of the immortal races that could speak to their parent. Until recently, there was still a surviving representative for the seraphs."

Shaman pointed at Ray. "Evelyn Raymond was the Monarch of Ages, the Bearer of the First Sin, and the Queen of Vampires. She was the First Daughter of Kraveloz and the last known person capable of speaking with a ruler."

Ray felt her heart beating faster and faster as Shaman recited her forgotten history.

"As you might imagine, Evelyn Raymond was the last hope of our world turning the tide against the false gods. I do not know what happened, but I am rather distressed to see the state that you are in now."

Ray bowed her head. It wasn't her fault that she had lost her memories and she couldn't exactly explain what Evelyn Raymond had been thinking when she performed the ritual. Her thoughts turned to the voice in her head. It was obsessed with animals and sometimes it seemed a little naggy, but he still wanted to help her, a monster.

It wasn't her fault that all the 'monsters' in the world collectively lost their only hope, but she could offer them an alternative.

"Shaman, if I could offer you a new possibility, would you be willing to hear me out?"

"If you could offer a possibility that I have not already considered and rejected, I would be most pleased. The centuries have not been kind to me, and I would like to leave this world knowing my children are moving towards a brighter future."

"What if there was a powerful entity who wanted to help us? A new god who rejects the ways of the invaders and persecutors?"

Shaman scoffed. "If such a being existed, why has he not shown himself until now?"

"He is a young god and was not a part of the events of the past. He did not fight against injustice because he did not yet exist. He desires to help the Glitterfart Goblins regain what they have lost."

Shaman's eyes dimmed. "What we have lost..." she repeated softly. "It seems this 'new god' has good eyes, though I suppose he could have heard it from another source."

The old goblin leaned back in her chair, lost in thought for several long minutes. The room was silent except for the occasional crackle from the firepit as the wood shifted and sparks, ashes, and embers scattered into the air.

Finally, she let out a troubled sigh. She pushed herself out of the chair and onto her feet, groaning faintly as her joints creaked and her bones ached. She leaned on her staff as she shuffled over to Ray and stared into her eyes.

"If we were to accept this 'new god', what would he ask of us?" Her tone was serious as her eyes studied Ray, searching for any signs of deceit.

Ray tilted her head for a moment as if listening to a voice.

Shaman took note of that and pursed her lips.

"He would like us to follow his teachings. He offers the same benefits that humans gain from their Overseers with similar conditions. He will write laws and commandments and, as we follow them, he will give us blessings, miracles, and power."

Shaman scratched her chin thoughtfully. "The same benefits, you say. Would that include their ability to resurrect nigh endlessly?"

"Of course."

Shaman turned to Lexi who was silently following the exchange with a confused expression.

"Meek one, I would hear your thoughts. Would you follow this 'new god'?"

Lexi met Shaman's gaze. "I would like to hear more about what this 'new god' has to offer. If his terms are bearable and the benefits are as great as he promises, then I would be more than willing to follow Ray."

Shaman examined the catgirl with a thoughtful expression. "So, it's not following this 'new god', but rather following her, is it?" The old goblin shuffled back over to her chair and carefully leaned back, plopping down onto the wooden seat. "I will ponder on this issue further. Know, however, that I am not the only one that you must convince. On paper, Glitter Goblins are as free to choose their own destiny as the humans let us be. In practice, however, I think you will discover that this is far from the truth. You may sojourn among us for a while. I recommend that you use the time to convince us that this 'new god' is worth following."

Ray let out a small chuckle. "If he can deliver on his promises, then I don't think that it will take very long."

Shaman shook her head. "The Gobber Goblins will almost certainly accept your proposal if you deliver it the same way you did to me. The Glitter Goblins are another matter. They hold to the traditional ways and worship only Demestrix."

Ray folded her arms and revealed a confident smile. "Challenge accepted."

Shaman nodded. She rapped her staff twice against the ground and Og faded out of the shadows, already kneeling in front of Shaman. "Og, take these two around and introduce them to those that she'll need to convince."

Og rose to his feet and then bowed. "Yes, oh venerable one."

They followed him outside the tent. Ray covered her eyes as the sunlight blinded her. As her eyes were adjusting, she bumped into Og who suddenly stopped walking.

"What is the meaning of this?" he muttered.

The camp was in chaos. The old, young, and other non-combatants were running away from the central area dominated by the large tent. A small group of fifteen... no, sixteen goblins surrounded the tent with weapons drawn. Three goblins stood between the sixteen goblins and the tent, spaced in an elongated triangle to cover all sides. They had their weapons drawn and were tense, ready to push back any who approached.

Ray recognized Vorg, the goblin who had approached them before. With a start, she noticed the goblin by his side and understood what had happened.

Og glanced back at her and saw the violent expression on her face. "What is it?"

She drew her sword out of her enchanted bag. As she observed the opponents who dared to threaten her, she revealed her fangs in a feral grin.

"Can I fight too?"

24

Another Way

"Absolutely not!"

Ray flinched in surprise. She had neither heard nor sensed the old goblin approaching, yet Shaman was suddenly right next to her. She lowered her sword, a bead of sweat forming on her brow as she felt an overwhelming pressure.

The old goblin was brimming with authority, her eyes a burning inferno as she stared Ray down.

"They have the tent surrounded with weapons drawn!" Ray protested.

"And what do you expect to do about it? Kill them all? Is that the solution that your 'new god' offers to problems?"

She glared at the old goblin. Her simmering bloodlust was palpable. She was confident that if she fought all of the goblins except Shaman, she could win. There were no problems. Ray was about to respond to Shaman but paused when when the voice in her head began to speak with a sharp, cold tone.

"What the hell do you think you're doing? You just offered them our religion. If you purge these attackers now, they'll see this as a 'crusade'. I will not create a religion that converts by the sword!"

"What about people that refuse to convert?" Her nostrils flared as her eyes roamed over the watching goblins.

"We will fight our enemies. But are these goblins our enemies? Or are they simply ignorant? This is a race of creatures that have been hunted as 'monsters' for over a thousand years! Remember that these goblins won't respawn. They will die if they are killed."

"Well?" Shaman demanded.

Ray hesitated, her mind filling with uncertainty. "I...I'm not sure..." she mumbled. In the few weeks since she had become 'Ray', she was faced with several difficult circumstances. Every time, she had been forced to make a choice and those choices led her to this point. This time she wasn't sure what the correct choice was. Her shoulders slumped and her bloodlust drained away.

Shaman stared at the dejected young woman for a moment and then donned a warm, kindly smile. She placed a gentle hand on Ray's shoulder. "Let me show you another way."

Her heart ached. A war was raging between her heart and her mind. She felt terrible and sad. She wanted to cry. She wanted to teach those goblins not to threaten her or her friend. She wanted to drink their blood and hear their agonized screams.

Amid her inner turmoil, she felt a comforting arm wrap around her. "Thanks, Lexi..." Ray whispered.

Her friend didn't respond. She didn't need to.

Ray's eyes focused on the crowd, and she felt a tinge of fear. Now that her head had cleared up a bit, she realized how badly outnumbered she was. Even with her regeneration, she would have to experience a lot of pain to win a fight against this many people.

And what about Lexi? Her friend wouldn't respawn if she died.

"Take a closer look at what's happening."

She carefully looked around. The sixteen goblins surrounding the tent were all armed. Vorg stood opposite the entrance flap, his eyes tilted up in a feral grin. He held a small, serrated dagger held out as he crouched, ready to pounce. Next to Vorg stood Jug with his twin swords held in his hands. Directly between the entrance and the group was Trog. Urg covered the back left side of the tent and Frog stood to the back right.

Her eyes settled on Shaman. The old goblin walked up beside Trog, her gait strong and confident - nothing like the struggled shambling she had shown inside of the tent. She raised her staff and rapped it against the ground. As if striking a hollow metal surface, the sound reverberated throughout the camp and drew all eyes to her. "What is the meaning of this?"

Vorg stepped forward. "I discovered that you were meeting with an immortal. I simply wished to take part in the meeting as a representative of the Gobber Goblins, but your assassin squad barred the path."

Shaman sighed. "Why did you draw your weapons? Who drew first?"

Trog grimaced. "It was my fault. I lost my temper and drew first," he admitted.

As Ray listened, she felt her heart sink. Because of a misunderstanding, she had almost jumped into a fight against people that simply wanted to speak with her!

"Don't worry about it. What matters is that you didn't do it. Nobody expects you to be perfect and I will always be here to help you. Let's build up a nice church full of good 'monsters' that can help you avoid any mistakes like this. You don't have to do this alone."

Ray felt a strange sensation as liquid rolled down her cheek. She reached up and touched it. Another drop formed at the edge of her eye and she realized what was happening. It was only the second time she had personally experienced it.

"Huh...?" she let out a gasp of surprise. She hadn't cried when her body was self-destructing. She did shed a single tear when she was being carried by the roc, but she hadn't cried since, even when she was being eaten alive. She hadn't cried when her head was cut off or when her heart got stabbed. She did cry a bit when she was helping Lexi back in Cairel, but that didn't count. Those emotions came from the old Evelyn Raymond, not her.

Crying was something that other people did. Now, it was something that Ray did as well. She couldn't explain why. It was like everything came crashing down on her in a single moment. The weight she was carrying suddenly seemed to be too much.

Lexi hugged Ray tighter, and Ray felt warmth fill her even as her frustration fled through her tears.

She wasn't alone.

All the goblins put their weapons away and Trog stepped back.

Vorg turned to look at Ray and then hesitated when he noticed her tears. "It seems that now is not a good time," he observed wryly. "I would speak with you when you have a moment." He signaled his Gobbers, and they backed off, moving towards another large tent that emitted the stench of food.

Shaman walked back over to Ray. "Violence doesn't solve everything. Simple misunderstandings and flared tempers can and should be resolved easily by figures of authority. If you walk this path that you are setting yourself on, you will lead many more than I do. You have much room to grow."

Ray nodded at Shaman's explanation. She wiped her tears on the sleeve of her robe.

"Og, take her to the training area and teach her how to let out her emotions the goblin way. When she is composed, introduce her officially to both Vorg and to the Glitter Court."

Og bowed and then motioned for Ray to follow him.

As they were leaving, Shaman grabbed Lexi by the arm and pulled her back towards the tent.

"Meek one, I would speak with you some more."

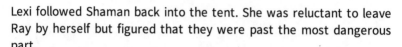

Lexi followed Shaman back into the tent. She was reluctant to leave Ray by herself but figured that they were past the most dangerous part.

She had only known Ray for a few weeks, but she knew that there were times when Ray became a little unstable. She didn't know all the reasons and she didn't care to ask. Ray was her savior and, more importantly, her friend. Lexi would respect and follow her until Ray didn't want her around anymore.

It was as simple as that. Ray had long since become her support.

"Meek one, the path of magic is difficult but rewarding. I can see that you have awakened your mana and are trying to study it. Your mana shows signs of frequent strain, yet it remains unrefined. Do you not have a proper teacher?"

Lexi shook her head, her shoulders trembling. "My tribe was destroyed before I could learn much. Ray rescued me but I am pretending to be a slave so that I can live with her in a human town. There is nobody to teach me properly."

"Hmm," Shaman pursed her lips. "You have a strong latent potential, but it will go unrealized if you tread without proper guidance. What magics do you seek to learn?"

"Enhancement and elemental magic," Lexi replied. "I also have an aptitude for holy magic but I'm not a human."

"What about your other aptitudes? Have you considered becoming an illusionist?"

Lexi stared at the old goblin with a confused expression. "I've never heard of that aptitude. Is it a branch of arcane magic?"

Shaman snorted. "Child, those things that you know of as 'aptitudes' refer to the magics that are known and understood by humans. Isn't it only natural that we, the original residents of this world, know more secrets of magic than they do?"

Lexi nodded hesitantly. It made sense logically.

"I am an illusionist," Shaman continued. "The closest human 'aptitude' to my magic would be a dominator warlock, but the medium, the operation, and the scale of the magic are all entirely different. I have been searching for many decades for one who has the ability to use illusion magic."

"Right…" Lexi responded, unsure where Shaman was going with this.

"Meek one, I feel that you have this capability. If you prefer the term, you might have an 'aptitude' for it. Your potential is simply astounding and given time, I believe you could surpass me."

Lexi's jaw dropped. The chain on her wrist rattled as she covered her mouth.

"If it is your desire to learn an art that no human or beastkin has ever touched, would you consider studying the art of illusions?"

Lexi purred with excitement. "Yes, of course I would!"

She started this morning with a satisfying revenge and now she was receiving the opportunity of a lifetime.

This was the best day ever!

"Hey Auto..."

"Yes?"

"What is a god?"

"Please provide context behind your inquiry."

I pointed at Ray's hunched form as she followed behind Og. "She is my Tether and my follower... and I am her god. I can feel her sadness and pain... and I can't do anything about it!" I took a moment to calm myself, then spoke again softly. "What is my purpose here? Why do Overseer's exist? Why did I become an Overseer?"

"I cannot answer."

"Cannot, or will not?"

"I cannot. I am not authorized to access data on the purpose of Overseers, and I do not know why you became one. They simply exist."

"I can't accept that. Who controls access to that data? It sounds like there is someone more powerful than Overseers running the show."

"Of course."

Seriously? You've got to be kidding me.

"What kind of entities could be greater than the gods?"

"Precursors. The entity known as 'Demestrix' that these goblins mentioned is one such being. There are currently four whole Precursors that reside on this world, as well as some fragments."

"Are any of those your boss?"

"Negative

I sighed. The more I learned about this world and the universe, the more curious I became about what else is out there and the more nervous I became about the future.

"At least gathering these goblins as followers shouldn't be too hard. I haven't used any holy power since I awakened, so I can probably use what I have to appear in front of them and do some magic tricks or something."

"Are you being serious?" Auto scoffed.

Huh?

"Wouldn't that work? The gods on Earth always did it the hard way. People are much more likely to believe in something they have seen, right?"

"Did you stop for a moment to consider that there might have been a reason *why* the Overseers of Earth rarely performed personal manifestations?"

Well, not really. I assumed that they were just being lazy.

"Haven't you wondered why your holy power isn't increasing despite Ray's knowledge of you?"

"Ah! Now that you mention it, that's true! It didn't even occur to me since I hadn't been thinking of Ray as a true follower."

"There is a difference between 'faith' and 'knowledge'. Faith is believing in things that you do not have a perfect knowledge of being true. They may have signs and reasons to believe but if they saw you directly or had a conversation with you, if they in any way gained an absolute, sure knowledge that you definitely exist, then you would no longer be able to harvest faith from that individual."

"Seriously?"

"Additionally, you cannot perform miracles without faith. Your holy power bar is charged by the faith of your followers. This is manifested in them following your tenets and by them beseeching you for aid." Auto paused, letting the full meaning of that statement sink in.

I frowned as Auto finished the explanation.

"A full-physical manifestation is a miracle as well. The amount of faith that must be present would be astronomical. There are ways that you can get around this but in general you should assume that you can only physically manifest yourself in areas where many followers are gathered. In so doing, you must be prepared to lose the ability to gather 'faith' from those individuals permanently."

Okay, so manifestations were a last resort. Damn it.

"So, I need to come up with a real way to convince the goblins that I exist and am worth following…"

"Good luck!"

25

The Glitter Court

Ray smashed her enhanced fist into the crumbling stone block. The already cracked and splintered surface shattered in a cascade of dust and rock. She stood amidst the range of shattered pillars, breathing deeply to catch her breath. Once she recovered, she dusted off her clothes and walked away.

Smashing things did wonders for her emotions. The sadness and anger already felt like distant memories. All that remained was a faint sense of embarrassment for shedding exactly five and a half tears.

She counted.

It was all thanks to Og's instruction on the 'goblin way' of dealing with emotions:

Breaking stuff until you feel better.

Technically, that was the Gobber Goblin method. Glitter Goblins played tricks on people and cracked jokes. Wisely, Og had recommended the more violent of the two options to her.

The magic users who were maintaining the field collapsed, exhausted. They had been desperately raising targets for her to smash. Once she got into a rhythm, it took four of them using everything they had to keep up with the rate at which she shattered the pillars.

Og noticed that Ray had stopped and approached her. "You worked it all out?"

Ray nodded sheepishly. "I feel a hundred times better."

"I've seen people go at it with zeal before, but I can't say I've seen many approach it with the same fervor that you did."

Ray snorted but otherwise chose not to respond.

"If you are ready, would you like to meet with Vorg or the Glitter Court first?" he asked.

She looked down at her disheveled dusty outfit. "I think I'll get cleaned up first. Then I'll see the Glitter Court, and after that I'll talk to

Vorg."

"Sounds good. I will let the Court know that you are coming. They will need about thirty minutes to assemble."

"Sweet. Where should I meet you when I'm ready?"

Og pointed at a small, fenced off area near the back end of the camp. "The Court meets there. Head over when you are cleaned up."

Ray nodded and reached for her enchanted bag, pulling out a tent, a rag, and a container full of water.

Half an hour later, Ray stood facing the Glitter Court, a group of five old goblins sitting in a semicircle around her. After cleaning up, she had donned a pair of dark, tight-fitted pants that stopped just below her knees and a comfortable, lacey shirt woven from bluish-grey fabric.

The old goblins of the Glitter Court wore matching outfits. Each of them wore a long, white robe that sparkled as if glitter was woven throughout. All of them had greyish-white, spindly beards.

Off to the side, Shaman, Vorg and Lexi sat as spectators. Og stood behind Ray as a form of translator. Though she understood the language, she didn't understand the culture or the flow of the proceedings.

"Kneel," Og hissed.

Ray hesitated. Like before, something within her violently rejected the idea. The idea of kneeling to someone else made her feel sick. She fought the feeling and forced herself down onto one knee. A wave of nausea filled her, and a sharp pain resonated within her head. The nausea was followed by rage and Ray struggled to push it back.

"You may rise," the goblin in the center droned.

She shot to her feet and the feelings of disgust evaporated. The lingering feelings from Evelyn Raymond were powerful, and they were frustrating to deal with because she couldn't understand their source. She wished the memories would just go away entirely if they didn't want to come back.

"Ray, Envoy of the 'New God', desires to share a message with the Glitter Court!" Og introduced.

The furthest goblin on the right raised his hand. "Why do we entertain a servant of the enemy?" he growled.

"Flynn, now is not the time for hostilities," the goblin in the center replied.

Flynn threw his arms up in disdain, but the other goblins shot him warning looks and he refrained from further response.

The center goblin motioned towards the goblin on the far right. "We shall introduce ourselves in accordance with the traditions of the ancients."

The rightmost goblin nodded, stood in place, and introduced himself. The goblin to his right, and then each goblin, in turn, also stood and introduced themselves.

"I am Tyrion, Lord of Commerce."

"Cosmo, Lord of the Hunt."

"Oberon, Lord of the Court."

"Cedric, the Martial Lord."

"Flynn, Secretary"

As Flynn retook his seat, Oberon resumed speaking. "We will hear your message, but that is all that we will promise for now."

"You may speak now," Og whispered to Ray.

Ray observed the five leaders for a moment. She ran a hand through her hair as she considered what to say first.

"Just repeat after me."

"Sure." If there was ever a time to rely on this 'New God', it was now. She started to relay the message he spoke into her mind, word for word.

"Honored Lords and Secretary," she began. "I am Ray. I bring a message from a new god who desires salvation for all those whom humans have termed 'monsters'."

"And what is this message?" Flynn demanded.

"This new god asks for your cooperation."

"What does he promise in return?" Tyrion asked.

"He is a new god and does not yet have much power. As he grows in power, he will use it to help his followers. As of right now, all he can promise is access to the 'respawn' system."

"Respawn?" Cedric said, leaning forward. "That's the system that resurrects the humans, no?"

"That is correct," Ray replied with a nod.

Cedric laughed incredulously. "That is amazing! You promise us immortality for merely agreeing to cooperate with a lesser god?"

Ray frowned. That didn't quite feel right... "Though he is not yet powerful, he promises that he will not be 'lesser' to any of the other Overseers."

Cosmo shook his head. "We do not refer to the Overseers with our comment. To us, they are also lesser gods. A greater god would be one of the rulers. You are a descendent of Kraveloz, no? Do you not worship your father?"

Ray shrugged and answered honestly. "I have no memory of such a being."

""..."" The goblins all froze.

"Hey, don't go off script!"

"We have been informed of your circumstances, but it is still difficult to believe that you, of all people, would reject your own creator..." Tyrion muttered in disbelief.

"I cannot reject him because I do not know him," Ray replied calmly. "I will make my judgment if he ever reveals himself to me."

"You're going to make them mad. Just listen to me..."

Oberon shook his head. "You do not understand. As is said in the records, never before has any individual from any of the origin races spoken against their creator."

Ray hissed in frustration. "Why are you so fixated on that? I am not Evelyn Raymond and I know nothing of the 'origin' races!"

The Court went silent.

"Now you've done it..."

"Shut up!" she thought back.

Shaman shook her head and covered her face with her palm. Lexi's eyes widened at the mention of a name that anybody would recognize, but she didn't understand Goblin, so she just looked back and forth without comprehending anything.

"She truly is no longer the First Daughter..." Tyrion sighed.

"My name is Ray," she replied firmly.

After a long, drawn-out silence, Cedric finally spoke.

"You do not seem to fully understand the significance of your position. Evelyn Raymond was known as the Monarch of Ages, though it was a symbolic title. Our Queen is declaring that she has abandoned our creators and is following an invader."

Ray was starting to feel like she messed up, though she wasn't sure where the conversation had gotten derailed. "It wasn't my fault! I didn't choose any of this!"

"That doesn't matter," Oberon retorted. "The idea that an individual bearing the name Evelyn Raymond does not serve Kraveloz, let alone any ruler, is tantamount to heresy!"

Ray clenched her fists as she fought down her urge to lash out. "I do not know of your ways, and I do not know your history," she started. "But where is this Kraveloz now? Where is this Demestrix? Humans have been dominating you for over a thousand years. If the Overseers are lesser, why are they still here? Why did the rulers abandon you?"

Cedric stomped to his feet. The ground shook and the chair behind him flew away. The blast of wind caused Ray to stumble backward and the tremors in the ground made it difficult to regain her balance. None of the other goblin leaders seemed affected by the display.

"Do not speak ill of the Great Mother!" Cedric roared. "You may blaspheme your own creator if you will, but I will slay you if you say another word against ours."

Ray trembled slightly as an overwhelming pressure tried to slam her into the ground. She met Cedric's enraged eyes with a defiant glare.

"Ray, please calm down and let me help you defuse this situation!"

She sighed. *"Sure."* She began to repeat the words that he put into her mind.

"I apologize if I have slandered Demestrix," she recited in a monotone voice. "I merely want you to consider that a new god can help you while you continue to search for her."

Cedric took a step forward, reaching for his sword.

"Stop." Oberon commanded calmly.

Cedric glanced back at him, and the overwhelming presence faded. He bowed towards Oberon and then returned to his position. Urg stepped out of a shadow and offered a new chair to the Martial Lord. He accepted it and sat down while Urg stepped back into the shadows, disappearing once more.

"We have heard your message," Oberon said. "We ask for ten days to allow us to deliberate amongst ourselves."

Ray nodded. "Take however long you will. I would like to give you a peace offering before I leave. I hope you take this into consideration during your deliberations."

"Oh?" Oberon raised an eyebrow, intrigued. "And what might this offering be?"

She cleared her throat. "It is information. There is a standing quest in Cairel, the nearby human fortress, to kill the goblins here. The adventurers know you are here. I don't know if they have found this village yet, but they know that there are goblins nearby."

She left the rest unsaid. The elders of the Glitter Court would understand the implication of her warning:

In the coming days, they just might have to choose between their loyalty and their lives.

Ray waited patiently near the training area with Og. Shaman and Vorg had stayed back to converse with the Glitter Court. After they were done, Vorg would come over here and speak with her.

Ray pulled out her shortsword that had been used to traumatize Jantzen and Peter. She also withdrew a whetstone, a rag, some oil, and some water. Using the methods Siegfried had taught her, she began to clean and sharpen the blade.

Og raised an eyebrow when he saw her maintaining her weapon, but he didn't comment.

As Ray finished her task, she looked around at the goblins in the training area. Everything was much the same as when she had first entered the camp and a question sprung into her mind.

"Why do none of the goblins wear metal armor?" she asked. "And not all of them have metal weapons either."

"We have been hunted for over a thousand years, never staying in one place for long. We have little to no trade with other races. It is rather difficult for us to obtain metal," Og explained.

Ray nodded in understanding. "So how did you obtain most of what you currently have?"

Og smiled as he motioned towards the training goblins. "That stuff mostly came from dead adventurers." Then he placed his hands reverently on the daggers he had hanging from his belt. "These ones were a gift from Master Evelyn."

'Master' Evelyn.

"I'm sorry that I'm not your Master. You seem to have liked her very much."

Og grunted but didn't respond.

Ray watched him for a moment as he stared at the daggers silently, seemingly lost in thought.

Finally, he spoke with a slightly husky voice. "Ah... I guess I miss her more than I thought I would. Since she was immortal, I always assumed that I would see her again... but fate is not so kind it seems." Og stood up and stretched his back with a low groan.

Ray followed suit, rolling her shoulders to work a kink out of her back.

"Evelyn Raymond found our camp a few years back. She stayed with us for a few months before moving on. During that time, she rigorously trained the five of us that are now referred to as assassins."

She tried to summon the relevant memories but, like always, they eluded her.

"She was a heartless master. She would beat us half to death and then drench us in healing potion," Og recalled, his voice full of nostalgia.

After that, they sat in silence. It was only broken when they heard shuffling steps and looked up to see Vorg approaching.

Vorg smiled as he stopped in front of them. "To think, the Monarch of Ages herself has once again graced us with her presence!"

Ray grimaced slightly. "You know that I'm not Evelyn Raymond."

"I know. However, the reputation of that body you are inhabiting will precede you until you overshadow it yourself."

Ray groaned.

Vorg's smile widened as he observed her discontent. He snapped his fingers and a stone chair rose out out the dirt across from Ray. He leaned back into the chair. "I will be quick and blunt in my statements," he started. "The Gobber Goblins are interested in the offer you presented to the Glitter Court."

Ray leaned forward in shock. "Wait, what?"

"The Gobber Goblins are interested in working with this new god."

Ray's mind reeled as she realized exactly what he was saying. "Why?" she blurted out.

Vorg laughed. "Why not?" he countered.

"The Glitter Goblins are hesitating. What makes the Gobber Goblins different?" Ray asked.

"The Glitter Goblins hesitate because they cling to the old ways. They expend all of their effort and worship for a greater god who disappeared over a thousand years ago. We Gobber Goblins have embraced our new form and moved on."

"New form?"

Vorg waved the question off. "It is old history and no longer important. The past is the past and we need to look to the future."

"So why do the Gobber Goblins want to follow the new god then?" Ray asked.

"It's the only logical decision," Vorg replied. "The Glitter Goblins know this and hesitate because it would require them to change their entire purpose. On the other hand, following this new god aligns perfectly with our purpose. There is no future fighting against humans as we are. It may take another thousand years but, eventually, all of the races labeled as 'monsters' will be overrun."

Ray nodded in understanding. "I can accept that."

"And so, we would like you to share the 'teachings' of your new god. We need miracles on our side."

"You hear that?"

"Yeah," the voice replied. *"I heard. Ask them if they would be willing to undergo a ritual to become one of my followers?"*

"He wants to know if you would be willing to undergo a ritual to become a follower. Every person who undergoes this ritual will increase his power."

Vorg shrugged. "If you give us some more details, I don't see why not."

26

Initiation

My voice trembled with barely concealed excitement.

"Auto, what kind of ritual do they have to undergo to become followers?"

"That is entirely your choice," the robo-voice responded. "There are only a few restrictions."

"What are they?"

"The ritual must be virtually impossible to accomplish by mistake. Also, the ritual must be performed by a sanctioned member of your religion. Currently, Ray is the only person who can perform the ritual. Later, the individuals you call as priests, paladins, monks, and templars will also be able to do so. The details of the initiation ritual should be listed as your first tenet."

I thought back to some of the rituals I was aware of on Earth. The most famous ones where I was from were probably 'baptism' and 'circumcision'.

As for baptism, some churches did it by sprinkling water and saying a prayer while others required full immersion in water in addition to a prayer.

Things that didn't happen by mistake.

Circumcision... well, one can only hope that something like that doesn't happen by mistake.

Putting baptism aside for its symbolic value, I decided to put a hard pass on circumcision. If I chose something like that, I imagined it would be much harder to find converts.

'All you have to do to join is get a circumcision!'

'What's that?'

'Well, you see... you just need to get this little surgery...'

Yup, circumcision would not be a religious requirement or initiation here. People could do that if they wanted to, but I would choose something else for my 'initiation' ritual.

What kind of criteria did I need to consider?

Acknowledging that my followers would be facilitating or performing this ritual, it should be something that isn't too difficult or embarrassing. Ideally, it would have some symbolic significance. Finally, it needed to be difficult to do by accident.

The third point could be easily accomplished by adding a 'prayer' component. The difficult part would be coming up with something symbolic. Baptism was generally held to be symbolic of 'rebirth'. It was starting a new life of religious devotion to God. I didn't really want to copy 'baptism' from Earth, though, so I needed to come up with something of my own.

What kind of church would I create? Remembering the types of religious people I met back on Earth, I preferred to stay away from crazy people who had enormous zeal and fervor about living a new life. I wasn't trying to revolutionize the way of life of monsters, I just wanted people in this world to treat each other fairly. I wanted all the various races to get along without persecuting each other.

So maybe adapting the idea of baptism, but changing the contents to symbolize a new concept? Instead of beginning a new life, they would be receiving a new hope and covenanting into a new peace.

I tossed a few ideas around before settling on something that I liked.

Once all the details were ironed out, I called out to Ray. "Let's do it!"

While she was sitting alone in a grove just outside the camp, Lexi pondered on the fragmented information she had. It was clear that Ray somehow represented a god, likely one of the Overseers. She wasn't sure how she felt about that.

The Overseers were the reason her tribe was called monsters. The adventurers who massacred her people were evil, but the gods behind them were the real monsters. They had absolute power and authority and they used it to play with lives and lead people to destruction and sorrow. Even if they changed their mind and repented, she didn't think she could ever forgive them.

Her ears perked as she heard someone approach and she opened her eyes to see Ray arrive.

"Hey," Ray muttered as she sat down next to her and pulled her knees up against her chest.

Lexi examined her savior in silence for a long minute. In all the time she had known her, Ray acted like she was strong, powerful, and in control. There were times when she saw cracks in the façade, but she was always able to push through.

Now, she just looked tired.

"Busy day," Lexi observed, breaking the silence.

Ray didn't respond and the two of them sat in silence for a while longer, enjoying the feeling of the cool, mountain breeze. Though spring was around the corner, it was still chilly in the mountains.

"I have something I want to ask you," Ray finally said.

Lexi turned and gave her full attention to her friend.

"The new god that I was talking about earlier... he told me that he wants you specifically to be the first person to receive the ritual to become his follower."

The new god said what now?

"He says that he heard your prayer - the one asking for strength. He desires to give you peace if you would be willing to give him a chance."

Lexi closed her eyes, tears welling up in the corners.

A new god. Not one of the evil Overseers, but a new, brilliant, and kind god. One who knew her name and her deepest desires. A god who heard her prayers and wanted to answer them!

She didn't want to open her eyes. What if this was just a dream? What if she opened her eyes and found out this wasn't real?

The tears began to spill out through her closed eyelids. She let out a stuttered breath as her chest swelled with emotion. She didn't know what to say. Never in her wildest dreams did she think someone was listening.

She had prayed out of hope, but she knew in her heart that there were no gods for the beastkin.

Except somebody was there. Somebody was listening.

There was a god who wanted to answer her prayers.

As Lexi tried to sort through her thoughts and feelings, she kept coming back to that one, singular point.

He would answer her prayers.

If it were one of the other Overseers, she wouldn't even consider it. But if a new, innocent god was making the promise, she would have to be a fool to not give him a chance.

She raised her head and opened her eyes with renewed determination. She met Ray's questioning gaze and beamed. "What do I need to do?

"We wait for Mr. Animal-Obsessed Dark Void to finish coming up with the initiation ritual."

Lexi tilted her head in confusion. "That's… an interesting name."

Ray giggled while Lexi looked on with concern.

They sat together for several more minutes, enjoying the peaceful quiet while they waited. Finally, the god called out to Ray.

"He's ready," Ray informed Lexi. The two of them pushed themselves to their feet, brushing off the snow and mud that clung to their pants. They walked back into the village and Ray called out to Vorg, who was waiting off to the side with another goblin.

She said something to him in a weirdly fluid language. Lexi didn't know any Goblin, so she watched their body language for clues. She recognized Vorg and Og because of their interactions with Ray, but she hadn't spoken to any of them yet due to the language barrier. Were they not going to explain anything to her? Was she supposed to just follow blindly and hope for the best?

Og said something back to Ray, and then Vorg asked a question.

Ray abruptly looked over at Lexi. "You don't understand Goblin, do you?"

Lexi shook her head ruefully. "I'm okay at Orcish though," she replied.

Unfortunately, the only two languages she needed to learn were English and Orcish. It was enough to speak both common tongues.

Ray asked the goblins another question and then shook her head regretfully. "You'll be able to use Orcish to communicate with Gobbers, but the Glitters refuse to learn anything except Goblin or Ancient."

Lexi let out a regretful sigh. "How many of the goblins are 'Gobbers'?"

Surprisingly, it was Vorg who answered the question. "We are small in number," he answered.

"You speak English?!" Lexi blurted out.

Vorg shook his head. "I do not 'speak' English, I can speech. It is hard language to learn when speakers try kill you."

His English wasn't perfect, but it was more than enough to understand.

"Anyways," Ray interrupted. "If it's alright, I will explain in English so that Lexi can understand, and I will explain it again in Goblin so that the goblins know what they are getting into."

Lexi nodded gratefully. She had been starting to worry that she would be in the dark through the whole process, but she should have had more faith in Ray.

"Explain," Vorg agreed.

Ray raised a finger, pausing them as she tilted her head to the side. She scrunched her eyebrows.

"He says that I need to be the one who performs the ritual, because I am his prophet and inherently have the authority. After they are initiated, if they accept positions of responsibility, he will grant this authority to others."

After repeating the same message in their language, the goblins nodded.

"He says that each person must present a weapon to me. I will then say a prayer, split the weapon in half, bury one side in a field of white poppies, and then return the other half to you as a symbol and memento of your promise."

"White poppies?" Lexi asked. "Do those grow around here?"

"He says the white poppies are optional, but he thought it would enhance the symbolism if we added them whenever possible."

The two goblins both nodded and then Vorg asked a question that Ray translated. "Seeing as he is asking us to break 'weapons' specifically, I suppose there is some sort of meaning in this ritual?"

"He is not asking you to forsake your weapons, he is asking you to give one up as a symbol of your promise. Following him is a declaration that you will pursue peace. He understands that fighting is necessary at times, but his ultimate goal is a world where every race can live together in harmony."

Vorg commented something and nodded. Then he pulled an old, bone dagger out of the sheathe hanging from his belt. He raised it up and asked another question.

"An old weapon is fine. It just can't already be broken, and it should preferably be yours, or one that you can keep after it is broken," Ray replied.

Og withdrew one of the daggers strapped to his leg. Ray turned to Lexi and pulled out a dagger. Lexi recognized it as the weapon Jantzen used to stab Ray through the heart. Ray held it out to her, and she accepted it.

"Lexi, upon completion of your initiation, our god would like to bestow upon you the privileges and responsibilities of being a priestess. Will you accept this burden?"

"A priestess?" Lexi's eyes grew impossibly wider. She knew she had an aptitude for holy magic, but she had long since accepted that she would never be able to use it. "I will gladly accept!" she replied, her eyes shining.

They moved back out through the gate and into the small grove. Ray stood in the center of the grove and called Lexi forward.

"Leximea Bloodclaw."

Lexi approached and kneeled before her. She presented the dagger reverently, her head bowed. Ray reached out and took the dagger with her right hand. She raised it up for all to see.

"By the power and authority granted unto me, I accept your vow in the name of the 'New God'. Henceforth, you shall be a priestess and a guide unto your brothers and sisters. You shall be a light and a strength to those who seek peace. He will watch over you and give you the strength to accomplish your desires. Remember your covenant for as long as you live."

Reaching up with her left hand, Ray firmly grabbed the blade and snapped it off at the hilt. She returned the hilt to Lexi, who accepted it with shaking hands. Kneeling, Ray dug her hand into the ground with a smooth motion. She shifted the frozen mud out of the way and placed the blade of the dagger into the small hole before replacing the mud.

Lexi shuddered as she felt an overwhelming, warm sensation encompass her body. Peace and joy filled her soul and warm tears streamed from her eyes.

Ray reached out and hugged her. "Now that you are a priest, he says we need to set a precedent. I need you to initiate me as well," Ray whispered.

Lexi nodded to show her acceptance.

Ray pulled out Peter's dagger and applied pressure at the hilt, bending the blade until there was a visible crack near the hilt. She kneeled and held the blade out for Lexi.

The new priestess accepted the dagger with shaking hands.

"Call out her name," a masculine voice spoke in her head.

Lexi yelped and took a step back in shock.

"Call out her name," the voice repeated.

"R..Ray!" Lexi blurted out.

"Now repeat after me. By the power..."

"By the power and authority granted unto me, I accept your vow in the name of the New God. Henceforth and forever, you shall be a prophet and a guide unto your brothers and sisters. You shall be the light in the darkness and the living symbol of Him. You will become great and mighty as you raise up your brothers and sisters. He will always be watching over you. This is the covenant between Him and you that should always be remembered."

Lexi grabbed the blade at the bend and applied as much force as she could. The blade slowly bent further. After several seconds of applying pressure, it snapped. Lexi returned the hilt to Ray and kneeled, digging her hands into the dirt. She buried the blade of the dagger next to hers while smiling.

Ray rose to her feet and turned to the watching goblins who had uncertain expressions. Lexi mirrored her motion and flushed as she thought about what just happened. To those experiencing the ritual, it felt holy and sacred. To those watching it, she imagined that it looked incredibly awkward and silly.

Still, she had to do her part, no matter how embarrassing it was. She waited for Ray to call out a name. She would baptize the other goblin.

"Vorg," Ray motioned for the Gobber Goblin to approach her.

"Og," Lexi called out, waving him over to her.

Since they were not being initiated into the priesthood, both of their prayers were identical.

"By the power and authority granted unto me, I accept your vow in the name of the New God. Remember this covenant for as long as you live."

After both of their weapons were broken, with the hilts returned and the blades buried, the two of them rose.

Vorg said something and Og nodded in agreement

"That is the sensation you will feel whenever the New God has answered your prayers," Ray explained, once in each language. "Since none of you are Tethers, you will not likely hear his voice directly. If you ask him for advice and learn to interpret that feeling, he can do his best to help you make decisions."

Vorg whistled in appreciation and started chattering with Og.

Lexi raised her hand hesitantly. "That voice that spoke in my head... was that him?"

"Voice?" Ray paused for a moment, then shook her head. "That was sort of him, but also not him at the same time. It was his voice, but he could only speak fixed phrases that he determined beforehand. The prayer I used for you will be used for all who are ordained to the priesthood. If another prophet is chosen in the future, the prayer you used for me is the same one that will be used at that time."

"I see," Lexi replied, disappointed. She wanted to talk directly with him, but it seemed to be impossible for now. She would have to make do with praying and interpreting the warm feeling that she received when he responded.

Og and Vorg exchanged glances. "What we do now?" Vorg asked in broken English while looking at Ray.

Ray tilted her head, listening to the voice. "He says that I need to return to Cairel tomorrow to avoid raising suspicion amongst the humans. He will prepare a basic set of teachings and next time I am able to visit, we will deliver them."

Vorg nodded in acceptance.

"Is there anything he needs us to do in the meantime?" Lexi asked.

"See if you can convince other goblins to give him a chance. Since Lexi is studying magic under Shaman, he suggests that she should stay here and study while I return. She will be able to initiate any goblins who decide to join."

Lexi, Og, and Vorg all bowed their heads.

"We do our best," Vorg promised. "I hope god is good."

The two goblins turned to walk back into the town when Ray seemed to realize something. She called out to stop them and said something. Og started to laugh, while Vorg smiled and waved.

Ray turned back, the smile dropping off her face as she sauntered back over to the tree to sit down. "By the gods, it's finally over...!" she groaned.

"What did you say at the end there?" Lexi asked while following her.

Her new prophet let out a tired sigh. "'Even though you can respawn now, do your best not to die until we figure out the whole 'temple' situation. It would be a little difficult if goblins started respawning inside of Cairel,'" she recited.

"That's an oddly specific problem to think of right now," Lexi pointed out.

"I know," Ray muttered softly in reply. Her eyelids fluttered as she let out a yawn.

"Is it a warning from Legion? Like a prophecy?"

Ray shook her head and leaned back until she was resting comfortably. "He says he's just being cautious. 'Death is sudden, and you never know it's coming for you until it's too late.'"

Lexi felt chills roll down her spine at the ominous words. At the same time, she agreed one hundred percent. She never expected her whole tribe to be destroyed in a handful of days. In this world of humans, one could never predict when their life would end.

As Ray drifted off to sleep, Lexi stared up at the endless expanse of the heavens. Something was a little different this time. Despite the cold mountain breeze, the sky looked warm and inviting. The endless darkness beyond the horizon seemed filled with light. It only took her a few seconds to figure out what the difference was.

Somewhere out there, her god was watching over her.

As each person was initiated, it felt like a light turned on inside my head. I felt a connection form between me and the individual. If I focused on that connection, I could read their thoughts and emotions. I knew that gods obtained information about their followers, but this was far more than I expected from anybody other than Ray.

Focusing on Lexi, I could keenly feel how pleased she was to be chosen by me as my first follower and as a priestess. That was also how I found out about her learning to become an illusionist from Shaman.

Ray's initiation was technically a formality, but it was still important. I wanted to suppress disagreements that would inevitably appear down the line when people started debating technicalities in the details of the teachings. Because Ray, the first prophet, 'had' to be initiated, all followers must be initiated. The precedent was important, even if the details were fudged a little bit.

When Vorg and Og were each initiated, I peeked into their minds, curious about their motivations. Vorg had given good reasons for his decision beforehand, but Og had chosen to keep quiet.

Vorg was feeling... apprehensive. He had a bit of anxiety. Peeking into his thoughts revealed that he was desperate. He was clinging onto his last lifeline. He had chosen to embrace this chance because he genuinely believed that it was the only hope of the goblin race. But he was also scared. I was an unknown entity and even after being initiated, I still didn't reveal what my 'teachings' were. He was nervous that the teachings of the New God would be harmful.

A very sensical mindset, albeit tending towards the pessimistic side.

Og, on the other hand, had a remarkably simple motivation.

He worshipped Evelyn Raymond. He knew that Ray was a different person, but he believed that by following Ray and staying by her side he would one day meet the real Evelyn Raymond again.

I couldn't say whether that was true or not, but I had to tip my nonexistent hat off at his optimism.

Ray would return to Cairel in the morning. Before we returned here again, I needed to create at least some basic teachings and tenets that would define my religion.

I already found my end goal. I wanted to create a world where all the races could live together in harmony without persecution. I knew that this was not very practical. However, I recently started to realize that religion was never about being at the ideal it strives for. Religions were always about the process of reaching for that ideal. If the purpose that a religion strived for were easy to reach, then there would be no point in building a religion to focus on it.

Harmony. Like each of the other Overseers, I decided to pick three domains and harmony would be my first.

I started shooting some ideas back and forth with myself, playing with the phrasing and trying to anticipate possible loopholes and misunderstandings.

I would try my damnedest to make my teachings well-thought-out and inspiring. I knew that no matter what, people would find a way to poke holes in them, but as long as I tried my best, Ray could just smack those people with a hammer if push came to shove.

After fiddling with some words and phrasing for a while, I leaned back and took a moment to rest my mind. I couldn't help but let out a sigh.

When I last answered the question 'where do you see yourself in ten years', I said I would be married with a stable income. I missed the margin a little bit, though. I did get married, but then I died, became a god, and started my own cult.

There was bound to be backlash, and it would likely come sooner than we could ever expect. I just needed to keep my end goal in sight and deal with the problems as they came up.

Today was only the first step, after all. There was still a long, long road ahead of us.

<hr>

"Could you repeat that?" Eileen asked, narrowing her eyes.

"The girl, Ray, was ambushed by goblins and led away to their camp. I was unable to attempt a rescue operation before she reached the camp due to the strength of one of the goblins," Max reiterated.

Eileen tapped the edge of the couch restlessly as she scowled. "There was a goblin strong enough to make you, a High Templar, wary? And he kidnapped our little scapegoat?"

Max nodded wordlessly.

Eileen sighed. "You know what this means, right? We need her back before we find the core. There are only two weeks left until spring. I'm going to have to devote my whole attention to helping Phineas find it, you need to resolve this side of things on your own."

"Understood," Max replied, pushing himself to his feet tiredly.

He had rushed back as soon as he discovered the goblin camp and hadn't rested or eaten the entire way.

Eileen noticed his fatigue and the corners of her lips turned up in a faint smile. "And take better care of yourself. You still need food, water, and sleep for the time being."

Max smirked. "Yeah, for now. I'll make sure that Ray is usable in two weeks. You can devote yourself to finding the core without worry."

Eileen accepted his promise with a smile. "I will do just that. Thank you."

27

Return

"The art of illusions is the art of distorting reality. There are legends passed down from our ancestors that one may be called a true illusionist only when they can trick the world itself and cause their illusions to become real."

Lexi listened to Shaman's explanation with rapt attention. They were inside of Shaman's tent next to the crackling fire. The old goblin sat atop her rocking throne while Lexi sat cross-legged on the ground, her tail swishing on the ground behind her.

"Using illusion magic is not the same as the magic that humans use. It does not require a medium, faith, a contract with nature, or anything of the sort. Illusions are formed by magic in its purest form."

"If there is no catalyst or medium, what fuels the spell? People are limited by their mana capacity, right?"

The old goblin smiled wistfully. "That is precisely the problem. The 'mana' that is used today is too distorted and restricted, so only members of the immortal races are born with a large enough capacity to use ancient magic. There is no known method of increasing the total amount of mana a person can control so most people cannot learn this even if they want to."

"I thought that expending mana to the limit increased the maximum threshold? That's what the elementalists in my tribe taught me."

Shaman shook her head. "That is a common belief amongst the mortal races. However, they are just increasing the amount of their already existing capacity that they can control. By the Law of Conservation of Aeion, mana can neither be created nor destroyed. When you use a spell, you are just controlling a portion of mana that exists outside of yourself equal to some amount of mana that exists within you. The process accumulates mental fatigue but, otherwise, there are no benefits or detriments to using more or less mana in a spell. You cannot gain or lose mana."

Lexi interlocked her fingers as she took in this revolutionary information. It was so basic, yet it was the first time she was hearing such a thing. If what this old goblin was saying was true, then the world was much more unbalanced than most people knew.

"Truthfully, I am unsure if a member of the mortal races other than goblins can learn this magic, but I believe my intuition which tells me that you can do so," Shaman concluded.

Lexi nodded dutifully. "I will do my best!"

"Then we shall see if my intuition is right. First, summon your mana."

The young catgirl did as she was told, and the scent of fish filled the tent as her mana permeated the air around her. The only sound in the tent was the crackling of the fire. If she listened closely enough, they could hear the faint hubbub of many goblins moving about outside, far away from the tent.

"Good. Your mana has the potential to control magic from three of the human aptitudes. You may learn elemental magic, holy magic, and arcane magic. Though it is sealed, I see the possibility for you to learn the ancient magics. It will take you many years of intense practice. Are you prepared for this?"

"I am prepared," Lexi asserted confidently.

Shaman raised her staff and leaned forward, touching the end of the staff to Lexi's forehead. "Then I will guide you on the first step. Move your mana in the way that I will show you."

With the staff touching her head, Lexi felt a strange, overwhelming sensation flow into her from the wooden object. The sensation began to twist and turn within her and Lexi moved her mana to follow the motions. Soon, a roaring pain filled her mind and her back arched as she hissed. Her arms and legs spasmed and it felt as if every muscle in her body cramped simultaneously.

After a very brief moment of determined, agonized resistance, Lexi collapsed and welcomed unconsciousness.

If she had been awake, she would have heard Shaman sigh.

"Those damned Precursors... she will be powerful one day, but the path ahead of her is full of pain and tribulation."

⸺⬤⸺

Unlike her first time returning to Cairel, this trip was uneventful. While Ray was excited at the prospect of a fight with wild monsters, she didn't seek them out as she was already late in returning to Cairel for her report.

While she was walking, she examined the contents of the magic bag she took from Peter. She deliberately ignored Ven and Helen's bags to respect their privacy. She recalled that Peter frequently wrote in a journal that he kept stored in his enchanted bag. She pulled it out and flipped to the latest entry.

February 14, 7602

Today's conquest was the two barmaids in the inn. Unfortunately, the innkeeper kicked us out afterwards and refused us business. I guess his workers complained about me. Rather than take offense, I have decided to be optimistic about this - there are new conquests to be found!

I have never tried to conquer two at once before. Their names were Vera and Jen. Admittedly, I was slightly disappointed at how easy it was to enchant the two girls. With just a simple mind control spell and few magically enhanced words, I had them obeying my every command. After dinner, I led them to my room for a night of passion. After closing the door, I proceeded to...

Ray read the next sentence and then slammed the book closed, disgusted at the depravity found within. She tossed the book back into the enchanted bag. Though Peter probably wouldn't respawn, she decided to keep it until she knew for sure that he was gone. If brutal torture and dismemberment wasn't enough to keep him down, then she would need to try another form of attack.

She entered the town before noon. The streets were bustling with traffic as people moved about buying food for lunch. The orc, troll, and beastkin slaves shambled along beside or behind their masters, chains rattling softly, though the sound was overcome by the movement, talking, and shouting of hundreds of people.

Ray observed the slaves as she moved towards the Adventurer's Guild to file her report. She'd heard a few stories from Lexi about how slaves were treated, and it left a bad taste in her mouth. For the most part, their gazes were empty. There were a few that still carried a hint of defiance in their eyes or in their shoulders, but most of them seemed to have given up.

"We can't do anything yet, but I hope to fix this in the future."

Ray clenched her teeth and nodded. She moved on, ignoring the slaves for now. There were too many of them and she didn't want to start a war against the humans.

"By the way, Mr. New God. Do you still not have a name?" Ray asked, distracting herself from the depressing sight around her.

"I honestly haven't thought about it too much since I've been focused on my tenets. I'll add it to my list of things to do."

She entered the central plaza and moved over to the Adventurer's Guild on the left. The building was big yet plain and simple. The structure was little more than a rectangle large enough to have three or four floors, depending on the height of the ceilings. Ray entered without a second thought, and, for the first time, she observed the inside of the guild.

The first floor was organized into four sections. Immediately to her left was a reception desk and a waiting area. The receptionists stood behind the desk. Since it was noon, the waiting area wasn't very packed, but Ray had heard that there were long lines early in the morning as the adventurers who procrastinated had to wait in line before they could register for a quest.

Ray didn't fully understand why, but apparently procrastination was an extremely common problem. She would have to ask someone about that later.

The second area was in the far-left corner of the room from the entrance. It had a large notice board covering half of the left wall and half of the central wall. The request board was partitioned into difficulties - bronze, silver, gold, legendary, and mythical - and then further sorted into different types of quests - suppression, collection, delivery, escort, and experiment. Obviously, there were no requests in the legendary or mythical sections. If there were, Cairel would be in big trouble. The spots were more of a formality than anything else.

The third and fourth areas, both on the right side of the room, were a bar and a seating area for drinking, talking, and recruiting new party members. Ray had no idea what the second, third, or fourth floors were used for. Presumably, the Guild Master had his office on one of those floors, but she wasn't sure what else could be up there.

She approached a receptionist at the desk. Since there were not as many people looking to start new requests in the middle of the day, she didn't need to wait for an open station.

"How may I help you?" asked a friendly man wearing a suit and tie. He had his light-brown hair slicked back. That, combined with his square glasses and a friendly smile, gave him a professional appearance.

"My name is Ray, a trainee. I'm here to report about the excursion that I just returned from."

The man's eyes lit up with surprise. "May I presume that you are from the missing party led by Master Jantzen Rovar?"

Ray nodded. "I apologize for returning late. We ran into some trouble."

"Seeing as you, instead of Master Jantzen, are reporting, I can see that an accident must have occurred." He pulled out a piece of paper and a pen and passed them to her. "If you would please fill out all the details, leaving nothing out. Even if your party was inexperienced, we cannot ignore this. If this threat can kill a party of trainees, then merchants, farmers, and other civilians would be helpless against it."

Ray smiled and accepted the paper. She moved over to the waiting area and sat down at a table, biting the end of the pen lightly as she considered what she would write. She had already decided, for the most part, but she quintuple checked to make sure she couldn't find any inconsistencies or other issues with the details.

A summary of her report would be something like this: they were ambushed by Ax the Pony and his bandits soon after they entered the Voskeg Mountains. They suffered no casualties and the bandits fled by using spatial magic grenades. They attempted to search for the bandits before encountering goblins and being wiped out. Ray managed to escape but the goblins chased her through the mountains for a day before she finally lost them. She camped out for the night alone and returned to Cairel on the third day.

At first, she had considered hiding the existence of the goblins, but she suspected that Ven and Helen might have woken up and seen the goblins before they were killed. If they didn't corroborate her story, she would fall under suspicion for lying. The existence of the goblins would likely be revealed either way and, in fact, the guild already knew they were there since there was a standing request to hunt them.

After filling out the report, Ray made her way over to the magic quarter for Master Rambalt's training. If their team was back, Kelsey would be there for the day's lessons. Since Ray had taken care of Peter and Jantzen, and Lexi was currently staying with the goblins, Ray, Suzy, and Kelsey would be the only students left.

When she slammed open the double doors to the tower, Ray flinched as she heard a loud shriek. A moment later, she saw a streak of white rushing towards her, and her eyes widened.

Kelsey embraced her.

It was the biggest display of emotion that Ray had seen from the priestess. "What brought this on?" Ray asked, patting the girl lightly on the back.

The priestess quickly pulled back, her face flushed. "Our group got wiped out on the first day by the goblins. They were a lot stronger than we were expecting and I only survived by running and hiding," Kelsey muttered. "When your group didn't come back in time, I thought you all died as well..."

It was a surprisingly familiar story.

"We got ambushed by goblins as well. I was the only one who made it back..."

Kelsey covered her mouth as she gasped as she looked behind Ray. Her eyes started to water. "I'm sorry. You must be really sad about Lexi..."

Ray hid her surprise as she observed Kelsey with interest. The priestess seemed to be legitimately sorry that Lexi had 'died' and wouldn't be able to come back. She couldn't help but wonder why Kelsey was being so familiar and empathic. Was she just traumatized from her experience? Or did she have an ulterior motive?

"There's not much I can do about it," Ray muttered softly. "She fought with courage and ripped her enemies apart, but the end result was what it was."

Kelsey nodded, patting her on the head. She then motioned towards Master Rambalt who was observing the two of them with a piercing expression.

He was tapping his finger on the arm of his chair impatiently.

Ray approached the old elementalist and waved.

"Ray," he called out. "You said you wanted to learn dark magic, yes?"

She paused and nodded hesitantly. She wasn't expecting him to bring that topic up so soon in her training. "I would like to, yes. I am a bit interested in obliterator and dark healer magics."

Master Rambalt pursed his lips as he examined her from head to toe, his eyes seeming to look at something beyond her physical presence.

"Why do you want to learn dark healing?"

Ray glanced at Kelsey for a moment before replying honestly. "I have a rather unique ability to regenerate."

Master Rambalt's eyes furrowed. "Regeneration? To what extent?"

Ray shrugged and summoned her shortsword. She raised it over her left arm and calmly swung down. Kelsey cried out as soon as she realized what was happening, rushing forward in a vain attempt to stop her.

Her left arm fell to the floor.

28

Familiar

Crimson blood began to drip down and stain the stone.

Master Rambalt's eyes widened at the display and then grew even wider as he witnessed her arm regrowing from the stump at an unbelievable speed. He tried to speak but he could only let out a stupefied sound.

Kelsey stared at the pooling blood, her eyes filled with shock and confusion. Her face was pale, and her lips were trembling. Her mind seemed to have shut down as she stumbled over to a chair and plopped down onto the wooden support. She leaned her head down into her hands.

In no time, the arm was fully regrown, and Ray stretched her fingers experimentally, smirking at the two reactions. She knew this power was unnatural, but this was the first time she had shown it to someone other than Lexi.

The voice in her head sighed. *"Uhhh, that probably wasn't a good idea..."*

After a moment of silence, Master Rambalt recovered from his shock and then frowned as his eyes moved over to Kelsey. He sighed and then returned his attention to Ray. "It goes without saying that I believe you now. I can now say with absolute certainty that you have the potential to be the first person to tread the entire path of the dark healer and unlock all of its secrets."

Ray reached down and picked up the arm that was leaking blood. She tilted her head as she considered what to do with the appendage. She stored it in her enchanted bag for now and decided to think about it later.

The idea of being the first to explore the realm of the dark mage in depth sounded exciting. Her heart beat rapidly as she imagined herself unlocking the secrets of dark magic and bragging to Eileen,

Master Rambalt, and Siegfried. She imagined the three of them praising her.

As if electricity was running through her veins, she began to quiver with excitement. "Please teach me!" she half-shouted.

Master Rambalt smirked. He waved his hand and a chair sprung up from the floor. He motioned for her to take a seat. "Let's talk about familiars then."

Ray glanced over at Kelsey with a bit of concern before moving to the seat. The priestess was still recovering, her face green with nausea.

"As you know, there are five aptitudes of magic. These five aptitudes can be further designated by alignment."

"Alignment?"

"Take holy magic, for example. Holy magic can only be used by those ordained by a god. This magic can also be considered 'divine' in nature and, therefore, has an alignment with the gods."

Ray nodded in understanding. That matched what she had experienced after ordaining Lexi to be a priestess.

"Dark magic, on the other hand, is the opposite of holy magic. The source is still unclear, but it is speculated to be aligned with the enemies of the gods, or the demons."

"Demons?"

This was the first time she was hearing about them.

"Demons appeared in this world once nearly a century ago. Legends say that they were led by a being known as the Demon King. He was killed a little over seventy years ago, though. It's not well documented since the world was in shambles during the War of the Ancients, but most scholars believe that demons are the enemies of the gods and the origin of 'dark' magic."

"Huh…" Ray replied, uncertain.

The elementalist's words sounded familiar to her but she got the distinct feeling that the explanation was missing some critical details. She tried to pursue the feeling through her hazy memories, but she couldn't find the source.

"Nature magic, used by druids, is a combination of holy magic and dark magic and is considered to have alignment with both the gods and their antithesis simultaneously. This conclusion was reached because of an observable pattern -- in all of history, every person who could use both holy and dark magic could also use nature magic. There are no documented cases of individuals who only had aptitudes for two of the three."

Master Rambalt paused in his explanation and coughed to clear his throat. He flicked his fingers, and a stream of water flew from somewhere inside his robes and into his mouth. After wetting his throat, the elementalist continued his explanation. "The final two aptitudes, elemental magic and arcane magic, have a neutral alignment. They can pair up with any type of magic. Each type of magic has a different form in which it manifests. Holy magic is performed through faith, recitation of prayers, or by using blessed objects. Neutral magic is controlled directly with body movement or stored in physical objects, while nature magic is too complex to summarize, but it involves contracts. Dark magic is performed through a medium known as a familiar."

"But Peter is a warlock, and he doesn't have a familiar," Ray pointed out.

Master Rambalt scoffed. "That boy is but a warlock-in-training. He doesn't have a familiar because his sense for and control of mana is not at a high enough level to summon one. You, on the other hand, have already reached that level in a matter of weeks."

Ray lifted her chin up at the praise. "I've seen priests use spells without recitations or holy objects, and Peter could use some basic magic without a familiar. What is the function of these processes?"

"For one, they greatly increase the power of the magic. They also supplement your mana when casting highly advanced and draining spells. Very few mages have the mana capacity to cast advanced magic without using these methods."

Satisfied with the answer, Ray leaned forward. "Alrighty, let's do it. Teach me how to summon a familiar!"

Master Rambalt chuckled. "It's quite easy, actually. Summon your mana and explore the inside of your own body and mind. Since you have an aptitude for dark magic, there should be a place that feels odd, like it doesn't belong. Since you have been focusing all of your meditations on enhancing your arm, you probably won't have noticed it yet, but it will be there."

Ray closed her eyes and summoned her mana. She focused internally and followed the path of the mana as it circulated through her body, searching for a feeling of strangeness. As the mana entered her mind, she felt three spots surrounding a large 'void'. The void, she knew, was her connection to her god.

She hadn't noticed these three spots the first time she had found the void, though that might have been because she didn't know how to use mana yet.

"I found three of them," she informed her teacher.

"Three?" he asked, his voice trembling with shock. "I've heard of two before, but three?!"

"Does this mean I can summon three familiars?" Ray asked, her eyes still closed as she examined the three spots.

One of them seemed to be willing to let her approach but the other two seemed to move further away whenever she tried to get near them.

"Eventually, yes. The first familiar can be summoned whenever you can sense it, approach it, and draw it out. The second familiar, I'm told, can only be summoned if you obtain its recognition and approval. It is rare that warlocks can summon two familiars, so the exact details are a bit murky. I honestly have no idea how you would go about unlocking your third familiar."

Ray shrugged. "What's important is that I can only summon one for now. I'll figure out the rest later."

"That's right," Master Rambalt muttered. "The first familiar is said to be one that closely represents something that you fear. The second is said to represent something that you greatly desire. I hope you share with me what the third one represents when you discover it someday."

"Sure thing!" Ray promised.

"To summon your familiar, approach and grab it with your mana. Once you have a firm grasp, pull with all your might while willing it to manifest in the material world."

Ray reached out with her mana and latched onto the spot that would let her touch it. She felt a strange sensation fill her body. She shivered as a wave of excitement and anticipation that was not her own rolled through her. Sensing the familiar emotions, she knew that it *wanted* to be summoned. It was eager to finally leave.

She willed the entity to manifest and pulled as hard as she could. The odd spot distorted, and a strange energy leaked out and started to merge with her mana.

With an audible *pop*, Ray opened her eyes. A small black sphere with burgundy streaks appeared in front of her. The black orb began to writhe, and a small crack grew on the side. After a moment, the orb shattered.

A storm of feathers filled the air as a large, black bird emerged. It glided down into the space between her and her instructor and perched on her leg. Raising its wings dramatically, it bowed its head in a smooth, practiced motion.

Ray stared at the large black bird, her eyes following its fluttering wings. She felt a regal presence, like when she stood before Shaman.

"Greetings and salutations, Master." His voice was raspy and willowy, having an almost ancient feel.

Ray raised her eyebrows. "You can speak?"

"Indeed. I am the illustrious and magnanimous Lord of Ravens! Remember my name henceforth, for I am Lord Mortimer Perseus Raventon the Dark!"

Ray stared at the large raven with a blank expression. His surface-level thoughts and feelings flowed through their connection.

Lord Mortimer, sensing how lost she was, raised an olive branch out of the kindness overflowing from the depths of his dark heart. "That is, of course, unless you decide to change it... but I would highly recommend that you allow this distinguished lord to hold onto such a glorious and magnificent name."

Finally, Ray shook her head. "I won't change your name but that is way too long to say in a casual setting. I'll call you Mort."

The bird flinched and visibly deflated. "As you wish, my lady."

Master Rambalt cleared his throat, staring at the bird with a peculiar expression. "This is the first time I have seen a familiar that can speak. Lord Mortimer Perseus Raventon, may I ask you a few questions?"

The raven lord observed the human elementalist. "Your attempt to curry favor is noted but I would advise you to say my entire name if you want to gain my attention in the future. My name is not merely Lord Mortimer Perseus Raventon, but Lord Mortimer Perseus Raventon *the Dark*."

Master Rambalt bowed his head. "My apologies, esteemed lord. It was my mistake, and it will not happen again. May I ask you some questions?"

Mort straightened up noticeably upon seeing the human offering him such obvious respect. The raven raised a wing. "I will permit thy questions!"

"Lord, you are the first familiar I have heard of or seen that can communicate in English. Are there other familiars like you?"

"There are other lords, if that is what you are asking. I am the Lord of Ravens. I can only be summoned by the worthy descendants of the rulers."

"Rulers?"

"The ones who created this world and gifted it with the source of all creation, and the same ones who later regretted and took it away."

Master Rambalt's eyes lit up with comprehension. "Let us halt that line of discussion there," he replied hurriedly, glancing at Kelsey with a nervous expression. She was following the conversation intently, her complexion long since recovered.

Their teacher cupped his chin thoughtfully. "I am most intrigued by this new source of knowledge that I never knew existed. I hope to learn many things from you in the future, Lord Mortimer Perseus Raventon the Dark."

Mort tilted his head upwards. "I am not a tool for your amusement. I will only answer questions when it pleases me to do so."

Ray tapped the bird lightly. "What about *my* questions?" she asked.

Mort felt a shiver run up his spine and he ruffled his feathers nervously. A sense of imminent danger filled his mind, warning him to issue the proper response.

"O..of course, I will answer my lady's questions!" he replied confidently, despite a brief stutter. "I exist only to serve thee, Lady Raymond!"

Master Rambalt flinched, his eyes immediately moving towards Kelsey once again.

Ray shook her head. "My name is Ray, not Raymond," she corrected.

"Duly noted! Henceforth, I shall refer to thee as Lady Ray!"

She pushed herself to her feet and motioned for Mort to come with her. "Let's go! I still need to tell Sister Eileen that I've returned. Then I need to practice with my sword before the lesson tomorrow. I can't show up to a lesson without having improved in between, now, can I?" Ray turned and thanked Master Rambalt. "Thank you for the lesson!"

Master Rambalt shrugged and waved off her gratitude. "I'll teach you some basic spells tomorrow, so don't be late..." he muttered indifferently.

Ray nodded and rushed out the door, Lord Mortimer Perseus Raventon the Dark flying behind her.

They left behind a disgruntled old elementalist and a young priestess who was staring after them with wide-eyed interest.

29

Teachings

Ray's training the next day with Siegfried was a blast. Since she was the only student who returned alive, she had Siegfried's undivided attention. He decided to give up on teaching her to fight defensively with a sword and shield. Instead, he gave her a battle hammer and taught her some basic movements. He gave her a lot of advice and then he sparred with her.

The spar was a lot of fun.

She stood across from Siegfried, holding her new battle hammer above her head, poised to strike. The guardian trainer held a large, steel shield in his left hand and a battleaxe clenched in his right fist. His expression while sparring had been serious ever since she accidentally broke his shield. She did apologize, but it still seemed to bother him for some reason.

Master Jedediah Lion, the Echo Fist, was the referee for the sparring match.

"Begin!" he shouted.

Ray circled to her left, trying to move around the shield. Siegfried matched her steps and they circled around each other for several long seconds.

On the second rotation, Ray began inching forward, her eyes searching for openings in his stance. Of course, there were none, but she would search for them anyway. Even the most veteran of fighters could make mistakes.

After half a minute of circling, she started to grow impatient and decided that she would try and make an opening. She rushed forward and swung her heavy battle hammer down, holding back just enough that the shield shouldn't break. Siegfried sidestepped and tilted his shield so that the battle hammer would slide to the side. Ray nimbly matched his sidestepped and reversed the swing of the battle hammer with inhuman strength. Siegfried deflected the swing with his shield and grimaced. His shield held, though it was slightly deformed where the mace impacted.

Ray followed up with another downward crushing blow. Siegfried intercepted the swing with his battleaxe, catching the shaft of the battle hammer between the blade and shaft. He twisted and pulled her weapon towards himself, and her eyes widened as the battle hammer was skillfully wrenched from her hands. She kicked off the ground, pushing herself back to dodge the swing of Siegfried's battle axe by a hair's breadth. Beads of sweat began to form on the back of her neck, and she grinned.

"Do you concede?" Master Lion asked.

Ray shook her head. "I would like to practice recovering from situations such as these."

Master Lion and Siegfried both nodded approvingly.

"Continue!" the Echo Fist shouted.

Ray rushed forward, observing the position of Siegfried's body, his weapon, and his shield relative to her weapon on the ground. She could just pull another one out of her enchanted bag, but she wanted to practice the scenario when she only had one weapon left. While unlikely, it could potentially happen.

Siegfried watched her approaching form calmly and shifted his balance to intercept her. Ray saw his left foot step back and reinforced her left hand. Seeing the arcing battle axe, she reached out with her reinforced left hand and intercepted the swing with an open palm. She then grasped the blade of the axe and pushed it aside. Siegfried attempted to retain his hold on his weapon, forcing him to take a step to the side and backward to recover.

In that gap, Ray ducked down and swiped up her battle hammer. She kicked off of the ground and propelled herself up and forward, completing the motion with an upward swing that didn't allow her opponent to take advantage of the moment she was down.

She planted her foot firmly and chained the upward swing into a solid, downward smash.

Siegfried calmly deflected the strike but flinched as his shield buckled from the impact and a large fragment of steel spun into the air. He channeled his mana and began to reinforce his body. Ray knew that he was one of the few humans who had managed to perform a full-body reinforcement. His whole body went rigid, though his joints maintained their flexibility. Ray grit her teeth. This wasn't the first time this had happened, but unfortunately there wasn't anything she could do about it yet.

Siegfried rushed at her much faster than before, his axe containing even greater strength behind every swing. Ray struggled to dodge and parry his blows, barely matching him with her superior base physical abilities. Finally, Siegfried managed to catch the shaft of her battle hammer again and pulled the weapon out of her hands. Before Ray could properly react, she felt a cold sensation as the blade of the axe tapped her neck.

Ray raised her hands in defeat. "I concede."

Siegfried lowered his axe and released his reinforcement. She could see that he was sweating profusely and revealed a bitter smile.

She had forced him to go all out. She felt a little proud of that.

"Well done," Siegfried commented while bending down to pick up the battle hammer. He held the weapon out to her, and she accepted it. "Your performance is improving at an unbelievable rate."

Master Lion nodded his agreement. "Young miss, I almost wish you had chosen to learn martial arts. With your speed, strength, and the level of your reinforcement..."

Ray waved off their praise. "I'm strong, but I can be stronger."

"That is certainly true," Siegfried agreed. "Let's review the fight and see where you could have made better decisions."

Ray followed Siegfried as he led her to the review room beside the waterfall. Before they stepped inside, he briefly ducked his head into the waterfall to wash all the sweat away. After he stepped back, Ray copied his action, smiling as the sticky sweat on the back of her neck washed was replaced with cold water.

They moved into the side room and sat down at the table inside. Ray wrung out her hair as they started talking.

This was the pattern they followed for Ray's lessons with Siegfried while they waited the four to five days for the other students to respawn.

Building a set of teachings was harder than I expected.

My personal moral compass was formed by my environment and my personal experiences, but I wasn't so arrogant as to believe that I knew everything there was to know. I kept finding myself referencing the general teachings I had either learned or heard about from my time on Earth.

I found that most teachings and commandments fell into one of four types.

Some of the teachings were focused on criminalizing certain behaviors or practices. Oftentimes these would be things that might be considered obvious yet considering that there were often laws banning the same things, it was clear that they weren't. This would be things like general bans on murder and theft.

Many commandments and teachings in religions were often focused on being preventative. They wanted to target what they perceived as the fundamental cause of the bans they placed on certain behaviors. Examples would include cautions against anger, lust, greed, or pride.

The third type of teachings were those related to the nature of the deity who presided over the religion. These would often be ceremonies or ritual practices that were required for members of the religion to 'repent', or achieve ranks, or earn more authority, power, or blessings, or whatnot. This would include things like baptism, animal sacrifice, fasting, tithing, and other kinds of offerings.

The fourth, and last, kind of teachings that I recognized were those that were preventative in some way or form, yet the purpose and reasoning behind the teachings were often left unclear. Examples of this would include bans on 'unclean' foods that were often consumed in other religions and nations, or regulations regarding gender roles or sexual orientation. One could presume that the corresponding Overseer had a reason for issuing their stances, but oftentimes they just gave general explanations that were ambiguous or unsatisfactory to those who were targeted.

A consistency in every religion was the promise of a 'reward'. These were often termed as 'blessings' or 'miracles' and the most consistent was a promise of recompense in the afterlife. Of course, I now knew that this was just an elaborate scam to increase the harvest of faith and souls. While I wasn't wholly against manipulation, scamming people wasn't my style. My religion would focus more on the blessings and miracles that could be obtained during their current existence. If gods from Earth had spent more time performing visible miracles, their religions probably wouldn't have crumbled as fast as some of them did.

Then again, I hadn't met any of the Overseers from Earth yet, so even though I wasn't impressed with their results, I would reserve my judgment on their character until I did.

Regarding each of these four types of teachings, I decided to hold off on the fourth type for now. I couldn't think of any 'general' bans that I wanted to implement on food, and I had no interest in locking gender roles, racial supremacy, or anything like that. It would be empowering in the short term, but I didn't want to collapse and fail in the long term. Besides, restricting or eliminating entire classes or groups of people based on uncontrollable circumstances would be counterintuitive to my decision to become a God of Harmony.

In fact, I could do the opposite.

"Thou shalt strive to live in harmony with all creatures and with nature."

"Thou shalt not promote, participate in, or support slavery."

"Thou shalt not discriminate."

The first commandment immediately came to mind when I remembered the large number of depressed slaves living in Cairel. The second commandment was a preventative measure. Naturally, I didn't add a clause excluding the discrimination of humans by 'monsters'. Even if the monsters had been on the receiving end for a thousand years, returning that discrimination after obtaining a resolution on the current issue would be antithetical to harmony.

I briefly made note of these new teachings in the Tenets tab, under a section set aside for drafting. Above those were some of the more general commandments, such as 'thou shalt not kill' or 'thou shalt not steal'.

I was hesitant on some of those though. Normally, I would be averse to killing but I learned on Earth that it was necessary sometimes. I joined the resistance against the Director's Unification Army because I wanted to fight for freedom. It goes without saying that I had to take lives.

What would 'killing' even mean in this world? Killing monsters was a permanent death, like on Earth, but killing humans associated with Overseers was temporary. Since they would respawn, was this anywhere near the same level of 'sin' as it was on Earth?

Yet putting in a clause that it's okay to kill servants of Overseers seemed counterintuitive to my purpose of pursuing 'harmony'. Even though they would respawn, people didn't usually enjoy being killed.

The biggest reason I was concerned about a commandment like this one was because I knew that conflict and opposition were inevitable. I would overturn the status quo of this world by introducing the Overseer system to the native races. Not all of the native races would accept me, and I highly doubted many of the humans would embrace the change.

War was inevitable.

I didn't know what form that war would take, but I had no intention of condemning my followers for any actions they would take to win that war. Rape, murdering and torturing innocent civilians, and stuff like that would be unacceptable, but just about anything else would be within the bounds of reason.

Also, if I made all forms of killing a sin, I would be limiting myself during times of war. I wouldn't be able to obtain faith from followers who were breaking my commandments.

So, for now, I would leave that commandment on hold.

Thinking about the times I had to fight on Earth made my chest ache. It was purely a phantom pain since I didn't have a body, but it hurt to remember those that I left behind. Since I went down holding back the enemy, I had no way of knowing if any of them got out alive.

My brother Dexter, my sister Cassie, my friends, my wife, and my unborn child...

I left them all behind.

I died to protect them, but that didn't change the fact that I was gone.

Focusing on learning about this world and my new role had distracted me for a bit, but now that around a month had passed, I couldn't ignore it any longer. Regardless of my sacrifice, I knew that the resistance wouldn't be able to hold out much longer. The Director controlled every government that was still standing.

I still remembered my goal of returning to Earth to liberate it. However, there would be no point as I currently was. I wouldn't be able to obtain any power because there was no room for gods in a world ruled by the Director.

I would resolve the issues of this world and, once I had a sizable following of superhuman creatures with incredible magic and abilities, it should be more than possible to march on Earth with my indomitable legions and save the world.

Reaffirming my resolve, I started looking once more to the present and, through it, towards the future.

Indomitable 'Legion', huh? That would be a cool name. That was another issue that I needed to address. However, as cool as the name 'Legion' was, I struck the idea down. It sounded too oppressive.

"Name... what should my name be..." I mumbled aloud.

It needed to be something powerful yet comforting. The name had to stand out from others yet not seem too strange. It needed to evoke a feeling of harmony.

There was a name floating in my head that I really liked.

"Tremble, mortals, and bow before Steve, the Almighty God of Harmony!"

30

Growth

Kelsey Vale couldn't help but feel that this woman she befriended, Ray, was a rather strange individual. She was suspicious to an exceptional degree. From their very first meeting, Kelsey had been curious about her red eye and strange hair color, but she pushed aside her doubts because she had literally just seen Ray respawn. It was an irrevocable fact that only humans could respawn. That was the will of the goddess, and the will of the pantheon.

She had witnessed Ray's inhuman strength when she tossed Jantzen over her shoulder like a weightless doll. Ray then managed to lift a slave collar while its suppression enchantment was activated. Only some of the best enhancement magic users could do something like that and Ray was still learning enhancement magic.

Then there was Ray's absurd mana pool and her insane learning speed when it came to magic.

Any one of these things taken individually could be shrugged off as a coincidence, a blessing from the gods, or as talent. All of them combined, however, started to paint a picture in Kelsey's mind, though she didn't want to believe it despite all of the evidence in front of her.

The final straw was the day Ray returned from a failed excursion. Not only had she displayed an impossible ability to regenerate, but she then summoned a Lord-type familiar, which supposedly could only be summoned by the descendants of the 'rulers'. If it were only that, then Kelsey wouldn't have come to the conclusion that she did. She didn't know who these 'rulers' were.

However, the raven lord had called Ray by a different name: 'Lady Raymond'.

Kelsey felt a chill run down her spine when she heard that name. There was only one person in the world who used the name 'Raymond'. Any humans who had once had that name, whether as a first or last name, had changed it centuries ago. No human wanted their name associated with the archenemy of humanity. She had once read in a book that even monsters didn't dare to steal her name. Even her name itself, Ray, was a syllable of the legend's last name.

Her suspicions were blooming into certainty. She hadn't confirmed her hypothesis, but she was starting to think that Ray just might be the infamous Evelyn Raymond.

If Ray wasn't the Monarch of Ages herself, she was most likely an immortal. Even if that were the case, Kelsey wouldn't be all that bothered though. She had known Ray for several weeks now and considered her to be a friend. Based on what she had seen, either Ray was an incredibly skilled actor, or something had happened to her.

An immortal, let alone the real Evelyn Raymond, would not struggle with a full-body enhancement, nor would she be attempting to learn basic magic. It was recorded that the real Evelyn Raymond had already mastered elemental, arcane, dark, and nature magic to a level that humans could never reach before humans ever came to Hanulfall. Her skill in martial arts and assassination techniques, combined with her mastery of magic, had made her a figure so fearsome and powerful that she was the subject of many children's stories. Of course, she only appeared in the stories told by children trying to scare each other.

However, there was a problem that Kelsey couldn't get around no matter how much she thought about it -- Ray had respawned in the temple.

By divine decree, only humans had the right to respawn. If Ray were an immortal, and especially if she were Evelyn Raymond, there was absolutely no way that any of the four gods would ever allow her to respawn if she died. They would rejoice and shower blessings and miracles for life on whoever managed to accomplish the feat.

So, was Ray just a human after all? A very peculiar, gifted human? But there were too many things piled up that Kelsey couldn't make herself believe that Ray was a human. She felt like she was only missing one piece of the puzzle so that she could say definitively who or what Ray was.

There was only one way to obtain this magical piece of missing truth.

When Ray tried to visit Eileen in the temple, the High Priestess refused to see her. She left a message for her saying 'I'm busy right now so go play with your sword or something.'

Ray felt her heart tighten a bit when Sister Eileen refused to see her, but she pushed the feeling aside and trained her sword stances and practiced her enhancement. She hadn't shown it to Master Rambalt yet, but she succeeded in performing a full durability/flexibility enhancement of her arm the evening that she stayed in the goblin camp.

Instead of practicing to increase the area of the enhancement to her other limbs, she decided to further develop the enhancement that she would later apply to her entire body. As it was, she could move her arm and joints, but her skin was rigid. It was obvious at a glance that her arm was enhanced.

Not only did it look ugly, but her skin would tear if she punched things too hard. Because of her regeneration, it wasn't that big of a deal, but she wanted to complete a 'perfect' enhancement. For it to be visually perfect, her skin needed to be more elastic to keep up with the massive impact forces.

First, she performed her usual enhancement. After her arm stiffened, she confirmed that she could move each of her joints smoothly. Her fingers twitched and bent with no delay and her wrist, shoulder and elbow all felt normal as well.

She focused on the sensation of 'elasticity', imagining the stretchiness of rubber, and willed her skin to take on similar properties. Before her eyes, her skin seemed to snap into place. She reached out carefully and pinched her enhanced right arm with her left hand. The skin felt a little stiffer than usual, but it stretched between her fingers.

There was also no pain. She wasn't sure what part of the enhancement dulled the sensations in her arm, but it was a welcome change. Pain was unpleasant.

The edges of her mouth tilted upwards into a smile. Increasing the elasticity over a wide area was much easier than increasing flexibility in multiple small areas. Though she still needed a little more practice with the visualization to make her skin feel more natural, the result of her experiment was a resounding success.

Ray turned her attention to reinforcing both of her arms simultaneously. She could reinforce only her left arm or only her right arm with ease but doing both at the same time took exactly twice as many reinforcements to focus on and maintain, but the difficulty felt like it increased exponentially.

She struggled briefly to add durability to her left arm. She could easily do it if she let go of the elasticity enhancement on the right arm, but she refused to let it go. She would persevere and perfect a total body enhancement, no matter how long it would take.

Mort observed her quietly as she went about her practice. They could feel each other's general thoughts and feelings, so he knew how intently she was focusing, and he didn't want to interrupt that. She knew he was being considerate and paid him no attention. It gave him a much-needed opportunity to learn more about his new master. If he wanted to please her as her servant, he needed to know as much about her as he could.

When Ray went to her lessons with Master Rambalt, Kelsey wasn't there. It was the first time that the priestess had missed, which was a bit concerning. She recalled the priestess' overly familiar actions and worried that her absence was related to any possible ulterior motives.

Her concerns aside, she was secretly glad to get yet another one-on-one lesson with the grungy elementalist. She recognized the fact that Master Rambalt usually ignored the other students and only answered her questions, but she preferred it that way. It made her learn faster. He only helped other students if he felt like they were on the verge of a breakthrough. He told them that he needed to be a part of that process if he wanted his name associated with their future accomplishments.

Ray set aside her concerns about Kelsey and began to study dark magic.

"Dark magic is fundamentally different from the enhancement magic that you have been practicing," Master Rambalt explained. "Each of the three types of dark magic have the same foundation, but beyond that they are only vaguely related to each other. Obliterator magics are flashy and destructive, while dominator magics are sly and manipulative. Both are most effective when you use your familiar as a medium. You supply the mana and weave the spell while your familiar operates as the source. In practice, this will mean that you select a spell to cast and begin to cast it. Lord Mortimer Perseus Raventon the Dark will finish the cast and operate the spell for you. Naturally, the spell will also be cast from the raven lord's location, which has various applications in battle."

Mort looked up from preening his feathers.

"I will be a most reliable aide for thee!"

"The third branch of dark magic, becoming a dark mage, is a little different. It requires physical contact with the subject whose injuries you intend to take upon yourself. Physical contact with your familiar is also sufficient. You invade the subject's body with your mana, encase the injuries or source of ailment and convert them into mana, and then return it to yourself. Due to the laws of magic conservation, namely the conversion of material into mana, the converted mana will lose its form and return to its original state. This means that you will receive the injury yourself."

Ray nodded to show that she was following along.

Master Rambalt withdrew a small knife and held it against his finger. With a deft motion, he swiped the blade across the skin, drawing a red line.

"You will practice removing these paper cuts," he ordered.

Ray reached out and touched her instructor's palm with her finger. She pushed her mana out and into his hand and urged the mana to move towards his finger. Her mana rebelled, seeking to spread outwards wildly. Ray fought against the natural flow of the mana and forced it in the opposite direction with all of her might.

Finally, the mana began to inch towards the small cut and Ray enveloped the tip of her teacher's finger. She could feel a vast amount of information encompassed in that one finger and shuddered, turning her mind away from it since she couldn't process it all. She focused the mana on the cut and willed it to convert into mana. The edges of the cut started to closed and she felt a foreign substance seep into her own mana. She latched onto the foreign substance and followed it to its source, attempting to pull all of it out.

In the blink of an eye, the cut disappeared.

Ray withdrew her mana and raised her corresponding finger on her right hand, waiting. A cut appeared on the tip of her finger and then regenerated.

Success!

Ray looked up at Master Rambalt, hoping for praise.

"Not bad for a first attempt," he observed dryly. "You couldn't use that on a battlefield though. It took you three minutes to remove a paper cut."

Ray grimaced. "It wouldn't kill you to give me a real compliment..." She turned around and stomped away to start meditating.

Hearing her grumble, Mort decided it was his chance to improve her impression of him. "Lady Ray, your performance was absolutely superb!"

"Shut it, you stupid bird." Ray spat out, waving him off.

Lord Mortimer Perseus Raventon the Dark fluttered in the air helplessly. Though he would never admit it, he felt like he had just made the first mistake in his life. The problem was that he didn't know what he did wrong, and Ray didn't feel like telling him. Her feelings made no sense to him.

The next couple of days were the same for Ray. Her concern grew as Kelsey continued to ditch her lessons in the magic tower, but Ray couldn't seem to find the priestess when she wandered in the temple. When she asked, the other priests simply replied that they didn't know where she was.

She attempted to consult Sister Eileen, but the High Priestess continued to refuse to see her.

Ray felt uneasy but there didn't seem to be anything she could do for now.

Every morning, she practiced fighting with her longsword and her battle hammer. Siegfried said that he would teach her to fight with a two-handed greataxe and a bec de corbin once she became more proficient with those weapons.

At first, she had wondered what the difference between her current training and a warrior's training was. Siegfried explained that warriors trained to master one or two different weapons and fight using that style. What he was teaching her was the guardian's style of using any large weapon to turn the tide of a battle. With her strength, agility, and seemingly bottomless endurance, she could charge into armies as a whirling tide of destruction. Towards that end, he encouraged her to also learn berserker techniques if she ever met a person who could teach her.

Honestly, she couldn't really call herself a guardian-in-training, as she wasn't learning any of the purely defensive techniques. Rather, she was more like a juggernaut-in-training. If she learned berserker techniques and a full-body enhancement and then combined all three of those with her unnatural regeneration and her superhuman basic stats, she would be a demigod on any battlefield.

And that wasn't the only thing she was learning. She continued to practice her dark magic under Master Rambalt's tutelage. She resolved that she would start learning obliterator spells after she had the ability to convert a wound the size of a standard sword cut in under twenty seconds.

She wasn't even close yet though. At best, she managed to convert a 'paper cut' in under a minute. Her enhancement was progressing at a snail's pace as well, from her perspective. After three more evenings of diligent practice and meditation, she could perform two more simultaneous enhancements than before.

Ray was aware that the speed of her growth was so unnaturally fast by human standards that she had already progressed far more than she should have in a year of study, but it wasn't enough to satisfy her.

Finally, on the fourth day after Ray returned to Cairel, the dead trainee adventurers began to respawn.

All the trainees were summoned to the training grounds in the martial quarter for a discussion led by the teachers.

Ray went merrily, humming to herself as she strode through the streets. She entered the training quarter and stopped as she felt a host of eyes settle on her. Most of them were doubtful but one set of eyes was particularly angry and terrified at the same time.

She turned to meet the eyes of the man glaring at her with deep resentment. Her eyes widened.

Oh shoot.

"I told you not to take the risk," the voice in her head chimed in.

Ray noticed the doubtful expressions on the eyes of almost every other person in the room and shuddered as she felt a chill roll down her spine.

Her god had been right. She'd made a mistake.

She would try her damnedest, but she wasn't sure how to get out of this one.

31

Consequences

"It was her!" She's the one who t..t..tortured me!"

"Who is that rude bundle of sticks?" Mort muttered, displeased.

"Don't worry about it," Ray whispered back. "And don't talk where others can hear you."

She returned her attention to the group and observed the conflicted expressions of each of the people standing in the room. Jonathan, Vick, and Bill all looked at her with disgust while the corners of Suzy's mouth were twitching upwards. She shivered as she saw the crazy gleam in the girl's eyes.

Siegfried and Master Rambalt didn't seem bothered. Similarly, Master Lion and Rick were expressionless, standing back and observing the situation.

Helen stared at her with a curious expression, though Ray couldn't detect even a hint of judgment in the archer's gaze. She squared her shoulders when she saw that and smiled, taking strength from the assumption that the situation wasn't hopeless yet.

As usual, Ven was impossible to read because of the silver mask underneath his ever-present dark hood, she turned to Kelsey with a hopeful expression. She felt her hopes crash violently as she saw her face.

Kelsey was staring at her with her brow furled. However, the priestess had her lips pursed and her eyes screamed of confusion rather than the support that she was hoping to find there.

"She's in league with goblins!" Peter continued. "It was her and that cursed slave that tortured us. It's her fault that Jantzen is..." His voice trailed off, choking up as tears streamed down his face.

Jonathan reached out and patted the young warlock on the shoulder. As he did so, his furious gaze never left the woman standing near the doorway. "What are you?" he spat out. "You have a red eye and when I fought you before, I'm sure I saw fangs. You can't be a vampire though, so what are you?"

Ray remained silent, unsure of how to respond. She knew what she was, but he would go batshit crazy if she told him.

"Keep quiet for a moment... don't reveal anything incriminating. The only evidence they have is that idiot crying over there."

She decided to listen to her god's advice.

"Well? Why don't you answer the question?" Suzy shouted, her voice rising with jubilation.

She shook her head. "Even if you ask, I don't know what I'm supposed to say."

"There's no need for riddles here. If you did it, admit it. If you didn't, you just need to prove your innocence," Bill interrupted.

Ray grimaced. They stared at each other silently for what felt like an eternity.

"Isn't the burden of proof on the accuser, not the defender?" Helen joined the conversation, breaking the silence.

All eyes turned towards her.

"I saw her retire to her tent before the goblins appeared. The goblins snuck into our camp and killed us in our sleep. I didn't see all of the goblins, but I also never saw her attacking us."

Ray felt a warm feeling rising inside her chest. Her bright smile returned as she met Helen's gaze and nodded her thanks.

"In fact, I did see both Peter and Jantzen attack Ray while she was asleep. Not only did she escape unharmed, but she graciously let the two of them live, although she did bruise them a little bit and knock them unconscious."

Siegfried and Master Rambalt turned their gazes towards Peter. "Is this true?" Master Rambalt asked, raising an eyebrow. "Did you attack your fellow student in her sleep?"

Peter flinched and his shoulders began to quiver. "Sh..sh..she killed me! She stabbed me over and over again with a sword... she broke my bones one at a time... she's a m...monster!"

"Are you sure it wasn't just a nightmare?" Helen challenged.

Peter shook his head vehemently. "She did it to Jantzen too!" he shouted, his voice bordering on hysteria.

"Did you see it?" Ven asked quietly.

Peter shook his head. "They k..killed me first. I didn't see it."

"Then how do you know?"

Peter's eyes went wide. "You're trying to defend her?" he shouted incredulously. He pointed a finger at Ray. "She isn't human! I stabbed her in the heart and Jantzen cut off her head. I saw her head roll away! And then a minute later she walked out of the tent covered in blood with no injuries!"

"So, you admit that you tried to kill her," Siegfried observed.

Peter froze. "What?! What is wrong with you people?!"

"He's right!" Jonathan jumped in. "She killed Suzy and Bill before and now she killed Peter and Jantzen. Even with an endorsement from Sister Eileen, she is way too dangerous. Even if you refuse to punish her, nobody here will ever team up with her again."

Helen raised a hand. "I would team up with her."

Jonathan stared at her in disbelief. "You would trust her over the testimony of my whole team and the warlock apprentice?"

Helen smirked and shook her head. "I trust her character after I saw the way she dealt with an ambush by her own teammates. There is no proof that she did what Peter says she did. On the other hand, Peter already testified that he committed the crime that I accused him of. As I said before, the burden of proof is on the accuser, not the defender." She stepped away from the group and walked until she stood beside Ray. She turned to face the students and instructors as she put an arm around Ray and patted her shoulder comfortingly.

"Thanks," Ray whispered, quiet enough that only the two of them could hear.

"Don't mention it. This is my way of apologizing for not stepping up and helping you before," Helen whispered back.

"B..but what about Jantzen?!" Peter shouted, his voice cracking.

"What about him?" Ven asked.

"How do you explain that he didn't respawn?"

Ven shook his head. "We all know that it happens sometimes. Nobody knows why some people fail to respawn. All we have are theories that haven't been proven yet." He stepped away from the group and walked over to stand on Ray's other side.

She watched him approach with surprise. She hadn't expected Ven to help her. She had never really had a conversation with the guy, so she didn't know anything about him. She turned her attention back to the crowd and then focused her hopeful gaze on one person.

Kelsey noticed her staring with the purest pleading gaze that she could muster and sighed. The priestess took a step forward and shuffled towards her.

Ray's eyes lit up with unadulterated joy. There were people other than Lexi who accepted her and stood by her. She revealed a beaming smile.

The four of them then turned and faced Peter and Jonathan's team.

Peter stared at the three people supporting her with disbelief. "There's no way. This is a dream, right?"

For Ray, the result was vindicating. Not only had Peter failed to ostracize her, but he, himself, had just become ostracized and lost his team. This was proof that her actions were correct.

Siegfried clapped his hands, drawing everybody's attention. "We have confirmation from Peter himself that he and Jantzen attempted to murder their teammate. There is a standing accusation that Ray murdered the two of them. Ray, do you have anything you would like to add?"

She shook her head. "I have nothing to add. My friends here have said more than enough."

"Then let us continue with the debriefing." He stepped back and Rick took over the stage.

Peter fell to his knees, defeated, yet only Jonathan spared the warlock another glance. Everybody else focused their eyes on the warrior instructor.

"Both teams failed to complete their missions. The team led by Jonathan suffered a near-total defeat, with only Kelsey surviving by hiding. The team led by Jantzen encountered the bandits but allowed them to escape and was later ambushed by goblins and annihilated except for Ray, who also survived by hiding. It is presumed that both teams were defeated by the same group of goblins and the difficulty of the request in the Adventurer's Guild has been raised to silver-rank."

Most of the students nodded in understanding. Any group of goblins that could wipe out two separate groups of adventurers in different places in a single night, even if they were trainees, was dangerous. Ray knew more than anybody else here and she agreed that the difficulty was much too high for a bronze-rank mission, let alone a trainee mission.

"Finally, Jantzen, the leader of the second party, respawned as a drone. In the next few days, we will be organizing a new party from the current students. There will be no excursions while we wait for a team to complete the goblin extermination request. In the meantime, we intend to increase the intensity of your training. This is the second excursion in a row that we have had several students die and this is unacceptable."

Jonathan hung his head in shame. Like everybody else, Ray knew the jab was mainly targeted at him. Not only had he experienced a full party wipe on the first of the two excursions, but he had rushed back out and lost half his party again. In the second excursion, he lost all but a single member.

"You all need to be more wary of death. Even if you can respawn, remember that it doesn't always work. Jantzen did not respawn this time. Next time, that might be you. Train harder! Prepare more! Strategize and study your targets! We aren't teaching you so that you can spend time in limbo, waiting to respawn. We are teaching you so that you can win and bring glory to the gods and to humanity!"

Rick stepped back and turned the stage over to Master Rambalt.

The old elementalist cleared his throat. "Kelsey and Ray, well done for surviving. The rest of you suck." Then the elementalist returned to his original position.

The air around the students seemed to thicken as the mood sank further. They were already somber listening to Rick's passionate speech but now they were just depressed.

Ray giggled as she sensed the mood falling.

"Dismissed!" Master Lion declared.

Ray turned her attention to the three people standing around her. These were her new friends who had supported her. "Thank you all so much!"

Helen and Kelsey smiled and Ven nodded his acceptance.

"What do you guys think of making this our new party?" Helen suggested. "We've got a guardian, a rogue, a priest, and a ranger."

Ray raised her hand. "I'm also studying enhancement magic and dark magic."

Helen raised an eyebrow. "An arcane guardian and a warlock, then? Are you aiming to be a dark knight?"

She shrugged. "I honestly haven't planned it out that much. I'm just learning whatever I want to."

Helen nodded in understanding. "So, what do you all think? I like the potential of this team more than my last one."

Kelsey half raised her hand. "I only have one condition. I need a team for lessons, but I do not want to be an adventurer. If you're okay with me leaving the team when we graduate, then I have no objections. I wasn't officially part of a team before anyways."

The three of them looked at Ven.

The cloaked man's shoulders sagged. "But then I would be the only male..." he muttered.

"Is that a problem?" Ray asked, tilting her head to the side.

Ven shook his head.

Helen smiled. "It's settled then! Who wants to be the leader?"

All of them exchanged glances but nobody volunteered.

Ray motioned towards Helen. "Why don't you do it"

"I'm a ranger. It's best if I'm in a position like vice-leader. My focus is tracking, scouting, detecting enemies, and long-range shooting. Oftentimes, I will be moving separately from the team so it's best if someone else is the leader."

"Same issue for me," Ven commented.

Kelsey and Ray exchanged a glance. Ray opened her mouth to speak but Kelsey beat her to the punch.

"I nominate Ray, all in favor, raise your hand!"

Kelsey, Helen, and Ven each raised their hand.

Ray opened her mouth to protest but Helen cut her off.

"It's settled then. I'm off to train so I'll see you all later!"

Helen rushed off towards the training dummies and the three of them watched her leave.

Ray returned her attention to the other two, and then her eyes widened in surprise. Ven disappeared while she was focusing on Helen. Only Kelsey was left.

Kelsey laughed when she saw Ray's flustered expression.

"What did you expect? We all gathered to support you. As the one who brought us together, whatever the reason may be, doesn't that make you our leader?"

Ray sighed in defeat. "I suppose so."

Kelsey took a step closer to Ray and started to whisper. "Will you tell me the truth later?" she asked, her tone turning serious.

Ray's eyes widened. "About Peter and Jantzen?" she clarified.

Kelsey shook her head. "I want to know how you can be an immortal and still respawn."

Ray pursed her lips as she chewed on her reply.

"Tell her yes. She's figured out this much and it doesn't look like she told anybody else yet."

She nodded slowly and Kelsey's smile widened. "I'll visit you tonight. Tell me then."

The priestess turned and left through the open doorway, ascending into the daylight of the streets above.

Ray withdrew her battle hammer as she pondered what to say to Kelsey while moving towards the training dummies to practice.

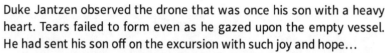

Duke Jantzen observed the drone that was once his son with a heavy heart. Tears failed to form even as he gazed upon the empty vessel. He had sent his son off on the excursion with such joy and hope…

"A report from the only survivor of his party, a trainee called Ray, indicates that they were ambushed by goblins. The reports of the other three who respawned corroborate the story," his butler reported. "However…" The butler hesitated.

Duke Jantzen noticed. "However?" he prompted.

"A boy by the name of Peter was hysterical when he respawned. He claimed that the woman called 'Ray' and her catkin slave were in league with the goblins and murdered him and Jantzen by torturing them to death."

There were a few points there that caught the duke's interest. "A catkin slave?" The slave he recently took from his son and sold was a catkin. There were multiple catkin slaves in the town, but his intuition told him it wasn't a coincidence. Was this 'Ray' the mysterious benefactor he thought had beaten sense into his son? "Have you determined the veracity of his claims?" If the boy's claims were true, then he needed to act. However, he knew the types of people his son surrounded himself with. He couldn't trust this 'Peter's' words at face value.

The butler shook his head. "My apologies, but I have not been able to yet. The students were summoned to report to their teachers, and I intend to investigate as soon as they return."

Duke Jantzen nodded. His shoulders sagged as he turned around, unable to bear the sight before him. "Investigate thoroughly," he ordered, moving through the doorway.

"By your will," the butler replied with a bow.

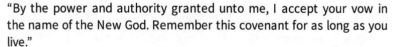

"By the power and authority granted unto me, I accept your vow in the name of the New God. Remember this covenant for as long as you live."

Lexi smiled as a familiar burst of energy filled her arms just long enough for her to cleanly snap the blade near the hilt of the small dagger in her hands. When she had first performed the ceremony, she had been a little worried that she would be unable to break the blade by herself, but it seemed that her new god would miraculously provide her with the strength necessary to accomplish the task.

The blade snapped cleanly, and Lexi buried it in the dirt, before returning the hilt to its owner, a young goblin with a long, crooked nose and sharp eyes. The goblin stepped back into the slowly growing crowd as the final goblin of the group stepped forward to make their covenant. This group of ten had approached her in secret and asked to be initiated after Vorg spoke to them.

Lexi was more than happy to accommodate them and performed the ritual. The tenth goblin, Jug, smiled as he kneeled and offered her one of his twin swords. Lexi accepted the blade reverently and baptized him in the name of the new god.

As she returned the hilt of the blade to the goblin assassin, a familiar voice interrupted the holy event, shouting angrily in fluent English.

"What is the meaning of this?"

Lexi sought out the source of the voice and her ears twitched nervously as she recognized Flynn of the Glitter Court.

"The Glitter Court has not allowed these radical elements to preach their dogma nor has the Court authorized the existence of proselytes amongst our kin."

The goblins behind Lexi began to shift and mutter amongst themselves with unease.

Vorg moved until he stood beside Lexi and addressed the grumpy Court Secretary in Goblin.

Flynn snorted, angling his chin up. "The decision of the Court was made before that perfidious false-god worshiper delivered her ultimatum. We will never abandon our heritage. The only god we worship is the Fae Mother and thus it shall be. Any of our race who opposes this fundamental state of our beings is a mistake and a heretic."

Did he just call Ray a 'perfidious false-god worshiper'? Lexi grit her teeth, her tail going stiff as her claws started to reveal themselves.

The recent converts grumbled in confusion and Lexi bit her lip, shoving down her anger as she observed them nervously. She knew that none of them were proficient enough in English to follow the conversation, but they should understand enough from the tone of the conversation that the Glitter Goblins disapproved of their actions. They were all part of the Gobber faction and were very aware of the closed-mindedness of the Glitter Goblins.

"We don't want to abandon great Demestrix," Vorg reasoned in English. "We believe to accept help. We need miracles if survive until we discover Fae Mother and why she disappear."

Lexi wasn't sure why they were speaking in English. The only possible reason was because they wanted her to understand what they were saying, but this was internal goblin politics, and she was an outsider.

"I see that you have fully become a heretic. I am disappointed in you," Flynn growled.

"A heretic?" Vorg coughed out in surprise.

"I bring an official declaration from the Glitter Court. We demand that you cease leading your fellows into condemnation until after the Court has released our decision. These brothers and sisters should be making an informed decision. Do not condemn the innocent to a life of heresy before the official stance has been made clear. It is already embarrassing that we have to exile some heretics from our tribe, we would much prefer to exile only those who would intentionally brand themselves and reject their divine heritage."

Vorg was speechless.

"Innocents? A life of heresy?" Lexi muttered; her eyes filled with fury.

From the moment Flynn had insulted Ray, calling her friend perfidious, Lexi's anger had been rising. He insulted the new god that had answered her prayers and acknowledged her. He was threatening those who sought her out to receive the blessings and miracles of this new god.

But, most importantly, he insulted Ray.

Lexi took a step forward and her mana released itself, directed by her rage. Flynn examined the furious beastkin for a moment with a critical eye before sighing.

"You're way out of your league, cursed human. These false gods are the gods of your people and I would never deny you the privilege of worshiping them. I just ask that you refrain from leading my people astray and destroying the fragile peace that exists here."

Lexi blinked in surprise, her simmering anger temporarily overwhelmed by her curiosity.

"Didn't you hate us?" she asked cautiously.

Flynn shook his head. "I do not and neither does the Court. We deny that seditious imposter who has rejected her heritage as the First Daughter of Kraveloz. We deny these malcontents who reject our own heritage. You, however, are more than welcome to embrace your heritage and follow one of the false gods who has invaded this world."

Lexi stared at the Court Secretary with a baffled expression, her anger all but completely drained away. She struggled to wrap her mind around the goblin's viewpoint.

Vorg shook his head. "The Glitter Goblins are only think on the past. Heritage and culture is not as important as our lives. We are goblins now. Fae Mother is gone now for many years."

Flynn spat a glob of coagulated glitter at the faction leader's feet. The shiny mass writhed on the ground as it mixed with the dirt.

"When your band of refugees sought our protection, we graciously provided it. We took you in and treated you as our own. You brought nothing with you but mouths to feed and dissidence. I voted against you then and you can be assured that I will be voting against you this time as well."

The Court Secretary turned and walked off. The small group of recent converts watched him leave with distaste in their eyes but none of them seemed all that worried.

Vorg looked tired as he turned to Lexi. "I'm sorry. The Glitter Court does not like other opinions."

Lexi's forehead wrinkled as she furrowed her brow. Her tail and ears twitched anxiously. "Don't worry about it. I've been treated worse than dirt before and I am prepared to be treated poorly again if it means I can return a portion of what I owe to my friend."

Vorg grinned, taking on a feral expression as he revealed his long, pointy teeth. "Good. I can respect. There are few days before Court can do anything. We will grow our numbers and support."

Lexi nodded her assent.

Vorg looked at the ten goblins who had just been baptized and repeated his statement in Goblin. Each of them nodded their understanding, splitting up throughout the camp to spread the message to those they trusted. Vorg left as well.

Lexi returned to her meditation, practicing controlling her mana. On top of the exercises Shaman taught her to train her mana to take on physical properties, she also practiced enhancement daily. She had reached the point where she could enhance her arm and bend the elbow, albeit stiffly. With a few more months of practice, Lexi hoped to reach the level where Ray was - the ability to perfectly enhance a single limb.

The other practice she had recently begun was attempting to utilize holy power. She discovered a new source connected to the well of mana within her. She instinctively felt that it was holy power and that she had obtained it as a gift. This source was the difference between a person who had an aptitude for holy magic and a person who could use holy magic.

Without the source, it was fundamentally impossible to channel divine power.

Lexi could access the source without any issue. When she did so, her mana changed until it felt bright and cleansing. She reached that step without any training or instruction. However, she had no idea what to do from there. She had little experience with using magic outside of some elemental magic she learned from her tribesmen, and the enhancement magic she was currently learning.

As a beastkin, she was not familiar with the types of spells that a person could cast with holy magic. She knew there were healing spells, cleansing spells, and smiting spells but that was the extent of her knowledge.

She spent some time focusing on teaching herself daily, but she knew it would take her a long time to make a breakthrough without guidance. Resolving to consult Ray about the issue the next time her friend visited, Lexi continued to practice.

32

Declaration

The very same day that Ray promised to explain her circumstances to Kelsey, the two met up in Ray's quarters in the temple. Ray explained everything, leaving out some of the more graphic details of her introduction to the world and, of course, skipping over the truth of what had happened with Jantzen and Peter.

She also left out the part about her encountering the goblins for now. She felt a degree of trust towards Kelsey, but she didn't trust her unconditionally yet.

Kelsey listened as Ray explained her story, her eyes going wide when Ray told of the encounter with the roc, nearly being enslaved by Jonathan's team, and being saved by Max near the gate. She bore a thoughtful expression when Ray told the priestess of how Sister Eileen had been protecting her.

However, the part that interested Kelsey the most was when Ray told her about the new god who was speaking to her.

"You're a Tether..." Kelsey breathed, her eyes alight with wonder.

Ray simply nodded.

"A Tether! A chosen representative of a god! If you are a Tether, then everything makes sense!" The young priestess grabbed Ray by the shoulders and shook her with excitement. "I understand your circumstances now. Since you trusted me, I will keep your secret until you're ready to reveal it, even if it condemns my soul to Hell!"

Ray nodded in gratitude as Kelsey released her.

"Still, it seems that times are changing," Kelsey noted while twirling a finger in her long, blonde hair thoughtfully. "A god who accepts monsters. Who would have thought that there would ever be a god of monsters?"

Ray shook her head. "We're not monsters, just different."

Kelsey snorted. "I know that. Humans are just scared. Vampires are faster than us. Trolls are stronger. Beastkin have better senses, and immortals are wiser and live forever. Hell, humans don't even have the advantage in numbers. Orcs are far more numerous. All we can rely on to survive in this world is our religion."

"Haven't they ever considered peaceful relations?"

Ray repeated the question.

"What race would be willing to speak with us? By the command of our leaders, we kill and enslave any non-human sentient race that we encounter. The neighboring United Federation has a standing order to enslave or execute humans on sight. The dwarves disappeared from the Voskeg Mountains many years ago and nobody knows where they went. The Empire of the Dragon King closed its borders. The lanterns burn our ships if the merfolk don't get to them first. Nagataur is occupied with maintaining their border with the Realm of the Mad God. Even Mad God's servants won't negotiate with us. Though we humans have never touched them, they have a strange, pervading hatred of us that goes beyond any distrust or suspicion."

"The Mad God?" Ray asked with interest.

"He's not actually a god, I think, but he is ancient and mysterious. The few eyewitness accounts say that he looks like a reaper. He wears a black robe, has glowing red eyes, and carries a large scythe. He was active in the Nightmare War fifteen-hundred years ago and has made a few appearances since, the most recent ones being about three-hundred years ago near the Forsaken Marshes, and seventy-ish years ago during the War of the Ages."

"You are well-informed," Ray observed.

Kelsey shook her head. "I just spend a lot of time in the temple library. There are all sorts of scholarly accounts in there and they are fascinating. There is so much that we don't know about this world because humans have mostly kept to themselves when they weren't invading and massacring the natives."

Ray examined Kelsey thoughtfully for a long moment, chewing on her words. Then she opened her mouth. "Would you be interested in joining us?"

Kelsey froze, her eyes going wide. "You mean, changing gods?"

Ray nodded cautiously.

Kelsey seemed to consider the question for a moment before rejecting the idea. "The idea is tempting, being able to follow a god who doesn't discriminate. I do respect the goddess very much, but not so much that I could never turn away from her."

"Then why?"

"I don't know anything about this new god yet, other than that it chose you as a Tether."

"Ah..."

Ray knew she was right. She, herself, didn't know all that much about her new god. She had a general idea that he wanted some vague concept of harmony, and that he liked beastkin for some reason, but that was all she knew about his ideals. The biggest factor that made her want to work with him was that he was always there, and he sometimes helped her with advice.

But this new god hadn't yet done anything for people like Kelsey. They had no reason to follow him when they already had another god that they followed.

"How rude," Mort muttered. "To reject the benevolent invitation of one such as my master. My lady, you must educate her most thoroughly..."

"Quiet." Ray ordered, shushing the raven lord.

Lord Mortimer sighed as he was once again quieted by his master. She felt a little guilty because she kept forcing him to be quiet. He was speaking less and less in her presence, even during the times when they were alone.

"I understand," Ray replied. "I'll ask you again once he has established his teachings."

Kelsey stood up, waving goodbye as she moved towards the door. "I'll listen when the time comes," she promised. Just before she opened the door, she paused. "Thanks for trusting me," she said softly. Then she swung the door open and left the room, closing it quietly behind her.

Ray stared at the door long after the priestess had left. She had entrusted Kelsey with important information that she understood would cause conflict if it spread. She resolved to herself that she wouldn't regret placing her trust in the priestess, no matter what happened as a result.

The next few days of training were more of the same. Kelsey started showing up to lessons with Master Rambalt again, though Peter refused to make an appearance. Ray continued her drills under Siegfried and sparred with him on occasion. Though she never managed to scrape a victory, she always forced him to fight at a hundred percent. If she increased her skills in fighting or in magic a little bit more, she thought that she might be able to beat him.

After five days of training had passed, Ray could almost fully enhance two arms simultaneously. She just needed another day or two and she would be able to start reinforcing her legs. Her dark healing speed had tripled, and she could now heal a paper cut in under twenty seconds. Once she could heal a paper cut consistently in two to four seconds, she planned to move on to larger wounds.

On the sixth day, there was a significant change. All the trainees were gathered in the underground training room again. Ray felt a brief sense of déjà vu as she observed the members of the Earthbreakers standing on a stone platform alongside the instructors.

After every student arrived, Siegfried stepped forward and began the announcement. "A week and a half ago, the Adventurer's Guild received an anonymous tip detailing the location of the nearby goblin camp."

Ray stiffened. "The informant gave detailed information that the goblins possess an assassin of a similar caliber to a High Templar. He requested the immediate dispatch of a silver-ranked team or higher, with a priority request to save the trainee he witnessed being captured."

Siegfried's eyes settled on Ray for a moment before returning to survey the crowd as he spoke. "The guild has decided to dispatch the trainee groups alongside the Earthbreakers for this mission. Both of your teams will be required to participate in a subjugation request under the leadership of Edwin Weston."

Ray felt her heart sink as the full extent of the task thrust upon her settled in. She glanced around and saw the determination in the eyes of her fellow trainees and forced herself to smile as well.

"That was the official stance of the Adventurer's Guild. However, Lord Rambalt and I personally interviewed the informant and have determined that only one team of trainees will be necessary as a support group. We have decided to send Jonathan's team while Ray's team remains on standby. If they send a distress signal, you will rush to the scene via teleportation gate."

Ray barely restrained herself from letting out a sigh of relief. That gave her some room to work with.

"The operation begins in three days. Use the remaining time to prepare for a full-scale extermination."

As Siegfried stepped back, the students burst into action as the members of each party surrounded their respective leaders. Edwin and his party stepped down and approached Jonathan's group while Helen, Ven, and Kelsey surrounded Ray.

Before Ray could start speaking, her god delivered more bad news. Her shoulders stiffened when she heard what he had to say.

"Ray, we've got another problem. The goblins are in trouble."

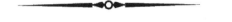

Over the next five days after Flynn had delivered his warning, Vorg, Og, and the other recent converts had managed to subtly raise the total of baptized goblins to thirty in groups of two or three. Almost all of them were Gobber Goblins, though a few were Glitter Goblins who had been wavering as the two factions intermingled over the last several months.

Finally, the fateful day when the Glitter Court would release their official statement came. As Lord Oberon took the stage, every goblin in the camp held their breath, awaiting his verdict.

"Ten days ago, our tribe was approached with a proposition," the old goblin began. "This proposition was to change the direction of our focus as a tribe from finding and serving our creator to following the edicts of a new god. We were promised the ability to respawn, something offered only to humans thus far, as well as miracles and guidance from this new god. Additionally, he promised to help us find Demestrix. In return, he asked for our faith and for our allegiance."

Lord Oberon paused, assessing the reactions of the crowd. Most of the goblins seemed interested in the proposal, though a few visibly showed signs of disgust by spitting on the ground or gnashing their teeth and scowling.

"The opinion of the Court was varied, and we debated this topic for ten days, the period set by our ancestors as the standard for resolving potentially life-changing and difficult conundrums. As a Court, we came to an inconclusive vote of two votes for and two votes against. As the deciding vote, I thought long and hard about what decision I should make for the benefit of our tribe." He stroked his long, grey beard thoughtfully, his expression showing his distaste as he released his verdict.

"I now declare the official stance of the Glitter Court. We will allow the presence and proselytizing of missionaries for this new god, but we will not tolerate conversion by the sword, nor will we allow missionaries or proselytes to exercise dominion amongst our people. Additionally, we will not tolerate secret practices or seditious elements."

Vorg and Og exchanged glances.

Og nodded and stepped back into the shadows. He moved over and tugged on the sleeve of Lexi's shirt, alerting her to his presence.

She didn't understand Goblin so they had decided that Og would let her know if things were getting dangerous.

"Time to go," he muttered in garbled English.

"It has come to our attention that there is a group of goblins who have embraced this new god. This, by itself, would be fine. However, they moved about secretly and gathered their forces behind closed doors. It is concerning to the Court that this group would strive so much to act without our knowledge, and we must question their motives. To that end, we have decided to temporarily suppress this group while we investigate. Fortunately, our informant provided a list of the names of each goblin who is participating. I will now read aloud this list and I will ask the goblins surrounding these individuals to suppress them if they refuse to cooperate."

Before Og and Lexi could move far, Og felt a hand grab his shoulder despite his concealment. He looked back and saw Trog staring at him sadly.

"Og and Vorg," Oberon called out.

Og sighed, raising his hands to show that he would go willingly.

"Jug, Yog, Rogog, Pog, Frank, Irg, Nogg..." the Lord began listing off names. As each name was called, the goblin raised their hands and allowed themselves to be taken. In accordance with their vows to the new god, they would do what it took to live in harmony. They had decided beforehand that they would accept whatever decision the Glitter Court made.

As this continued, Lord Cedric came up beside Lexi. "As our guest who is allowed to proselytize by law, you may choose to remain free or to be detained with them. We will respect your decision, but we would ask that you refrain from operating in secret in the future."

Lexi felt lost as she watched the people she had baptized one by one being rounded up. She felt a tinge of guilt welling up, realizing that if she hadn't performed the ordinance, none of these goblins would be in trouble. If she had waited a few more days or perhaps if they had operated more openly, this oppressive atmosphere might have been avoided.

"I will stay with them for now," she replied.

The Martial Lord reached out and gently grasped her wrist with his clawed fingers. "If you would follow me, I will guide you."

Lexi allowed herself to be dragged, shuffling behind him as they moved towards an area near where the Glitter Court met. The area was being cordoned off with slabs of stone that were being manipulated by goblin elementalists while the goblins whose names were called were led into the enclosure.

Cedric released her, motioning for the young beastkin to enter. Lexi stepped into the prison and watched as the walls moved higher and higher. After the stone reached a height twice that of the average grown human, the stone began to stretch out over the area to form a roof.

Lexi stroked the shackle on her wrist and the rattling of the chain mingled with the scenery to bring back unpleasant memories.

Vorg tapped her arm, pulling her attention away from the prison being formed around them. "I'm sorry, Lady Leximea. I did not guess this."

"It's fine," Lexi muttered in reply. "I can understand their reasoning. My father despised secret organizations forming in our tribe because it undermined his authority and often led to trouble and death."

Vorg let out a deep sigh, chuckling to himself scornfully. "This time is the same."

"What do you mean?" Lexi asked, tilting her head to the side as her ears twitched anxiously.

Vorg scratched the side of his head. "Ahh, how should I say…? Did you see Flynn out there?"

Lexi shook her head. She hadn't seen Flynn or the other two members of the Court. She hadn't seen Shaman either, despite the importance of the event.

"Glitter Goblins are not all of same opinion. Flynn is extreme but Lord Oberon and Shaman are middle. Glitter Court has three middle and two extreme. This cause many fights."

Lexi furrowed her brow as she tried to guess what Vorg was hinting at. "So, the extremists were overruled by the moderates and that led to our current circumstances. Is there more to it than that?"

Vorg let out another deep sigh. "Your father was a leader?"

Lexi nodded. "He was chief of the Bloodclaw tribe."

"Then you know. Politics is dirty. Losers do not like losing."

Lexi cast her mind back to her childhood years. People had different opinions that they believed were facts, and when they didn't get what they wanted they would cause problems. Her father had always seemed stressed dealing with one problem or another. The issues would pile on top of each other and, if he failed to manage them properly, things got out of hand.

Comparing that to their current situation and layering in Flynn's words from several days ago, Lexi gasped.

"How long do we have?" she asked, fidgeting with her tail nervously.

"Maybe tonight."

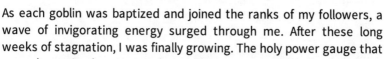

As each goblin was baptized and joined the ranks of my followers, a wave of invigorating energy surged through me. After these long weeks of stagnation, I was finally growing. The holy power gauge that was always in the corner of my vision was expanding and growing denser. The total holy power available increased with each person who was baptized, and the gauge filled up as I received their prayers.

Interestingly, after roughly ten or so people were baptized, I stopped receiving prayers directed towards nobody. I still received prayers from Steve because he was directing them towards me, though he wasn't fully aware that I existed yet.

My theory was that the system aid for finding potential followers was removed now that I had a basis for expanding my religion.

I would have confirmed this with Auto, but...

"Hey Auto, you there buddy?"

Silence. Auto hadn't spoken to me for a while. I was absorbed in building my teachings and following the events happening on the surface, so I hadn't spoken to him in a while either. I couldn't say when he left but the fact was that he was no longer here, and he hadn't said a word before disappearing.

He called himself a training and observation unit. While I wasn't sure why he would no longer need to observe me, I felt a sense of pressure from the realization that my 'training' was apparently finished. Simultaneously, it felt like a burden was lifted. Ever since I came to this world, I was out of my element. I had to be careful and timid because I couldn't accurately predict the consequences of my actions.

With Auto leaving, it was proof that I now knew enough. My training was finished, and it was time for me to become more active. I wasn't sure if he would ever come back, but it didn't matter. Listening in on the conversations around Ray in Cairel and around my followers in the goblin camp, I was very aware that something big was about to go down.

It pained me to see that the reason the goblins were being detained was that they had become my followers. I had seen enough corrupt politics back on Earth leading up to the rise of the Director. Extremists never got anything done on the surface because they are too busy slandering the opposing side. Even if they pretended to compromise, it was just another way of saying that they would get their way outside of the public's attention.

I would wait and see before forming my opinion on Oberon, but Flynn was exactly the kind of degenerate that pervaded the governments of Earth before the Director cleansed the system. It was because of people like him that the general population initially embraced that dictator's rise to power. I was also his follower until he went crazy with power. We all did, every member of the resistance.

We realized it too late, and he gained some sort of power from the gateway. After that, he personally took to the battlefield and wiped out every army that faced him. The gateway was destroyed so that no one else could obtain the power that he did. He bulldozed through politics with overwhelming force and overturned all his opposition with bloodshed.

The ethics of his methods aside, I had to give credit where it was due. The man got things done.

Personally, I had mixed feelings when thinking about the Director. If he had died after he cleansed the government of America, he probably would have gone down in history as a great man. Had he died after he conquered the rest of North America, he still would have been a great man, but flawed.

But alas, he didn't die and now every person on Earth could see him for who he was - a ruthless, cold-blooded killer, and a dictator. When he inevitably traveled down the path of all dictators in history, he would only be remembered for his cruelty and not for the great acts that elevated him to his position.

It had been a long time since I had thought about the time before the Director started rising to power, but the actions of the goblins reminded me. There was a reason I had supported that man and his radical ideas.

If there was one thing I hated, it was deception. Hiding small things wasn't a big deal. Having Ray hide the fact that she was a Tether... that kind of thing didn't bother me either. What bothered me was the type of deception that was happening right now before my eyes.

I felt my form begin to vibrate as anger welled up inside of me.

"Ray, we've got another problem. The goblins are in trouble." I spat out.

I looked around the goblin camp and saw Flynn speaking to Cosmo, Lord of the Hunt. Since they were outside of earshot of any of my followers, I couldn't distinguish any of their words, but it was obvious from their vicious expressions and barely concealed anger that they were planning something.

I used to look the other way and say I didn't know enough, but that wouldn't work this time. My training was finished. I knew enough, even if it didn't feel like it.

Whatever was going to happen, it was going to happen soon, and I would not look the other way.

33

The First Miracle

That evening, after lessons ended and she was finally separated from all the people that might interfere, Ray bolted for the gate with Mort gliding smoothly through the air behind her. She ran over the rooftops to avoid the annoying task of weaving around people. As she jumped from roof to roof, she couldn't help but remember the previous time she had left town this way. Back then, she had just become aware, and she was confused. She wasn't acting rationally.

This time, Ray knew exactly where she was going and why. She had a purpose. Though she wasn't fully aware of the details, something was happening in the goblin camp. On top of that, the adventurers knew where the camp was and were preparing to raid it. She needed to warn them.

She kicked off the final building and launched herself towards the gate. The guard waved as he recognized her flying form. It was Jerrick, someone that she hadn't seen in a while. Ray waved back as she sailed over his head and into the tunnel. She rushed out of the gate and into the farmland. At her pace, she would reach the goblin camp before it got too dark outside.

Ray cried out as something caught her leg and she tumbled forward, crashing face first into the cold, hard ground. There was a sharp pain in the area around her nose as she stood up, and she grimaced as her nose straightened itself back out. She ignored the blood dribbling down her chin and searched for the cause of her tumble.

"Where do you think you are going?" a cold voice whispered from the shadows.

The voice seemed to be coming from all around her.

"Who are you?" she coughed out. Her voice sounded reminiscent of a human who had a cold. Her nose twitched uncomfortably as it reformed and Ray took a deep breath as she reached up, pinching the bridge of her nose. She snorted mightily and launched the congealed blood out.

A figure appeared before her, stepping out of the shadows.

Ray blinked in surprise when she recognized him. "Max? What are you doing here?" She hadn't seen since he helped her through the gate.

"I'm making sure you don't do anything foolish. Go back to the temple."

Ray's eyes narrowed at the strange order. "Why do you think I'm doing something foolish?"

"You're going to warn the goblins, correct? That is foolish. You must remain in Cairel for the next few days while this situation resolves itself."

"Why?"

Lord Mortimer descended and alighted himself on Ray's arm that she extended as a perch. "My Lady, allow me to terminate this depraved creature who dared to harm your beautiful face."

Ray smirked while stroking Mort's back. "Max, if you don't give me a suitable explanation, I'm going."

Max ran a hand through his short-cropped hair, mumbling inaudibly to himself. Ray thought she heard something about 'three more days', but she wasn't quite sure.

"The Lady asked you a question!" Mort shouted, spreading his wings wide in a regal manner. "Answer or suffer the consequences!"

Max focused his attention on the bird. His eyes narrowed. "Quincy did mention that you had a talking bird. It's quite annoying."

"A t..talking bird?!" Mort spluttered, outraged. "I am not merely a 'talking bird', I am Lord Mortimer Perseus Raventon the Dark, the Lord of Ravens and faithful servant of Lady Ray!"

"Yes, yes," Ray stroked the back of his head. "You are great and mighty."

Mort calmed down as he received the attention of his master. He began to preen his feathers, keeping an eye on the rude man who spoke like an ill-bred savage. If the brute tried anything, he would curse the man's luck so thoroughly that he would die before he realized how unlucky he was. Ray wasn't quite sure what that meant, but Max was close to Eileen, so she didn't want to risk something bad happening to him.

Max returned his attention to Ray. "Miss, as worried as you may be about the situation, it is best to leave it to resolve itself naturally.

Humans and monsters fight. That's just how it is. The gods have ordained it and until someone takes their place, that is how it will be."

"And you're okay with that?"

"Of course I'm not okay with it! Why do you think I've...? Ah..." Max cut himself off. He glared at her warily.

"Why are you so flustered?" Ray pressed.

He closed his eyes, taking a deep breath to calm himself. When he reopened his eyes, he observed the young lady with a more relaxed expression.

"I apologize. I let my emotions control me. Please strike it from your mind."

"Is something wrong?" Ray asked, taking on a softer tone. "Is there something that you need my help with?"

He shook his head. "My worries are my own. If you truly desire to help me, then please... stay in Cairel for three more days. You need to be inside the town during the attack on the goblin village."

Ray frowned. "I don't understand. Why do you care so much?"

Max ground his teeth in frustration. "Stop asking me 'why'! If I were going to tell you, I would have answered the first time!"

"If it's so important that you remain in Cairel, ask him why he reported the location of the goblin village."

Ray repeated the question.

His eyes widened. "Why do you think that?"

She remained silent, waiting for his explanation.

The High Templar sighed, seeing that she wasn't going to answer. "I reported it because I need you to be in Cairel three days from now. At the time, I thought that it would be necessary to send a group of adventurers to bring you back. I didn't expect you to waltz back into town a day later."

Ray chewed on his words for a moment.

"What do you think I should do?" she asked in her mind.

"Leave Lexi, Vorg, and the others to me. You can't get there in time to help them anyways. Send Mort ahead to deliver the message that adventurers are coming. We'll set up plans after that."

Ray clenched her fists, deciding to trust the ever-present voice in her head. She turned and looked at the large bird perched on her arm. "Mort, I have a mission for you."

The raven lord perked up. "Finally! I mean, how may I serve?"

"Fly to the goblin village hidden near the base of the second peak in those mountains over there. Find a catkin named Leximea Bloodclaw and deliver a warning that adventurers will be attacking in three days.

I trust that you have been paying attention and will be able to answer any questions that she might have."

The raven lord raised a wing and saluted. "Thy will be done!" he declared, stepping off her arm and gliding up into the sky before turning towards the Voskeg Mountains.

"I will accomplish this task without fail!" Ray flinched when the raven lord's voice spoke directly to her mind even though he was already a dark speck in the sky.

"I didn't know he could speak in my mind..." she muttered. She returned her attention to Max who was staring off into the distance where the raven had disappeared. "I'll be heading back!" she announced, startling him.

A relieved smile slowly spread across the man's face and Ray felt a seed of unease sprouting within her. She had no idea why he was so insistent that she stay in Cairel, but she wondered if it was related to why Eileen was refusing to meet with her.

Ray turned and allowed Lord Maxwell to escort her back into the town.

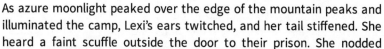

As azure moonlight peaked over the edge of the mountain peaks and illuminated the camp, Lexi's ears twitched, and her tail stiffened. She heard a faint scuffle outside the door to their prison. She nodded towards Og and Jug and the two of them stepped back into the shadows, prepared to ambush whoever came through the entrance.

The stone door began to tremble as it slowly sank into the ground. Moonlight peaked over the widening gap, hiding the identity of the intruder behind a dark shadow. The small figure slid through the gap once it was large enough, drawing out a small, two-handed mace. Several more goblins began pouring in behind him. Without any words, they drew their weapons and charged.

The goblins inside the prison began to shout as they pulled out whatever hidden weapons they had managed to sneak into the prison with them. Some of them cowered, rushing towards the back while others stood firm, ready to defend their lives. The dark tide rushing towards them faltered as several of the invading goblins in the lead keeled over, bleeding from gashes in their throats.

The goblin in the lead swung his hammer towards an empty space and a loud *clang* resounded as it was parried by something invisible to the naked eye. Lexi sniffed carefully and she could barely detect Og's scent coming from that space.

The rest of the invading goblins set upon the defenders and began to slaughter them in silence. The defenders cried out desperately as they fought back. The fight wasn't entirely one-sided as some of the defenders managed to repel their attackers, but the ones who lacked weapons found it difficult to deal a killing blow while avoiding the flailing knives.

Lexi flinched as a goblin rushed towards her, his face distorted with an angry sneer. She took a step back into a stance. As he neared her, she stepped forward, firmly planting her foot on the ground as she took advantage of her superior reach to spin and hook her heel into the goblin's neck.

The goblin's head snapped to the side with a sickening crunch and the creature fell, his momentum carrying forward for a few more steps until he crashed to the ground at her feet. Lexi reached down and picked up the bone knife he was holding. She rushed back to a weaponless female goblin hiding near the back of the room and passed her the weapon.

"Take this and use it to defend yourself," she urged.

The goblin accepted the weapon gingerly, looking up at the beastkin who was helping her. She didn't understand her words, but she could see the priestess' unwavering eyes. The goblin clenched her claws around the hilt and directed her fury towards their assailants. She charged out with the dagger and stabbed a goblin who was attacking one of her brethren. Her dagger took him in the back, and he keeled over, releasing his blade.

The female goblin leaned over to grab the new dagger when a mace spun out of the darkness and smashed her in the head, caving in her skull.

"Pog!" the goblin she had just saved shouted out.

Trog was launched out of the shadows by a kick and Og followed him out, striking furiously with his daggers. The two assassins clashed over the corpse of Pog while the goblin that she saved snatched the two daggers and crawled away from the scene, looking for another goblin ally to arm.

Lexi cast her eyes over the chaos. The frequent clanging of weapons and the cries of pain and anguish filled the air. She closed her eyes and began to pray.

"Please help us!"

She felt a warm sensation as if she were being embraced and a sense of peace washed over her.

Then all hell broke loose.

The ground began to rumble. All the goblins stumbled away from each other, pausing combat as they felt the world shaking. A loud *crack* resounded, and Lexi craned her neck to see a large, dark tear in the ceiling. The gap slowly widened, allowing moonlight to enter and light up her surroundings. In front of the large, azure moon, she saw dark clouds gathering.

A drop of rain struck her face and she flinched, her nose twitching. The goblins rushed towards the opening of the prison as rocks began to crash down from the crumbling ceiling. Many of them tripped and fell as they failed to maintain their balance on the flowing surface. Lexi stared at the scene in a daze.

Was this the answer to her prayers?

A sudden downpour descended from the sky, instantly soaking Lexi and every goblin. Lightning crackled in the clouds and the beastkin priestess sensed what was coming. She dived towards the corner of the prison as a flash of light illuminated the world behind her, followed by roaring thunder.

Cries of fear filled the night. Another flash and then the smell of burnt flesh permeated the air. The earthquake eased and the building stabilized. Lexi huddled down, covering her ears as the deafening roar of a raging dragon shook the world once more.

A flash struck a building near the other side of the camp, melting through the structure like butter and frying the goblin within.

Lexi quivered in her hiding place, occasionally glancing at the sky fearfully. She flinched at each flash of light and peel of thunder.

Truly, her prayer had been answered. Normally she would feel thankful, but in the moment, Lexi could only feel fear.

Amidst the raging storm, a large, black raven descended into the building and alighted himself on a piece of rubble lying near her. Lexi sensed the presence and turned her terrified gaze on it.

The raven opened its mouth, and, to Lexi's surprise, it spoke in English. "Quivering feline, this magnanimous and glorious Lord of Ravens brings a message from his master, Lady Ray!"

Lexi's eyes widened. "From Ray...?" Her fear temporarily settled as she focused her attention on the bird in front of her, ignoring the screams of terror and violent flashes of lightning in the background.

"The adventurers are coming to attack in three days!"

Her heart sank. "Wonderful..." she droned sarcastically. With a sigh, she pushed herself to her feet and wobbled into the rain. She stepped past the corpses of goblins she had baptized. She scoffed at the charred remains of their assailants and kicked them aside. She hadn't realized it while she was overcome with fear, but the lightning discriminated. It only struck those who had attacked the prison and it sought them out ruthlessly.

"Great One! Please stay your wrath," Lexi prayed.

Immediately, the rain ceased, and the dark clouds faded away as if some unseen being was wiping it away with an eraser. The goblins who were hiding near her and overheard her prayer stared at her in awe. They didn't understand the words that she spoke, but they understood the most important point.

Her prayer calmed the storm. She spared their lives.

Lexi ignored them as she strode towards the tent where she knew Shaman dwelled.

Og appeared beside her, his expression blank. His knees were shaking, and his gait was unsteady.

She continued forward and he followed behind her. Lexi observed the camp as she walked. As expected, every goblin was now awake. Many of them were on their knees, praying to the Fae Mother while others were staring at the night sky with dazed eyes. The few goblins remaining from the group that had attacked her cowered under her sharp gaze, crawling away from her path.

Other than the prison and the one building on the other side of the camp, none of the structures were harmed. Lexi figured this was some other miracle performed by the powerful god who was watching over her. She shivered as the cold, winter chill settled over the camp once more, reminding her that she was still soaked.

As they approached the old goblin's tent, they found her waiting outside. Her tired eyes focused on them and noted the large, black raven following behind Lexi.

Shaman sighed and motioned for them to enter. "It seems that we have much to talk about."

Lexi entered the tent and shuddered with delight as the warm air rushed over her. She shook off the droplets of water clinging to her body and moved closer to the fire.

The old goblin shuffled over to her rocking throne and plopped down. After a long, drawn-out silence, she closed her eyes and clenched her teeth before spitting out her question. "Please inform me as to why an angry god is smiting my people?"

"It is because we were attacked within the prison by assailants during the night," she answered. "I prayed for salvation, and he delivered us."

Shaman opened her eyes and stared at Lexi accusingly. "You called down the wrath of your god on my tribe? Even if their choice was wrong, those goblins who were smitten won't respawn like those who accepted your god. It was too much to continue smiting them long after they lost the will to fight."

Lexi shook her head. "He stopped because I asked him to. Under normal circumstances, I would have waited until all of the attackers were dead, but there will soon be a need for every goblin in this camp."

"What do you mean?" Shaman asked, her eyes narrowing.

Lexi motioned towards the raven lord who had followed her into the tent and was now perched on a pole near the roof.

"Accursed, clawed menaces and the fallen race...! The company my lady keeps is unbecoming of her illustrious self," the bird murmured.

"Ahem," Lexi cleared her throat.

The bird focused its beady eyes on the priestess and the old goblin. "Greetings, I am Lord Mortimer Perseus Raventon the Dark, loyal servant and familiar to the great Lady Ray."

Shaman nodded in greeting. "It is nice to meet you once more, Lord of Ravens. I did not expect to see you again."

The raven lord cocked his head as he examined Shaman more closely. "Ah...!" he sighed, ruffling his feathers uncomfortably. "I did not expect to meet you again either."

Shaman grimaced. "It is a bad omen if you have reentered this world. You claim to have come as a familiar to young Ray?"

Lord Mortimer raised his wing. "I do not merely claim so, for it is a fact that I have come in the aforementioned capacity."

The old goblin closed her eyes, leaning her head forward into her staff. She seemed to age a decade in a moment as she pondered. Finally, she opened her eyes, focusing on the ground below as she asked the question that she knew she didn't want to know the answer to. "And to what, pray tell, do we owe the pleasure of your visit?"

Lord Mortimer descended from his perch and hovered above the fire, keeping himself aloft through some unknown method. As the smoke curled around his dark feathers, he raised his wings dramatically and declared in the regalest voice that he could muster.

"The adventurers are coming!"

Keeping an ear on the ground as Lexi, Mort, and Shaman discussed the impending attack, I thought about the actions I had just taken. My holy power bar was nearly empty now. It had taken almost everything I had stockpiled to channel that localized earthquake and summon a thunderstorm. Once the storm was already present, each lightning bolt only took a small amount of power but summoning the storm itself consumed almost half.

Considering that I had thirty-one followers, that wasn't too bad. If I had over a million, I could probably summon as many lightning storms as I wanted, assuming that I was willing to forgo other miracles that might cost even more.

I knew that Flynn was going to act in some manner.

I knew that it was possible that some of my followers could die.

However, there was a difference between knowing it was possible and seeing it happen. I taught my followers to be peaceful and to seek harmony. They followed my will, and they were slaughtered.

What was the meaning of harmony then?

Clearly, pacifism was not harmony. While I was busy trying to play god, I nearly forgot some of the lessons that I already learned in my past life. Sometimes, peace could only be won with the sword. Striving too hard to avoid conflict would often result in the peace-seekers receiving violence and persecution.

I looked over the destruction below me, the scorch marks on the ground, the crumbled prison, and the blood mixed with pooling rainwater.

This was the result of avoiding open conflict.

If I wanted to move forward and bring true peace and harmony, then I had to learn from this experience. If I wanted to help the people of either world, then I couldn't shy away from fighting. I already knew this, but I had forgotten it.

I opened my tenets tab and selected the 'domain' button. Then I adjusted the draft that had been waiting for my final decision - the one that would determine my direction and focus for as long as I ruled on this world.

God of Harmony. God of Freedom.

These were the two domains I had settled on thus far. Selecting the space in front of God of Harmony, I pushed it down to second place.

If I wasn't going to shy away from conflict, then I needed to embrace and control it. My people would need to fight on my terms. My teachings would reflect it. They would know that sometimes peace could only be obtained through fighting.

Carefully, as if writing the lines of destiny, I typed in my first and final of my three domains.

God of War.

I hit submit before I could second guess my decision and my three domains locked in.

God of War, God of Harmony, God of Freedom.

These three concepts would define me. They would define my religion and my church. These concepts would lie at the center of my teachings and would outline the form and the core of the afterlife that I would design.

Now that I had a direction, followers, and a prophet who was willing to cooperate with me, it was time to move on. It was time to stop 'playing god'.

It was time to become the real thing.

34

Initial Assault

Melissa had just about had it with the scrubs that her team was carrying through this mission. The party of trainees was so unfocused and incapable that her head ached every time that she heard them speak. Twice in the last hour, the overzealous priestess and the playboy warlock had devolved into competing to see who could come up with a more offensive insult.

She and her fellow silver-rankers were traveling near the edge of the Voskeg Mountains. They had been assigned by the Guild Master to purge the goblins and rescue a trainee that had allegedly been captured. It was clearly bullshit since none of the trainees were missing, but a mission was a mission. This same group of goblins was said to have an assassin unit with a leader capable of fighting on par with Lord Maxwell Rovar, a High Templar.

If it were just that goblin alone, she wouldn't be very worried. She trusted her teammates and they had faced difficult foes in the past. They were veterans of many battlefields.

It was her past experiences fighting goblins that made her wary.

It wasn't uncommon for goblins to have assassins, but assassins were never the leader. If this tribe had assassins that were that powerful, their leaders were likely to be even more frightening.

A gentle hand tapped her shoulder, pulling Melissa from her thoughts. She turned and saw Edwin looking at her with a concerned look.

"How're you holding up?" he asked.

Melissa rolled her eyes. "I'll live, though my mental state might be permanently affected."

He chuckled. "Everybody has to start somewhere."

She shook her head, motioning slightly towards idiots one and two. "Maybe so, but *that* is a bit much."

They looked at the party walking down the path with them. Though Samantha and Sage were keeping an eye on their surroundings, the fools that should have been helping watch for roaming monsters or enemy scouts were showing their mediocrity and lack of training. Their party had a ranger *and* a rogue, for crying out loud! There was literally no excuse for them to be so inattentive to their surroundings.

The group had a general idea as to where the goblin camp was located due to the anonymous informant, but they didn't know exactly where it was. Melissa had never been to the area before either, so she didn't have a relay point to tie her teleportation artifact to, which was a shame because she was looking forward to showing off her level a bit to the newbies. Thus, they had been roaming around the hill for over an hour.

There was an itch in the back of Melissa's mind that told her something was wrong with their surroundings, but she couldn't quite place it...

"Shut it, you judgmental prick!" a voice shouted from behind them.

Melissa sighed while Edwin just shook his head. They stopped, turning to address whatever happened before it turned into another fight.

The warlock was bearing down on Suzy, who was in turn gathering mana to cast some sort of spell. Suzy raised a hand and gathered holy light.

"*Divine Retri---*" she started when a flash of crimson crossed her vision.

Samantha appeared behind her, her red hair billowing as she smacked the purge-happy priestess on the back of her head.

"Oww! What was that for?" Suzy demanded, covering the throbbing spot with her hand.

"Don't use holy purge spells on your allies. It's inefficient," Samantha reprimanded sternly.

"It's more than just inefficient. It's unacceptable. Why the hell would you attack a teammate?" Melissa demanded.

On a personal level, she understood Suzy's dislike of the playboy. He laced too many of his words with mind control magic for any magic-user to feel comfortable around him. Outwardly, he seemed like a nice enough person, but her intuition warned her that he was actually a weak predator.

"This creep just tried to use magic on me again. Let me purge him just once! He'll respawn...!" Suzy growled, miffed at being stopped mid-cast.

Melissa's eyes softened. As a girl, she understood Suzy's feelings but as an adventurer...

"This behavior is unprofessional. You may do as you wish after the completion of the quest," Samantha said in her typical monotone.

Melissa had been adventuring with the methodical rogue for almost a decade and she honestly couldn't remember the woman ever displaying more than the most basic level of emotion.

"Now, now" Edwin interjected. "There are bound to be tensions when working with new faces. Both of you have a bone to pick with these goblins, right?"

Suzy and the warlock both nodded.

"Then you should work together until they are dead." He looked at Suzy. "That will help you appease your god." Then he looked at the warlock. "And it should help you get the revenge that you desire." He turned to Melissa and Samantha. "Either of you have any ideas on what's going on? The intel said the camp would be around here."

Samantha shrugged indifferently. "The paths are strange."

"What do you mean?"

She pointed at the road they were following. It angled off to the right and continued as far as the eye could see. There were a few trees lining the path and budding flowers amongst the rocks, but nothing stood out to Melissa.

"The trees are the same. Somehow, we are walking in a loop," Samantha supplied.

The itching feeling in the back of Melissa's mind returned and then her eyes widened in understanding. That feeling was her mind reacting to the use of magic! All things considered that had to mean...

"Illusion!" Melissa shouted. "We've been wandering under an illusion barrier for over an hour."

Edwin clasped his gauntleted hands together, the chainmail on his arms rattling from the impact. "There we go! An illusionist! If it took us this long to detect it, then the little bugger must be pretty powerful." He glanced at Melissa. "Can you break it?"

She smirked at the obvious challenge. "Easily." She closed her eyes and focused on sensing the magic in the air around her. The magic had an almost 'tangy' taste to it that made her mouth water. She ignored the feeling as she drew upon her own internal mana supply. After a moment of gathering mana, she condensed it into a fine point and thrust it into the barrier around them. A faint buzzing sound reached her ears and then her vision distorted. Their surroundings began to blur and shift as the path bent into its normal position. The barrier had been surprisingly easy to break. Whoever the illusionist was, they had powerful skills, but their mana supply was probably small.

The trainee adventurers all gaped at their surroundings, mouths wide with amazement. Melissa squared her shoulders smugly as she took in their silent complements.

And then all hell broke loose. An arrow flew from a nearby tree and struck Melissa in the shoulder. Burning pain clouded her mind for a moment and she cried out as she ducked down, covering her head with her uninjured arm. A scream from nearby alerted them to the presence of multiple attackers.

"Defensive positions!" Edwin shouted, donning his shield and mace in seconds. He stepped in between Melissa and the attacker and smoothly defected a hail of arrows.

Samantha followed the direction the arrows were coming from and ran towards the tree line, dodging any arrows aimed at her as she looked for the source. Suzy and the warlock were both face-first on the ground, Suzy was crying with a large slash on her back while the Warlock was out cold, a bloody gash on his head.

"They were waiting to ambush us as soon as we broke the barrier...!" Melissa realized, dazed. "They weren't supposed to know that we were coming though!"

"Get a hold of yourself. We need your magic!" Edwin ordered.

Melissa shook her head and slapped herself to clear her thoughts. She pulled a health potion out of her bag and started to drink it while yanking the arrow out with her free hand. The sharp pain was instantly muted by soothing relief as the injury healed.

She looked around, gathering information about their new surroundings. The trainees were scattered, running about like chickens with their heads cut off. They had no sense of order or discipline.

Samantha was moving through the trees, chasing some sort of blur that Melissa couldn't make out distinctly, but she thought it might be a goblin. A really, really fast goblin.

"*Mana Well*," she muttered, using the short incantation to focus her thoughts on her magic. The air around her seemed to thicken, filling with the overpowering smell of roses. She channeled her mana into the well, multiplying the output manyfold. As she reached the amount that she needed, she projected the mana into the surrounding forest.

The mana condensed around each of the adventurers, protecting them from the hail of arrows and any other attack that might come.

A few more arrows were absorbed by the barrier before the hail stopped. Then, as quickly as the attack had started, the attackers disappeared. Even Samantha paused as she was unable to find any trace of them.

They waited for several more seconds of tense silence, prepared to defend against any attacks. Sage used her nature magic to heal the injured trainees while Samantha, Bill, and Vick swept their surroundings.

Finally, the three returned, assuring everybody that the attackers were gone for now.

Melissa sank to the ground. "What the hell was that..." she groaned, massaging her shoulder where she had been injured. Lowest-quality healing potions were great, but she would still have a bruise.

"Someone told them we were coming," Samantha observed. "There is a traitor or a spy in Cairel."

Sage grimaced as she finished treating Suzy's back. The young priestess was sobbing, clutching her hands together in prayer as she mumbled incoherently.

"Why would any human try to protect goblins?" Sage asked, her lips quivering as her normally smooth and melodic voice was betrayed by a slight tremble.

Edwin reached into his bag and pulled out a bottle of water, guzzling it to wet his throat. "We'll have to worry about that later as well. For now, we need to make a plan of attack. We can expect that the rest of the path will have various traps and ambushes laid out for us."

"Can't we just use magic to detect the traps?" Jonathan asked as he approached. He pointed at the barrier surrounding them. "This seems like it could keep us safe from almost anything."

Edwin motioned for Samantha to explain.

"Our opponents are a skilled group of assassins. If they use magic to set a trap, then it would be possible to detect its magic signature using magic ourselves. However, they will probably have set their traps manually. If so, we will also have to find and avoid or disable them manually," she recited dutifully.

"And the barrier?" Jonathan pressed. As he motioned towards it again, the barrier folded in on itself and collapsed, the mana dispersing into the air.

Melissa shook her head. "It's not all-powerful. As you just saw, I can only maintain it for a handful of seconds... perhaps a minute if I strain myself. Also, it won't stop any traps that go off inside of the barrier."

Jonathan frowned. "What's the point of detection magic if it can't sense things done without magic?"

Edwin smiled. "Good question. Magic can be used to automate processes; therefore magic is often predictable and easy to counter. As we just noted, if you simply use magic to simplify processes in combat, there is a tradeoff. You are basically advertising your position, your abilities, or your method of attack. While it has limited uses as a feint, you won't see veteran assassins using magic to set their traps."

"Templars and arcane tricksters, on the other hand..." Sage jumped in when she was interrupted.

"We can continue this lesson another time," Melissa pressed. "We're in enemy territory and they know we are here. We need to end this quickly."

Edwin nodded in agreement. He turned to Samantha. "I want you to find the exact location of their base. With the illusion barrier down, it should be simple enough. Then, find out as much information about their numbers and equipment, and as much of the layout of the camp as you can." He turned to address the rabble of weakling trainees. "As for the rest of you, let's talk about a little something that I like to call 'teamwork.'"

⸺◆⸺

Lexi stood behind a barricade on a raised platform near the center of the camp. This relatively centralized area served as the strategic command center for the goblin defensive forces. She had a small, patchy straw hat covering her ears and her tail was tucked into her pants. Though uncomfortable, she endured because it was part of the plan.

On a small table in front of her sat a hand-drawn map of the village and its surroundings. Aside from Lexi, there were four others sitting around the table - Shaman, Lord Cedric, Frog, and another goblin called Nag. Frog was the strategist for the Glitterfart goblins while Nag used some sort of magic that she didn't understand. It allowed him to relay instructions quickly and easily.

Though Lord Cedric was the Martial Lord, he was only in the command center because he was awaiting deployment. He was much better at fighting than coordinating troops.

She looked out over the camp once more, noting that the sun was reaching its highest point in the sky. The alarm sounded hours earlier, but the adventurers had yet to reveal themselves to the camp. Nag was receiving steady reports about the movements of the adventurers from Og's assassin troupe, but it wasn't clear why they were waiting.

On the other side of the palisade, she could just make out the craggy trees. The newly budding branches remained relatively still.

"They broke through the barrier, right? What are they doing? Why aren't they attacking?" Lexi asked, with a hint of annoyance.

Frog tapped his finger on the table while observing the map with a critical eye. There were small stones marking the positions of the various defensive groups. There were offensive and defensive lines, archers, assassins, magical bombardment and support groups, and supply lines set up in a series of circles around the camp. Lexi didn't fully understand the purpose of it, but there was an offensive line and a defensive line in the center of the camp behind all the mages.

"They must be gathering information. As far as they know, we aren't supposed to be aware of this attack," Frog replied, his voice tense.

"Why are we giving them time to plan? Shouldn't we act while we have more information?"

"Og and his group are already engaging in guerrilla fighting but we can't move our entire force into the forest. If this turns into an unorganized brawl, we'll lose."

Lexi hissed, balling her hands into fists. Her claws dug into her palms. "We should be doing something. I dislike this waiting game."

Shaman placed a calming hand over Lexi's clenched fists. "Relax, child. All things in their proper time. The only information they have is that which their senses can detect. They will fall for our traps."

Lexi took a deep breath and forced herself to relax. "Will these 'traps' be enough, though? Og told me a bit about silver-rankers."

Shaman shook her head, smiling uneasily. "There is nothing we can do that will guarantee our victory; however, we have no choice but to try."

"The enemy has split up," Nag reported. "Also, the assassins have lost sight of most of the members. They assume some sort of teleportation magic is involved."

A flicker at the edge of her vision caught Lexi's eye and she turned in time to see a hail of snow fall from the hanging limbs of a tree. The horn sounded once more and all the goblins immediately tensed up, searching for the enemy.

Frog clasped his hands, rubbing them together with a gleam in his eyes. "Looks like things are getting started. Let's wreck some faces."

He turned to Nag. "Fire the warning shot."

Nag nodded and then placed a glowing hand to his ear. He started speaking, though Lexi heard no sound.

After a brief pause, a wave of fire launched over the palisade and into the trees where the snow had fallen. Some of the dead branches briefly lit up but the flames were quickly smothered by a wall of steam from the melted snow.

"Anything?" Frog asked through clenched teeth.

Nag tilted his head, listening to reports. "One of the elementalists reported movement in the trees. It is unclear if we caused any damage, though."

Frog pursed his lips. "Good."

Lexi watched the exchange silently. Though the reports they received were obviously in Goblin, they were carrying out the discussion here in English for her benefit. She was grateful for their consideration though she wasn't sure why they were going that far. She had zero experience with large scale conflict like this one and so everything was new to her. She wasn't sure that she could contribute anything up here in the command structure.

She observed the wall of steam that was slowly dissipating. Three forms stepped out of the mist and approached the front gate.

Edwin stood in the center, covered in heavy-looking steel armor. He had a large kite shield adorning his left arm and his right hand held a mace. The one on the right was Jonathan, the trainee fighter and to the left of the steel-armored man was Bill, the trainee ranger.

Lexi fiddled with the edge of her hat, tipping it forward slightly to hide her face as she observed the adventurers. "I know them…!" she muttered. She felt a tinge of hesitation taking root inside of her, but she shook the feeling off. She didn't have time to be doubting her course.

Shaman and Frog looked at Lexi curiously.

She returned a grin. "The man in the center is Edwin Weston, leader of the silver-ranked party Earthbreakers. The other warrior is Jonathan, leader of one of the trainee adventurer parties. Bill, the ranger, is also a trainee."

"You knew about their party compilation beforehand, and you didn't share this information?" Shaman asked, displeased.

Lexi shrugged. "I had no idea who was coming. I'm just as surprised as you are that I know the teams. I don't know much beyond the names and faces of the silver-ranked team, but I know a lot about the trainees."

"Tell us quickly then. If necessary, we might have to adjust the strategy with the new information," Frog urged.

The three enemies approached the gate. The goblins on the palisade fired a few arrows but they were all expertly deflected by the steel armored man.

"Lexi, what are we facing?" Shaman repeated the question urgently. "This information could save many lives."

Lexi scratched her head. "Umm, as I said before, that one there is called Jonathan. He is a trainee warrior, specialized as a frontline fighter. His party includes a rogue, a ranger, and a priestess." Then she pointed at Edwin. "He is a silver-ranked frontliner. I've heard that he trained as a warrior, but I never confirmed it. His party consists of a rogue who may or may not be an assassin, an arcanist, and a druid." She pursed her lips for a moment as she considered whether to speak about the other trainees, then decided it couldn't hurt to have extra info just in case. "I don't know if they are also here, but the other team of trainees had a ranger and a rogue, and there was an unaffiliated priestess. If Peter or Jantzen somehow survived, then another priest or a dominator warlock could be here as well."

Frog took note of the info. "I'm not sure if they have any other surprises up their sleeves, but at least this is something to work with."

While they were talking, the three adventurers had reached the gate. Edwin raised his mace and it started to glow with a strange blue light. After a brief delay, he struck out with the head of the mace and blew the door off its hinges. The wooden slab splintered into pieces as it crashed into the ground.

Frog frowned. "Offensive line engage the enemy. We need to get a better grasp of what we're dealing with. Bombardment squads launch a line of fire into the tree line encircling our camp. We'll smoke out the rogues and rangers if they are hiding in the trees." Then he turned towards Lord Cedric. "Martial Lord, after observing the result, prepare to intercept the silver-ranked warrior."

Lexi gently stroked the chain on her wrist, taking comfort from the symbol of her freedom.

Shaman noticed the motion and the old goblin's eyes softened. "It will soon be time for you to go out, child."

Lexi leaned on the barricade; her eyes glued to the goblins that were now approaching the three humans. "I am prepared. I don't want to sit back and watch the goblins die," Lexi replied, her eyes filled with determination.

Frog came up on her other side and watched the first offensive line move forward. "That is one burden of leadership. If you and your god truly desire to bring salvation to monsters, then you have to be prepared."

The first goblins reached the adventurers and were smashed down in a series of smooth motions. The silver-ranker moved through the goblins, ending lives with every swing of his mace.

"I am prepared to kill anybody who tries to stop us. Is that not enough?"

Shaman shook her head. "You must also be prepared to be a leader. Sometimes that means watching others die for you."

Lexi flinched as unpleasant memories danced at the edge of her mind. "What meaning is there in 'salvation' if it's built on the bodies of hundreds?" She turned and looked at Shaman and froze as she saw tears roll down the old goblin's cheeks.

Shaman met her eyes with a hollow gaze. "That is for us to decide," she declared forcefully. It almost looked like the old goblin was trying to convince herself of her own words.

The silver-ranker finished smashing down the first offensive line without suffering a single injury and then paused, assessing the lines of goblins around him. Jonathan and Bill stayed back near the gate, not yet participating in the battle but also preventing any goblins from attempting to flee.

Another wave of fire flew out from the bombardment squads, but this time it completely ringed the camp. A wall of steam erupted from the trees. A scream sounded from behind the camp and Frog clapped his hands.

"There we go! Report!"

"One body fell from the trees and is currently not moving. Seems to be a rogue."

"That should flush out their backline a little bit," Frog said, glancing down at the map.

A strange buzzing sound filled their ears. A flowing, violet rectangle appeared behind the line of mages.

Lexi noticed it first and pointed at it, tapping Frog on the shoulder. "What is that?" she asked.

"Damn it!" Frog cursed when he saw it. "It seems the silver-ranked arcanist is incredibly skilled..."

"What does it do?"

Frog pointed at the humans stepping out of the portal. "That."

There were four of them. Sage in a very nature-y robe decorated with green and brown leaves, Melissa wearing skin-tight black pants and a purple blouse, Peter in his standard black robes, and Suzy in her white priestess garb.

Shaman grabbed her staff with one hand and the edge of the chain dangling from Lexi's wrist with the other. "Now it is our turn."

Lexi verified that her ears were covered by her hat and that her tail was not visible. She looked at Frog and he nodded in assent. As she and Shaman started to descend from the platform, she overheard Frog's next instruction.

"Begin Operation: Skyfart."

35

Overwhelmed

Ray stood by herself, a short distance away from the small camp her team had set up. They didn't pull out anything expensive since they might teleport away at a moment's notice, but they did make a small campfire and set up a few tents. She was fiddling with the little artifact that Melissa had given her before the other two teams had left for the Voskeg Mountains. It was a simple, small cylinder that fit comfortably in the palm of her hand.

The arcanist had instructed her that if the orb began to glow purple and vibrate, then she could teleport into the vicinity of a paired artifact that would be on Melissa's person.

A short distance away from her team, she paced anxiously around the camp while ignoring their worried looks. She didn't want them to see when the artifact started glowing. Once the artifact was activated, she intended to find a way to move in while leaving her team behind. She would come up with some sort of excuse later.

Her god had relayed the events of the massacre to her, so she had mixed feelings about rescuing the goblins.

Those mixed feelings didn't extend to Lexi, though. Her friend was in the middle of that battlefield. The goblins who trusted her were there, too.

Ray stroked the artifact softly as she waited.

She didn't know what to expect once she walked through that gate, but whatever she encountered, she would stand where her heart told her to.

<hr />

As she walked through the portal and into the camp, Melissa fought down the normal wave of nausea and looked around. The protection spell cast on the group by Sage would give them time to adjust to their surroundings, but they were still in the middle of the enemy forces.

Since they had teleported a good distance into the camp, there were several lines of goblins between them and Edwin. In front of her group was a line of goblins and a barricade that they guessed was protecting the goblin command center.

Everything was within expectations. She needed to distract the goblins long enough for Samantha to do her job.

Vick was supposed to help the assassin, but, like a typical useless trainee, the idiot got caught in the random firestorms and died before he did anything useful.

She heard a battle cry from the goblins standing between her and the barricade as they charged forward. The little monsters were poorly equipped. Some of them held sharpened sticks and bones, and most of them were only wearing rags for armor. She shook her head as she raised her hand. "*Mana Blast.*"

The mana condensed in front of her and then she interrupted the cast and willed the magic to split and multiply. Her specialization in arcane magic meant that she was used to dealing with magic in its purest, unmodified form. The condensed ball of mana split into a dozen narrow bolts which she promptly flung towards the approaching monsters. Each bolt struck true and a dozen goblins fell in the blink of an eye.

Melissa felt a twinge in her heart as more than half of the approaching line died from her attack. She disliked culling the weak, whether they were humans or monsters. As far as she knew, these goblins had been living here peacefully for a while. But it was her job to eliminate the threat and rescue the hostage that the goblins were presumed to be holding. Whether the goblins were weak or not, she would do her job. She was a professional, after all.

As she fired out another string of compressed mana bolts, she saw a small figure leap from the barricade, erasing the projectiles with a wave of her staff. Dragging behind the figure was a human teenager wearing simple clothes and a straw hat. The poor girl had a chain on her wrist which was being held by the magic-using goblin.

She observed the goblin that was now moving towards her group. She appeared to be ancient, with gray hair and eyes that looked down upon the world as if she had moved beyond it long ago. Melissa immediately recognized that this was this tribe's Shaman, the oldest and most powerful magic-user.

Shaman stalked towards Melissa, a sinister smile playing at the edge of her lips as she revealed her sharp teeth.

Suzy, who had been quiet thus far, squealed at the terrifying sight.

"So there really was a hostage," Sage observed. "Though isn't she a bit strange? They said she was a trainee, but I don't recognize her."

Melissa narrowed her eyes. "That's a slave collar on her wrist. I've never seen monsters using them and it's illegal to enslave humans. There's definitely something else going on here..."

"She looks kind of familiar..." Peter muttered, coming up beside them. "It's that feeling like something is on the tip of your tongue, but you can't quite remember..."

"But you do recognize her?" Melissa asked, turning her sharp glare on the boy.

Peter shrunk under her gaze. "I... uh... I think so, though I don't know who she is..." he stuttered, refusing to meet her eyes.

Melissa shivered as she felt the oppressive force approaching them. "If you recognize her then she really might have been a trainee. We'll rescue her first and then investigate later. Let's focus on the ancient magic user for now."

Ancient magic users were terrifying opponents. They used magic that humans could never hope to understand which made planning against them terribly difficult. Most ancient magic users required a minimum of a full silver-ranked adventurer team to be able to fight head-on. They didn't know anything about the abilities or magic of the one in front of them, though Melissa suspected that she was the illusionist.

Shaman stopped several steps away from them and tilted her head. "Why do you hesitate?" she asked in fluent English, her voice a bit deeper and smoother than her looks would lead one to expect. "Are you finished with your conversation?"

"D..Divine Retri..." Suzy started to shout but Sage silenced the purge-happy priestess with a sharp glare.

Melissa raised an arm, preparing another strike. "I take it you're Shaman here. I have to admit we're interested in your unique magic. Are you the illusionist?"

Shaman shrugged. "Maybe, maybe not. I know this is a bit late, but could I ask you to leave? If this goes on, a lot of people will die, and my side doesn't resurrect."

Melissa stared at the old goblin incredulously. "You're asking us to just... leave?"

Shaman smiled, baring her sharp teeth.

The viciousness carried in her grin caused Melissa to falter for just a moment. She took a deep breath to calm her mind. She slowly reached an arm into a pouch at her side and channeled mana into the artifact resting inside. If this camp had an ancient magic user and an assassin on the level of a High Templar, they needed more fodder to provide opportunities to strike.

"If you don't leave now, then I will have to ask you again with a little bit of force," Shaman warned.

"Y..you're just a monster!" Suzy screamed back. She folded her hands together as if in prayer while glaring at the old goblin with wild eyes.

"Seriously, what is wrong with this girl..." Melissa muttered.

Peter stepped up beside Suzy and summoned his mana. "I'll protect the healer; you guys can fight without worry."

Melissa nodded without taking her attention away from Shaman. She finished preparing and several dozen mana bolts formed in the air around her, each of them aimed at different targets. With a flick of her wrist, each of the bolts launched. A few dozen of them flew towards the line of goblins behind them, another dozen flew towards Shaman, while yet another dozen flew towards the goblin commanders hiding behind the barricade.

Shaman clenched her teeth. She struggled to maintain her illusion while blocking as many of the bolts as she could. She ignored the bolts aimed towards her, and instead focused on the ones moving towards her kin in the command center and in the defensive lines. The two sets of bolts evaporated while the final set descended upon the old goblin. She desperately evaded, but one of them struck the shoulder of the arm holding the chain while another two pinned her leg. Shaman groaned as the condensed mana seared her skin and cauterized the wounds. With another wave of her staff, the bolts disappeared, and she stumbled. She released the chain as her left arm dangled uselessly at her side.

The hostage noticed the opportunity and immediately acted, running away from her captor and towards the adventurers who came to save her. As she ran, she raised a hand to hold her patchwork straw hat in place.

Shaman watched helplessly; her eyes furious as their precious hostage escaped.

Seeing the old goblin cornered so easily, Melissa couldn't help but smile.

The hostage passed beside Melissa and their arms touched briefly before she moved to hide near Sage, Suzy, and Peter. The arcanist didn't even spare the girl a second glance as she prepared another attack to launch at the wounded creature before her. "You look a little tired. Perhaps you've grown too old to fight?" she taunted, attempting to distract the old goblin while focusing intently on forming her spell.

Shaman scoffed. "Young one, you know nothing. I have been fighting humans for over a hundred years. Sometimes sacrifices are necessary for victory. I believe you humans have an expression for it -- 'to lose the battle but win the war'?"

Melissa giggled. "So, you admit that you will lose this battle then?"

Shaman raised her staff. "We shall see."

Sage stepped up beside Melissa and channeled her mana. The ground shook slightly as large cracks began to spread out around them. Roots inched out, exposing themselves to the dry mountain air. With a gesture, the roots swirled around Shaman and closed in on her.

Shaman raised her staff and smacked the edge of it into the ground.

Melissa gasped as the world began to twist around her. She stumbled to the side, attempting to regain her balance as the ground rose beneath her and the roots vanished into thin air. The mana she was gathering dispersed as she lost her focus. "Damn it!" she growled.

In the next moment, her vision went black. One by one, each of her senses faded. All sounds disappeared, the smell of sweat and blood drained away, her skin became numb to the chilly mountain air. Even her sense of taste died.

Melissa was alone, floating in an endless, dark world of nothing.

This was her second time experiencing an illusion spell of this level. She knew how to break it, but it would take her some time. She was more concerned with how the illusionist had cast this spell in the first place. Something this powerful and immersive would require either physical contact or a medium.

Ah...

Melissa checked her arm and found that the magic originated from a speck of mana there. It was so small that she would only notice it if she were looking for it. The only time it could have been placed there was when the hostage had touched her. She mentally sighed as she gathered her mana and focused her mind on the speck that served as the source of the illusion. Using the source as an anchor, she projected her mana into the illusion surrounding her and willed it to disperse. She encountered an unexpectedly powerful resistance and clicked her tongue.

Tsk. This old illusionist was too damn powerful.

Melissa growled as she released another layer of mana and shot it directly into the barrier. She channeled her anger into the mana and bore down on the mind of her oppressor, suppressing it with as much force as she could muster. Gradually, her senses faded back into reality, and she blinked at the unexpected brightness that filled her vision. Her ears and nose twitched, her tongue tingled, and she felt a strange itch on her skin as if insects were crawling all over her body.

A wave of mental exhaustion ran through her, and she shuddered. A quick glance revealed that Sage had been in the same predicament. Chills ran down her spine as she realized that they had only escaped because it was two against one.

They had been gone for approximately ten seconds.

And in those ten seconds, the flow of the battle had changed.

Right before her eyes, the 'hostage' twisted Peter's head, and snapped his neck. Suzy had already collapsed with her head similarly tilted at an odd angle. The straw hat was on the ground, and she could see black, triangular ears peeking out from the hostage's dark hair.

Fortunately, they had escaped before the beastkin could do anything to either her or Sage.

"Phew, that was dangerous," Melissa wheezed, pulling a staff out of her enchanted bag to lean on.

Sage snapped her fingers, causing warm mana to seep into both of their bodies. It spread throughout her body, relaxing the tension in her muscles. She felt the burden on her mind lessen as the mana reinvigorated her.

Melissa sighed in relief. As her clarity filled her mind, a wave of energy rolled through her body.

"I think we've let this go on for far too long," Sage said, her calm voice contrasting with her annoyed expression.

The arcanist formed another wave of mana, this time leaving it as one large, concentrated orb. "I agree."

Sage extended her arms out and pushed her mana into the ground. As she slowly raised her arms, little mushrooms began to pop out of the dirt around her.

Melissa threw her mana orb at the illusionist. The druid snapped her fingers and the mushrooms burst, filling the air with a poisonous mist. The mist avoided Melissa and it spread outwards towards both the beastkin and Shaman.

Shaman pointed her staff at the mana orb. "Begone!" she declared.

Melissa's jaw dropped as the orb obeyed the command and disappeared. "What? How is that even possible? I didn't sense any mana in your voice..."

Shaman took a step back as the poison mist approached her. She wiped her sweaty palms on her robe, fighting against the mental exhaustion that threatened to overwhelm her.

Melissa felt the artifact in her pouch vibrate. "Finally...!" she muttered, aiming another blast towards the beastkin behind her.

With reinforcements on the way, they would be able to easily win this fight.

A small portal opened beside Melissa. The arcanist thinned the orb into a fine blade and fired it towards the beastkin. The young girl tried to jump out of the way. Before the mana blade could strike, a shadow darted across her vision, stepping between the blade and the catkin.

The mana blade sliced into the stomach of the platinum-haired lady with heterochromatic eyes. To Melissa's eyes, it didn't look like she had stepped in the way intentionally. It was more like she had launched herself through the portal quickly without regard for what might be on the other side.

Ray split in half. Her eyes were frozen wide with surprise and her expression was clearly asking 'what the hell?'

Melissa sighed, turning away from the dead fool to check on the state of the rest of the reinforcements. To her dismay, the portal closed without any other trainees coming through.

"What the hell?!" she shouted.

"That's my line..." a new, yet familiar voice called out from behind her.

Melissa flinched and turned back to see Ray's torso crawling towards her lower half.

The young adventurer reoriented herself and held the edges of the lower half against her severed stomach. Unbelievably, the intestines, muscles, bones, skin... everything began reattaching itself.

Sage and Melissa stared at Ray with wide eyes, their spells and opponents temporarily forgotten. "What are you...?"

Ray smiled. "I suppose you could call me an independent third party."

"Huh?"

Ray pointed at Melissa and Sage. "I disagree with you attacking this camp." Then she pointed towards the goblins. "And I have a bone to pick with the goblins who attacked my friend." She took a step towards the arcanist and drew a longsword from her enchanted bag. "What issue do you have with this attack? We're just doing our job...!" Melissa muttered.

Ray shook her head and pointed towards the defensive lines. "You may or may not have noticed, but every goblin in this camp is mobilized to fight you. There are goblins that I don't want to die, and others who haven't made their choices yet. Monsters don't respawn when they die, so I would rather you not kill them just yet."

"Choices? They killed the trainee adventurer teams! They wiped out your team as well!" Sage pointed out.

Ray giggled and motioned towards the trainees who attacked the camp. "And all but one of those trainees are still alive. Even if the goblins win this fight somehow, they will have lost. Those that you kill won't come back, whereas you can keep trying repeatedly until you win."

Melissa aimed another mana blade at the rebelling trainee. Her arm was trembling. She had never intentionally attacked a fellow adventurer before. She knew that if she didn't, her life would be in danger, but she still hesitated.

Ray took another step and Melissa released the blade. The mana arced towards the young woman and slashed into her neck, decapitating her in a smooth motion. Blood spewed from the wound, yet a slender arm reached up, caught the head before it could fall too far, and firmly reattached it in its rightful place.

Melissa stumbled, trying to move back but her legs were shaking. It had been a long time since she'd felt fear. She fell to the ground, trembling as she threw burst after burst of mana at the demonic entity approaching her.

A root erupted from the ground and attempted to grab the demon, but she simply stomped on the root, grinding it into dust.

Ray stopped, hovering over Melissa's shivering form. She bent down onto one knee and leaned down to whisper into Melissa's ear. "My name is Ray. If I catch you doing something like this again, there won't be a next time."

Melissa's mind went into overdrive. She shuddered as confusion and fear warred within her. She began to laugh. It wasn't a mere chuckle or an amused laugh but rather the laughter one might expect when realizing how unfair the world could be. Everything that she had just witnessed was beyond expectations. More than that, it was simply impossible.

A blade swung down and pierced her neck.

The world tumbled.

And then there was darkness.

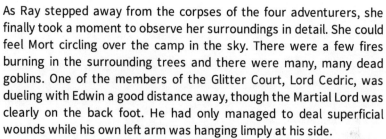

As Ray stepped away from the corpses of the four adventurers, she finally took a moment to observe her surroundings in detail. She could feel Mort circling over the camp in the sky. There were a few fires burning in the surrounding trees and there were many, many dead goblins. One of the members of the Glitter Court, Lord Cedric, was dueling with Edwin a good distance away, though the Martial Lord was clearly on the back foot. He had only managed to deal superficial wounds while his own left arm was hanging limply at his side.

Lexi stood nearby, holding a strange, patchwork straw hat. When Ray looked her way, her friend raised a hand in greeting. She returned the gesture with a smile and a nod.

"Good work," Shaman said, coming up beside her. "I was not expecting your aid, but it was timely."

Ray shrugged. "It was easy because I caught them by surprise."

Shaman smirked. "Oh, they were definitely surprised. I doubt there is an entity on this planet that wouldn't hesitate after seeing someone recover so quickly from decapitation."

Ray rubbed her neck sheepishly. The blood on her shirt still hadn't dried all the way, so it was a little uncomfortable. That blood was the only remaining proof that the injury had happened.

"Still, I wonder why only magic users came through the portal...?" Shaman muttered.

Understanding lit up her face and she turned towards the strategic command center in time to see Nag's body tumble over the edge.

Ray looked up, her eyes barely catching a cloaked figure as they disappeared.

"Well damn," Shaman cursed. "We're in trouble now..."

Ray returned her attention to the form of the steel-clad warrior. "Let's deal with one problem at a time."

Shaman nodded. "I'm a bit tapped out, so I won't be of much help in this fight. I overexerted myself keeping up the illusions as long as I did."

Ray winced internally. "Alright."

She ran forward, breezing past the Martial Lord as she prepared to swing her sword. Her sword arced downwards in an overhead strike. Edwin smoothly raised his shield and deflected the strike to the side.

Ray stumbled, expecting to feel more resistance. A crushing force slammed into her side and shattered her left arm. She hissed as she kicked off the ground, jumping back and away from her opponent. A red haze covered her vision as she observed the warrior's calm stance.

"Hmm, aren't you that promising trainee?" Edwin asked, examining her curiously.

Ray bit her lip, drawing blood. She knew this wasn't going to be easy, but she had a bad premonition about this fight. She spit the blood at his feet. "I don't know anything about that. Please stop what you are doing and leave."

Edwin smiled and raised his sword and shield. "It's a pleasure to fight you. I am quite tired of culling bystanders."

They circled, looking for an opening. Ray felt like she was dueling against an armored version of Siegfried. Not only did his stance leave no obvious openings, but his armor covered all his vitals, and he clearly knew how to use his shield. She ran forward, initiating the first strike.

Edwin planted his feet firmly and once again aimed to redirect Ray's overhead blow. However, this time Ray flicked her wrist and, in a monstrous display of strength, completely altered the trajectory of her swing. Edwin grimaced as the blade struck the center of his shield. The steel bent from the impact and her sword snapped in half, the blade spinning up into the sky. He swung his mace and Ray intercepted the blow with an enhanced right arm.

She deflected the mace and it seemed to bounce off her arm.

Edwin blinked in surprise, though he didn't slow down for even a moment. He swung down and Ray moved to block the strike, putting her entire weight behind her enhanced fist. He changed the angle mid-strike and Ray stumbled forward, expecting resistance but finding none. The mace came up and clipped her chin, shattering her teeth.

The world went dark.

Ray fought the blackness, willing herself to remain conscious as she righted her head and forced a smile. Blood trickled from her mouth, oozing out from between the gap left by the broken and missing teeth. As her awareness fully resurfaced, she took a hesitant step forward, swaying as if she were drunk. Her vision slowly recovered, though everything was spinning. She closed her eyes and took a deep breath as she tried to reorient herself.

"I'm impressed that you're still standing," Edwin's voice came from in front of her. "Your willpower is incredible."

Ray growled and fell to one knee. Willpower or no, she couldn't fight like this.

"Even so, I am surprised you got the better of my companions. If this is all you have, you aren't nearly strong enough to take those two on."

A hand reached under her chin and lifted it up. She opened her eyes and found herself staring into the gaze of Edwin Weston. In his clear, blue eyes she saw confidence and curiosity, but there was no hint of anger or desire for vengeance.

Then again, his friends would respawn, so he really had no reason to get angry.

She moved her jaw experimentally as she felt it shifting back into its natural place. Her gums itched as fresh teeth began to sprout into the empty gaps while the shattered teeth were pushed out of their places.

"Why...?" she groaned, blood dribbling down her chin. "Why are you killing the goblins? Did they do something to you? Do you hate them?"

Edwin released her and stepped to the side. "That's an interesting question. I have no grudge against you or any of these little creatures."

"Then why?" Ray demanded, coughing to release the crimson liquid from her throat.

Edwin shook his head. "We're following orders. If you're asking why our superiors want these goblins dead, then I don't know why."

Ray tilted her head. Her eyes followed his movement as he looked around the camp. "I'm not talking to your superiors; I'm talking to you. I don't care why they ordered it, I want to know why you would follow such an order."

Edwin shrugged indifferently. "Isn't that the natural thing to do? I was ordered to kill the goblins, so I will. I wasn't ordered to kill you, so I will happily let you go."

Ray spread her arms and motioned to the death and destruction surrounding them. The living goblins wailed even as they moved to execute the final orders they received. There were few goblins who were not crying, and there were none that were not struggling to survive. "If this is natural to you, then maybe you should reconsider who the real 'monsters' are."

Edwin pursed his lips. "I'll take note of it. Goodbye."

He raised his mace to deal the final blow.

Ray pushed herself back up to her feet. Her regeneration had finally healed the internal damage to her brain, and the world stabilized around her. She spit out a cracked tooth.

"Mr. Following Orders, I'm sorry to say but we are just getting started."

36

Legion, God of Monsters

Ray leapt back, putting a little bit of distance between her and Edwin. After her dramatic statement, the act probably seemed a little cowardly, but she didn't want to be anywhere near the warrior for what was coming next.

A quick glance told her that the goblins had moved into position around them. Seeing several of them reaching for the flaps on the back of their pants, Ray could guess exactly what was about to happen.

She felt her regeneration finish fixing her face into its proper shape. She moved her jaw a bit, trying to relieve the stiffness caused by having the bones shattered and then put back together.

As she did so, she looked up. Several goblins were flying over Edwin. In near-perfect sync, they released the flaps covering their butts and then a horrible stench filled the air. A rainbow of sparkles rained down in abundance on Edwin, covering him in the goblin's characteristic glitter.

At the time when Ray had personally experienced the colorful deluge, she hadn't suffered from any side effects, other than horrendously damaged pride.

However, Edwin seemed to be suffering from side effects now. He fell to his knees, pounding his chest with his fist as he began to cough. His eyes were swimming with tears and filled with terror as his gaze settled on Ray. It took her a moment to realize that he wasn't seeing her, he was staring at something that only he could see.

"Operation: Skyfart," Lexi commented as she came up beside Ray.

The young woman raised an eyebrow at the ridiculous, yet apt, name.

Lexi patted Ray on the shoulder and then rushed past the temporarily incapacitated warrior to take on Jonathan and Bill who were standing nervously near the gate. A group of ten goblins, including Vorg and Tyrion, the Lord of Commerce, followed her charge. Shaman came up beside Ray as they observed Edwin for a moment. There were three lines of goblins behind her. Og and his team signaled from the opposite side.

She wasn't alone in this fight.

Ray started to laugh. This was the first time she had fought an opponent with other people.

Shaman placed a hand on her shoulder. "Are you... alright? Every hit you received there looked lethal."

Ray shook her head, dispelling her own strange laughter.

Shaman tilted her head to the side in confusion but moved past it without further question. "Og's group and I will assist you as best as we can. If we can stop this warrior here, then the remaining kin might be saved."

Ray motioned as if to leave but then she paused. "If you die in this fight, you won't respawn. Are you sure you want to participate further?"

Shaman smiled and waved off the inane question. "This is where I must stand. We will speak of this again after you have saved my family. Go."

Ray charged towards Edwin once more. Though he was still under the effects of some illusion, he still reacted towards Ray's approach.

Lexi charged with Vorg and Lord Tyrion at her side. They had been assigned to work with the converted Gobber Goblins for the remainder of the battle and the job they had been given before strategic command went silent was to secure the gate.

Jonathan and Bill were the two enemies blocking the gate.

The blonde-haired blue-eyed warrior stood in front of the dark-haired archer. Lexi had never interacted with either of them before, but she had seen them training many times. She hadn't seen their training in over a week though, so she would need to test the waters a little bit to get a complete grasp of their capabilities.

The two of them noticed the approaching force and prepared to receive the goblins. Jonathan raised his shield while holding his sword poised to strike. Bill knocked an arrow on his bow, sighting it on the catkin in the lead.

Lexi released her mana and channeled the only elemental spell that she knew, one that she had learned just a week before she became a slave.

Gathering fire to her hands, she charged straight at Jonathan with two goblins at her side while Vorg took four goblins to the right and Tyrion took another four goblins and circled to the left.

As Bill released his arrow, Lexi relied on the magic users amongst the goblins to protect her. A small barrier appeared in the air, halting the arrow in its path.

Lexi sidestepped the projectile and continued moving forward while lashing out with her claws. Five flaming slashes burst towards Jonathan. The fire sputtered against his raised shield and left scorch marks on the smooth metal surface.

"Isn't this Ray's slave?" Jonathan called back to Bill.

"I believe it is," Bill replied dryly. "Yet another piece of evidence against that feral bitch."

Lexi raised an eyebrow at their commentary but otherwise ignored it.

Jonathan observed Lexi appraisingly while the goblins finished surrounding the two adventurers. "Could she always use magic? It would cost a lot of money to keep her restrained now."

Bill shrugged indifferently. "Doesn't really matter. We don't need goods that don't know their place."

Lexi's ears stood on end. "You talk as if you think I can't hear you."

Jonathan waved her comment away. "She's still worth money though. Should we take her alive?"

Lexi hissed, thoroughly irritated with the nonchalant attitude of the two adventurers. She stalked forward, gathering mana into her right hand. As she moved, the goblin encirclement started to collapse inwards.

Jonathan met her enhanced punch with his shield. Lexi twisted, narrowly avoiding the shortsword by a hair's breadth as she hooked her heel towards his head.

He ducked under the blow and struck out with his sword. Lexi backed off and avoided the blow. She glanced at Bill to see how the goblin's charge had fared. In mere seconds, two goblins fell to arrows despite the best attempts of the magicians to block them with barriers. However, they now had the ranger engaged in melee and he was quickly getting overwhelmed.

Small daggers flashed under the sunlight and the air was filled with severed limbs. Arms were sundered, weapons broke, heads rolled.

And then Bill was knocked to the ground by the wave of goblins who leapt onto him, tearing into him with their nails and teeth. The ranger screamed as he desperately tried to pull the crawling creatures from his body.

Lexi grinned, baring her canines. While she would have preferred that less goblins died in the charge, every single one that had gone down was a baptized follower of the new god. Every single one of them would respawn.

She returned her attention to Jonathan just in time to duck under a wide swing. She stepped forward, closing her fingers in like a tiger's palm as she thrust her hand out and struck his chin. His head snapped back, and he stumbled, falling to his knees.

Lexi glared at his weakened form. She gathered mana into her claws and reached for his neck. "You're too weak to be this closed-minded."

An immortal, a master Illusionist, and four assassins against a single silver-ranked warrior. Ray, Og, Trog, Urg, and Jug were keeping Edwin pressured. Urg moved from structure to structure, firing arrows with pinpoint accuracy that weaved between Ray, Og, Trog, and Jug to strike at joints. Edwin had a single arrow jutting out from the back of his left knee, severely limiting his movement. A normal person would have been taken out of the fight with that attack, but he somehow persisted. He took extra care to deflect the arrows while holding off the four melee attackers.

Og, Trog, and Jug were like wraiths. Any time one of Edwin's attacks seemed to hit one of the goblins, they would disappear, only to strike from a shadow. They would use Edwin's own shadow or those cast by the other two goblins to move around - Og, with his twin daggers, Trog with his two-handed mace, and Jug with his sword.

The sight of the three goblins moving in and out of each other's shadows looked to Ray like they were performing a beautiful and deadly dance.

It was unclear to her exactly how much Shaman was contributing to the flow of the combat before her. The old goblin was sweating profusely and looked to be in pain as she channeled some sort of spell. A trickle of blood ran from her nose. Ray couldn't see any illusions herself, but she did notice that Edwin occasionally flinched or moved to block an attack where none was coming.

Ray sprinted forward and struck with her battle hammer. The warrior raised his shield to intercept the blow and the edges quivered as the center of the shield caved even further. The shape of the metal board was no longer conducive to deflecting, so Edwin was forced to 'block' more and more often.

She pressed the attack and swung another overhead strike.

Simultaneously, Og appeared behind the warrior while an arrow flew in from the side. Edwin flinched, presumably reacting to yet another illusion.

He caught Ray's strike with his shield and then spun, throwing her off balance. He took a step to the side to dodge the arrow and, continuing the momentum of his spin, the warrior thrust his mace out towards Og.

The goblin assassin ducked under the blow and jabbed his dagger into the gap of Edwin's armor over his elbow. He kicked off Edwin's chest, leapt back, and vanished.

Ray backed away, taking a moment to call out and check on Shaman's condition. "You okay?"

Shaman grunted in response. Ray glanced back in time to see the old goblin collapse down onto her hands and knees, gasping for breath. Seeing that Og and the others had renewed their attack, Ray rushed towards the old goblin and pulled a piece of cloth out of her enchanted bag. She dropped to one knee beside Shaman and held the cloth out to her.

The old goblin accepted the cloth, using it first to wipe the sweat off her forehead and then the blood from her nose. "Have you seen the assassin?" Shaman asked, swaying unsteadily.

Ray shook her head. "She disappeared after she cleared out the command post. She's probably hanging around here somewhere waiting for the right opportunity."

Shaman groaned weakly. "I've been standing here with my back wide open for a while now and she hasn't taken the bait."

Ray shrugged, feeling a hint of unease. "If we don't know what she's doing then we can't do much about it. Let's end this fight here and take care of whatever happens."

Shaman coughed, flecks of blood scattering on the ground in front of her. "You'll have to finish this one without me."

Ray nodded and donned a reassuring smile. "Leave it to me." She stood up and directed a glare at Edwin. The warrior was facing away from her, heavily occupied dealing with his four attackers. She took a second to calm her mind and then she rushed forward, her hammer poised to strike.

The four assassins noticed her approach and readjusted their rhythm. Jug jumped forward and swung his sword.

Edwin caught the blow with his shield and deflected it.

Trog rolled out of Jug's shadow and ducked underneath the shield. He struck the warrior's knee with his mace and the warrior stumbled as his armor caved in.

He swept out with his own mace, but Trog disappeared.

Ray approached in an arc, keeping to the man's blind spot.

Edwin seemed to sense something as he quickly spun around. His eyes widened in surprise as he took in Ray's charging figure. The surprise quickly transformed into an amused expression as he turned to deflect an arrow coming from the right.

Trog and Jug pressed the attack from behind while Ray shifted to the left. She enhanced her left arm and intercepted the mace that swung at her. She grabbed the mace just below the head and held it in place.

Edwin grinned, a line of sweat running down his face.

"Good, now disarm him!" Trog shouted from behind the warrior.

Ray yanked the mace towards her. Edwin maintained his grip on the weapon and was forced to lurch forward, caught off guard by her unexpected superhuman strength. Urg ducked out of Edwin's shadow and his sword curved up towards the small gap under his shoulder.

As her prize came loose, Ray jumped back and held the mace in the air to display the bloody appendage.

Edwin stared at Ray for a long moment, his eyes moving between her triumphant figure and his arm still grasping firmly onto the mace. He started to laugh. "Hah.. haha. 'Disarm'... that's a good one!"

Ray felt her spirit dampening. "Are you even taking this seriously? I haven't seen you use magic once yet."

His smile twitched. "It's not fun if you take it too seriously."

Ray clenched her teeth. "Are you implying that we're not strong enough to make you get serious?"

He shrugged and waved her comment away. "Thank whatever god you worship that I didn't go all out, or you would have all died a long time ago. They call me a silver-ranker, but I'm pretty close to my promotion."

Ray quivered, anger rising inside of her as her vision tinted red. She took a step forward. "If you won't get serious then you're going to die!"

Edwin sighed. "So be it."

Ray paused. "...what?"

"There's a reason my team is called the Earthbreakers. If you want me to get serious, then goodbye."

"…"

The warrior's figure blurred and then he jumped impossibly high. Then he accelerated towards the ground unnaturally fast. "*Earthbreak!*"

As he hit the ground it caved beneath his feet. A wave of cracks appeared around the warrior as the ground seemed to roll away from the epicenter, flattening everything in its path. Every structure in the camp collapsed and every one of the few remaining goblins fell to the ground.

Ray stood dumbfounded. She could only watch as Edwin took a red vial out of his bag and drank it. Immediately, his arm regrew from the stump and then he pulled a two-handed mace out of his bag while storing his shield.

This mace was glowing with a faint blue hue. An enchanted weapon.

He was a real adventurer. He wasn't restricted to measly training weapons like she was.

Ray slapped herself, jolting her body into action. She ran forward while enhancing her left arm.

Edwin casually swung the weapon down with one hand.

Just before she intercepted it, she felt a wave of mana enter the weapon. The mace took on a dark and eerie glow. Her arm bent oddly, though it quickly snapped back into place like a tight rubber band due to her reinforcement and her regeneration.

Edwin swung a glowing left gauntlet towards her face.

Ray's nose splattered and her skull crumbled as her head snapped back. Her eyes filled with tears involuntarily and she stumbled away from the warrior.

"*Earthquake!*" Edwin called out again as he stomped a foot into the ground. This time, the earth ruptured in a cone. The same amount of destructive force that had levelled the camp was now all focused in a single direction.

Ray was blown away. Cries of pain filled the air as dozens of goblins fell with shattered bones. At least a dozen more died instantly from the attack. She crashed into the ground, tumbling uncontrollably as agony surged through her body.

She came to a stop and rolled over, coughing out blood as she pushed herself onto her hands and knees. She glared towards Edwin's stationary form.

He hadn't moved after blasting her away. "See?" he sighed. "This isn't any fun."

Ray chuckled weakly. "He's a monster," she muttered.

Og crawled out of her shadow beside her. "Are you okay?" he asked, concern in his eyes.

Ray shook her head and motioned towards Edwin. "We have to get out of here. We can't beat that."

"My offer still stands young lady!" Edwin shouted. "We don't have to fight. My job is to kill the goblins, not you."

Ray unsteadily lifted herself to her feet.

Og placed a hand on her arm to stop her. "Don't do it. This is our fight and, as you said, it's impossible. There is no reason for you to continue to suffer."

She shook his hand off. "I know." Her face itched as her nose reformed. She felt a sharp pain in her chest telling her that her ribs were moving back into place. She let out a sigh of relief as the various sensations of pain that had been nagging her slowly faded away.

Edwin started walking towards her. He had a hand outstretched as if expecting her to go with him.

What kind of idiot would believe his claim after all of this?

Ray rushed forward, screaming with all of her might as she swung her battle hammer.

Edwin shook his head sadly. He swung his enchanted mace and smashed the head of her weapon aside, shattering the mass into little pieces.

"Oh..." Ray unintentionally let out a surprised sound as her momentum continued to propel her forward.

He discarded his mace and grabbed her by the neck. He lifted her into the air and looked into her eyes. He saw only defiance. "So be it," Edwin sighed.

A large, black blur descended from the sky and Edwin nonchalantly backhanded it with his gauntlet. Lord Mortimer crumbled to the ground and then faded away.

He turned Ray around, showing her the camp.

She cried out as she saw a blur. The assassin appeared behind Shaman, stabbed forward with her blades.

Another blurry figure jumped out of Shaman's shadow, intercepting the blades with their body. Urg fired the arrow on his bow into the assassin's chest as he fell to the ground. The light faded from his eyes.

The assassin stumbled. As she fell forward, she reached out with her dagger and jabbed it into Shaman's leg.

"Hmm," Edwin muttered, a hint of surprise in his voice. "Though Samantha is pretty new to the assassination gig, I wasn't expecting that."

Edwin turned, noting that Lexi, Tyrion, and their six remaining goblins had managed to take out Bill and Jonathan. The victorious group was now watching him warily from beside the destroyed gate.

"Am I really the only one left?" he sighed. "I guess I'll have to increase their training. I didn't expect my teammates to die today." He let out a tired sigh. "Though it's been fun, I doubt you have much else to show. Why don't we just end this?" He motioned as if to walk towards the gate but then paused as the goblins took battle stances.

Lexi raised her arms and summoned a ball of fire.

The warrior looked back and saw Og, Trog, and Jug ready to attack.

Edwin raised Ray high into the sky, examining her struggling form with interest. "This is in my way. I guess I don't *have* to take her back alive..." he muttered. He ignored her desperate punches and kicks that dented his armor as if he was merely being stung by an insect. He swapped his enchanted mace for a large sword, threw her to the ground, and placed a foot on her back to hold her in place while he raised the sword, poised to strike.

Lexi yelled in protest. She rushed forward along with several dozen goblins as the sword descended.

"Don't be angry when you respawn, you chose this!" Edwin warned. His enchanted sword arced down smoothly and separated Ray's head from her shoulders. He bent down and grabbed it, holding it up by the hair to display it to all the watchers. "Come and get me!" he roared.

Lexi, Vorg, and the five other surviving converts rushed towards the warrior. Og and Trog danced out of his shadow, aiming for the moment right before the charging force crashed into him.

As if he had eyes on the back of his head, Edwin thrust his fist back and smashed Trog aside.

The goblin assassin soared through the air. His weapon flew out of his hands as he rolled across the ground.

Simultaneously, Edwin tossed Ray's head at the charging beastkin and the girl flinched, releasing her magic as she caught the flying bundle of silver and blood. He spun in place and his now empty hand snatched Og by the neck like a viper. He squeezed, crushing the goblin like an egg. He tossed the corpse aside, laughing as he stomped his foot, once again pushing mana into the ground. He caused the surface to quake, throwing the attacking goblins off balance. He raised his glowing sword once more and, with five sharp movements, five heads rolled. Then he threw his sword like an arrow and pierced Jug through the heart with uncanny accuracy.

Edwin turned his attention to the last surviving member of the final attack force.

The cursed beastkin hugged the severed head against her chest, backing away slowly with fear in her eyes.

"So, you were the 'hostage', eh?" Edwin muttered nonchalantly as he observed her for a moment. "I'm not really sure how the anonymous tip missed the fact that you were a beastkin, but whatever. Technically, I don't have to kill you since you aren't a goblin. You can leave. Take that head if you want it." He turned, as if to walk away.

Lexi growled in defiance. She raised her right arm, the one shackled by the chain that once represented her bondage. Now, that chain represented her freedom. She grasped the chain in her right hand while cuddling Ray's head softly with her left. She leapt forward and swung the chain towards the warrior's head.

Edwin reached up, as if to grab the chain out of the air..

For the first time since obtaining the authority, Lexi channeled her mana into the chain and activated the master's disciplinary measure. She cried out in pain as her shoulder was wrenched out of its socket. The chain smashed into the warrior's outstretched hand and his arm bent underneath the weight.

His eyes went wide with shock as his arm snapped despite his use of enhancement magic.

Despite the pain, Lexi smiled as she fell to the ground. Her shoulder throbbed and tears streamed down her dirt and bloodstained face.

Edwin examined his broken arm for a moment with interest before turning back to the sobbing catgirl. He lifted a glowing boot and smashed her head into the dirt. Her head burst like a melon and her crying stopped.

He turned to move back towards the illusionist who was lying on the ground, dying. Then, he heard an unexpected voice behind him.

"There, you happy?" the voice muttered, her tone obviously pissed.

A brilliant, golden light filled the sky.

Edwin turned around to see Ray's body dusting off the head that Lexi had been holding tightly until the moment of her death. The unbelievable sight was perpetuated as she reached up and placed her head back onto her shoulders, her neck seeming to reach out of its own accord.

The light descended and enveloped Ray's body.

"H...how...?!" Edwin spluttered, fear in his eyes.

Ray placed a hand on her neck, feeling the space where it had reconnected. It was smooth, as if there had never been an injury. She craned her neck to the side and popped it to relieve some tension. "The term is 'mortally' wounded for a reason. What did you think would happen if you cut off my head?" she taunted.

"W..what?" he asked, confused and afraid.

"Who knows?" she replied mystically. "Judging from your reaction, you didn't see when I pulled the same trick on Melissa."

Then a voice rang out that Ray immediately recognized.

"Edwin Weston, I am thoroughly vexed with you."

"Who are you?" Edwin challenged, his eyes wandering throughout the camp. He was unable to identify the source.

"Who am I indeed?" the voice thundered. "You and your 'adventurers' waltzed into this camp and executed every single one of my followers. Having done so, you still have the gall to ask that question?"

"Followers? Are you supposed to be some kind of god?"

"Indeed, I am. More specifically, I am the God of War, I am the God of Harmony, and I am the God of Freedom."

The voice paused for a moment as understanding started to dawn on Edwin's face.

Ray looked on with a miffed expression.

"Amongst the goblins that you slew, several of them were my followers. I am thoroughly pissed off."

"Well damn," Edwin muttered. "Leave it to the higher-ups to pick a fight with a damn *god*, of all things."

"You dared to lay a hand on my prophet. You dared to kill my priestess. You dared to slaughter those who have placed their trust in me. However, I fail to see a point in killing you as you would simply respawn. I have thought of another task for you."

"Oh?" He raised an eyebrow, intrigued.

"Edwin Weston," the voice uttered. "I would have you deliver a message for me."

"A message?"

"You will be a messenger - a harbinger if you will. You will first return to Cairel and deliver this message, and then you will spread the word as far as you can."

"And what message might this be?" Edwin humored him.

"I will place a curse upon you as a sign of your calling. If you fail to accomplish the task that I have granted unto you, your soul will wither in eternal torment!"

He flinched. His eyes narrowed and he started paying much closer attention to what the voice was saying.

"This is the contents of the message you will deliver. Tell the world that there is a new god. Tell them that I am the God of War, the God of Harmony, and the God of Freedom. Tell them that I have taken it upon myself to be the god of all those who are oppressed and persecuted. Tell them that I will not stand for slavery, persecution of races, or the slaughter of innocents. Tell them that I will bring harmony to this world."

Edwin nodded furiously, revealing his willingness.

"Other gods have dubbed the non-human species 'monsters'. We will embrace that title and turn it against them. If these races are to be known as 'monsters', then tell all who hear my call to come unto me!"

The voice paused and Edwin gulped nervously.

In a calmer, commanding tone, the voice issued its final edict before disappearing.

"Tell them that I am Legion, God of Monsters!"

37

Endings and Beginnings

"Phew," I let out as I withdrew my partial manifestation. I wanted to do a full-blown physical manifestation, but that would have cost more than my maximum holy power capacity. This little 'miracle' was draining enough to wipe out pretty much all the holy power I had left. No wonder they didn't happen frequently in most of the religious stories of my old world.

The conjured light faded from the sky, and the small aura surrounding Ray faded away as well.

I was keeping an eye on Edwin but if he decided to act up then I would let the curse that I placed on him take care of it. Of course, I didn't have nearly enough holy power to place the curse that I spoke of. The curse that I placed on him would only activate once and only when I manually activated it, but it would make him suffer excruciating pain.

As long as he didn't know the restrictions, I figured it would serve as sufficient motivation to keep him going for a while.

Though when he started proclaiming my message, it was possible that whatever Overseer he was aligned with might smite him. Whether or not I would help him at that time would depend on how fervently he showed his repentance.

"Work hard, Edwin!" I cheered him on, though he wouldn't be able to hear me anymore.

I examined the devastation below me and recalled how absurdly powerful Edwin had been once he got serious. These goblins didn't stand a chance at all. The difference in strength was beyond absurd.

Looking around, I could count the number of survivors on one hand. Though all the ones who followed me would respawn, it was still a depressing result and I had to admit that I felt a little bit guilty. From the start, I had been more focused on saving my followers than the others, despite their ability to respawn. Because my options were limited, I waited until I was sure my help was necessary.

Even after the battle had taken a turn for the worse, there were so few surviving followers that I decided to wait until after they all died to intervene. I only had a small number of followers, after all, and I couldn't obtain faith from those who gained a sure knowledge of my existence.

However, seeing the results, I felt a tinge of regret. The goblins who survived looked hopeless as they stared at the ruins of their home and the corpses of their kin.

This scene struck a chord within me. It was too similar to what happened to my home town, albeit on a different scale. This was the same thing that was happening on Earth. Even now, this same thing could be happening somewhere else on this continent.

That was why I picked the name that I did.

There was a story from one of the now-dead religions of Earth. The story of a man who bore the burden and weight of many souls in a single body. He could not be restrained with shackles and chains, and no one had the strength to subdue him.

Legion.

It was powerful. It was a name that would represent me for many thousands of years. It would inspire fear in my enemies and hope in my allies. This name would reflect my purpose and my ideals.

The resistance of Earth failed. Therefore, I was the last hope of Earth.

This name would represent the weight of my burden. This name would belong to both me and everyone who followed me. We would break the chains on this world and shatter the chains winding around Earth.

It might have been arrogant of me to take this burden upon myself. It might have been naïve to want to save the world when I didn't even have a church yet and only had thirty-one followers.

I knew as well as the next guy that dreams betrayed many.

However, I passionately believed that hard work betrayed none. I would make my hopes into reality and bear the weight of the fight that my brothers and sisters could not finish. I would liberate this world and establish myself as an absolute power.

Today, tomorrow, and forever, I would be Legion.

After Legion, as she now knew he was called, ended his manifestation, Ray examined Edwin carefully to judge what actions she was safe to take. The warrior completely ignored her as he collapsed to the ground, his arms and legs spread wide in an x-shape while he stared up at the cloudy, blue sky.

She watched him warily for over a minute, unsure of how to act. Just a few minutes ago they had been fighting to the death and now...

Now, she had no idea how she was supposed to feel about him.

Was he an ally? Definitely not.

A friend? As if.

There was no way that she could put him in the same category as Lexi. Kelsey, Helen, and Ven were tentatively on that list, but this man was far from it.

Yet she didn't think she could still call him an enemy either. Just one look made it obvious that he had no more will to fight.

Edwin chuckled, breaking the awkward silence. "Young miss, go and tend to the illusionist. Our fight is over."

"Illusionist?" Ray asked, turning to look towards Shaman.

The old goblin lay on the ground where she had collapsed a short distance from the bodies of Urg and the silver-ranked assassin.

"Samantha coats her blades with poison. It might already be too late," Edwin warned. He reached for his enchanted bag, pulled out a red vial, and tossed it to her. "This is a medium-quality healing potion. Use it if it's not too late."

Ray caught the potion smoothly and ran towards Shaman's prone form.

The old goblin was barely breathing. Foam spilled from the corners of her mouth as the light in her eyes flickered.

She kneeled beside the old goblin, uncorked the bottle, and lifted the rim to Shaman's lips.

"D..don't..." Shaman whispered.

Ray hesitated as the old goblin started speaking.

"Healing potions... cannot... save... me... anymore. Do not... prolong... the pain..." Shaman's body convulsed as she started to cough. When the coughing fit subsided, she looked up at Ray. Her eyes were filled with a mixture of sadness and contentment.

Ray looked around desperately, hoping against hope that someone had a way to save Shaman.

All she found was death and destruction.

Trog limped over, holding a broken arm against his chest.

Lords Cedric and Tyrion, who stood back during the final charge, approached as well. As they met her inquiring gaze, they shook their heads sadly.

Ray could only see two other surviving goblins, and both were in critical condition. She knew without anyone telling her that they would die soon. She returned her attention to the old goblin.

Shaman smiled kindly and reached up with her hand, searching.

Ray tossed the potion aside and immediately seized it with both of her hands, holding it tightly.

The old goblin reached into a normal bag hanging from her belt with her free hand and withdrew a small candle. "It is... inconvenient... to do this without illusions," she wheezed.

She looked at Trog and the goblin assassin walked over. He lit the wick of the candle in Shaman's hand.

Shaman pushed the candle towards Ray. Her body seemed to flicker for a moment but Ray dismissed it as a trick of the light.

"This wax is fate, and this flame is my burden."

Ray tilted her head to the side, not quite understanding.

"The flame is now yours to carry. For over three centuries, I have carried this burden but I... I could not save our race. I could not burn either strong enough or long enough to overcome our fate. My time has come, but your time is just beginning."

Ray accepted the candle and held it tightly against her chest as the wax began to melt, a small tendril oozing down the side. She ignored the pain as it burned her skin, her entire focus on the dying goblin leader. "Shaman, I... I can perform a baptism right now! If you swear to Legion, then you can respawn!" Ray urged, a hint of desperation entering her voice.

"No, young one. I... will not be shackled... to this world. My soul... shall be... free...!" As she breathed out the last word, she closed her eyes. She almost looked as if she were asleep.

And then she was still. Her body slowly crumbled to dust and drifted away in the wind.

Ray leaned back and craned her neck to look at the sky. There was a peculiar tightness in her chest and her eyes stung the slightest bit. She hadn't known Shaman for very long, but the old goblin was still someone who had treated her well. She looked down at the burning candle as hot, melted wax ran over her hand. "The flame is mine to carry? What does that mean?"

"It's an ancient tradition," Trog supplied, his voice shaking with suppressed grief. "Though she couldn't change herself, she believed that your coming was a sign that it was time for the goblins to move on. She passed the mantle to you."

She pushed herself to her feet. She looked around, taking in the hundreds of goblin corpses scattered throughout the camp. She met the eyes of each of the silent goblins surrounding her. Each of them had tears streaming down their faces but their eyes held no hint of despair. Rather, she saw a cold fury.

Trog's hands were shaking, and he clenched his teeth.

Ray finally understood what it really meant to be called 'monsters' by the humans. This was the goblin's plight. An entire tribe was wiped out almost to the last goblin in just this one assault. Because they didn't all have Legion, most of those who died wouldn't come back. Shaman, Urg, and Frog wouldn't come back yet every single one of the adventurers who died today would respawn.

What had this fight even accomplished then?

These goblins spent their lives running and hiding in the woods. They spent their lives praying to a creator that disappeared over a thousand years ago, begging for a salvation that never came.

This was the plight of all monsters.

Ray was surprised when Legion declared his intent to be the god of monsters. He reached out his hand and offered a new way.

As she looked around the goblin camp and took in the destruction once more, she knew that some lives were saved because she had followed his requests and offered them a new path. She clenched the candle tightly, crushing it as she pushed herself to her feet. "Until now, I did not understand," she started.

She was met with questioning glances, and she cleared her throat to continue. "I did not understand what it meant to be a 'monster'. I thought I knew when adventurers tried to capture and sell me. I thought I knew when I saw other 'monsters' in chains."

Trog, Cedric, and Tyrion focused their eyes on her.

"What does it mean to be a 'monster'?" Ray asked. "Is this what it means?" She gestured to the destruction surrounding them - the wrecked houses and walls, the hundreds of dead goblins, the scorch marks, and the blood staining the dirt. "Does it mean that we must be hunted by quasi-immortal zombies for our entire lives?" She shook her head. "I cannot accept that. We have our own god now. No longer will 'monsters' be seen as lesser creatures, fit only to be playthings or a source of income."

Trog growled, his eyes narrowing fiercely.

Tyrion squared his shoulders and wiped the tears from his eyes.

Cedric grinned and revealed his sharp teeth.

"They call us 'monsters'?" she smirked, baring her fangs. "As Legion has declared, we will embrace the name that they have given us and turn it against them! If they call us 'monsters', then let us become monsters!" She paused and heard a few grunts of approval. "If they persecute us, we will return it tenfold, and if they murder us we will return it a hundred times over!" Ray raised the crushed candle up high, displaying it for the remaining three goblins to see.

Trog fell to one knee and bowed his head. Tyrion and Cedric followed.

In front of all of them, the candle and the flame also crumbled into dust and drifted away like an illusion.

"Let's get this place cleaned up and then get out of here."

"By your command," Trog replied.

"We have to gather and bury the dead and then search for a new place to set up camp. Oh, and we have to figure out what to do with Edwin... Also, we're going to have to figure out how to rescue the goblins who respawn in the temple..."

Trog cut her off. "Let's focus on the problem in front of us and take it one step at a time."

She nodded at the suggestion. Before they could go much further, she held out healing potions that she found in her enchanted bag. "Trog and Cedric, both of you have broken arms. If you use these, it should help you recover."

Trog accepted the vial and raised it to his lips, downing half of it. His arm straightened out and the various cuts and bruises on his body recovered. Cedric downed the other vial with similar results. Tyrion fought Bill, but he stayed back for the rest of the fight and was lucky to avoid Edwin's 'Earthquakes'.

The three of them split up and began to gather the corpses.

"Good job down there. My little seraph is starting to become a leader."

"So you knew I was a seraph?"

"You're an immortal, but you're not a dragon, an elf, a fae, or a slime. Wasn't it obvious?"

She pursed her lips. "Seraph..." she tried out the word, testing how it felt. It was a familiar word and evoked fuzzy memories that had remained dormant for weeks now. Maybe it was time to openly claim her race.

"As I was saying, that was a decent speech. I'm happy that we're finally both moving in the same direction," Legion continued.

Ray shook her head, her anger rising. *"Don't get ahead of yourself, buddy. I'm still a little annoyed that you waited so long to intervene. Why the hell did you ask me to let Lexi die?"*

"An excellent question. Now that we've finally taken our first real step forward, I think it's time that we take a moment to sit down and talk. I will explain what I can do and what my limitations are, and I will make sure that you are educated in my teachings that I came up with."

Her anger simmered away. *"As long as you have a good explanation..."*

"Anyways, now that we have more followers, we will also need to talk about the next step."

"The next step?" she muttered aloud.

"See if you can't convince those three to get baptized. Our next task is figuring out how to get those goblins out of the temple after they respawn."

"You got any ideas?"

"Have you ever heard of Moses?"

"No...?" She felt amusement channel through their connection. If she could see him, she was certain that Legion would be smirking.

"Good," he replied simply.

Ray looked towards the distant town of Cairel. Once her final few tasks in the goblin village came to an end, she would return. There were lots of questions to answer and problems to solve.

However, she knew that she wouldn't be doing it alone. The young seraph began humming to herself as she strode through the destruction while avoiding the scattered remains.

It felt to her as if many things had ended but, as with any ending, this was really just the beginning.

Epilogue: Behind the Scenes

On a wagon rumbling down the road towards the inner region of the Kingdom of Rovar, four individuals sat hunched, their features covered by dark cloaks.

"Not only did we fail to find the core, but our plan to cover our escape failed as well," Eileen Vanis groaned, pinching the bridge of her nose as if holding back a headache.

"I'm sorry," Maxwell Rovar muttered, unable to meet the eyes of his compatriots.

"It's fine, it's fine," Quincy Rambalt replied while waving the apology away. "Not finding the core aside, the second plan wasn't particularly good in the first place. She may have been a seraph, but that young lady didn't qualify to be used yet. There's no way anybody would believe that she killed the four of us."

Siegfried Lancaster nodded his agreement. "At the level of strength we revealed in Cairel, they *might* have believed that she beat one of us. All four of us, though? Definitely not."

Eileen shook her head. "The point was that people needed to have an excuse for our disappearance. It's too early to let people know about our plans and things will get really complicated if anybody starts searching for us. Our efforts were entirely wasted, though. We left a way to find her when we need her again later, so for now let's focus on finding the core."

The wagon jolted as a wheel rolled over a divot in the road.

"So where are we meeting up with the brat?" Quincy asked.

She responded with a glare.

"Where are we meeting *His Holiness*?" he corrected with a sigh.

"He may be crazy, a coward, and self-centered, but he is the only person that the Dark Lady will speak to. It's better to be accustomed to speaking respectfully so that there aren't any accidental slip-ups," Eileen reprimanded him.

"I know, I know…" Quincy muttered. "I just can't stand the guy."

Siegfried grit his teeth. "None of us can, but we have to for now. He knows that which is why he refuses to let us know any more details beyond the next step in the process. We're all only sticking around because we want the Dark Lady's gift."

Max nodded silently. "Still, I've been slaving away for that guy for a decade now and we haven't seen a lot of progress. Where the hell could the dungeon core be?" Quincy grumbled.

"We'll ask Phineas when we get to the capital. He said he'll meet us there," Eileen replied.

Siegfried, Max, and Quincy all jolted in their seats, staring at her with wide eyes.

"He's leaving the base? That guy? I've never seen him outside his stupid throne room before!" Quincy half-shouted in amazement.

Eileen shrugged. "He said something was happening and he needed to leave before it got worse. I didn't ask for any details, but he was complaining about 'dead mana experiments' and some angsty 'summoned hero.'"

The four of them exchanged glances.

They each knew that they were all thinking the same thing.

If that guy was jumping ship, then they didn't want to go anywhere near the New American Empire for at least a decade.

That guy was a prophet, after all.

To be continued in Legion, God of Monsters: Contagion.

Acknowledgments

Thank you for reading Legion, God of Monsters: Awakening.

I hope you enjoyed it as much as I enjoyed writing it. I would like to take a moment to encourage you to review the book.

Every review helps others find this book, and both compliments and critiques are helpful for me as I seek to improve my craft.

Want to discuss my books with other readers and the author?

Join my Discord server at and be a part of the Legion community.
https://discord.gg/XEA2z7WcTg

As a blatant bribe, you'll also be able to receive a free copy of The Transcendent World: Origins - Alice, a four chapter short story dated roughly ten years before the events of Legion, God of Monsters: Awakening.

If Discord isn't your thing, you can also follow my author page on Facebook for updates on upcoming novels.

About the Author

Kyle J. Forthman was a missionary, an Electrical Engineering major, and an avid gamer. He decided to try mixing those things together with a little bit of magic and see what happened.

To discuss Legion, God of Monsters, meet other fans, or contact the author, join K. J. Forthman's Discord!

Made in the USA
Middletown, DE
27 July 2023

35810168R00189